My Lily

by *Brigitta Barnes*

Order this book online at www.trafford.com
or email orders@trafford.com

Most Trafford titles are also available at major online book retailers.

Printed in the United States of America.

ISBN: 978-1-4269-6207-3 (sc)
ISBN: 978-1-4269-6208-0 (e)

Library of Congress Control Number: 2011904422

Trafford rev. 03/30/2011

 www.trafford.com

North America & international
toll-free: 1 888 232 4444 (USA & Canada)
phone: 250 383 6864 ♦ fax: 812 355 4082

This book is dedicated to all the females in my life.

First of all, my daughter Andrea, who is now an Angel in God's care. Although she will never read the book, I felt her sitting on my shoulder so many nights while I was writing. Thanks for the memories, they are all good.

Andrea's two wonderful daughters, Abby and Emma, who light up my world.

My daughter Amanda who makes me realize what love a mother has for her child. I enjoy the laughter, gossip and confidences. Her daughter. Brianna, who was my first granddaughter and introduced me to the joys of grandchildren. As she grows, it only becomes more special.

My wonderful friends for over forty years. Barbara is always there for me and has been the best friend anyone could have! Betty who is always encouraging me and Joann, who never has a bad word to say about anything. Their contribution to my life has enriched it more that I deserve. My friends are my treasure. Their children are as close to me as my own and we have shared so much. And, I cannot forget Kas who left us much too soon.

My adopted daughter-in-law Jen, thanks for all you do for my grandsons.

My sister-in-laws. Nancy, who has a heart bigger than Texas and is the Matriarch of the family and Linda who I do not get to see nearly enough.

My two nieces, Beth who is an angel walking on earth and of course, MY Tracy. We always laugh that she should have been my daughter but there was a mix-up in Heaven. She is always there for me and so much like me, it's scary.

I know the list is long but hey, my first book is as special as the women who touch my life. Without them, I would not be the person I am!

The Early Years

Chapter 1

The young child woke up from a fitful sleep. Her attention was drawn to the window. She noticed the sun had fully risen and was coming in the only window in the room. Because the unadorned window was closed, and stuck shut, there was no air circulating in the room. She was covered in sweat. She rose quickly to get outside to rid herself of the stuffy room. As she walked through the two-room shack, she noticed the old man sitting in the other room. She did not say anything to him as she passed on her way outside and he never acknowledged her presence.

She relieved herself and went to begin her day. As usual, she would spend the daylight hours entertaining herself. She learned a lot from watching rabbits and birds and found flowers and nuts to eat. She often wandered off in search of something to occupy her time and today she repeated the pattern by heading away from where she slept. She never thought of it as home. She knew she needed to get up each day and leave as soon as she was awake because she did not like the way the man looked at her. Today she was tired because she had not slept well. Waking up drenched in sweat was uncomfortable. No one suggested she take a bath to cool-off. That idea was foreign to her. She did stop at the pump and get some water to quench her thirst but that was the only meaning the water had for her.

The old man looked up as the girl passed. It never occurred to him that this was his daughter. He never spoke to her unless she did something to irritate him. He looked around his small shack and decided to go into town. It never occurred to him to take her with him. He shook his head as if to console himself for the misfortune that entered his life. He never thought of ways to improve his circumstances. He had settled into a life of just existing from one day to the next. His only pleasure was contained in a pint of whiskey. The only ambition he possessed was to make sure he always had a bottle on hand.

When he returned from town, he was feeling good. He brought some canned food so the girl could eat and he had enough whiskey to last a few days. He opened the can and put a spoon in it. When the child tipped over the can as she was trying to eat out of it, the man told the girl she was clumsy like her mother. For a long time, the child thought that was a good thing. She barely remembered her Mother, but being told she was like her, made her Mother real to her. Tonight she could smell the whiskey on his breath and knew she would not do anything to draw his attention to her.

When her father was sober, he talked about his first wife. He told her they had been married and they had a little girl. She ran off with someone and took the kid with her. Never heard a word from her after that. Never knew if they were divorced. He told her he didn't really care. He rarely spoke of Lily's own mother. When he did, it was to criticize her. She soon learned not to question him when he talked; so the information she gained from him, was often relayed in a drunken stupor.

One day someone came to the house and inquired about her. The old man was really mad after that. Pretty soon after that visit, she was sent off to school. As soon as she entered the schoolyard, she experienced a feeling of awe and fear. The schoolhouse looked so large and the children looked so different from her. Yet this was the first time she had left her familiar surroundings and her excitement overcame her fear.

When class started, the teacher introduced herself to the students and called out the names of the children assigned to her. No one had called Lily by her name. The old man called her "Girl" when he spoke to her. Therefore, Lily did not respond when her name was called. The teacher looked at her and said, "Lily when I call your name, please respond by saying *Present.*"

Laughter and giggles broke out in the classroom. The teacher looked around the room and called for everyone to be quiet. The teacher then looked at Lily and realized the child was not being difficult. Her face displayed innocence and puzzlement at the instructions.

Lily loved both the teacher and learning. What she didn't like, was how the other kids made fun of her. They said she smelled. They made fun of how she was dressed and they were always trying to get her in trouble. When the teacher noticed that Lily never brought a lunch to school, she reminded her to pack a lunch to bring with her each day. She soon realized that Lily had no one at home who seemed to care if she ate or not; so she always gave her half of her sandwich. She told her she was too full to finish the lunch she brought for herself. Lily wondered how anyone could ever be too full since she was always hungry.

Her teacher often made an excuse to keep her after school. When all the other children had left, and it was just her and her teacher, she learned much more than school work. Her teacher showed her how to wash herself outside from the outdoor spigot. She brought Lily a bar of soap, washcloth and towel and explained how she could get clean without actually getting a bath. Her teacher also managed to bring some clothes and shoes for her to wear. She was well aware of the treatment Lily received from the other children because of her appearance. Because of Lily's exceptional mind and her thirst for knowledge, she was clearly the smartest child the teacher had encountered in quite a while. Most of the children would only stay in school until they were strong and old enough to help their families out on the farm. It was not unusual for the students to be uncommitted to school work because so many had to focus on farm chores. The parents sent them to school, but gave little encouragement to their children to succeed. They all knew they would end up as farmers, just as the generation before them. There was no aspiration to gain a higher education.

This was why the teacher tried to do all she could for Lily. She often spoke of Lily to her husband. About how unfair the children were to her. "The first day as school began, when I looked at all the faces in the room, Lily stood out to me. She had this innocent look to her but I could see intelligence in her eyes. Of all the students I was given this year, I knew many were only entrusted to me until the fields needed them. Lily, however, was so different. From her appearance, she had the look of neglect. Not just from poverty, but as if no one cared. That and the smile that lit up her face, as it mirrored her innocence. I cannot help but to look out for her. She has such a sweet nature; she never causes trouble and doesn't seem to understand why her schoolmates are so cruel. She is so innocent; I have to do whatever I can for her". Her husband knew his wife well and agreed.

She found out that Lily didn't even have a bed to sleep in. She slept on a pile of rags and plastic bags. Her father did not provide anything past a roof over her head (if you could call it that). When it rained, it was hard to keep dry inside, but it never seemed to bother her father. He never did anything to correct the leaks in the roof or anything else for that matter. She never had a hot meal. Whatever they ate was out of a can. The teacher drove her home one day and decided to talk to her father. He was outraged that she tried to interfere with his life and told her if she didn't like how things were, he would keep Lily home from school. The teacher looked at Lily and noticed the tears running down her cheeks. She decided it would be useless to try to call in the authorities. Because, in this poverty ridden town, no one would want to take Lily into their care. The system was so overwhelmed with the amount of resources available versus the amount of help needed; it may be years before anything could be done to help Lily. Therefore, she made a point of helping her, the best she could. She gathered up old blankets and pillows and gave them to Lily. She drove her to the end of the road so she did not have to carry them all the way home, but she never approached Lily's father again. She and her husband agreed that Lily was probably better off staying in school and getting what little help they could give her instead of going into the system.

One day after class, the teacher decided to give Lily extra help in reading and writing. "Lily whatever your life brings, if you are proficient in reading and writing, you have the tools to keep learning".

Although the teacher knew the other children were cruel to her, she admired the determination that Lily displayed in order to overcome all the obstacles she encountered. She would do anything to learn. This was a rare occurrence for the teacher. In her experience teaching here, most of the students were just content to wait until the day they could leave. None had much interest in learning. For the first time in a long time, she was challenged to make a difference in someone's life. Not only did she assume the role of schoolteacher, but also took on the job of teaching Lily the basic necessities of life.

As the year passed, Lily took books home with her to read and she wrote stories about what she had read. She was so engrossed in learning during class that the taunts from the other children were often not even heard. She hung onto every word the teacher spoke and absorbed everything that she was taught. Lily had never been as happy in her short life as she was during school hours. She hated the weekends because there was no school, but she always took work home to do. Her school hours and time spent with her teacher were the focus of her life. This was the first time she did anything other than try to exist. She had a purpose and a reason to face each day.

The old man never cared what she did. He did not work the land so there were no chores for Lily. In fact, the only chore she had was to stay out of his way. He barely spoke to her and had no actual feelings for her. They just existed together. He left her alone and ignored her existence as long as it did not bring attention to him. He viewed her as another obstacle that life dealt him. It never occurred to him to try to make a better life for Lily or himself.

The Marriage

Chapter 2

The summer when Lily was 13, her father told her she was getting too big. She looked like a whore. Lily really didn't know what that meant, only the way he said it, she knew it wasn't a good thing to be. Of course, she could never ask him because he didn't like her to talk to him.

One night he came home and told her it was time she moved along in life. Lily didn't know what he meant. Soon she found out.

Her father brought another old man to her house one day and told Lily to brush her hair and get cleaned up. She was excited and surprised because her father never brought anyone home before or cared how she looked for that matter. She was told the man's name was Clyde. He talked to her and she liked that.

A couple days later, her father told her she was getting married. Lily was surprised and wondered what being married was like. Two days later, Clyde came back and her father told her to pack. She thought they were all going somewhere together and she had never been anywhere but here and school.

When she had her clothes, hairbrush, nightgown and books in a paper bag Lily was surprised to see her father take some money from the other man. He looked at Lily and told her to enjoy married life. He just laughed when she drove off alone with the man called Clyde.

Clyde was nice enough on the ride. He told her they were getting married. Since she had no birth certificate, they were going to tell the judge she was 16. Lily knew better than to question grownups, so she just nodded her head.

They headed into town and stopped at a house that had a sign, *Justice of the Peace*. Lily thought peace sounded pleasant. Once they were inside, a man talked to Clyde and the woman came over to her. She asked her how old she was and Lily remembered to say 16. The woman said she had such a young face but looking at her body, she could tell she was older. The woman gave her some wildflowers and told her to hold them when the man spoke to them. She said to answer, "I do" when he asked her a question.

After she did what the woman said, she heard Clyde say "I do" and she said that too. Everyone was smiling so she knew she did everything right. She and Clyde signed a paper and the man gave it to her. She thanked him and put it in her pocket.

On the ride out of town, Clyde told Lily that she was his wife now. He needed someone to cook and clean. He reached out, grabbed her breast and said, "Looks like I got a ripe one. Did your Daddy ever touch you there?" Lily told him no one had. He smiled and whistled a little tune. He told her she was to tell everyone from now on, she was 16. He told Lily that the only reason he married her was to make sure he wouldn't get jail time for having sex with her. She was confused about the jail time and sex but kept quiet. She was scared after he had touched her but realized she had no one to turn to.

Once they arrived to Clyde' house, Lily thought it was a mansion. It had so much room, a separate kitchen, sitting room and an indoor bathroom. She asked if she was going back to school. He laughed and said he would be her teacher from now on. She never had a man teacher before but guessed that was ok. He told her to go into the bedroom and put her bag away. The room was big and the bed looked like it would hold two people. She sat on the edge of the bed and thought how much she was going to enjoy living here.

Clyde called out and told her he was hungry. She walked into the kitchen and stood there looking at the table. Nothing was sitting there to eat. He said 'Girlie, cook up some grub." Lily stood there not sure what to do. "Don't tell me you don't know how to cook? Your Daddy told me you were a good cook. What did you eat at his house?"

Lily told him mostly out of cans. He told her that wasn't going to cut it. He'll give her a few lessons but it was going to be her job. He showed her how to fry up bacon and scramble eggs. She had never had bacon but it sure smelled good. He told her to make toast and again she was unsure what to do. He muttered some profanity and showed her that too.

After dinner, he showed her how to do the dishes and he went outside to check on the animals. Lily was excited to see them but he told her to stay inside and do the dishes and take a bath. She had never had a bath inside before.

When Lily came out of the bathroom, Clyde gave her a toothbrush. She didn't know how it would work on her hair. He muttered again, took her into the bathroom and showed her how to use it on her teeth. He told her he would see her in the bedroom.

She walked into the bedroom and saw him naked in bed. She covered her eyes and said, "I'm sorry, where do I sleep?"

"With me. Don't you know nothing?"

"I don't know what you mean. I never slept in a bed with anyone before."

""Well little Lily, from now on that's what wives do. Take off your clothes."

Lily was shaking but did what she was told. As she sat on the bed, he pulled her down on top of him, fondled her breast and started kissing her. Soon he tried to ram something between her legs and she started to cry. Clyde said, "Shut up. This here is normal married stuff. Just follow my lead and it will all work out."

She tried but could not enjoy any part of that. She held her breath and tried to think of other things to get her mind off what he was doing. Soon he jumped up and down on top of her and she had intense pain. Something ran down her leg. She thought he peed on her. She was so humiliated she didn't know what to do. She just wanted to die.

"Well little girl. You was a virgin alright. Hard to break that cherry. Now go to sleep, it will be easier tomorrow night."

Lily cried herself to sleep.

Soon it was morning and she woke up confused. *Where was she?* She remembered. She was full of fear. She eased herself up and went to get dressed. She noticed the blood on the bed. She was so ashamed. She walked out to the bathroom and was immediately in pain. Her insides felt like they were going to fall out and she was so sore down there.

No one was in the house. She didn't know what to do so she sat at the kitchen table. She decided to walk outside and maybe see the animals. She saw Clyde shoveling hay inside a barn and walked over.

"Well my little bride, did you survive the night?" She blushed and turned away. He grabbed her arm and said, "Guess you didn't expect to have to grow up so fast but then I didn't expect to get such a baby."

He kept shoveling and told her to get in the kitchen and fix breakfast. She stood there not sure what she was expected to fix.

"Did you learn anything last night? There is still bacon in the fridge. We can have pancakes and bacon."

She said "Pancakes?"

Clyde threw down the shovel and said, "I could kill your father."

They went inside and he showed her how to put the flour, sugar, eggs and milk in a bowl and mix it all together. She was determined to learn fast. He got out two black pans and told her to put the bacon in one and grease the other one for the pancakes.

After breakfast, Clyde told her to come into the barn and he would show her how to take care of the animals. He told her he did not make a living off them, but kept them for the food they provided. There were chickens to provide eggs, two cows to provide milk and butter and hogs to provide the meat they ate. The hogs were raised for slaughter but he sold them in town to get a credit at the general store. "I've worked out an arrangement with the owner to take one hog each year. No money is exchanged. I get enough credit in their store to buy meat and the supplies that I need, so it works out ok. Messy and smelly creatures, but worth the trouble just for the peace of mind. I know I'll be able to eat even if the crops are not successful. This is why you have to take good care of the animals, girl."

Lily looked around at the animals and knew she would do her best. She had never had any animals before so she was grateful that Clyde had them. Plus, she was glad to know she would not go hungry again. At least Clyde made it sound that way.

Things went well for the next few weeks. Although she didn't like the sex part, she was grateful for all the food she ate. She enjoyed tending to the animals and sometimes played with them. She always talked to the cows and made a game of feeding the hogs. They were smarter that she thought. She learned how to do the laundry and her cooking was getting better. Clyde even promised that he would let her buy some store bought shoes and clothes for winter. She never had store bought clothes. The only clothes she ever got were used.

She missed school. When she asked if he was going to teach her, he told her this was her education. She was a wife now and no longer had the luxury of being a kid. Lily tried to learn things fast because she didn't like it when Clyde got mad. When he got upset about something on the farm, he told Lily his sons had deserted him. One time she got the nerve up to ask about his boys. He told her one left to join the army and the other one left right after that to go to Detroit and get a job in a car factory. He said that was a while ago. That's when he decided he needed a wife.

Twice a year he had to hire outside help. In the spring, to plow and plant the field, and in the fall, to harvest the crops. He told Lily during those times she was to keep close to the house and not venture out to the fields because they were savages. She remembered hearing about savages in school. She wondered how Clyde found Indians to work for him?

Clyde took her outside and told her she was going to have her own garden to plant vegetables to grow for them to eat. She was excited because she never had anything that was hers before, unless you counted clothes. They dug up the ground and hoed the rows; and planted the seeds. Finally, the area was fenced off. He told her how important it was to keep weeds and animals out if she wanted to continue having food on the table. Lily was fascinated by the amount and variety of things they planted. She made up her mind that she would make him proud of her. She worked in the garden every day, and kept an eye on it out the kitchen window to make sure no animals got in to eat the plants.

Since Lily had never had anything of her own, actually anything she could control and nurture, she looked at her garden as her first real commitment. Something that would give back as much as she gave to it. By keeping the weeds out, protecting the plants and giving them enough water, she would be rewarded for her hard work with nothing else asked for in return. This, as much as anything, made Lily determined to succeed.

Although Clyde never thought to compliment her on her hard work, he often stopped and surveyed the garden. He watched its progress as it grew. He was actually surprised that Lily had done so well since he knew she had never planted anything before. He didn't even feel the need to help out or make suggestions, which surprised him even more.

Chapter 3

Soon the days had a routine to them. Lily was no longer unhappy. She learned to get through the sex part. If she ever thought about her life, it was to appreciate all the things she had now. It seemed so long ago that she had lived with the old man and attended school. She never thought about him because there was never any affection between them so there was nothing to miss. The only thing she did miss was her teacher and learning new things.

One day Lily noticed blood in her underwear. She had started to bleed and was very upset and most of all, scared. She ran outside and hid. Clyde found her hiding in the barn and couldn't figure out what was wrong. He came over and asked what was going on. She cried and told him she was dying.

He said, "What the Hell are you talking about girl?"

"I'm bleeding out my sex part."

"What sex part?"

"My bottom".

"Is this the first time you had blood".

"I cut my leg once."

Clyde again cussed her father. She was getting scared. He told her to come in the house with him because she had some learning to do. He took out two jelly glasses and poured whiskey in both. "Drink this, then I guess I have to tell you the facts of life." Clyde explained as best he could. "There are men and women. They are built different so they can have sex. Do you know what I mean?"

She nodded her head.

"Well sometimes women get pregnant when they have sex."

Lily's eyes got huge and she looked at him. "Am I having a baby?"

"No. The bleeding is to wash out the sex thing when you are not pregnant. If a woman is pregnant, the bleeding stops because the baby is plugging up the thing that makes blood. As long as you bleed, everything is ok" He got up and poured himself more whiskey. Told her to drink up. This was her first taste of alcohol. She didn't like the smell, the taste or how it burned her throat but was afraid to tell him, so she drank it.

Lily felt him looking at her. He said, "Sometimes I wondered why I took on such a burden. You are beautiful, with a body that makes me want to have it even right now. Your large breast are perfectly shaped, and not an ounce of fat on you." He glanced down and he was growing hard. "I know you would have never chosen me if you had a choice. Fate just gave you to me. So I have to take the good with the bad."

He stopped talking. She was visibly scared. Then he said, "I guessed if I was a better man, I should feel unworthy of you. But I paid for you and you are mine." He shook his head as if clearing his thoughts and then told her, "Well, you can't go bleeding on everything so go into the bathroom and put some clean rags in your underpants to catch the blood. When it gets full, wash it out and put another rag down there. I think it should only last four to five days. Usually women bleed once a month. If you don't bleed, you have to tell me right away."

Clyde sat alone at the table. He realized he didn't know for sure how old she actually was. Didn't even know when her birthday was. Doubted if she did either. She had the body of a woman but the innocence of a child. After Lily emerged from the bathroom, Clyde asked her if she took care of things ok. She nodded and then he got up from the table and told her he had work to do.

Soon she learned that the bleeding was a good thing. She did not have to have sex while she bled. Clyde kept a close eye on her to make sure she continued to bleed each month. He was not sure what he would do if she stopped but he would have to do something. He wasn't educated enough to realize there were ways to prevent a pregnancy, just to terminate one when it was necessary,

Lily's garden grew and under her care gave back the abundance of vegetables. She loved fixing dinner using her own food and was always proud when Clyde complimented her on something she fixed. They settled into a harmonious relationship and Lily was proving to be a big help with the chores. Since she never complained, Clyde gave her more responsibilities. If he would have thought about it, he would have wondered how he ever did all this alone. The chores now were manageable and the work she did, was always done right. Not like his worthless sons who took shortcuts and often had to be reminded what to do. Once he told Lily something, he never had to remind her.

Soon it was time for the harvest. Clyde went into town to look for seasonal help. He did not offer to take Lily with him. Didn't even think to tell her why he didn't want her to go. Truth was; he did not want her to be seen. If you are looking for help, you don't want someone signing on who has ideas in their head. She knew she should not question him. She decided to take this rare day being alone, to explore the farm. Places she had never had time to explore. Lily knew Clyde would confine her to the house when the workers came, so this might be her only chance to look around. She tried to imagine teepees set up for the savages. She spent her day walking through the fields. The corn was very high and the hay fields were ready to bale. It took her almost three hours to walk around the farm. She was amazed that Clyde had so much land. Lily never thought of anything as belonging to both of them. She was never told that once you were married, this was hers too. Of course, Clyde would never think it was hers either. That was just the way things were.

Clyde returned home in time for supper. He was in a good mood and had brought back a piece of candy for Lily. She was like a kid when he gave it to her. She never had candy before. He told her not to eat it until after supper because the candy was very sweet and it would make her supper taste bad. After supper was the best time to eat it. She realized that she had never been given a gift before.

As they ate, he told her he had been able to hire enough help to get the harvesting done. Things were looking good. She asked when they were coming and he told her they should be here by the next week. "Where do they set up the teepees?"

"What in tarnation are you talking about girl?"

"You know the savages. Don't they sleep in teepees?"

Clyde started laughing and she thought he was going to choke on his food. "Lily, my girl. When I said savages I meant like bad people, not Indians."

"Oh!" Lily was secretly disappointed because she had never seen an Indian and really wanted to. Clyde told her to clean up the supper dishes and then to enjoy the candy.

Soon the wait was over. The migrant workers began arriving and Clyde pointed out where they could set up camp. Usually, he had them close to the barn where he could keep an eye out and watch them to make sure they behaved. This year he wanted them as far away from Lily and the house as possible. He led them to the far end of the fields close to the pond. He had not planted on that location this year because he liked to rotate the crops. He always felt this was why his crops were better than other farmer's. This would work out well for him this year because the laborers could wash in the pond and stay away from his private space.

Lily crept out and climbed the tree she had found. It offered the perfect cover to watch what was going on and was high enough to see clear down the field. She wanted to see what the workers looked like. Since she had never seen many strangers, it was fascinating to know what other grownups looked like. Clyde had warned her to stay in the house and out of sight. She didn't want to disobey him but figured if she stayed out of sight, that was what mattered most.

She had never seen so many people. Some with dark skin, some with tan skin and some women in the group. Lily was so fascinated, she sat very still and watched until Clyde took them to the field and pointed out directions to them. When she saw him head back, she quickly jumped out of the tree and ran in the house.

As she sat dinner on the table, Clyde said "Well did you get a good look?"

"What?" she didn't know what he meant.

"I saw you in the tree looking at everyone. Don't go denying it. You disobeyed my order. This is the last time I'm going to tolerate that. Do you understand, girl?"

Lily was surprised he saw her because she had been so careful. She was also disappointed that she couldn't do it again. It wasn't fair. For the first time Lily felt her temper rise. It was a new emotion for her and it surprised her to have these feelings.

Chapter 4

For the next week, Clyde worked hard. He arose before the sun and fell into an exhausted sleep as soon as the animals were tended to at night. He required a large breakfast so Lily got up at the same time. Usually he took a sack with him with something to eat for lunch. He rarely came back to the house to eat. Therefore, she had the entire day to herself. Because she was getting very good at doing chores, she often could do them faster than Clyde realized. She was starting to get bored because she had stopped learning any new things. Her mind craved knowledge and adventure. She didn't know how to direct these needs or what to do about them. She often felt isolated and alone. Funny, for the first time in her life she actually had a home but craved more. There was no one to talk to besides Clyde. He was working so hard, the last thing he wanted to do at night, was talk. He often fell asleep early and they didn't even have sex much anymore.

Clyde never told Lily he loved her. In reality he probably didn't. She had never known love or affection as a child or now as a wife. The only thing she knew was sex. That was like going to the bathroom, fixing dinner or taking care of the animals. She looked at it as just something you do.

Eventually, the Harvest was done. Clyde seemed pleased and the workers all left. They walked out to the field where the workers had camped out and cleaned up what trash was left behind. She saw the pond and asked if she could go into the water.

"Pretty cold this time of the year. Go put your feet in it and see for yourself."

She walked over and felt the cool water on her legs. The bottom of the pond felt strange between her toes, soft and smooth. She told Clyde it felt good. He told her that she could take off her clothes and go all the way in. "Do you know how to swim?"

"I've never been in this kind of water before."

Clyde sighed to himself and said, "Wait a minute. I'll come in with you. No use in you drowning." They both went in and Clyde tried to show her how to swim. She was so happy. She started trying to imitate him and was doing pretty well. He watched her as she swam around the pond. The cold water caused her breast to become hard and her nipples erect. He scared her as he grabbed her around the waist and started to caress her breast. Even in the cold, he felt himself grow hard.

"God, girl, you have no idea what you do to me." He quickly thrust himself in her, holding her on his hips. Clyde never thought to tell Lily how beautiful he thought she was or offer any endearments. To him it wasn't necessary. It was just lust. He liked her fine, but he had never had affection himself, so he thought sex was affection. After he was finished, he told her to get her clothes on and head back to the house. Lily looked at him and wanted to ask if the sex had been bad. She had been having so much fun until after he stuck his thing in her. She thought she must have done something wrong. Afraid to ask, she did what she was told.

Chapter 5

The next day Clyde told her he was going into town and she could go with him. She could get some clothes in the General Store because she didn't have anything for the winter months. Lily was excited to be able to go in a store and then to actually buy something. On the drive into town, he told her that she needed to buy some underpants and some bras. She had never worn a bra in her life, but remembered her teacher used to. She had asked her once, what the strap under her dress was for. He told her to ask the woman in the clothing department for help. "Remember, you say you are eighteen now."

Lily thought it was strange since he said she was sixteen when they got married and it didn't seem that long ago. She didn't think much of it or think to question him but she really didn't know her actual age. She thought she was thirteen or fourteen, but really didn't care.

Once in the store, Clyde took Lily into the clothing end of the store. He saw a grandmotherly type woman folding some clothes. He went up to her and said, "Can you help my girl here find some winter clothes and underwear? I'll be upfront getting some other supplies. Send her to me when it's time to pay." The woman looked at Lily and smiled. Lily felt her looking at her so long that she blushed.

The saleswoman asked Lily what she was looking for. Lily looked at her and glanced wide eyed around the store. The woman noticed her confusion and said, "Well let's start with the basics. What size bra and underwear do you take?"

"I don't know."

"What size are you wearing?"

"I don't know."

18

Now the saleswoman looked at Lily as if she wasn't right in the head.

"Does your Mother usually buy your clothes for you?"

"My mother is dead."

"Well that explains it", said the saleswomen. "What do men know? Well let me get a few bras and have you try them on behind the curtain."

She took a handful of different size bras and led her in to the dressing room. Lily looked at them and said, "I don't know how they work, can you show me?" The saleswoman got the bras out of the box and told her to take off her shirt. She did a quick intake of breath when she saw Lily was naked.

She was soon in possession of two new bras. She also had five new panties as the saleswoman called them. As they checked out the clothes, the saleswoman recommended things for school and church. Since Lily didn't go to either, she asked for some clothes to wear at home. If the saleslady thought it was strange, she didn't say anything. Soon Lily had two pairs of jeans, some sweaters and sweatshirts. She even tried on a winter coat but wasn't sure Clyde would buy that too. She went over, looked at the shoes, and chose a sturdy pair that she thought would work on the farm. The saleswoman asked if she needed socks and she said, "I guess."

Finished with shopping, Lily went to get Clyde. She told him she picked out things the saleswoman said she needed and hoped that was ok. Clyde walked back with her and looked at the things on the counter. Said it looked ok to him.

"Don't you have a coat for the girl?"

"I saw your daughter try one on. She seemed unsure of the price,"

Clyde scowled and looked at Lily conveying the signal that she was not to dispute the saleswoman's remark about being his daughter.

"Well, we will take that coat, she'll be needing one this winter."

The saleswoman bagged up the purchases and Clyde paid in cash. Clyde told Lily to get in the truck and wait for him. He had a few more things to pick up and then they would head home. Lily was so thrilled with the trip into town. She had never picked out her own clothes before. She felt lucky to have Clyde. She smiled at him as they rode home. Once they arrived home, Clyde gave her some store bought pads for her period. He explained that she could use these instead of rags and throw them away once they were full. That evening before bed, he told her to come into the bathroom and watch him shave. She was fascinated and wondered how he kept from cutting himself. Once he was done, he took out a bag and handed it to her. Inside was a Lady's razor.

"I guess it is up to me to tell you what women do to get rid of the hair under their arms and on their legs. Good thing you have light hair or you would look like an ape. Now, you follow what I did on my face. Put some of this shaving cream on your legs and then run the razor up your leg. It should remove the hair."

Lily did not realize she shouldn't have hair in those places. She did what Clyde told her to do, but soon nicked her leg and blood ran out of a cut.

Clyde cursed, but told her, "Soon you will learn how much pressure to put on the razor against your skin. I cut myself when I started to shave too. Now try to get under your arms but be more careful."

Lily finished and washed the rest of the lather off her legs. She liked how smooth they felt and was pleased with the results. Clyde checked under her arms and was satisfied with the job she did.

He looked at her innocent face and lush body and soon was growing hard. "Damn, Lily, why can't I ever touch you without growing hard and losing control? Your body drives my wild."

He reached out and removed the rest of her clothes. He was soon lost in the throes of passion. She never understood what she did to cause this reaction in Clyde. She wanted to please him and gave into his needs. He had taught her what pleased him and soon learned what to do to satisfy him. Neither one of them ever gave a thought to finding out what aroused or pleased Lily. It was as if sex was done, only to bring pleasure to one person, Clyde.

Chapter 6

Two weeks later the farm had some light snow. Lily was helping out with the animals and was grateful she had the coat to keep her warm. They heard a car coming down the road to the farm.

"Get into the barn. I don't know who this is. I'm not expecting anyone."

Lily did as she was told. But she climbed up to the hayloft where she could look out.

The car stopped and a young man got out. He walked over to Clyde and they talked. Lily couldn't see his face or hear his words. She knew Clyde well enough to take in his body language and he did not seem pleased to see the man. He stiffened his shoulders and balled his hands into a fist. That was always a sign for Lily to get out of his way until he cooled off. Suddenly he raised his voice, "Who the hell do you think you are kidding, you ungrateful bastard? You know harvest is over and now expect to hit me up for money. Well if you wanted money so bad, you would've come home to help with the harvest. You are not getting a penny."

Lily was scared. She had never heard Clyde so angry. Even when she first came and had to learn to cook, he was not this mad. She shrank back and hoped they didn't look up and spot her hiding. She still remembered being caught in the tree. The other man said something she couldn't hear and then Clyde answered him back. Clyde was no longer shouting so she couldn't hear anymore. Suddenly they went into the house. She didn't know what to do now. Better stay here in the barn, until he called her to return to the house.

She climbed down from the hayloft and finished out the chores they had started in the barn. She finished and then sat down to wait for Clyde to come after her or for the other man to leave. Soon with nothing to do, she fell asleep in the fresh hay.

She awoke to someone shaking her shoulder. "Well what do we have here?" She knew right away from the look in his eyes, he was trouble. She had seen this look before from the boys at school.

"Who are you?"

"Funny, thought you might recognize me."

"I never saw you before."

"Not me, my dad. People say I'm the spitting image of him."

She glanced at him again and gave a small gasp.

"You see it, don't you?"

"Where is Clyde?"

"What I want to know little lady, is where is the money?"

"What money?"

"The money Clyde has."

"Ask Clyde. He doesn't tell me about money and I don't have any."

He hauled off and hit Lily across the face. She was suddenly very afraid. Too scared to talk and too scared to run. She just sat there. Her face was stinging but she was afraid to cry out.

"Well, I think we can find a way to make you talk." He began to slap her again. Then he reached up and ripped her blouse off. He leered at her breast. "Looks like Papa got himself a prize."

Lily tried to cover herself and it only seemed to excite him more. He suddenly was consumed with such rage for his father, that his only thought was to hurt her. He reacted in anger at all his father appeared to have, that should be his. The farm, money and now this young girl. He was so focused on his hatred, that he was unprepared for Lily's sudden movement. She kicked out at him and rolled away. He immediately ran after her and shouted, "Give it up; you are no match for me. I'll make you pay".

The more she fought, the more he enjoyed himself. She managed to put a bale of hay between then and looked around for any escape. Suddenly, she spotted the shovel. She tried to ease toward it but he immediately caught her looking at it. He laughed and headed for the shovel. She used that distraction to run toward the back of the barn. As she reached the back door that led out to the animals, she felt a pain in the back of her head as the shovel made contact. Her immediate thought was that he was going to kill her. She was thrown off balance, reached out to catch herself, but strong arms yanked on her hair. He threw her down and kicked her in the ribs. She had trouble breathing and knew she was unable to defend herself. He lay on top of her and took her nipple in his mouth. She cried and he clamped down until she thought he would bite it off. The pain was unbearable. He laughed. "Now, I think I have your attention. If you want to save those nipples, you better lay here and take what is coming to you."

Lily was convinced he was going to kill her no matter what she did. She was in such pain and her body was unable to fight back. She was close to losing consciousness. He slapped her again. "You are not passing out on me bitch. You are going to know what I am capable of…" He finished ripping her clothes off and savagely raped her. When he was sated, he hit her hard in her stomach and said, "Now if you want to live, you will tell me where dear old Dad keeps his money."

Lily found it hard to talk. Her mouth was starting to swell and her lips were bleeding. She was not sure what to do. She had never seen any money. She muttered, "Don't know" and passed out. He kicked her again in her back and walked out.

It was dark when Lily regained consciousness. She immediately remembered that man and what he had done to her. *Where was Clyde?* She forced herself to get up. As she stumbled to her feet, she looked outside. The car was gone. She was in so much pain she forgot she was cold and naked. She made her way to the house. It was dark inside and she turned on the light. She saw Clyde lying on the floor. She ran over to him and felt him. Still warm. That was a good sign. She remembered when she came across animals and they were dead, they go cold. She gently shook him and called his name. He stirred and opened his eyes.

He had trouble focusing his eyes. Then he realized Lily had what was the beginning of black eyes, swollen and bleeding lips and she was naked. *Dear God, did his son do that?* She was crying and calling his name over and over. He knew he had to try to get up and see what shape he was in. It was dark outside so he had been out a while.

"Lily, get yourself cleaned up and get dressed. Then come back and I'll try to get up." He had a pain shooting in his chest and passed out again. Lily did what she was told and was soon back to help him. Clyde pulled on Lily to try to get up. It took a while to get him on his unsteady feet and both were covered in sweat from the effort it took. He took a few steps and said, "I think the bastard broke my ribs." He moved his arms and legs. They were sore but he didn't think they were broken. He then focused his attention on Lily. "You ok?"

"He hit me and then he did the sex thing. He kicked me too."

23

"I'll take care of it. I bet he'll be back but I'll be prepared. Let's try to eat something and go to bed. Can you bring my rifle in from the barn? I'll keep it close to the bed."

That night Clyde slept lightly and kept his rifle loaded and ready to use. He would do all he could to protect himself and what was his. Son, be dammed. The next day they were both sore. Lily looked the worse because she had been hit in the face but she felt ok. Her back and stomach were very sore and Clyde said she was covered in bruises. As they were eating oatmeal and toast, she asked him what his son was after. She told him that he kept asking her about money. She wasn't sure why.

"Good thing I don't tell you anything or he might have beaten it out of you. That's a good reason for you not to know anything."

Lily was not sure why money was so important. It was hard for her to understand. She never had any dealings with money and was never educated in the importance of how it related to life. She could not understand why it created violence in people. Lily went out to the barn to check on the animals. She climbed up to the hayloft with difficulty and had to lie down until the muscle spasms subsided in her back. Once she could get up, she looked in her hiding place. She had the piece of paper the Judge had given her when she and Clyde got married. Also, a favorite rock that looked like a turtle and an old piece of chain she found in the field. Her lone possessions but they were hers. Maybe that's how Clyde felt about his money. It's his and he doesn't want someone taking it. She could understand a little better now.

She climbed back down, finished the chores and headed back to the house. The house was quiet and she walked back to the bedroom. She saw Clyde on the floor by the dresser. He had pulled away the dresser and the rug. His back was to her. Something told her to be quiet and not get noticed. She caught a glimpse of a tin can being placed in a hole in the floor. She then saw Clyde put a board back and start to rise up. Lily quickly ducked out of sight and made her way back to the kitchen. She quietly opened the kitchen door and shut it hard. She walked heavily back through the house and ran into Clyde in the hallway. "I did the chores in the barn. Anything else you want me to do?" Clyde came the closest to compassion as he ever had and almost gave her a hug. Her poor face was a mess yet she didn't complain.

"No, we eat lunch and we wait."

While they ate, Clyde told her that his son was no good. He had always been in trouble and he was glad when he left to work in the car factory. He had been fired and now he was back looking for money. He wasn't going to let him have any or give him a chance to hurt them again. He explained what they were going to do when he came back. Once they heard the car, Lily was to go out in the barn and call out to him. Then tell him the money was hidden in there, to take it and leave. That Clyde was unable to walk after the beating. He was counting on his son's greed to get him in the barn. Clyde was going to be hiding and scare him off.

Lily agreed. She never questioned Clyde. After lunch, he sent her out to the barn and then he went to get his gun and followed soon after that. It wasn't long until they heard the car coming down the drive. Clyde reminded Lily to wait in the barn until she heard the car door close.

Once the car stopped, she heard the car door. She walked out and stood in the open barn door. He saw her and started over. The look on his face caused her to shutter but she felt safe because Clyde was inside. Lily backed into the barn and when he approached her, she said, "I found the money. Now take it and leave."

"Well, well, little lady you sure changed your tune after yesterday. Must have been being with a real man. You liked it, didn't you? Give me the money and then take off your clothes; I have time to give you what my father can't."

Lily suddenly was scared and started to back away. That seemed to excite him even more. Suddenly, Clyde stood up and aimed his shotgun at his son's chest.

"You don't have the guts old man. I'm taking you out and then I'm going to have fun with your little whore."

He reached in and pulled a gun out of his pocket. Before he had a chance to move his arm all the way up, Clyde fired two-shotgun blast into his chest. It created gaping holes and blood poured out of the wounds. Lily fainted.

Chapter 7

When she came to, she saw Clyde outside. She went out and ran to him. He put his arm around her and told her she had to help him. He went to get the plow. They were going to bury the body. He showed her where. Under *her* garden. He explained that the garden would only be plowed so deep for vegetables. They needed to dig deep to bury the body. He was going to put fertilizer on the body and other chemicals to make it disappear. The bloody hay left in the barn where he fell, would also go in the grave and no one would ever know. They worked late in the night and finally it looked like it was cleaned up. Clyde said, "Let's wait until daylight just to make sure we didn't leave any trace in the barn, then we'll close up the grave. Tomorrow I will drive his car to the next town and leave it there."

"How will you get back?"

"You will drive my truck right behind me. Stop outside of town and wait for me."

"But I don't know how to drive."

"You are a fast learner. I'll give you a few lessons before we leave."

As soon as it was light outside, Clyde woke Lily. They both were still sore from their injuries. It was difficult getting up and dressed. He put on a pot of coffee and they sat at the table drinking it before heading outside. "I want to make sure the barn is clean. We will rake up all the hay in the area to get rid of any soiled hay. Then I want you to get a bucket and bleach and clean the floor before we put down fresh hay. I'm still trying to figure the best way to get rid of the car. I don't think my first idea is that good. We'll wait on that for a spell."

Clyde told her they would not take the clothes off the body before they put it in the grave. He would wrap it in a sheet so she wouldn't have to look at it, but she would have to help carry it from the barn to the grave. Lily was shaking but knew this was the only way. Once they had dumped the body in the grave, he sent her back in the barn. He covered the body in lye and started to shovel in the dirt. He went in the barn to check on the remainder of the hay. He found a few spots they had missed the night before and shoveled it in the wheelbarrow with the hay sitting there from last night.

He emptied the hay into the grave and began to finish filling it with dirt. Before he was finished, Lily came out and started to help. Soon, it was all filled in. He took the stalks of the vegetables he had moved aside last night and put them on top of the dirt. This way, it looked like they had started clearing out the area for the next season. He replaced the fence to keep the animals out. They stepped back and looked at what they had done. To the casual observer it looked like a garden. The extra dirt had been spread out over the entire area so it all looked the same and all the dirt was accounted for.

"Good, now let's check out the barn." Clyde was pleased at the job Lily had done. The floor was clean and no blood was visible. They got the pitchforks and began to lay down fresh hay. He sent her into the house to start breakfast and he tended to the animals. As Lily was cooking, she realized she didn't even know the name of the man that was killed. She should ask Clyde.

After they ate, he told her he decided they should drown the car in the river. Their pond was too shallow. Besides, the migrant workers used it to bathe and may find it. He figured they could make it to the Smoky Hill River and back in the same day. He would check to see if his truck and the car had enough gas. Before they would leave, he would have Lily practice driving up and down their road.

They practiced for an hour and Clyde felt sure Lily could manage the truck. Both had enough gas and they decided to leave. Lily was to follow him and he would keep an eye out for her in his rearview mirror. If she encountered any problems, she would honk her horn twice. They started out and soon were at their destination. Lily did a good job of driving and shifting gears. Since there was little traffic and no stop signs or intersections on the road they chose, she only had to shift three times and that went pretty good. He had her park a half-mile from the river. She got in the car with him and they drove up to the overlook. No one was there. He removed the license tags and emptied the glove compartment. He had checked the trunk at home so that was empty.

He looked around for a large rock and drove the car as close to the cliff of the overlook as possible before getting out. He placed the rock on the accelerator and they both got behind the car and gave it a push. It went over the cliff, bounced a few times on jagged cliff rocks before landing in the middle of the river. They turned and walked back to the truck. As they drove home, Clyde looked at Lily and said, "Thank you. Now we will never mention this again. It never happened."

This was the first time Clyde had ever said thank you to her. He didn't realize it when he said it, but this gesture would change their lives together forever.

Chapter 8

They settled into their routine. Lily kept the house immaculate and her cooking actually became good. Everything had changed on that one day when she could have lost it all. She appreciated the little things and she was less restless. In fact, she became closer to Clyde and actually initiated sex as her way of pleasing him. She never thought of this as lovemaking between a husband and wife. It was all to satisfy him. Lily had never experienced sexual pleasure for her body. She did not know that was possible and therefore, never realized women should enjoy sex. Clyde had begun to show her affection that surprised even him. He kissed her when he left the house and hugged her when he returned.

Clyde drove into town to pick up supplies. Lily did not want to go, so he left early in the morning. The store was advertising Christmas items for sale and he realized she had never had a Christmas. He decided to buy her a magazine so she could look at all the decorations and recipes for Christmas.

Lily wasn't feeling well so she laid down while Clyde was at the store. She sure was tired lately. I hope I am not getting sick, she thought. When she heard him return, she quickly ran into the bathroom to throw water on her face. He was putting things away when she walked into the kitchen and he handed her a bag.

She was pleased that he had thought of her. Inside was a magazine with beautiful trees and decorations on the cover. He said, "I decided we are going to have Christmas this year. We will get a tree and lights. You can pick out a few decorations to put on it. There may be some recipes you can use for Christmas dinner." She ran over and jumped in his arms almost knocking him down. "I never had a Christmas before. In school we talked about it but I never saw one."

He was glad he could give her some pleasure. He realized what a great person she was. He had never known anyone like her. She was genuine in her feelings, a hard worker and appreciated everything he did for her. He was amazed at how much he liked her and how she had made him enjoy life.

Soon it was Christmas and the house was decorated. Lily had made decorations from the directions she found in the magazine. She almost had the print worn off the paper because she looked it every spare minute. Clyde told her, "If I can't find you, all I have to do is look for the magazine and you'll be there." He was glad he got the magazine for her. The smallest thing made her happy and she appreciated everything that was done for her.

Christmas was wonderful for Lily. Her first was all she had imagined. She made a gift for Clyde. It was a craft idea she copied from the magazine and really looked amateur but he thought it was the most wonderful gift he had ever received. He gave Lily a box to open. Inside was a wedding ring and a bag of candy. She was thrilled. He lit a fire in the fireplace and they enjoyed a mug of hot chocolate to celebrate her first Christmas.

Time passed and it was five months since 'the incident'. It was never spoken about between them. So far, no one had been to the farm questioning the disappearance of the man either. After dinner one evening, Lily felt sick. Clyde looked at her and noticed she was very pale. She said, "I think I have to lie down for a few minutes. My stomach is killing me, I either ate too much or am about to bleed." He looked at her. He couldn't remember when she last had her monthly. He asked, "Is it time for that?" She looked at him and said, "I forgot about it. I guess it is time."

Clyde had cleaned up the dishes and was putting everything away, when he heard a groan, then a shrill scream. He ran to the bedroom. "What is the matter?"

"The pain, the pain! Make it go away".

He felt her stomach and it was hard. He kept his hand there and he could feel it tighten each time she cried out in pain. Dear God! She was pregnant. It looked like she was about to lose the baby. He better prepare her for this. He checked and she was not bleeding. He went in and got some towels to lay under her. He explained that it looked like she was pregnant. "Can you think back to when you last bled"?

She thought a minute but was gripped by another contraction before she could speak. "It was before that thing we don't talk about. I have been so happy after that, I forgot all about it."

"I don't think the baby can live this young. We'll hope for the best."

After twelve hours of labor, Lily delivered a boy. It was fully developed but was born dead. Clyde took the baby to the kitchen and washed it off. He looked at its feet and then he knew. This was not his child. It was a result of the rape. Her son was born with six toes. No one on his side of the family had that. Just his son's Mother. He laid the baby on the table and went into see Lily. She was exhausted and looked at him. "Where is the baby?"

"In the Kitchen"

"What was it?"

"A boy?"

"Can I see him?"

"He died. Do you still want to see him?"

"Yes or I'll wonder about him the rest of my life."

He brought the baby in wrapped in a towel. She uncovered him, looked at his little body and started to cry.

"Well bury him near your garden."

"I don't want him anywhere near that man."

"Look at his feet."

"Oh, no. He has six toes."

"Yes. I am not his father. The other one was."

""Please take him away, I need to rest."

He took the baby back to the kitchen. He looked at him and realized this was his grandson. Then he cried. His tears consumed him. He felt such terrible pain for Lily and this innocent child, his grandson.

He sat at the kitchen table and drank a glass of whiskey. He went in to check on Lily. She was still awake but lying very still. He went and got fresh towels and cleaned her up. Then he went back into the kitchen to pour her a glass of whiskey. He thought back to the last time he had done this; how different the circumstances were now. He took it in to her and told her to drink the whole glass. It would relax her and allow her to rest. She had been through a lot and she needed to sleep.

Lily felt numb. She drained the glass and laid back down. She didn't even know she was going to have a baby but now she felt such a sense of loss. All her strength left her. Soon she fell asleep. Clyde left the room and went out to the barn. He gathered some wood and built a box. The baby

31

was so small; the box was no bigger than a shoebox. He went in the kitchen and brought the baby out wrapped in a towel and laid it down in the box and covered it with the lid. They would bury him when Lily was ready.

The baby was not buried with his father. Lily wanted him buried under the tree she climbed that day to watch the migrant workers arrive. She thought he would be safer there and closer to heaven. They would plant flowers when spring came.

Chapter 9

Things took a long time to get back to where they had been before the baby. Both Clyde and Lily grieved in their own way. They never talked about it the way they would have if it had been their baby. It was too painful for both of them. Poor innocent baby. Not his fault. But, the fact could not be ignored of how he was conceived.

Spring came and it was time to plant the fields. Clyde drove into town to look for workers to help out with the planting. Lily cleaned the house from top to bottom and took care of the animals while he was gone. He came back late and told her he didn't have much luck. Only half of what he needed to hire, were available. He would need to try again next weekend. He unloaded the seed while she heated up his supper.

Finally, he was able to hire close to the amount of workers that he needed. Luckily, a few of the families had been there for the fall harvest, so they knew the land. He decided to set the camp up in the same field as before. Not so much as to hide Lily, but to allow her more freedom, in the barn and outside the house.

And each time he went into town, he brought back a magazine for Lily.

Again the farm was filled with workers and Clyde worked long hours with them. The weather cooperated and planting was done, right on schedule. Clyde had tilled the soil in Lily's personal garden and helped her start planting her vegetables. If the thought of what was lying underneath bothered her, she never showed it. She planted flowers under the tree. She sat there thinking about all that had happened and realized she had never known the baby's father's name or had named the baby. It would always be *baby* to her. She had never had a chance to have him look at her or to look into his eyes. She felt a sense of loss. Not because she missed the baby she had never known, but because something that could have been, would never be.

The planting was finished and the workers left. Lily was not as interested in them as she had been in the fall. She worked in her garden and tended to the animals. She kept busy and time passed quickly. She often went outside, sat underneath her tree, and read the magazines over and over. She loved looking at the pretty clothes and the pictures of different places throughout the country. The farthest she had ever been was into town and they didn't have any clothes like that, since most of their customers were farmers. It was exciting to see places so unlike anything she had ever known. She marveled at the clothes pictured and the high heels fascinated her. She wondered how anyone could work in them. Of course it didn't look like any of them lived on a farm. She did not feel inferior to the glamorous women she read about, just in awe of whom they actually were.

Now that the weather was warm, she and Clyde often swam in the pond. She was becoming a good swimmer and enjoyed the calm feeling she always had in the water. She was never fearful of drowning because she had never known anyone who had drowned so it did not seem like a possibility. Clyde had relaxed his fear for her when he realized how well she adapted to the water. He often relented and let her swim alone if he was working on the crops closest to the pond. She enjoyed the solitude and the feeling of freedom her swimming gave her.

Her vegetable garden was growing even better this year. Once or twice, the thought of what happened 'that day' came back to her but she quickly dismissed it. She occasionally saw Clyde stop and stare at her garden. She had the feeling he was thinking about that too. But it was never mentioned. It was as if, if they didn't talk about it, then it never happened.

Clyde noticed that Lily bled very infrequently since the baby. He wondered if it had damaged her in any way. She never complained about having pain. She never mentioned missing the baby or wanting another one. If asked, he probably would want a baby, if that was what Lily wanted. He had always been adamant about never having more children after the disappointment his sons gave him. He was sure they were conceived by the devil. He never could understand why they were so mean. Even as kids, he caught them killing cats and dogs, then gutting them. That is why he never wanted any more pets. He still felt the pain they caused him. He could not even mourn his son's death. At least he wasn't free to hurt anyone again. He decided to wait for Lily to say something to him if she was concerned about her woman parts. He didn't want to scare her if it was nothing. He never thought to take her to a Doctor. Farm people helped their own. Only if someone got hurt real bad by farm equipment, did they seek help from a doctor. Usually by then, it was too late anyway.

A doctor would probably tell them that Lily's body at thirteen was not ready to accept the pregnancy after the brutal rape. She may never have a baby again because of internal damage, which may have caused the miscarriage, when the baby started to grow. Of course, they would never see a doctor about this. They would never tell him she was thirteen, because neither of them knew if that was her actual age. Clyde and Lily would both be surprised if they knew she was going to be fourteen on her birthday. Her body and her approach to life were much older than the years would have indicated.

One day the Sheriff came by. Clyde sent Lily in the house and went out to meet him. "What can I do for you Sheriff?"

"I got someone looking for your son. Wanted me to check with you to see if he was here."

"Did they say he was supposed to be here?"

"Not really, just checking."

"Well he came by right after harvest a year ago. Not this harvest. He wanted money but did not want to stay and live here. I kind of got the impression his job at the automobile factory didn't work out, never said, just a feeling I got."

"Did he say where he was heading?"

"Nope. Just interested in hitting me up for money. I didn't have much on hand. The crops were harvested but not sold yet. I still hadn't gotten the money for them. Which was a good thing for me." He laughed and added, "If you know what I mean. That kid never wanted to work for anything."

"That's all?"

"Yep, came one day gave me his sad story about needing money. Had another place to go that night and came back the next day to get the money on his ways out of town. That's all, he said. Didn't feel the need to know anymore. I was actually glad to see him leave. Haven't seen him since. That all I know Sheriff."

They made chitchat and the Sheriff climbed back in his car. Clyde felt relief that someone had finally come out and checked. He felt sure he bought his story. The Sheriff had to remember what a hellion his son was when he lived here. In fact, everyone was glad to see him move on. He looked at the Sherriff before he left and the Sheriff stopped and leaned out the window. "No offense, but I'm actually glad that boy moved on. You should be too."

Clyde looked at him and said, "No offense taken. I know what you mean."

He went back in the house and told Lily what had happened. He seemed satisfied that the conversation went well. That should be the end of any questions about the son being at the farm.

"Who is looking for him?" asked Lily

"Not sure. Didn't say."

"Is that strange?"

"We can only hope when we are gone, someone would miss us. Although with that boy, I am surprised anyone would. Maybe his brother."

"I forgot he had a brother." The look on Lily's face displayed absolute terror.

"He is in the Army. He may be dead. I guess if that was the case, they would send a letter and I haven't gotten one. Don't worry about him showing up. He hated me and the farm. Would have gone when his Mama died but he was too young. Left as soon as he turned sixteen. Only told his brother when he left. They fought all the time. Never thought they were particularly close. I don't see him as a threat to us."

Lily could not get the thought out of her mind. She was very fearful for the next few days and found it difficult to sleep. She even asked Clyde to bring the shotgun into the bedroom to protect them while they slept. He told her the Army keeps their soldiers for three years and he wouldn't be able to come home. She still could not shake the fear, so he decided the best thing was to bring it in, and pray she was wrong.

Chapter 10

Clyde looked at her one day and said, "We've been married three years already. I got to thinking; we don't know when your birthday is. I think we should make up one because everyone should have a birthday."

Lily didn't know what the big thing was with birthdays but she wanted to do anything to make him happy. "How do you do that?"

"Well, first we pick a month. What is your favorite time of the year?"

"I like when I can go swimming the best."

"Ok, how about July or August?"

"OK."

"I'll pick July. Now what is your favorite number? Pick between one and thirty-one."

"How about 16?" She chose that number thinking it was the age she was supposed to be, when she married him.

"Ok that's settled. Your birthday is July 16th."

"How old am I?"

"Now that's a tricky one. We don't know for sure but let's make you 18 on your next birthday."

"OK."

"Well you picked good because that's next week."

"Oh, ok."

Lily didn't know people had birthday celebrations or why it was important to have one. Then, she remembered the good part of Christmas and she never had that before either.

On July 16, Clyde told her today was her birthday. He was taking her to town and she could pick out a present. He handed her some money and told her she could buy it herself. She knew how to count numbers but had never even touched money before. She had no idea what the money meant. Clyde told her if something was listed as cents, then she would use a one-dollar bill. There were one hundred cents in one dollar. That was the hardest part. If it was listed in dollars, she should count the one-dollar bills to see if they equaled the amount of the item. If not, move up to the five-dollar bill.

"You know how numbers climb. One, then five, then ten. The higher the number the more you can buy. Does that make sense?"

"I think so."

Clyde wrote numbers on pieces of paper and told her to pretend the paper was something she wanted to buy. He then had her count out the right amount of money to buy it. Soon she got the concept right and clapped her hands. She got so excited he looked at her in wonderment. He still couldn't understand why God had sent her to him. He didn't deserve such joy.

Lily came out of the store carrying a bag. Inside she had a pair of jeans and two magazines. Clyde asked how she made out.

"I did great. It was so much fun. But I still have money left." She handed it to Clyde. He handed it back. "Keep it for the next time you come with me. You may want to shop again."

Lily could not imagine having her own money. She was going to keep it and play with it until she was sure she knew how to count out the right amount for things. She even had coins. He took her across the street and bought her an ice cream cone to eat on the way home. There were so many flavors; she didn't know which one to choose. Clyde chose two scoops for her. A chocolate and a vanilla. "This is the most common. Next time maybe you will want a different flavor."

"This was a wonderful day. Thank you for my birthday!" Just the look on Lily's face made Clyde realize he had done the perfect thing for her first official birthday.

Soon it was harvest time again. Lily went into town each time Clyde made trips to find workers. She used this time to walk around town and to explore. She was fascinated at how close the houses in town were to each other. You could almost touch the neighbor's house from your front porch. She found a secondhand store and went in. She went to the book section and found a cookbook. She spent time looking through the other books and decided to buy one on travel. She loved reading about other places, even though she had no desire to go anywhere. She also bought a recipe book.

This year they had to make three trips before they found enough workers. Clyde complained how hard it was getting to find people to help on farms. The younger people wanted to get away from farming. Lily couldn't understand this. She loved the land and the animals. The life they had. Each time she went into town she took some of her change and bought a new magazine. No one in the magazines lived on a farm, so she guessed Clyde was right.

Lily had used her recipe book many times. She was excited each time she made something new and Clyde said it was good. Sometimes he told her not to make something again but he never blamed it on her cooking, just the recipe. She was able to find new ways to use her vegetables and change how they tasted.

After her chores were done each day, she headed out to her tree, as she always thought of it now. She took her travel book, read the stories and looked at the pictures. She rarely thought of the baby. In fact, if she did, she never thought of it as her baby and never her son. It was just *'the baby'*. This may have been because she had never known she was pregnant and never thought about being pregnant, or for that matter being a mother. Since she had never had a mother to relate to, it was not something she was familiar with or thought was a normal thing to be. Just like she never had friends, so not having any now, never made her wish for any. Clyde fulfilled any need she had for other people and she was content being by herself. When he was working out in the fields, she never really missed him. It was just something he did, like the chores she did.

Her reading was not a wish to change her life. It was just something to fulfill her quest for knowledge. If anyone were to ask Lily why she read, she wouldn't have an answer. She rarely analyzed anything. She just accepted things as they were.

One day she was up in the hayloft and looking through her treasure box. She decided to put the rock under her tree and take the box inside and put it in her bedroom drawer. She would keep her money in it. She glanced at the chain and paper. They no longer seemed like hidden treasures. Clyde had given her so many things of her own; she no longer felt the need to hoard her possessions. She didn't know the reason or have the ability to put her thoughts into words, but she was feeling safe for the first time in her life. She knew her possessions were safe with Clyde.

The Harvest time was the favorite time of the year for Clyde. Once the worry of getting enough workers to help him was behind him, he loved seeing the result of his hard work in planting and working the fields. It was as tangible as anything he had ever known. It secured his hope for another year. He could sell his crop. The profits let him pay the workers, buy seeds for the next year and have enough money to carry the household for necessary living expenses. They kept enough animals to satisfy their food supply. The hens laid eggs, the cows gave milk and the pigs kept for slaughter. Once a year, Clyde loaded up one or two of the pigs and took them to town. The profit he made on the pigs was enough to pay his yearly expenses at the General Store. He bought all his meats and staples there since he decided to stop butchering his own years ago. It was too much time and money invested, to make it worth the effort, since he did not have a family to feed. Although there was not much extra money left over, he was frugal and could provide a comfortable living. It never occurred to him to credit Lily for her free labor and lack of demands for money or material things.

The years passed and soon four more harvests and plantings were successfully completed. Their fear had become a distant memory. Clyde made sure Christmas and her birthday were still celebrated because he felt that's how things should be done.

Chapter 11

One day Clyde went out to the barn to tend to the animals and Lily made pancakes for breakfast. She was pleased because she thought back to the first pancakes she made and how awful they looked and tasted. Now they are light and fluffy and tasted as good as they looked. She went out to check on Clyde. He was taking a long time and the pancakes were getting cold. As she walked into the barn, she saw him lying on the floor. She ran to him and felt his head. He was burning up. She managed to get him to his feet and help him into the house.

He said, "I need to lie down. I feel awful." They struggled to get him in the bedroom. He was weak and had difficulty moving his legs. Lily had to do most of the work. Once she got him into the room, they both collapsed on the bed. She went into the bathroom and got some cold wet towels to cool him down. After she got him out of his clothes and rubbed him down, he fell asleep. She returned to the kitchen and started to clean up the remains of breakfast. She had lost her appetite and put everything away without eating. For the first time since she had been with Clyde, she saw that he was not invincible, and felt a sense of loss. What had always given her security, was now in jeopardy. Not in the romantic sense, but the fear any child would have with a sick parent.

Lily went out to the barn to make sure he had completed tending to the animals before he got sick. She finished the undone ones and headed back to check on Clyde. She felt his head and it seemed cooler. He was fast asleep so she left him alone. She sat in the kitchen reading her books so she would be close if he called out. She didn't want to go out to her tree and not hear him.

Clyde laid in the bed for three days. Lily nursed him the best she could, giving him sponge baths and trying to get him to eat. Finally, the fever broke and he got out of bed. He was still weak and could only walk with Lily's help. She could see he was scared and trying to be strong for her. They sat at the table. Lily told him what she had been doing, and that the animals had been taken care of.

It took several days before Clyde was able to get around on his own. Even then, he looked stooped and older. His pallor was not good and his voice not as strong or authoritative. If he or Lily noticed, they never discussed it. She started doing most of the chores while he attempted to help. That soon became the norm and they adjusted to the new arrangement.

After several months, Clyde realized he would not get better. In fact, he knew he would only get worse in the coming months. Soon it would be time for planting. Even if he could manage the planting, he didn't think he would be around for harvest. He did not want Lily trying to manage it by herself. Now, what to do about this? He has some serious thinking to do. No need to worry Lily until he had a plan.

For the next week, he had Lily show him her travel books. By now, she had three she had purchased from the secondhand stores on their trips to town. They looked at the pictures together and she told him all she had learned about each place. He listened carefully to what she said and asked questions about what she liked best in each place she told him about.

The following week, he told her he was going into town and she was going with him. He told her he had business to take care of and she could walk around the town and look in the stores. Once they arrived in town, Clyde and Lily separated. She went for a walk and he headed to the Doctor's office. He did not have an appointment but this town was so small, no one was required to have one in order to see the Doctor. There was only one person in the office when he took a seat so he did not have to wait long until the Doctor called him in.

After the exam, the Doctor confirmed his fears. He was dying. "How long Doc?

"Well since I have not seen you before or had the opportunity to follow your illness before this, I have to generalize. Most likely, three to six month. Could be sooner but not much later than that."

"Anything I need to do?"

"Get your affairs in order. I will give you some morphine to take toward the end to help with the pain. You can come in anytime and see me if you are getting worse and need something stronger. Is there any way I can help you with this? Someone I need to talk to?"

"Just me. I appreciate your time, Doc."

He paid his bill and left the office.

Now that he knew what he suspected was true, he went to a lawyer.

Again, because it was a small town, he did not have an appointment and it did not present a problem. He was granted a visit right away. He explained what he wanted and agreed to the financial arrangements. He needed to get Lily a Birth Certificate. He doubted her birth was registered or even if her father remembered when she was born. He wanted her birthday to be July 16th. The year was sometime before her mother died. Maybe two or three years? The death may have been registered. He gave the location of her father's house although he didn't know if he was still there or even if he was alive. The Lawyer promised to do what he could.

Next, he went to the General Store. He looked around and did not see Lily. *Good.* He headed back to the ladies department and told the salesclerk what he needed. Soon all his business was finished. He sat outside on the bench after he placed his purchases in the back of the truck, and waited for Lily. He decided he would buy her a Coke or an ice cream cone on this trip. He'd let her choose. He sat there for thirty minutes and spotted Lily coming across the street toward the truck. She waved at him to let him know she was on her way.

"Did you have a good time?"

"Yes, I always do."

"I don't see any books this time."

"I didn't see anything I wanted. Nothing new came in."

"Well so it's not a wasted trip, let's get you a treat. What will it be, coke cola or ice cream?"

Lily had a hard time deciding. She thought a few minutes and then said, "Nothing today".

Suddenly it dawned on Clyde that she looked sad. "How about I buy a bottle of coke and we can take it home with us for later?"

"Ok." Lily spoke without her usual enthusiasm.

They were both quiet on the way home and by the time they arrived; Clyde was exhausted from the activities of the day. "Lily, can you see to things? I want to rest before dinner."

Lily agreed. She had been doing all the chores by herself for a while now, so it was nothing she couldn't handle. But, the scared feelings came back. Clyde did not get up for dinner that night. Lily ate leftovers alone at the kitchen table. Confusion and uncertainty washed over her.

The next morning she had the chores done and breakfast almost ready before Clyde got out of bed. She watched him approach the table and it hit her. He was sick. Really sick. They needed to get him to the Doctor. She decided that once the breakfast and dishes were done, she would talk to him about getting him better. Clyde continued to sit at the table while she cleaned up the kitchen. When she finished, she sat down beside him and said, "Should I get my Travel book now?"

"No. Not now. We need to talk."

"About you being sick?"

"Yes."

"I want you to go to the Doctors and get medicine."

"Lily, I went yesterday."

"You did? Did he give you something so you can get better?"

"I want you to listen to me. I have some things we need to discuss." Clyde explained what the Doctor said.

Lily began to cry. "It can't be true."

"Lily, it is. Now, I want to tell you what we are going to do. Especially, what you are going to do. I have some plans made out to take care of you and we only have a short time to start. I want you to go out to the truck and get the bag out of the back. I forgot to bring it in last night."

Once Lily brought it in to him, he opened it up and pulled out a purse. "See how long this strap is? I want you to try it on and wear it across your shoulder like half of an X. This will keep it from falling off your shoulder. Now try it out." He stood up and showed her how to put the strap over her head and have the bag rest on her hip.

"It feels funny. Why do I have this?"

"I want you to get used to using this bag. I want you to take it wherever you go and whatever you do until you don't feel comfortable without it. Even to bed for the first couple of days. Do you understand?"

"Yes." Lily really did not understand at all, but decided she better do as he said because he had always told her the right things to do. Clyde then told her they would look at the Travel book later. He needed to lie down. He went into the bedroom and realized he would probably be lucky to see three month so he needed to get Lily ready. But not now. He was drained from the morning and needed to rest to keep up his strength. During the night, he reached out to Lily. He smiled to himself when he realized that she was wearing the purse. *"The girl is going to be ok,"* he thought to himself.

The next morning he felt rested and had more strength. He went out to the kitchen and poured a cup of coffee. Lily was already out in the barn taking care of the chores. He walked over to see her. She was almost finished and had a basket of eggs in her hands.

"How's it going today?"

"Fine"

She didn't look happy.

"What's the matter?"

"This dang bag keeps getting in the way."

"You'll get used to it."

· "No I won't", she pouted.

He laughed and said, "Let's go eat some of those eggs".

After breakfast and dishes were done, she sat at the table.

"Can I take this thing off to get my bath"?

"Of course. It's not a punishment. I want you to get use to having it with you at all times. You need to know where it is and never leave it out of your sight. That's why I want you to wear it, until you get to the point you feel naked without it. Like part of you is missing. Always aware that you should have it. Never forgetting. Do you understand?"

"I guess so".

"Ok. Now we are going to talk about why. You are going to keep your money in there. And, most importantly, your papers. Just like you do now with your treasure box."

"Why?"

"I will not be here long. I want to teach you to protect yourself and what is yours."

Lily looked at him. She still could not believe he would not be with her every day. She had never been alone before. Never had anyone taken care of her before. What would she do? She nodded ok. Clyde laid out his plan.

He owned the farm. He had gone into the Lawyer's office and put her name on the deed. The farm would belong to her. Now he told her to listen carefully until he finished.

"I am going to sell the animals. All but the chickens for now. You cannot stay here by yourself. It's too isolated and dangerous for such a young girl. In order to make money, the fields have to be planted and harvested. You cannot do that by yourself. I've arranged to rent the farm.

45

The rent money will pay the taxes on this place and the extra money will go into a bank account for you. We will decide where you want to go and buy you a bus ticket so you can start a new life. We looked at the Travel book and I think I know where you like best. I have some cash put away and you will take that with you to pay for what you need until you get a job."

He looked at Lily. He felt sad she had to start over again. Poor girl had not had much of a life so far. But that can't be helped. No time for sentiment now. They had to plan. He wanted to give her as much help as he could while he still had time.

He pulled out a small leather bag with a zipper on the top. He gave it to her and told her to open it. Inside was more money than she had ever seen. "Take it out and count it." She got to one hundred and then got confused. "Ok. You have to be able to keep track of every dollar. We are going to practice until we get it right."

He told her he was going to write down prices on pieces of paper and she was to put the money to pay for each price on the paper. He would give her time by herself to do it and then come back and check. He would sit on the porch until she felt she had each one right. He wrote out numbers on ten pieces of paper and left her alone. Lily had so much going through her mind that she found it difficult to concentrate. The tears were running down her cheek. She realized she was losing Clyde, her home and the animals. It was almost too much to bear.

Clyde sat outside to give Lily a chance to think through what he had told her. He was concerned about the money, but he had seen how she spent her money, when she had some. He had checked and she still had money left from when he had given her the birthday money. That was the least of his worries. He had to make her as safe as he could.

They worked each day after breakfast getting her proficient in counting and keeping track of money. What she spent, what she had left. Finally, he was satisfied. "Now it's time to move on to the next thing, Lily. You did good with the money. Now get me a knife and spoon." He drew a large circle on paper and made a clock face. He took the knife and told her this would be the hour. The hour on the dial was always the longest part that was on the clock. "Some people call this the hands of the clock." He took the spoon. "This will be the minutes. See how it is shorter?"

She nodded *yes.*

"The spoon or the little hand will have to move all around the numbers before the big hand moves to the next number. The little hand counts out sixty minutes." He showed her by moving the little spoon, then the knife, when it passed the number twelve on the clock. He had her practice repeating each number of minutes represented by five. She was a very attentive student. He never realized how smart she was. If she were a man, she would go far. Too bad his sons never had her brain. He thought how unfair life could be. Then he looked at Lily and smiled. "I'm going to write down some times on paper and I want you to move the knife and spoon to that time."

He was surprised at how quickly she finished. She got each one right. Then he went through minutes and had her count the minutes between each space on the clock to make sixty minutes. She struggled with this, but was determined to get it right. She loved learning new things. She was so absorbed in learning; she forgot why she was learning.

Suddenly he was tired. "I have to lie down. You did good today."

The next day, he brought out a calendar he got at the feed and grain store. "I want you to remember the months, days and weeks of the year. We will mark the dates for you to remember on the calendar, ok?" He had her find the month of her birthday. She didn't recognize any of the months. The spent the next hour getting her to know the months and soon she could tell him the winter months, spring, summer, and fall one's. They moved onto the days of the week. Then the different days in each month. He explained how not all months were the same number of days.

When he was confident that she was sure how to read the calendar, he had her mark her birthday. Then he had her mark their wedding date. Neither really remembered, so she went and got the sheet of paper, he called the Marriage Certificate. He asked her if there was any other date she wanted to put on there and she said, "Christmas."

He forgot about the Holidays. He went through each month and explained holidays to her. Since they were all marked, she wouldn't have to remember to write those down. He was extremely pleased how fast she had learned the basic things she should have learned in school, if she had been allowed to attend long enough.

He then had her place the calendar in her purse so she would have it with her. She now slept with the purse beside the bed but put it on each morning after she dressed. She rarely noticed it.

"Our next thing will be to decide where you are going and what you are going to do once you get there. Now get your book, go outside under your tree, and decide what place you like best. It is time for my rest."

Over the next couple of weeks Lily practiced all that she had learned when she got some free time from the chores. Clyde's health continued to decline and he realized that it was soon time to send her away. One more trip to town to get her a suitcase and meet with the lawyer. Time to off load the livestock. Just loose ends to clear up while he was still capable. They would check out the bus schedules and plan her trip. He was glad she had decided on heading west. He feared she was too naïve to head east and get lost in a big city.

Finally, the day before she was to leave, arrived. Her clothes were packed and plans were finalized. He gave her the Birth Certificate the lawyer had managed to obtain for her. He reminded her to keep the Marriage Certificate because it would give her legal right to the farm. They decided she would go as far as California. She would look for a room in a private home or boarding house. Then she would look for a job. He told her she should be able to get a job as a waitress or as a clerk in a store. She had enough skills for those. He knew she was a quick learner and would adapt to anything she undertook.

Lily cooked up extra meals for Clyde to eat and washed all the clothes and sheets. She did not want to leave him. More from leaving something comfortable and moving to the unknown, was what held her to him. She was married to him, but had never felt the romantic feeling toward him, that married people should experience. If anyone was to examine their relationship, it resembled the feelings of father and daughter. Although they had sex as a married couple, it had never resembled making love.

That night, they held each other in bed all night. They both knew they would never see each other again in this lifetime. Clyde went over the instructions and one of the last things he reminded her, was to never talk about what happened. She was to forget about it, and if anyone asked her any questions, which he doubted, she was to say she didn't know anything about it. What's done, is done and forgotten. He made her promise she would forget about the bad times and remember the good ones.

"When you get sad, think of your birthday or Travel books. Remember to trust your instincts when you face a new situation."

They got dressed in the morning and ate breakfast. Clyde was glad the animals were gone and no longer required his attention. He was also glad that Lily was leaving today because he doubted it would be long before he could no longer drive. He was glad he could die peacefully and not worry about her being a target of thieves or worse. Although the farm was isolated, it would not be long until the townspeople knew he was dead and she was alone on the farm. He had always tried to protect her and keep her safe. Now, that was no longer possible. Yes, he thought, this was best. She had now been with him six years and in some ways was still as innocent as when he first brought her home. He owed her this much.

They did not talk on the ride into town. Lily was both scared and sad and did not want to worry Clyde. He was desperately trying to keep his attention on the road. He was getting weaker and the pain had started to intensify. If was difficult to concentrate. He decided while he was in town he would see the Doctor one last time and get stronger pain medicine.

Once Lily was on the bus, she waved out the window to Clyde. As the bus drove through towns and countryside, she was suddenly excited for the adventure and looking forward to what lay ahead of her.

Clyde went to the Doctor's office and gave him some money. He arranged for the Doctor to send someone out once a week to see if he was dead. He was to be buried in the family plot at the edge of the field. His coffin would be in the barn. Then the Doctor would hire someone to dig his grave and notify the Lawyer that the farm was ready to be rented out. He felt pleased that it was almost over so he could leave this earth in peace and enter his next journey. He had never been a churchgoer so he didn't know if God wanted him or not. He had lived his life the best way he knew how. Made some bad mistakes but hoped he had done some things right too.

The next week he went out to the barn when he had the strength. He worked on his coffin and hoped he could last until it was finished. He could no longer eat. He finally decided to stay in the barn because going back and forth to the house was too much trouble. True to his word, the Doctor sent his son out to check on him. He told him to tell the Doc it would be soon and to look in the barn. He was staying there now.

On the day before the next expected visit, Clyde put the last nail in the coffin. It was complete. He took the pills for the pain and washed them down with the last of his whiskey. His last thoughts were of Lily. He laid down and went to meet God.

Lily's New Life

Chapter 12

Lily was enjoying her bus ride. She was following the instructions Clyde had given her. She kept her purse on her at all times. She always made sure to eat a big breakfast because he told her that was the cheapest meal. She washed up in the bathrooms at the restaurants and bought the cheapest item on the menu for supper. She did have to put her suitcase in the storage compartment under the bus, but the driver promised her it would be safe, because only the drivers could get to it. Many passengers got on and off but she stayed on. The drivers changed along with the buses. She had several layovers. Because of the remoteness of the town she started from; it was difficult to get to her new destination without taking several different routes.

On her second day on the bus, she was sitting down to breakfast and the bus driver sat across from her. He had a kind face and she was grateful for the company. "I hope you don't mind my sitting with you. You remind me of my daughter."

The word was passed down by each bus driver, that she was traveling alone. Each new driver would keep an eye out for her. Hank, the current driver, had noticed her when he first took over the bus she was already on. He became aware of how she kept to herself and did not talk to anyone. He was glad because that was a safe thing to do. "Where are you going little lady?"

Lily looked at him and was not sure how to answer him. Clyde had coached her of what to say to people about her personal life but not about questions about where she was going. "I want to go to California to find a job."

"What kind of job?"

"Either waitress, or to work in a store."

"Where in California?"

"I just thought when I saw the town, I'd know."

He thought that was strange but she acted skittish and he did not want to scare her. "Well there are a lot of pretty places out there. We have another day to go until we reach the start of the state. Maybe something will look good to you."

The bus driver kept thinking of the conversation while he drove. He had raised three daughters and two sons and still worried about kids when he had them on his bus. She sure looked young but he had noticed a wedding ring on her finger. He did not question her about her life because it was none of his business. He did not want to scare her off from talking to him. His wife always told him he could not take every lost "youngun' under his wing. If he had his way, they would have had a dozen kids but God had not seen it that way, so he was grateful for the five they had. Still he couldn't let go of the notion that he needed to protect every young passenger he had on his bus.

He always stopped at his sister's restaurant, on each trip through the small mountain town in Colorado, where she lived. Although it wasn't on the authorized list of designated stops, the bus company preferred, he was never reprimanded for making the detour. Lily got off the bus and looked around. She was standing out in front of the diner because she was not really hungry and thought she'd just wait until the stop was over. The bus driver noticed her and suddenly had a thought. "Why don't you take a look around this town and see if it appeals to you? We should be here for thirty minutes or so and I will not leave without you."

Lily thought she would take that suggestion and walk up and down the street. Not too far because she wanted to make sure she could see the bus at all times. If she noticed passenger boarding the bus, she knew she could get back quickly.

The bus driver went into the diner to greet his sister. He sat at the counter so they could talk as she worked. He explained his idea to her. She thought about what he said. Lord knows she didn't want trouble, but she did need to find dependable help. The town was growing, business was growing and she was not getting any younger. She agreed to talk to his passenger. She knew what his wife meant when she complained about his big heart getting in the way of his head. He didn't even know the girl's name for goodness sake. He went outside and looked around for Lily. She was up at the end of the street and when he waved to her, she quickly ran back. "How do you like this town?"

"It looks nice."

"Well, you could do worse than stay on here."

"Stay here?"

"Did you have another place in mind?"

"Not yet."

"Come on in and meet my sister. She is the owner of this place." He held the door for her. As Lily stepped through the door, she immediately felt at home. The place was clean and had an inviting look. She had never been in a restaurant before this bus trip but from her limited knowledge, she liked it.

The bus driver introduced her to his sister. "This is my sister Bea. I'm sorry but I don't know your name."

Lily told them her name. It was funny saying it out loud. She rarely heard her name and she couldn't remember the last time she told it to anyone.

"My you look just like a Lily", exclaimed the woman with the plump figure and graying hair.

The bus driver laughed out loud, and said, "That she does".

He explained his name was Hank and he always stopped in to see his sister every couple of weeks. Since she did not have a definite destination in mind, why doesn't she consider staying here and work for his sister? She needs help and Lily needed a job so it looked like a good fit for both of them. Bea explained that there was a room available with Mrs. Thomas, a few blocks over.

Hank said "Tell you what. If you don't like being here, I will pick you up the next time I am in town and take you anywhere you want to go. That way, your ticket will still be good, if you want to leave. What do you say?"

Lily was overcome with emotion. No one had ever acted like they wanted her. Well, maybe Clyde, but never a woman. She knew this was not the town Clyde had suggested, but it sounded like it would work. Hadn't he told her to trust her instincts?

"Ok. I'd like that." Lily spoke so softly they both had to strain to hear her. Then they both started laughing and told her they would watch over her. Hank left to get her bag off the bus and Bea told her she would take her over to see the room, after the bus left, and business slowed down.

Lily was very pleased with the room. It was clean and decorated very pretty. Mrs. Thomas told her where the bathroom was and if she wanted to use the kitchen, it would be an extra five dollars a week. Bea told Mrs. Thomas she was crazy. Lily would eat all her meals at the diner and maybe, just maybe, use it once in a while to heat water for tea. Was she out of her mind to charge the poor girl five extra dollars? Mrs. Thomas and Bea yelled back and forth for a couple of minutes. Lily was sure she was going to be thrown out of the house, and she would lose her room. When Lily was close to shaking, they both burst out laughing. They called each other some names and then hugged each other and said in unison, "Agreed!"

Lily had her room. She was not used to relationships and did not understand what had just happened. But, they both seemed happy.

Lily walked back to the diner and Bea showed her around the kitchen. Then she explained the menu and the daily specials. Since she would waitress, she would need a uniform. Bea went in the back room and brought one out. "This belonged to Peg but she ran off with a truck driver. Go into the storeroom and see if it fits."

Lily came back wearing the uniform.

"Little snug across the top but otherwise it will do. You'll have on an apron anyway. Now let's finish up here and then you can go home and rest up. You need to be here at six a.m. sharp. And you can't wear that damn purse while you work."

Lily went back to the storeroom, removed her uniform and hung it back up on the hook. She put on her own clothes and carefully counted out the money to give to Mrs. Thomas, who Bea called her landlord. She would be careful not to let anyone know where she kept her money.

As Lily walked back to her room, she took in the sights and sounds generated by the town and the people that lived here. So unlike anything she had ever known. The air smelled different and the land was so different. The land was not farmland but just like a place out of a picture in her magazines and books. Houses were close together and all shapes and sizes. All looked warm and inviting. Like people cared about them. So different from the town she and Clyde went to. She saw people walking up and down the streets on their way to some place close by. Children could be heard calling to each other and playing together. The sky even looked different as if the activity taking place on the streets had an influence on the clouds. They were all white and puffy as if they were swelling with pride over the town reflected below. She decided she liked it. Mrs. Thomas seemed nice, the house was even larger than Clyde's and she was actually going to have a job. She also liked that she would be sleeping in a bed all by herself. She had never had her own bed or her own room.

She did not think of Clyde anymore than she thought of her chores and animals. She was focused solely on learning her job and doing what she was told at work. She smiled as she pulled the cover up, this is something I could really get used to, and she yawned and fell quickly into a peaceful sleep. That night she fell into a sound sleep. Not the result of exhaustion; but from the realization she was in control of her life, for the first time ever. She had worked hard on the farm but this was going to be different. It would not be at her own pace, but at a structured one. She smiled to herself and thought *I feel like I'm looking out from inside of one of the pages in my magazine. I never thought I would be in a place like this*

Chapter 13

After a week had passed, Bea was very pleased at how well Lily was working out. She never complained, she was polite and patient with the customers and did not bother with the men like other waitresses. She never flirted. In fact, she seemed to be unaware of how attractive she was. She did nothing to enhance her looks; she did not even wear lipstick. Little did anyone know; Lily didn't even own any cosmetics. Lily solved her concern over her handbag. She took out the smaller pouch that Clyde had given her and kept her cash and papers in that. She put that in the pocket of her uniform under her apron.

At first, Lily was surprised that people left money on the table when they left the restaurant. She started to run after a customer but Bea stopped her. She told Lily that was a tip left for the waitress who waited on them. Since Lily had taken care of that customer, the money was hers to keep. This made Lily uncomfortable but Bea admonished her every time she noticed that Lily did not pick up the money left for her. She soon became comfortable accepting the money left as a tip.

At the end of the week when her shift ended, Bea handed her an envelope. Inside was money. Lily's face was blank when she looked at Bea. "What is this? I took all the money; I mean tips off my tables like you said, so this money isn't mine."

Bea laughed. "Honey, this is your pay. I admit it is not much more than a day's worth of tips, but you are paid by the restaurant to serve food. You don't work just for the tips."

"I get more money than I need. You keep this" She thrust the envelope back to Bea.

"If you don't need it now, maybe one day you will. Best save it for a rainy day."

"But it doesn't cost anything to have rain".

"Lordy girl, what planet did you come from?" Bea shook her head. Her first thought was that this girl was *'touched'* as her Mama used to say when someone was not right. But, she thought this over, and then decided that can't be. The girl was smart. She caught on fast, she made change correctly and then it hit her. This girl was innocent of the ways of the world. Where did she come from? What had her life been like? Well, whatever happened before, Bea was going to make sure she kept an eye on her so no one took advantage of her. She rationalized that since she never had any children maybe the dear Lord had sent this angel to her to look out for. She was determined not to let Him down.

Bea reminded Lily that she needed to pay her landlord today for her rent. She also reminded her, she did not have to work for the next two days. She only worked five days a week. Lily looked crestfallen. "What's the matter Honey?"

"I don't know what to do for two days if I don't come to work."

"Boy, wouldn't a lot of people wish you worked for them! Tell you what. Explore the town. Look in the shops. Spend some of your money on yourself."

"Ok." Lily had no idea what to buy. There was nothing she needed. She decided to explore the town and see if she could find something to do. She really had no choice.

Bea noticed Lily had left her uniform hanging in the storeroom. She was tempted to call after her and tell her it needed to be washed and ironed. Then she shrugged and thought the poor girl doesn't have a washing machine let alone an iron. I better try to teach her how to use the Laundromat. Then she though, *and I guess a lot of other things too*!

Lily woke up the same time the next morning. She greeted her landlord as she walked down the stairs. "Good morning, Mrs. Thomas."

"Good Morning to you too. Come into the kitchen and have some cereal and coffee with me."

"Ok". Lily reached for her money to give her five dollars to use the kitchen.

"Honey, the five dollar thing was between me and Bea. We go way back to when we were both in diapers. We always see who can get the best of each other. Now you can use the kitchen anytime you like. If you do cooking, you need to supply your own food to cook but I can spare coffee and cereal."

As they ate breakfast, Mrs. Thomas kept a steady stream of chatter going. It was hard for Lily to keep track of what she was saying because she kept talking of people and things Lily didn't know. Then she stopped and looked at Lily. "I bet you don't know where the church is now, do you? Are you Baptist?"

Lily shook her head *'no'* because she didn't know what Baptist was so she was sure she wasn't one.

"Good. You can go with me tomorrow to the Community Christian Church. I go to the eight o'clock service. I can introduce you around if you like."

Lily had never been to church. She couldn't tell this to Mrs. Thomas because then she may not like her, so she said, "I'd like that very much."

Lily took off to explore the town. She was careful to take note of what she passed so she could find her way home. It was a beautiful fall day and it was fun to have nothing to do. At the end of the street, she came to a big sign *Welcome to Relay Community Park*. She had never been to a Park before and was excited to see what was there. She walked in and saw Ducks swimming in the water. Without thinking, she walked over and took her shoes off. It was cold, too cold to swim. Then she thought of what Clyde had told her one day when they were swimming in their *pond "Lily, it's ok to swim without clothes here in our own pond but if you ever swim anywhere else we have to get you a bathing suit. People don't like to see naked people swimming in public places."* So, I guess this is a public place she thought.

She sat on the bank and watched the ducks. She thought back to their pond and the ducks that sometimes swam there. Once she had taken some chicken feed out to feed them and Clyde had gotten mad. He said not to feed them because he didn't want ducks making a home in the cornfield. She glanced over when she heard children playing. There were swings and other playground equipment like they had at her school. She decided to go over and get on them. Good thing I have on pants she thought. When she got on the swings at school, the boys were always trying to look up her dress. She found an empty swing and got on. She started to swing higher and higher. Soon she noticed the adults were looking at her. They were there with their children and resented teenagers who often hogged the swings. Lily soon felt uncomfortable with the attention she was getting and got off the swings and walked away.

It was now close to lunchtime so she decided to go to the diner for lunch. She would decide what to do after that. She ordered a cheeseburger and fries. This was something she had never had, and found out she loved it best of all the foods they made here. She watched the customers. Something she couldn't do when she was working. She was too busy then making sure drinks were refilled and people were waited on quickly. She was fascinated with the families that came in with their kids. How nice it was to have a mama and daddy. She watched more with interest than envy. Every day she was discovering new experiences and encountering things she had never seen before. She was content.

After lunch, she walked down the other way and looked in store windows. She found a secondhand store and went inside. They had a book section and she wanted something different to read. She selected several books and paid for them then headed home. As she reached the house, she saw her landlady outside at the clothesline. She headed back to see if she could help. "Can I help? I know how to hang up the wash."

Mrs. Thomas looked at her in surprise. None of her boarders had ever offered to help. Heck, most of them act like I'm hired help and they can mess up all they want to. "Now, I'd appreciate that Lily."

She watched Lily hang up the clothes. The poor girl was throwing them over the lines like she never used clothespins before. She went over and showed Lily the way the pins held the clothes.

"This way, they are not doubled over and they dry faster. Remember, we wash the sheets first and hang them on the outside of the lines. Then we have to turn them around and make sure they dry on each side before going back on the beds. Then we wash the underclothes and make sure they are hung in the middle lines so the sheets hide them from the neighbors. They don't like seeing underwear flapping in the breeze. Plus, I don't like the nosey neighbors knowing what I wear under my clothes. Then the clothes are hung on the inside lines closest to the sheets. Once you get the hang of it, it works out easier."

"Oh, Ok." Lily thought that was a good idea and soon got the laundry hung up. She thought Mrs. Thomas was nice. She looked at her and smiled. "Do you have any more chores I can do?" Her landlady looked at her. Was she serious? "Well you can't do chores instead of paying rent, if that's what you have in mind."

Lily didn't understand why she thought that. "I'm used to chores and I'd like to have some. I'm not working today so I have nothing to do. I didn't mean I wouldn't pay you for my room."

The look on Lily's face convinced her this was true. *God Bless this innocent child,* she thought. "Well Lily, I have washed all the sheets and things I needed to do. Do you have anything you want to wash? You can use my machine if you want."

Lily was grateful. She was wondering how she would clean her clothes. The landlady watched over her and instructed her on what to do. "Each machine is different, so I'll explain how mine works." She didn't want to embarrass Lily, but could tell the poor girl was clueless.

After the laundry was done, she went out and sat on the front porch with her book. She told her landlady she would take down the laundry and fold it when it was dry. She was so engrossed in reading she didn't see anything going on around her. She discovered she loved reading books. It was magical. A way to escape into something and someplace different than she had ever known. As the afternoon wore on, Lily realized the laundry must be dry, laid her book down and went to check. She folded the sheets and towels and then went back to get the clothes off the line. Mrs. Thomas watched her out the kitchen window. When Lily came in with the folded laundry, she spotted her landlady by the sink. "Where do you want me to put these?"

"Just set the basket down. I'll need to iron some things before they are put away."

"Iron?"

"Honey, don't you ever iron?"

Lily looked puzzled.

"Well, I can teach you. It's something every woman needs to learn." She got out the ironing board and plugged in the iron. Once it was heated, she showed Lily how to put the clothes on the board and smooth out the wrinkles. She ironed a dress, then an apron. "Do you want to try?"

Lily was surprised how heavy the iron felt in her hand. She burnt her fingers several time but Mrs. Thomas was surprised that she never complained. In fact, looking at her face, she was in deep concentration and trying her best to do it right. Soon Lily had all her clothes ironed and folded. Although there were still plenty of wrinkles ironed in, both she and Mrs. Thomas were pleased at what she had accomplished.

"Can I do this again?"

"Of course. I appreciate your help. Now go do something young people do."

Lily again looked puzzled. She didn't know what young people did. She thought she was doing what she should be doing. She went back on the porch to catch the rest of the daylight available to read her new books.

Each night before bed, she took out the calendar Clyde had given her and crossed off the date. He had told her to put an X in each square once the day was done. That way she would always know what the date was and the day of the week.

When Lily awoke in the morning, she realized she was going to church with her landlady. She was excited because she had never been to church before. When she went downstairs, she saw her landlady.

"Lordy, girl. You can't wear blue jeans to the house of the Lord. You got a dress or skirt you can wear?"

Lily looked down at her clothes. She did have one dress. Not sure how it fit but she turned around to go change.

When she came down the stairs, her landlady frowned. "Is that your only dress?"

"Yes."

The dress was two sizes too small and very childish looking. She was sure to be stared at if she walked in to church in that. "Come with me, I might have something that would fit."

Mrs. Thomas rummaged through a closet. She had a bag of clothes that a tenant had left behind when she skipped out on her rent. She was saving it in case the girl ever came back to pay her. Not that, that was likely to happen. Now she was glad she had decided to keep them. She dumped the clothes out on the dining room table. "Now let's see what we have here."

There were several nice outfits and she selected two for Lily to try on. "Just step in my bedroom and see which one you like and what fits the best." Lily chose the simplest one. She put it on and walked back out to Mrs. Thomas.

"Honey, you look beautiful. That blue dress matches your eyes and fits you like it was made for you. You'll turn heads alright, but in a good way. Now let's have a quick breakfast of toast and coffee and get to church on time. When we get back, we'll look over the rest of the clothes and see what shape they are in. If nothing needs repaired , you can take them. I have no need to hold on to them anymore. They will be out of style soon enough and if the person who owned them wanted them back, she would have come back for them before now."

They walked to the church. Lily was in awe of all the people heading in the door. As they entered, she was struck by the calm that washed over her. She sat down beside Mrs. Thomas and looked around the room. She was transfixed by the cross above the table and the candles burning.

Soon the Pastor came up to the altar and everyone took out a book from the shelf in front of them. Everyone began to sing. Lily thought this was the most wonderful sound she had ever heard. She just stood there and took everything in. Mrs. Thomas looked over at her and wondered why she was not singing along. But when she looked at Lily's face, she was struck at how angelic she looked. Again she was amazed by this girl. She secretly wondered where she had been before she came here. Could God be testing her faith by sending this girl to her home? She shook her head *"Forgive me God; I must be seeing things that are not there. I know she is a mortal person."*

Lily sat very quiet and listened to every word the Pastor spoke. She was so absorbed she was almost in a trance. Mrs. Thomas nudged her several times when it was time to stand for parts of the service. When it was over, they went outside. Lily was introduced to several parishioners and then the Pastor. She was still in awe of what had happened during the service, she found it hard to speak.

"Welcome to our church. We hope you become a member." He shook her hand and moved on.

As they walked back to the house, Lily asked what becoming a member meant. Her landlady looked at her for a minute and explained what being a Christian and a member of the Church meant to her. She also explained about contributing to the church in the collection each Sunday and about the Bible Study that was held every Tuesday evening. Lily was very excited and wanted to learn more about God and being a Christian.

"Well, I put in extra money this week for you so don't fret about that. And if you want to join me on Tuesday night, we can walk over together at seven-thirty."

"I would love that. Can you let me know when it is seven-thirty? I get off work earlier and don't want to be late."

"Don't you have a clock?"

"No"

"Well how do you get to work on time?"

"I don't know I just do. I get up when daylight comes. It wakes me up."

"Well, we will fix that. Come on in to the storage closet. I know I have one in there that someone left behind."

They found an old electric clock with an alarm on it. She showed Lily how to set the time and the alarm. Lily spent the next half hour playing with it and getting to know how the alarm would work when she set it for different times. She was very grateful and took it up to her room. After she changed into her everyday clothes, she came down to sit on the porch and read.

Mrs. Thomas came out to remind her that the clothes were still sitting out for her to look at. They inspected the clothes together and decided they were all suitable for Lily.

"You are very nice to me Mrs. Thomas. Is there anything I can do for you?"

"Yes, let's drop the Mrs. Thomas and call me Madge."

Lily grinned, she was glad she moved to this town. She really liked it here.

Chapter 14

The weather cooled and winter arrived. One nice thing about living here, it was easy to walk around even in the snow. People who have houses facing the streets shoveled the sidewalks and a truck plowed the streets. Lily was now working different shifts and different days of the week. It made her sad to miss church on the Sundays she worked. But usually, if she worked on the weekend she had Tuesday off, and she still was able to go to Bible Study. All in all, Lily was beginning to think of this place as home. Her memories of her previous life were fading and she rarely thought back to those times. She had removed her wedding ring and put it in with her papers. She no longer wanted a constant reminder of her previous life. Not that she felt it was something to be ashamed of but in her hear, she knew that it was over and a new life was beginning for her.

Usually Bea worked the same schedule as Lily. Recently she told her she was doing such a good job, she didn't need to be watched or instructed anymore. Lily was pleased at the compliment but missed Bea when she didn't see her. The other waitresses were kind to Lily because they knew she was special to Bea. Although she never openly displayed favoritism toward Lily, the employees knew to be careful and not cause any trouble for her and get Bea mad at them.

Lily had now been in town over six months. She knew most of the customers, either by name, or by what they drank. They liked that about her. She remembered what they drank and what they liked. She always told them when the cook had made their favorite soup that day and always had a smile on her face. If they talked about her at all, they would say they had never seen her in a bad mood.

Hank had been back through several times to see his sister. He always said to Lily, "Ready to take me up on that bus ride to another town?"

Lily always replied with the same answer, "Not this time Hank, I like it here" and laughed with him.

He was always glad he had found her a *'home'*. His sister seemed really pleased with the arrangement and he always told his wife the story over and over but she never seemed to grow tire of hearing it. She knew she was lucky to have married such a compassionate man.

Lily was working the Saturday evening shift with the waitress named Sue. Since Sue was interested in the men, Lily did most of the work that evening. Especially if it was a family, women or teenagers. Sue hung around the young single men. Lily didn't mind or even think about it. She liked keeping busy. Besides sometimes the single men tried to grab at her when Bea wasn't around. She hated that and it made her uncomfortable. She didn't know how to act when that happened so she didn't make them mad. She tried to avoid any unpleasant situation.

Later that night, Sue slipped outside with one of the men. She told Lily she would be right back and to take care of all the tables while she was gone. Before she got back, a man came in and Lily smelt the whiskey on him. Memories of her father kept drifting back. She had no choice but to wait on him. She tried to keep her distance but when she delivered his food she had to lean over the table. He grabbed at her and ran his hand along her leg. "Bet you like that, don't ya, honey?"

Lily froze. The nightmare returned. She turned and ran out of the diner and ran all the way home. Madge saw her come in and run up the stairs. It was so unlike Lily that she went after her to check what was wrong. She heard her sobbing before she reached the door to her room. She knocked but did not wait for an answer before she went in the room. She automatically took Lily in her arms to find out what had happened to her.

"He touched me. He scared me. I don't want the sex thing anymore."

"Calm down honey. Who touched you? What sex thing?"

"The customer in the restaurant. When I put his food down he grabbed me and ran his hand up under my dress."

"Wasn't anyone else there? Where was the other waitress?"

"It was close to the time we close and she went outside for a minute. I was alone and scared like the last time."

"What last time?"

Lily did not realize that memory was still there. Panic gripped her that she had said the words out loud. Now she cried harder.

"Lily, tell me."

"I can't. I promised. Don't make me!"

Madge realized she would not get anything else out of Lily tonight.

"Tell you what. Go take a nice bath. I'll bring you up some tea to help you rest. I promise this will not happen again. It's not right."

While Lily took her bath, Madge called Bea. She told her how Lily had been attacked by some heathen drunk when she was left alone in the restaurant. By the time she got off the phone it was lucky they both didn't have a stroke. They were both that mad.

The next day Lily went back to work. She refused to discuss it any further with either Madge or Bea but they both noticed that some part of her had closed up. Like she was hurting but could not face talking about it. Bea did all she could to give Lily earlier shifts and avoid the ones that drew the drinkers. She also made sure Sue was scheduled for those shifts. Neither she nor Lily ever discussed that night but Sue knew something had happened. She decided not to ask and admit she may have been responsible for leaving Lily alone.

Soon it was spring and nothing else had happened to worry Lily. She had gotten a new calendar for Christmas from Madge and a Timex watch from Bea. She was so surprised that she still kept the wrapping paper and ribbon to remind her of that day. She had gotten Bea a new apron and Madge a cookbook. She hadn't wrapped them in the nice paper because she didn't know that was how it was done. They were both very happy with their gifts.

She thought about this as she walked to work in the cool spring day. It had almost been a year since that day she arrived here and her life had changed so much. Lily was grateful for the life she had now. She enjoyed her job and her two women friends. She also had developed a faith in God that she never had before. In fact, she remembered to thank Him for giving her such a good life.

Lily was settled into a peaceful existence. One day Madge suggested they go to the department store together.

"I noticed you never buy yourself any clothes. I also know your underwear is getting pretty ragged because I see it on the clothesline when you do your laundry."

Lily looked at Madge to see if she was making fun of her. Instead, all she saw was someone trying to take care of her.

"Ok, I guess you are right."

Once in the store Madge went with her to the clothing department. She insisted Lily buy seven panties and three bras. She made her try on the bras to make sure they had the right size. Then she went over to the dresses and they picked out two that they both liked. They also picked out three skirts and three blouses. Then Madge selected a sweater and raincoat. This should be a good start. Lily had never had this many clothes in her life. She had never spent this much money on herself. The saleslady rang up the purchases and told Lily the amount she owed. Lily reached into her pouch and brought out her money. She counted it out and put the rest back in her pouch before putting the pouch in her handbag.

Once they got outside, Madge had her sit down on the bench.

"Lily it is none of my business but I couldn't help but notice you have a lot of money in your purse. Do you always carry all your money with you? "

"Yes."

"Is that all the money you have earned since you started working?"

Again, Lily answered, "Yes."

Madge shook her head. She again called upon the Lord to look over this poor girl.

"Honey, this is not safe. Why, when you took all that money out in there, I almost fainted. You should have seen the saleslady's face. I bet half the store knows by now and the other half will know soon enough. You cannot carry all that money around on you. Someone could rob you; maybe even kill you for your money."

Lily thought back the last time someone had tried to take money. She shuddered.Madge felt bad when she saw Lily's reaction but knew she had to protect this girl. "We are going to the Bank across the street and open a savings account for you."

"Noooooo, my money has to stay with me."

"Why."

"That's what I was told."

"Well whoever told you that certainly did not think you would keep adding to the money you had in there when you came into town. I'm sure if they saw how much money you had, they would agree with me."

"You think so?"

"I know so. Now you don't have to put everything in the bank. Keep some out in case you want to buy something. Of course knowing you, you don't spend much but keep enough to feel comfortable. Remember, you get tips everyday you work so you will be getting more. Now the Bank will give you a book when you give them money. It is called a passbook. You can add more money whenever you want or take it out whenever you need to. They will even pay you to keep your money there. It is called interest. When you get paid and then pay for your room, count your money and see what's left over. This is called budgeting. That way if you think you have more than you need, you can put more in the Bank. It will keep adding up. One day you may want to buy something big and you will have the money to pay for it."

Lily thought over what Madge told her. She was still unsure that was the right thing to do because Clyde had been so insistent she never let it out of her sight. But then she remembered that thing she never was supposed to talk about. It had all started because of money. Maybe Madge was right. That way no one could attack her for her money. Lily told Madge she would do it. Madge let out a sigh of relief and walked her across the street to the bank and she introduced her to Mr. Ottoman. He showed her around the bank and took her into the safe. He explained how the bank called this the bank vault and that it was locked each night and everyone's money, even the banks was kept safe and secure. Lily looked at everything and agreed it was much safer than her purse.

Once everything was done, Lily looked at the bank book they gave to her. It fit nicely in her pouch and she could still keep it close to her. They had assured her in the Bank that she could get her money out anytime she wanted to. She just had to bring in the book and sign a withdrawal slip and she would get cash. She could also add money to her account and they would give her a receipt and keep her book up to date for her.

Lily settled into a contented life in the church and the community. Soon she had been here almost two years. It was hard to imagine she had a life someplace else. This was the place she felt was home. She rarely thought of the time before she came to live here.

One day on the way home from shopping, Madge talked about her son and his family. She was going to visit them next month. She only got to see them twice a year. They had not been able to make it out to see her this past year but she was going to go see them. She talked about her granddaughter the rest of the way home.

The following week, Lily came in from work and saw Madge crying. She was scared. She went over to Madge and stood there too afraid to speak. Madge looked up and said, "Lily, my son just called and his wife is dead. She was hit by a car and died instantly. I don't know what to do."

Lily wasn't sure what to do either. What do you do when someone dies? Bury them she thought. She didn't say anything instead; she walked over and wrapped her arms around Madge who cried uncontrollable for a while.

After a while, Madge stood up. "Well enough of this, let's get some tea and maybe something a little bit stronger and then I'll see about getting a way to my son's house."

She heard Madge on the phone later talking to Bea. Luckily Hank was due to stop by sometime tomorrow and she could get the bus at the diner. Since her son lived in California, the bus headed in that direction and she should have no trouble getting to where she needed to go. She called her son and told him her plans and he would pick her up when she got off the bus. Everything was in place. She asked Lily if she would look after things while she was gone. Usually she had someone come in and stay when she went away but the lady wasn't available at this short notice.

"All you have to do is make sure all the doors are opened in the morning and closed at night. The only other thing is to change the sheets and towels once a week and do the laundry. By now you know where everything is kept. Do you feel alright doing this?"

"Of course. I'd like to do that for you. You are always so kind to me, I can never repay your for that."

"Thank you. Now promise you will not tell Bea the kind part about me. I have my reputation to uphold with that old biddy." They both burst out laughing and hugged each other.

Lily enjoyed taking care of the house. She almost felt like she did on the farm when the chores were done. She dusted and vacuumed inside and kept the porch swept outside. She was never too tired. It was great to be needed. She even started humming and singing the church hymns when she was alone in the house.

Madge ended up staying with her son for three weeks. Lily collected the rent from the other tenants and added her money to the envelope she kept in her pouch. Since Madge did not offer meals or the use of her kitchen anymore, it was easy to keep everything running smooth.

Madge finally returned and was exhausted from the travel and the grief. She explained that she had never been real close to her daughter-in-law but she was so sorry for her poor granddaughter had lost her Mommy. Lily helped her into bed and laid the rent envelope on her dresser. I'll lock up. You get your rest. Then she did something that surprised then both, she kissed her on the cheek.

Max and Rosie

Chapter 15

For the next year, Madge traveled back and forth between her home and her son's. It was hard on her to leave her son and granddaughter and hard on them to see her go. She was not sure how long she could keep up the pace. Of course, with Lily now living with her, she never had to worry about the house when she was gone. She had just returned from her last trip. Lily told her two tenants had given their notice and were moving out in two weeks.

"Which ones?"

"The two rooms at the other end of the hallway from my room."

"Well that doesn't surprise me. I always thought there was hanky-panky going on between those two. Maybe they are getting married."

"They didn't tell me. Just paid their rent and said they would only be here two more weeks."

Madge was weary. With all the traveling and now the loss of income on two rooms, she wasn't sure what to do. Lily still paid her rent each week even though Madge told her it wasn't necessary because Lily did so much work and took care of the place when she was gone. Lily insisted and told her she didn't have any other expenses. It was only fair to pay rent.

The next day Madge called her son to let him know she was home and she mentioned the renters that were moving out. Her son said, "Mom, I have been thinking about my life now. Yours and Rosie's too. Since Helen died, we have all been in turmoil. I was thinking about asking you to move out here with us. But to be honest, I think Rosie and I both need a change. Too much here to remind her of her mother. How about we come out and rent your two empty rooms? If it works out, I might be able to find a job and buy a house close by. What do you think?"

"I think that would be wonderful! But you don't have to pay rent."

"Of course I do. I have enough money to get by. I didn't realize how much Helen spent until she died. After a year, we are debt free. I am excited and if you can stand an inquisitive three year old living there full time, we will leave as soon as I can make arrangements to close the house."

"Just do it Max! I am so excited. This sounds like the best plan for both of us!"

Madge could not wait for Lily to get home so she could tell her the good news. However when Madge told Lily, she was surprised at the reaction. "Do you want me to move?" She could see the fear in her face.

"Of course not honey. Why I feel like I'll have all my children with me then!"

She could tell Lily still did not understand.

"Lily, when will you realize I love you like a daughter?"

"You do?"

"Yes, I love you." She reached out and embraced her in a hug. "There is enough love for everyone. One day I hope you can see what I mean. I hope you can have a large family."

Tears spilled down Lily's face. She had never felt a woman's love before.

Lily and Madge spent three days cleaning the entire house. The renters had moved out at the beginning of the week and Max and Rosie were due here by the weekend. It was an exciting time for Madge. She could hardly keep the excitement out of her voice. She had insisted that Lily start eating her meals with her when Lily wasn't working. Lily enjoyed spending time with Madge and started to wonder what her own Mother would have been like had she lived. It was strange; she rarely thought of her Mother and did not remember what she looked like or anything about her. It was so long ago.

Suddenly it was Saturday and Madge could not sit still. She kept running back and forth looking out the door. Lily had all the sheets and towels changed and the laundry washed and hanging on the clothesline. She was glad for the diversion because Madge was making her nervous.

Finally, she heard a loud shout and the front door bang shut. She came out of the kitchen and saw Madge running down the sidewalk. They must be here. Lily returned to the kitchen. She was cooking dinner today and was just finished peeling carrots, onions, and celery to put in with the roast. It was almost ready to go into the oven. She had dough rising on the counter. Madge had taught her how to make bread and rolls and Lily loved the smell of the yeast in the dough as it sat out to rise.

She heard them come in the house and the giggle of a little girl. Soon they all came into the kitchen. Madge came over and put her arm around Lily. "Max and Rosie, this is Lily. She lives with me and I don't know what I'd do without her."

Max smiled the most gorgeous smile she had ever seen. He walked over to her and took her hand "My mother talks about you all the time when she comes home. I was prepared to be jealous of you because I thought she loved you more than me" he laughed "But now I can see why. It smells wonderful in here."

Lily blushed. "Glad to meet you too. Hi, Rosie. We are both named after flowers. How about that?"

Rosie ran over and wrapped her little arms around Lily's legs. Lily had never held a child and had no idea what to do but instinct took over and she picked her up. She kissed her on the cheek and said, "You are a beautiful Rose. Much prettier than a Lily."

They all laughed. She put Rosie down so she could run off to explore the house.

"Max, we should show you the rooms that you and Rosie will have. Luckily they have connecting doors". She winked at Lily. "No wonder our last tenants were so chummy."

It didn't take long for everyone to settle in. Max surprised his mother by telling her he had changed his mind and put his house on the market so it was definite. He and Rosie were staying in town. He just needed to decide what he wanted to do. He couldn't decide if he wanted to teach at the local school or to open a business. One would allow him more time with Rosie but the other was something he always wanted to do. So he had a lot of thinking to do.

Lily enjoyed the company of Rosie. She played with her every chance she got. She had never had any playmates growing up and found she could act like a kid around Rosie and she never judged her. They loved to go to the park. She took scraps of bread to feed the ducks and they played on the swings and slide. Life was good. She never resented her occasional temper tantrums and seemed to have the knack of soothing her when her grandmother and father had about given up. She loved playing with her dolls and toys because she had never had any herself. Max and Madge were amazed at how patient Lily was with Rosie and always told her to let them know if Rosie was bothering her. Of course, Lily could not imagine a time that she would be bothered by Rose's company and was grateful for the unconditional love she always felt from the child.

Soon Christmas was coming. Madge explained all about Santa Claus to Lily and how it would be different this year with Rosie in the house. Madge had adopted the habit of explaining things to Lily when she suspected she didn't know about them. She was sure she had never had a real family Christmas complete with stockings, toys and gifts. She noticed that when Lily gave her the cookbook one Christmas. Actually, she was just as excited for Lily as she was for Rosie. She laughed to herself; she would have two excited kids this year. What a blessing!

They all decided to go out in the outskirts of town to cut down their own Christmas tree. Rosie and Lily were so excited when the morning arrived to go, they could hardly wait. Max looked at both of them and smiled. How glad he was that he had decided to move. He had never seen Rosie so happy, even when her mother was alive. Why couldn't Helen been more like Lily?

Once they got the tree home, Max began the chore of getting it in the stand and trimmed so it stood just right. Madge sent Lily up to the attic to bring down the boxes of decorations for the tree. The tree was sitting majestically in the tree stand and Max was finishing up the lights when Lily came down the steps with the last of the boxes. She stood on the last step and gasped. They all stopped what they were doing and looked at her. Two big tears ran down her cheeks. "This is the most beautiful thing I have ever seen."

Madge laughed and came over to give her a hug.

"Just you wait until we get the decorations on it. Then you will see beautiful!"

Max laughed and said, "Then I guess I better step up the pace and get the lights done."

Rosie and Lily took the lids off the boxes and looked at the colored balls. There were so many to choose from Lily liked them all. Rosie wanted the red ones. Soon everyone was choosing their favorites to hang on the tree. Once it was finished Madge served Hot Chocolate to everyone then they all sat in front of the fire and enjoyed the warm glow of the fire and the twinkling of the tree as the flames bounced off the ornaments.

The next day they all helped bake cookies. Lily had never baked Christmas cookies before but soon got the hang of it and was having a great time. She loved to roll out the dough and she and Rosie used the cookie cutters to make the shapes and sprinkled colored sugar on the top of each one. It was hard to say who ended up with more flour on them, Lily or Rosie.

All the talk at work and at home was about Christmas. Shopping decorating and baking were the only topics anyone discussed. Lily was excited. Her first *"Santa Claus"* Christmas. Lily wanted to get gifts for everyone and wrap them this year. One day when she worked the early shift, she stopped at the department store on her way home. She picked out a wool scarf for Max, a toy for Rosie, a hat and gloves for Bea, and a flannel night gown and robe for Madge. She took up the store's offer to wrap them for her and chose different paper for each gift. The woman handed her gift tags when she finished wrapping the packages and told her all she had to do was write the names and attach them to the gifts before they went under the tree.

When she arrived home, she quickly ran up to her room before anyone saw her packages. She went down to the kitchen to see where everyone was. To her surprise, Bea was in the kitchen with Rosie. "Why are you here? Is everything ok?"

Bea laughed. "Can't I visit sometimes?"

"Yes, but where is everyone?"

"By everyone, if you mean Madge and Max, they are out picking up a few things. If you get my drift. Too many little ears."

Lily looked at Rosie and laughed. "I know what you mean. I keep forgetting how difficult that must be, a little elf in the kitchen."

Rosie looked at Lily. "I want the elf."

"Ok, you finish up in the kitchen with Aunt Bea and we can go read about the Christmas Elves."

Soon it was Christmas Eve. Before bedtime, Madge brought out stockings for everyone. She had made a special one for everybody and each stocking had a name on it. They had a ceremony where each picked out their stocking and hung it on the mantle above the fireplace. Then Max sat with Rosie on his lap and read *"The Night before Christmas"* story. Lily had never heard the story and hung on each word to the point Max thought he had two little girls listening intently instead of just one.

Max took Rosie up to bed after explaining that if she didn't go to sleep, then Santa would not come. Madge told Lily she should go to bed too because it would be a busy morning soon enough. She told Max she was going to bed too. Lily went upstairs to read before falling asleep.

Madge gestured to Max when the girls were safely upstairs. They went into Madge's bedroom and gathered the presents from their hiding places.

Then they quietly placed them under the tree, turned off the lights and went to bed themselves.

The next morning Lily was awakened by Rosie. "Hurry, hurry, Lily. Santa came and there are presents under the tree and the stockings are filled!"

"Is your daddy and grandmother awake."

"I woke them too. Daddy said to wait for you. Hurry, hurry!" Her little voice was so excited. Lily jumped out of bed and grabbed on her robe.

Max was standing at the top of the stairs so they could all go down together. "Merry Christmas, Lily."

"Merry Christmas, to you too. Let's not hold up Rosie any longer!"

They hurried down the stairs. As Lily got to the bottom of the steps, she was unable to move. This was definitely what the Bible described as Heaven. Never had she seen such a sight.

Madge came over and gave Lily a hug and kiss. "Merry Christmas, Lily."

Lily returned her kiss and hugged her tight. "This is wonderful!"

"Welcome to a child's Christmas. Sure different from last year, right?"

Lily laughed, "It sure is."

Rosie didn't know what to open first. Max sat beside her and said

"Why don't we see which ones have your name on them?"

Rosie agreed that was good. Soon she had a pile in front of her and opened each one with squeals of delight. There was a doll from Santa. A jack-in-the-box from grandma, then and a little tricycle from Daddy. Lily remembered she had not brought her presents down this morning. When she came back down, she handed Rosie her gift and placed the rest under the tree. Rosie opened Lily's gift. It was a music box with a ballerina inside. Rosie ran over and jumped into Lily's lap and hugged her tight. "I love it. Thank you Lily."

Lily had tears in her eyes and hugged her back. "I would say we have a lot of new toys to play with now."

Max called Rosie over to give out the other presents. He read the names and Rosie handed them the presents. Max and Madge watched as Lily opened her presents. There was a winter coat from Madge and a pair of winter snow boots from Max and Rosie. She was happy because she really needed both to get back and forth in the snow.

"Thank you all for everything. These are the best thing you could have given me."

Max called Rosie back to the tree. "I see another gift I missed. Can you get it for me?" Rosie pulled it out and handed it to him. He looked at the tag and said, "It looks like Santa left this for Lily."

When Lily opened it, it was an identical doll to the one Rosie got except Rosie's had brown hair and brown eyes and Lily's doll had blond hair and blue eyes. Both dolls looked like their owners. Lily and Rosie hugged each other and laughed. Rosie said, "I will call my doll Lily and you can call yours Rosie."

She told her that was a great idea and glanced over at Madge. She knew she bought it for her to make up for the ones she never had as a child. Lily had never felt so much love as she did that first Christmas morning as part of a real family.

Madge reminded everyone the real reason for Christmas. We need to get dressed for church and thank God for all our blessings. Lily knew she would be giving thanks for the rest of her life for the happiness He gave her today.

Soon it was a new year. Bea had given her a new calendar. It was time to mark her special dates and throw away the old calendar. This would be the third year she was in her new life. She thought she would be twenty something this year but had forgotten how old she really was. Not that it mattered to her. Max had made the announcement that he had decided to start his own business. He was going to open a furniture and appliance store in the building down by the diner. He was buying the building since it had the storefront and an apartment upstairs over the store. He thought it would fit his needs for a home and business. The previous owner was retiring and Max was taking over his building. He was anxious to get the place spruced up and order new merchandise. He would sell off the old furniture at discounted prices and he hoped to bring a better and more up to date selection. He doubted if the current furniture in the store was less than ten years old. Madge thought it was a wonderful idea. Lily was glad for him.

Lily had never painted before but she and Madge helped Max freshen up the inside of the store. He had gotten rid of most of the old furniture and was anxious to get the walls done before his new stock arrived. She discovered she loved painting. She loved how the room changed before your eyes with just the addition of paint.

Rosie had her fourth birthday in May. Lily had never seen a decorated birthday cake and candles. She had seen them pictured in her cookbook but never like this. Rosie blew out her candles and Madge said the first piece of cake goes to the Birthday Girl and next one goes to the person with the closest birthday. Rosie said "When is your birthday Lily."

"July sixteenth"

"How old are you?"

"I'm not sure."

Rosie laughed. "Everyone knows how old they are silly."

Max said "Rosie that is not polite. Only little children need to tell their age."

Max and Madge exchanged puzzled glances with each other.

Danny

Chapter 16

The first week in June, Bea came to work all excited. She told everyone her nephew, who was Hank's son, was coming to town to be a Deputy Sheriff. Then two days later, Lily went home after work and Madge told her that they were having Bea and her nephew over for dinner. She wanted him to meet the family.

Bea came in with her nephew Danny. She introduced him to everyone and he shook hands. When his hand touched Lily's she had an electric shock go through her body. She felt sensations she had never experienced before. They looked into each other's eyes and both could feel the connection unlike either had experienced before.

He said, "You are all I ever hear my dad and Aunt Bea talk about. You must be one special girl."

She blushed and found it hard to speak. Danny kept holding her hand and kept his gaze on her eyes as if they were the only people in the room. They stayed this way until Madge called everyone in for dinner.

Rosie was her usual chatty self and wanted to monopolize Lily's attention. Danny and Max both new to town were discussing the pros and cons of the town. Madge and Bea were discussing mutual friends and townspeople. Danny was to start work the next day. He was twenty-eight and had graduated from college. He decided to pursue police work and had worked with the state police for five years. He wanted more interaction with people so he started looking into small towns and his dad suggested here. Since Aunt Bea was living here, it seemed like a good choice and there was an opening.

"Like it was meant to be," said Danny as he glanced at Lily. He raised his glass to hide his smile from everyone else.

Max and Rosie had settled into life with Madge. He never spoke of buying a house or moving into his apartment over the store and Madge had not taken on any other tenants. Once the current tenants moved out, the rooms were taken over by things Max had brought with him. He made a playroom for Rosie's toys and took over the bathroom by their bedrooms. With the other tenants gone, it was almost as if they had their own apartment inside Madge's house.

It worked out great for Lily because she now had the bathroom by her bedroom all to herself. Actually, when he bought his business, he had decided to move in the apartment on the second floor. He even went as far as fixing it up with new appliances and furniture. He had a change of heart when Rosie cried and said she did not want to leave her grandmother and Lily. He decided she had been through enough changes already and did not want to disrupt her life again. So they continued to live with Madge.

Madge took care of Rosie when Max worked. Sometimes he took her to the store because he was rarely too busy to keep an eye on her. Since Madge no longer had anyone renting rooms beside Lily, she also had more time to devote to Rosie instead of household chores. Max helped out with expenses so it was a satisfactory arrangement all around. Therefore, it did not surprise anyone when Max told Danny he had an apartment he could rent if he wanted to. Danny was excited and Max offered to walk down with him to show the apartment after dinner.

Bea and Danny left with Max to see the apartment together because they would head over to Bea's place from there. Everyone had to work tomorrow. Max came home and said Danny liked the apartment and was moving his things in after work the next day. He was actually pleased because if anyone tried to break into his store, he had a police officer on site. He laughed and said, "I'm sure Bea will be glad to have her place to herself again too."

Since Danny lived next door to the diner, he got into the habit of coming in to eat. Depending on what shift Lily worked, she saw him at either breakfast or dinner. Often he stopped by as she was leaving to walk her home. She was grateful for that, especially when it was dark outside. She still remembered the drunken old man who had grabbed her so it made her cautious. They settled into a comfortable friendship but her heart still did flips when she saw him.

Danny was enjoying his new job. For the first time, he was having interactions with people instead of cars and he felt he was making a difference. He had the usual police matters. Husband and wife fights, rowdy teenagers and men who had too much to drink causing fights. Because he always treated everyone with respect and had a professional way of dealing with problems, he was well liked and respected in just a short time on the job. He had a lot of the single women and for that matter some married ones too, trying to hit on him. He had plenty of opportunity to date but he was hooked on Lily. He knew she had a troubled past from what his Dad, Aunt Bea and Madge had told him. He had decided to win her friendship before making any romantic feeling known to her.

One day he received a call about a rape. He was the first to arrive and was sick to see it was a twelve-year-old child. Her mother had found her bleeding when she returned from work. The girl stayed alone in the house after school. They lived in a remote part of town and there were no close neighbors to have seen or heard anything. The girl was incoherent and could not talk to describe her assailant. Danny collected what evidence he could and called for an ambulance to take the girl to the hospital.

He was busy for the next few days and did not have time to spend on anything but the case. He canvassed the area around the child's house and walked thru the woods looking for clues. He discovered a shack on the edge of the woods but did not find any evidence that it was recently occupied. He decided to keep an eye on it. He could not find any unsolved cases with similarities to this one. The little girl recovered quicker physically than she did emotionally. She was unable to provide any other description except that he was an old man. Danny realized that anyone over thirty-five was probably and old man to her.

Things quieted down and he had the usual police calls but nothing could get the sight of that little girl out of his mind. He thought he had a lead one day when a woman called in a peeping tom in her neighborhood. He watched the houses each night after dark. He got out of his car and walked around each house. Finally one night, he spotted the peeping tom or as he referred to them as the peeking toms. Next to the neighbor who called in the report, he spotted three boys sitting in some bushes drinking beer and looking at the Brown's house. He looked up and saw a light in the bedroom window. He then saw their sixteen-year-old daughter putting on a show for the boys below. It was not hard to see what she was doing. It even embarrassed him to watch. He decided the best approach to this is the direct approach. He walked over to the boys.

"We have two choices the way I see it. Number one is the one I recommend. We all go over and knock on the door and explain what you boys have been watching and apologize to Mrs. Brown. If you don't like that option Number two is we all go down to the police station and I fingerprint you, put you in a cell and call your parents. Course if a call comes in and I have to leave the Station; I may not be able to call your folks until morning. Then the school has to be informed why you're absent. So gentlemen, which is it? Number one or Number two?"

They all chose Number one.

As he drove the boys home, he laughed at the scene at the Brown's house. He had Mrs. Brown step outside and see what the attraction was for the boys. He could still hear her yelling as they pulled away from the house. They did apologize to her alright but she did not seem upset with the boys at all. Her daughter on the other hand was another story. He was sure this solution resolved itself without bringing any of the boys into the police station but just to be sure when he dropped them off at home he told them "Next time gentlemen, if you chose a next time, there will only be door Number two. You've used up door Number one. It is up to you to decide if it's worth it."

The boys scrambled out of the car and in unison said "Yes sir."

Saturday nights were the worse for troublemakers. There were two bars in town. One was just a bar that catered to the married men and the old timers. The other was a bar and dance hall. This one catered to the single men and women looking to hook up. The only thing he had to worry about from the first one was when they stumbled out drunk and decided to use the sidewalk as a bathroom or when they got into an argument with each other and decided to settle it with their fist. He had his usual regular a man called Mr. Moon. He always managed to get touchy about his name when he got a few beers in him but Danny thought if my name was Moon, I wouldn't like being called "Old Man Moon' either. He always took pity on him and either got him sobered up with coffee at the station house or let him sleep it off in a cell overnight. His wife was often grateful when he chose the second choice.

Of course most were too old or too drunk to do much damage. However, the dance hall crowd had to be watched. Occasionally one of them would forget they were married and go in the wrong bar and the spouse would find them in the arms of someone other than their own wife. Or two men chose the same women and decided to duke it out. He hated it when the women were the ones fighting. It was hard to reason with them and even harder to pull them apart. Wow, they really could fight.

Chapter 17

In the fall, the Bank Manager, Mr. Ottoman, came into the diner for lunch. "Lily, when you get a chance, can you come over to my office and see me?"

"Is my money ok?"

"Nothing like that. Just want to tell you how much interest you made on the money." Lily was relieved and said she would be over after the lunch crowd was gone. She got there right before two and was shown into his office.

"So how much money do I have?"

"Lily, it isn't really about your money. I'm sorry if I misled you but I didn't want anyone knowing the real reason and I wanted to see you today."

"Why?"

"I don't know how to start, so I guess I'll start at the beginning"

"I had a man come in asking questions. I don't know much about you but from what he said, you came to mind."

"Why Me? What did he say?"

"He gave me a story that frankly I didn't believe. Said he was looking for a young girl that was either married or living with his father before he died. Said she lit out of town and he was able to trace her heading this way. Really couldn't describe the girl too well. Said he never actually met her but had some business to settle with her."

Lily felt a minute of sadness. So Clyde was dead. He said he was dying but it just became real. She was very quiet and Mr. Ottoman sensed her distress. "What's the matter Lily, did I upset you?"

"No, I'm just confused."

She could not think exactly what to say. She sat there a few minutes gathering her thoughts. "Well, what made you think of me?"

"To be honest, you did come into town out of nowhere. You are the only girl that we have had move into town in the last few years. No one seems to know much about you. I'm not trying to interfere, but people in this town look out for each other. I'm not asking you to break any confidences. As far as I know everyone likes you and you have been no trouble since you moved here. Sometimes, I even forget that you aren't related to Madge. Just that this man rubbed me the wrong way. Looked like trouble and I didn't really believe his explanation as to why he was looking for either you or whoever it is that he inquired about."

"So what did you tell him?"

"I told him that I do recall seeing a girl get off a bus a couple years ago. I ran into her in the drugstore and she was buying some things. She asked me where she was and how far it was to California. I figured she was headed there. I never saw her again or any other young girl for that matter."

"Did he believe you?"

"I checked and he went to the drugstore and asked around. No one remembered a thing but told him a bus comes by occasionally headed for California."

"Yea that would be Hank's bus."

"Well he won't get anything out of Hank. Bea would skin him alive." He laughed and looked at Lily.

She continued to sit in his office looking pale and scared. He felt guilty for causing her to be scared but still he consoled himself that she needed to know. If that man intended to harm her, he looked mean enough to carry it out. Now what to do next? He thought he should say or do something. "Lily, do you want to tell me anything? I can be very discrete and hold any information you tell me in confidence. That is what bankers do best."

He could tell Lily was thinking about it. Then he saw her stiffen. "Thank you Mr. Ottoman but I don't really have anything to hide. I don't know this man or who he is. I'm sure he is not looking for me but thanks for trying to help."

She got up and left his office. He sat there feeling he had let her down in some way. He thought of telling Bea or Madge but then felt foolish. He was sounding like a gossipy old woman and that after telling Lily he could keep her business confidential. *Shame on me!* He did decide to keep his ears open in case the man decided to come back.

Lily walked home. She wasn't sure just what to do. Her first reaction was to leave town. If he was anything like Clyde's son, he was not someone she wanted to mess with. The pain of that encounter hit her. Her eyes filled with tears. It had been so long since she had thought of Clyde or the *thing* that had happened. As she reached the porch, Max was leaving with Rosie. She said "Hi," but hurried into the house before they could see her tears. Just as luck would have it, Madge heard the door and thought Max had forgotten something and came out of the kitchen. "Oh Lily, it's just you. Max just left and I thought they forgot something. Rosie is going to the dentist."

Lily hurried up the steps to her room. She fell across the bed and began to cry as she had never cried before. She cried for Clyde, the baby and the sorrow that had entered her life. She cried because she had finally felt safe and had a real home and was in danger of losing it because of someone looking for her. She cried because she felt such despair.

Madge stood outside of her door and heard Lily crying. She had never seen her like this and was scared that something bad happened. "Lily honey, what's wrong. Did that Bea do something to upset you? I'll go right down and whip her a new ass!"

Lily thought how much she loved Madge. How could she live without her in her life? She cried harder.

"Lily, let me in. I'll take care of whatever it is that upset you. Please let me help you."

"Go away, no one can help."

"You should know me by now. I love you and I will do anything for you. Just don't block me out."

Lily got up and opened the door. She saw the look on Madge's face and cried harder. Madge reached out and enveloped her in her arms. "Now, now, it can't be that bad."

Lily looked so beaten; Madge had never seen her like this. It broke her heart. Lily was like the daughter she never had. She could not stand her to be in such pain. "What is it Lily? Let me help you. Tell me."

"I can't."

"Yes you can. Nothing is so bad that I can't hear it. I love you and I will protect you."

Lily had never had such kind words spoken to her. She wished she could confide in Madge. The very idea of telling all this to Madge was frightening. How could Madge like her after she knew the truth? "It's nothing. I'm sorry I upset you. Nothing wrong with Bea at work. Just having a bad day. I don't want you to worry. Thank you for your concern but it is really nothing."

Madge continued to hold her. She knew Lily was holding something back but she didn't want to pressure her now. It was not the time to confront her. Better to wait until she was calmer. Right now the girl just needed to be comforted. "I'll leave you alone to get yourself together. Take a nice relaxing bath. I am going downstairs to brew some tea. Come down when you are finished. We will have some chocolate. That will make you feel better too. As least it always works for me."

Lily did take her bath and stayed in until the water was almost frigid. She finally got out and put on warm clothes. She dried her hair and decided to go down to Madge; she had decided what she would tell her.

Madge was in the kitchen. "Are you feeling better now?"

"Yes, thank you for all you do for me."

"Lily, I love you. That is what we do when we love someone. We take care of them."

"I don't know what I'd do without you."

"Well don't think about that now. Just sit and have a cup of tea. I have some yummy cookies. It'll give me a chance to eat some too and not feel guilty. There is a difference in eating cookies with someone instead of sneaking some by myself." She laughed. Lily sat down and sipped her tea but left the cookie on her plate.

"Oh no you don't. You are going to eat a cookie. They have the best chocolate filling. Taste them and see!" Lily smiled and took a small bite. It was good.

They sat in silence for a few minutes before Lily spoke. "I want to tell you something. I can't tell you everything because it is too complicated. I heard something today that upset me. A man was in town looking for me. He is a man that I'm afraid of. I'm afraid he will hurt me. I don't know why he wants to find me but I can't let him."

"Someone from your past?"

"Someone who must have connections to my past. Not the best part of my past. That's why I am so scared."

"Do you want to tell me what happened?"

"No, I can't tell you anymore than that. If he comes back I have to leave before he finds me."

"So he's not here now?"

"No, I think he left to see if I am in California?"

"Why California?"

"Because someone told him that's where I went. But when he finds I'm not there, he may come back."

"Who told him?"

"I don't want to say anymore. But if you hear anyone asking around about me, you have to let me know."

"OK. Should we tell anyone else?"

"I don't think so."

"Ok, just let me know if I can do anything. Right now, I just appreciate you telling me that much. You know I'd do anything to protect you from harm. When and if you feel like telling me more, I'm here for you."

"Thanks Madge, that means a lot to me."

Just then, Rosie came running into the kitchen. She threw her arms around Lily. "Are you ok? You were sad and I told Daddy I want to stay with you but he made me go to the dentist."

She released her arms and stood back. She opened her mouth ,"See my clean teeth!"

Madge and Lily laughed and Lily reached out and hugged her to her chest. She kissed the top of Rosie's head. "I'm fine now, I love you so much. You are the best little girl I ever met."

It always amazed her how perceptive Rosie was. They had a deep connection that was unlike anything Lily had ever known.

Rosie laughed. "There are no other girls that live here."

"True but I see some that come into the diner. No one is as good as you!"

Max told them all about Rosie's visit to the dentist. "She was so well behaved; I think she surprised the dentist. She sat still and let him look at her teeth and use the magic toothbrush. I was so proud of her."

"You should be. I could tell you stories of your first visit and believe me, it was not a happy experience for anyone." She laughed.

"Now Mom, be nice. I am your favorite son."

"Yes, you are. Plus, my only son."

Lily absorbed all the love in the room. She prayed she would not have to leave it.

Rosie wanted to go feed the ducks. She and Lily took some old bread and left. "We may take some time for the swings too but we'll be back in plenty of time for dinner." Lily said as she and Rosie left the house holding hands.

Max looked at his mother. "I am so grateful for Lily. Do you realize Rosie never cries for her mother? Now I wonder if she ever had the love from her Mother that she gets from Lily. I was gone so much and I took so much for granted. I guess I gave too much responsibility to her mother and not enough to myself. Speaking of crying, what happened to Lily as I was leaving? She passed us so quickly that I didn't notice but Rosie sure did. It was tough getting her to go with me after she saw the tears in Lily's eyes."

"Well I'm glad you didn't bring it up when you came in. Yes, she was really upset. Something frightened her. I don't know if I should tell you what she told me or not. I ask her if we should tell anyone else and she said she didn't think so."

"Well, we both want to protect Lily. She didn't actually say no, did she?"

"She said she didn't think so."

"That's good enough. How are we going to protect her if we don't know how or what she is scared of?"

"She actually told me very little. If I tell you, you have to promise never to let Lily know you are aware of anything concerning today."

"Ok. I promise. I still think it's best if I know so I can help her."

"Apparently someone told her a man was in town asking around about her. Actually looking for her. Someone from her past. Someone she is terrified of. That's all I was able to get out of her. You know she never talks about her past. That may be why. I didn't push her to tell me more. I was grateful she confided in me at all."

"I agree it must be something painful she is suppressing. I think it is best if we are aware so we can be prepared. I think you should confide in Bea. Someone may come in the diner. That seems a logical place to go if you are looking for someone. That way Bea can be prepared and block any attempts to find Lily. I'm sure you can threaten Bea with one of her dark secrets to keep her mouth shut and not let Lily know that she knows."

"Bea loves Lily too. I know she would do anything she could do for her. No threats required on that, but I hate to let so many people in on her secret. She trusted me to keep it sacred. She trusts me."

"Mom, the more of us that know, the more of us out there to protect Lily."

"Ok, I'll think about telling Bea. But that's as far as it goes. Just you and Bea."

"Well at least she will have three of us looking out for her."

Lily was feeling better the next day as she walked to work. The time with Rosie always brightened her day. She felt renewed and decided she would put her fears to rest for now. If she needed to run, she could still do that, but right now she felt stronger and encouraged by the fact that he did leave town. Maybe he wouldn't be back.

No one let on to Lily that they were aware of the fear she had about being discovered by someone from her past. However, by now, Madge, Max, Bea and of course Hank had been told. Then Hank told his son Danny. She was being protected at home, at work and when she walked around the streets in town. No one should be able to get close to her. Hank would put the word out to his bus driver friends. They would point the trail to California and away from here.

Several weeks had passed and everything seemed back to normal. Bea made sure Lily only worked the morning shift. Madge and Max arranged for her to drop Rosie off in his store each day and have Lily pick her up on her way home. That way Lily was not alone. Max was able to talk to her as she stopped to pick up Rosie and could tell if anything was bothering her after work. Not that he asked her but he knew her well enough to observe her demeanor. Rosie was there to represent a family. Chances are anyone looking for her knew she did not have a child. Outward appearance would indicate a married woman stopping by her husband's store to pick up her child. Or at least that's what Madge and Max decided upon. The thought that Rosie would be in danger never entered their mind or it would not have been something to consider. It was a small town after all. It was a short walk from the store to the house and if they went to the park it was only a few blocks away. Now that was late fall, it was not always possible to go to the park as frequently as they would have liked because it was often raining.

Soon the winter bazaar would take place at Church. Everyone was busy making crafts to sell to make money for the church fund. Madge had Lily and even Rosie assigned to projects. Rosie was making scented balls by sticking cloves into Styrofoam balls that would eventually be covered by thin material and resemble a Christmas ornament. Lily was learning to sew. Her job was to make aprons plus kitchen towels with snaps to hang on appliance handles. Madge was tackling the more complicated task of knitting small animal shaped toys. Everyone was anxious to get home in the afternoon to begin the project that Madge had cut out and ready to sew or in Rosie's case, to assemble.

Even Max could not escape the bazaar. He was in charge of decorating the church hall for the bazaar and setting out the outside manger scene. Of course, all merchants were expected to donate money, time or sellable items.

Bea was donating cakes and pies to sell. That meant she was often in the kitchen baking and less often in the diner helping out with customers.

Lily was extremely capable of handling a restaurant full of customers by herself now. She could take orders, refill drinks, and deliver food in unbelievable speed yet it never appeared to the customers that they were not her sole priority. Everyone liked Lily. If you would ask anyone their opinion of her, most would say efficient, polite and professional. No one would call her a good friend. She blended into the background but appeared quickly if anyone needed anything. She never gossiped or joked with customers. Other waitresses did, but not Lily. She never thought about it. Just like some people had blond hair and others had brown hair, that's the way it was. She never thought she did more work than the other waitresses who stopped to chat or joke with customers. She was only interested in doing her job.

Bea often watched her and shook her head. She could never put Lily in charge because she did not have a competitive bone in her body. She took life as it came. The staff would walk all over her if she was in charge. That was a shame, thought Bea, because Lily was the one person she could trust.

Danny was busy now and rarely had time to stop by the diner. He occasionally ate breakfast there before his shift, but his time with Lily was sporadic. If she missed him walking her home, she never gave him any indication. He often thought about her, especially when he had to spend time alone on patrol. He had been in town about a year now and had adjusted to his way of life. He was lonely at times an ready to develop a relationship. Most of the women and girls in town were only interested in a quick, uncomplicated relationship. He was ready to settle down and start a family. He had one person in mind, and that person was Lily.

Often he saw her walking with Rosie. Those were the times she really seemed happy. He still wasn't sure what her relationship was with Max. No, what he hadn't determined was, what Max's relationship was with Lily. He loved her, that was for sure. But did he love her as a woman or as a friend? That was the difficult question. Pretty soon he was going to find out because he intended to marry Lily.

He had been busy during Halloween, tracking down town reports of vandalism, which amounted to kids harassing their teachers and pulling pranks on each other. He remembered his childhood. He found the kids he caught on the calls he received were not actually vicious, just mischievous. He usually gave them the choice of volunteer service or jail time. Not that he could have probably enforced jail time, but it was enough of a threat to gain the cooperation of the kids. Strangely, the parents mostly agreed. It worked out for the entire town. The leaves got raked in the yards of the victims and the windows were finally washed in the Police Station.

Everyone was murmuring about Danny taking over as Sheriff when the current Sheriff retired. A prospect Danny was considering. Not that the Sheriff was considering retirement, but he was becoming less and less involved in his job since Danny came to town. He usually stayed in his office and depended upon Danny to handle any situation that arose.

Danny was aware of the incident with Lily so he tried to keep a watch out for any strangers that came to town. He had asked several merchants to alert him of any newcomers with the explanation that he would rather check on new people before an incident happened. He had several occasions to use the information supplied by merchants. His inquiry of the new people was done without any suspicion directed toward them. In fact, most people did not realize he was investigating them. He also gained the respect of the merchants, because he gave no indication that they notified him of their arrival, except by his own observation.

Chapter 18

One evening, the dispatcher called Danny out to a traffic accident just outside of town. He discovered the accident had occurred when the driver apparently going at a high rate of speed, missed a turn, and ran off the road. The driver was barely conscious and bleeding badly. He called for an ambulance and started to administer first aid. As he reached into the car, he noticed a bag full of currency. He called the Sherriff and explained what was going on.

"Check and see if there was a robbery anywhere. Looks like this fellow was speeding for a reason. There is a lot of money in this car."

The ambulance arrived and removed the driver, then sped off toward the hospital. Danny had asked the Sheriff to meet him at the scene to help recover the money and he arrived just as the ambulance was loading the patient. They both approached the car and started gathering money from the seats and floor of the car. "Better check the trunk too, Danny."

"Doesn't appear to be any money in here, but there is another set of license plates."

"Call it into the dispatcher, both plate numbers and have him send a tow-truck. This thing isn't drivable."

As soon as the tow truck arrived, Danny left to meet the Sheriff in the station to count the money.

On the way back to town, he called Mr. Ottoman at home and explained the situation and asked if they could put the money in his bank until the owner was found. "How much you got there, Danny?"

"I honestly don't know. The Sheriff and I didn't count it yet. He took it back to the Station while I arranged for a tow for the car. I'm headed back there now and I'll give you a call back when it's counted and arrange to meet you at the bank. Just wanted to give you a heads up, while it was still early enough for you to still be up."

"Ok. I'll wait for your call before I head in."

Danny arrived at the Police Station and saw the money had been dumped out of the bags and was on the Sheriff's desk. As he sat down across from the sheriff he said, "I called Ottoman at the bank and told him we would have a deposit tonight. Guess we better count it to make sure how much is here. I bet we get notice tomorrow of either a store or bank robbery."

"Ok, I just dumped it out."

"Let's put it all in denominations first. That way we can see if there are consecutive numbers from a bank. Or random, which would most likely be a store robbery. But, from the looks of the money, it is far from new bills."

They separated and sorted into piles. The Sheriff left to go to the bathroom twice complaining of his damn prostrate. They had the ones, fives and tens counted when the Sheriff asked Danny to get him a drink. Danny went to the vending machine and brought back two cokes. They drank and then resumed counting twenties, fifties and a few hundreds.

"Looks like a store for sure. Not many high denominations. In fact, once it's been stacked and sorted, it looks like a lot less than it did loose in the car. Guess he would have got a surprise when he realized how little it probably is. Sure not worth wrecking his car and body over, right Sheriff?"

"Yeah, looks that way."

They finished counting. He called Ottoman. "Hate to bother you sir. We counted it and it is three thousand fifty-six dollars. He sure went to a lot of trouble for that amount of money."

"I'll be right down with the papers, for you and the Sheriff to sign, to release the money to me until it's claimed. Probably a small business, so they should notice it missing right away."

It was after midnight when Danny arrived home. He thought of the money and shook his head. Funny it had looked like a lot more in the dark in that car. You just never know.

The next morning, the dispatcher informed them that both plates were from cars reported stolen. Neither of the stolen cars matched the description of the wrecked car. They were still waiting on something to come over about reports of stolen money. The hospital said the guy in the wreck was patched up and doing fine. Danny headed over to place him under arrest for drunken driving until he could come up with a robbery charge.

The man was resting in bed and looked like his face had been pulverized. He had stitches across the forehead, down his cheek and on his chin. His nose looked broken. His face took most of the impact when the car ran off the road. Car was too old for air bags, thought Danny. "Buddy, looks like you aren't feeling too good. I'm Deputy Danny Mc Cain. I need to ask you a few questions. I'll read you your rights, just so you understand."

Danny then asked him his name and read him his rights. "Mr. Hill, how fast were you going when you had the accident?"

"Not fast, I didn't know the roads and missed the turn. You need better light out there."

'Well from the tire tracks sir, you were going pretty fast to take that long to stop."

"I don't know."

Danny looked at his notes. "Where were you coming from?"

"The next town over."

"Where were you headed?"

"Nowhere in particular. Just traveling, looking for a job."

"How much money did you have in the car?"

"Not sure, whatever is in my wallet."

"What about the bags of money in the car?"

"What money?"

"Ok Mr. Hill. Stop the bullshit. We found over three thousand dollars in paper bags in the car. Now you tell me............Where did you get that money?"

"I don't know what you are talking about."

"If you ever want to walk out of here, you better explain or your ass is going directly to jail."

"I don't have anything to say. I want a lawyer."

"I'll arrange to have one come see you as soon as I transfer you to jail. I'll check with the staff and see when that will be."

Danny left the room and had the nurse page the Doctor. When the Doctor came up to the floor, he pulled out the patient's chart. "Looks like his alcohol and drug screen were clean. He got a lot of stitches in his face and his ribs are sore but not broken. He can be discharged anytime. He's stable and most of the damage was external, which doesn't look pretty, but will heal in time. No reason to keep him in the hospital. I'll sign the release papers."

Danny called the Sheriff and filled him in. "I'll stay with him until he is discharged, then I'll bring him in for questioning. Let's hope we get a lead on missing money. His screens were clean for drunk driving so I can't charge him with that."

Danny walked back to the room. "Mr. Hill. I have good news and bad news. The good news is that you are being discharged; no serious injuries and you are getting a ride out of here. The bad news is that I have to take you to jail for questioning. We have to account for that money we found in your car. Until we find the owner, I'm afraid we have to keep you and the money. Get dressed."

The patient was discharged and transported to the station house for questioning. The District Attorney was contacted and a public defender was called in to represent the suspect. He was placed in a cell because he refused to answer any questions without a lawyer. The Sheriff contacted the police departments in the neighboring towns to check on recent robberies. He also checked the wire service.

"We are coming up blank, Danny. No one has reported a theft of three thousand dollars. Not even close." The District Attorney advised them that they had no grounds to hold him without a charge. He was not driving drunk or intoxicated, no money matching the amount found has been reported missing. Unless they came up with something to charge him with, he should be released within twenty-four hours. The Sheriff shrugged. "We could hold him on theft of license plates. At least impound his car."

Danny told the sheriff. "I am reluctant to just let him walk out of here. Something isn't right. I just have a feeling about this guy, and it isn't a good feeling."

"Danny, sometimes it goes like that. If you think about it, that three thousand dollars is really not that much money. Since he refuses to claim ownership of the money, we'll keep it here until we can track down the owner."

Danny did not like defeat. He felt something nagging at him but he wasn't sure what to do. He couldn't put his finger on what was bothering him about Mr. Hill but it was there. No matter how many times Danny tried to get an answer out of him, he didn't tell him anything. The Sherriff said "I talked to Bea. Her brother will be here tomorrow. The way I see it, we put Mr. Hill on the bus and he can travel as far as the money in his wallet will take him. We have to impound the car but that hasn't been reported stolen. We'll keep the money as evidence, but I doubt we will ever find out where it came from."

The next morning Danny kept the man in jail until Hank was ready to leave. He didn't want him anywhere near the diner or Lily. Better not take a chance. That man just rubbed him the wrong way. He had no choice but to let him go. He didn't like it, but he had no choice.

Soon the stores began decorating for the Christmas season. Bea complained to Lily that it seemed to get earlier every year. It wasn't Thanksgiving yet and the town was putting up the street decorations and encouraging the merchants to get their places ready for the Holidays. "If you want me to help with the window decorations, I'll be glad to stay after work. I helped Max do his, I know what to do."

"Lily, I may take you up on that. I hate that job. Let me look upstairs for the decorations and then I'll let you know."

Lily was happy to assist with anything related to the Holidays. This was fairly new to her and she couldn't imagine how anyone could get tired of decorating. Everything was so beautiful with the lights and decorations. Most of the crafts had been finished and Madge had moved on to making fudge. Lily got to sample a few pieces and knew that was what she was going to buy.

Rosie was starting to get excited about Christmas. She wanted Lily to take her to the department store every day.

"Rosie, we haven't had Thanksgiving yet. We can't go into the store every day."

"Yes we can. We have to check what toys they have so I know what to ask Santa for."

"But the stores don't get new toys in everyday."

"Yes they do!"

"Ok. Tell you what. We will go in today. I'll ask the people in the toy department when they get their new shipment of toys. That will be the day we go in."

Rosie was not happy to find out that the toy delivery was on Thursday but the stock was not put out until Friday. They told her the last few weeks before Christmas may increase deliveries but they wouldn't know until closer to that time.

"Ok, Rosie. We will come in on Fridays. If we find out they get toys at other times, we can come in then too. Take a look around today and then Friday you can tell me what's new. Do you have any idea of what you want this year?"

"Not yet. I have to make sure I don't miss something and forget to ask for it."

"Smart move. That way you will be sure you really want the toy and will play with it. I'm proud of you Rosie."Lily looked at her with love. She had never enjoyed the relationship with a child and found she was amazed at how they rationalized things and how smart they were.

As they came out of the store, Danny was driving up the street. "Mr. Deputy Danny" yelled Rosie. Danny pulled over to the curb. "Hi ladies. Rosie, I see you have taken over my job of walking Lily home."

"Yes, I did." They all laughed.

"How about I ride you home in the police car? I'm off duty and was just doing my last tour around town. Would you like that?"

"Lily, please say yes. I've never ridden in a police car before."

Danny looked at Lily. "Now you can't disappoint both me and Rosie, can you?"

Lily looked at both of them. "Well you make it hard to turn down and invitation from the likes of you two. Actually, I have never ridden in a police car either. Let's go Rosie." They both climbed into the back seat. Danny looked at Lily and said, "I was kinda hoping you would get in the front seat."

Lily laughed, "And give up the opportunity to see what a prisoner feels like? No way."

"Put on the siren, Mr. Deputy Danny." Rosie called from the back seat.

"Don't you dare do that Danny! Rosie, everyone will look at us."

"Rosie, I hate to disappoint you but I can only do that in an emergency situation. I don't think taking you home is an emergency. Tell you what I can do, is take you for a ride around town. We can pretend we are on the lookout for criminals and you can let me know if you find anyone suspicious. Does that sound ok?"

"That sounds like a great idea. I can't wait to tell Daddy and Grandma!"

They circled the town and all agreed that everything looked ok. They all agreed that no suspicious characters were observed and finally they pulled up in front of the house.

"Rosie, you did a fantastic job. Thanks for the help. I'm going to call you my Junior Deputy. Ok?"

"Sure!"

Madge was standing in the doorway. She came out and told them all to come inside and taste her latest recipe of fudge. Danny grinned and said, "How can I say no?"

Rosie could not get the words out fast enough to tell Madge about her adventures this afternoon. She described her trip to check out the toys, how she had discovered when new toys came in, her trip in the police car, her experience looking for criminals and her new title '*Junior Deputy*'.

"The only thing we didn't do, was use the siren."

They all laughed and Madge held her chest and said, "Why would you want to scare your Grandmother like that? They only use a siren in an emergency and that would make me scared that you were in danger."

Rosie looked thoughtful "That's what Mr. Deputy Danny said too." Madge led them all into the kitchen and gave them some of her latest fudge. Danny agreed he would go to the bazaar, if only to buy fudge.

"Lily and I made things for the bazaar. Won't you buy those too, please?"

"I had no idea. Of course I will."

Madge said, "Danny we hardly ever see you. You must stay for supper. Max will be home and I made a roast that is big enough for everyone."

"Please, please stay." Said Rosie.

"Only if it's ok with Lily."

"You want him to stay, don't you Lily?"

"Of course. That would be nice."

Lily excused herself to go change out of her uniform. Danny said he should change too and take the police car back. He would come over in his own car. "The neighbors are probably wondering what is going on that I had to bring these two ladies home in a police car. I hope you are up to some gossip Madge."

She laughed and said, "Bring it on. Nothing much happens in this town anyway."

When Danny got home, he stopped in the store to tell Max he was invited to dinner at his house. He suggested they ride home together, after he changed out of his uniform. When he headed back down to the store, he thought, *I am going to ask Max about Lily. I've put it off too long.*

"Max, before we leave, can we sit down and talk for a minute?"

"That sounds serious. Should I call my lawyer or is something wrong with your apartment?" he laughed.

"This is personal. I could really be serious about Lily but I've seen her with Rosie and your family and I know she loves you all very much. What I need to know is how you feel about her yourself."

Max looked surprised. "Well to be honest, I look at her as a member of my family. I've never given any thought to any romantic side of the relationship." He laughed "I'm sure I seem ancient to Lily. She must think I'm an old man. I'll tell you one thing, whoever Lily decides to choose, that will be one lucky guy. And I'll tell you another thing. If that someone does not treat her right, I'll tear him to shreds and once I'm finished, I'm sure my Mother and your Aunt will eat him for breakfast."

Danny laughed. "Wow, you don't mince words do you?"

"Not when Lily is concerned."

"So can I have your permission to date her?"

"That is entirely up to Lily. I honestly don't know how she feels about you or dating for that matter."

They got through dinner ok. Danny was still wondering about the conversation he had with Max and was replaying it in his mind, so he was distracted at times.

"Mr. Deputy Danny. Aren't you listening to me? I told Daddy about our ride today. He wants to know if you handcuffed me, isn't that silly?"

"Sorry, Rosie. I seem distracted tonight. Yes, that is silly because you are a law abiding citizen and also a Junior Deputy."

"See Daddy!"

"Ok. I see."

They cleaned off the table and Danny insisted he help clean up the dishes. Madge attempted to refuse but he reminded her she had spent all day cooking. First the fudge, then dinner. If Lily would help him, he was sure they could finish in no time.

Lily said "Of course. I'm sorry I didn't think of it. You must be tired. You have been baking nonstop for the bazaar. Danny and I can manage. Go sit down and prop your feet up. Max is giving Rosie her bath, so you should have some quiet time."

"Sounds good to me. I am a little tired to tell you the truth."

Danny and Lily made good time of the clean up. The pots were scrubbed and the dishwasher loaded before Rosie came back down. Danny asked if they could put on a pot of coffee and sit in the kitchen and talk for a few minutes before he left.

"Sure. I enjoyed today. You were so nice to Rosie. Thank You."

"Lily, I really like you. I think I could love you. I want to know if you would consider me as a boyfriend and date me?"

Lily looked stunned.

"Lily if you don't like me, just say so and I won't bother you. Or if there is someone else, just tell me."

Lily looked at Danny and saw a gentle man. *Could she ever be with a man again? Could she ever have a relationship? One that she chose?*

"Lily say something? Your killing me."

Lily opened her mouth to speak but she didn't know what to say.

"I like you Danny." Is what came out.

"Well what does that mean, Lily?"

"I never thought of having a relationship other than friendship with a man. You took me by surprise."

"Ok, does that mean I have a chance?"

"I have to think about it."

"Do you like Max instead of me?"

"Max, what makes you say that? Max is just like family."

"Ok. No pressure. How about we take it slow and easy? Would you like to go to the movies or to dinner in the next town? That way no one will see us and gossip. Then you can decide if you want to date and let everyone know. If you don't think it will work out. If you don't feel anything for me, no one will be the wiser. It will be just between us or anyone you decide to tell."

"Ok, I'd like that."

Danny leaned over and kissed her gently on the lips. He felt a jolt go through his entire body. He pulled away and looked at her. He got a smile on his face when he saw her expression. "I'd say from the look on your face, you got the same reaction. I may have a chance yet." He kissed her cheek and said goodbye to Madge and left.

Danny decided to drop in the diner on Tuesday and ask her to go out on Thursday. He was anxious to go out with her and wanted to do it soon before she changed her mind. He chose a booth instead of sitting at the counter so he could ask her without anyone knowing. When he got a chance to ask her, he was surprised at how quickly she agreed.

He decided they would leave early when they both got off work and went home and changed clothes. He also thought he would take her to a movie that was a comedy, nothing risqué or violent. Luckily, there was a new *Jennifer Aniston* movie playing. Since they both had to work the next day, they would see the movie first, then have dinner and be home early. He was pleased with his plans.

On Thursday, he went to the door to pick her up. Madge let him in and told him Lily would be down in a minute. Rosie was helping her get ready.

"Before she comes down, I want to lay down some ground rules. You may think I'm an interfering old biddy, but I guess I am when it comes to Lily. Don't ask her any personal questions. You'll scare her off. She'll tell you what she wants you to know soon enough. I don't know much of her life before she got here, but I do know, it wasn't something she wants to remember. The quickest way to end any relationship with her before it starts, is to pressure her in any way. There, I've said my piece. Enjoy your date."

Danny said, "Yes, ma'm." They both laughed.

Lily came down the stairs holding Rosie's hand. She had on a dress and Danny had a sharp intake of breath. My God, she was beautiful.

Danny handed her the flowers he had picked up at the florist. Lily blushed and said "Thank you, they are beautiful."

"I tried to get Lilies but they are not in season. So I got Roses because I know how much you love Rosie."

Rosie giggled and Madge said, "I'll put these in a vase of water and have them in your room when you get home. Now you two run off and have a good time."

Lily gave Rosie a kiss and thanked her for helping her get ready. She also gave Madge a kiss on her cheek. Funny, she thought, this is my first date!

Danny had no way of knowing Lily had never been to a movie before. She was so excited and could hardly sit still. Danny did not see much of the movie. He just kept watching her. She tensed when the love scene started and Danny could see a trace of fear in her eyes. God she must have been hurt. He felt so much rage against the person who caused this in her. Then he realized that he had to calm down for her sake. He couldn't let her know what he saw in her face. Soon the movie moved on and Lily was laughing with the antics that were going on in the movie. The rest of the movie was full of laughs and had a happy ending.

They walked to the restaurant down the street from the movie theater. Abruptly, she stopped and grabbed his arm. "Look, posters for our Church Bazaar! All the way out here!"

Danny said, "Well since most of the stuff for sale was either made or baked for the Bazaar by the people in town, I guess they figured no one would want to buy their own stuff so they are hoping for outsiders to come in and buy it. Except for us of course, we are buying all Madge's fudge, right?"

They both laughed as they entered the restaurant.

After they ordered, Lily started talking about the movie. He felt like he was out with Rosie. He had never been on a date where he was made to feel like he did such a wonderful thing. It was just a movie but she acted as if he had bought her the moon. He thought to himself, this is what I love about her.

She loved the dinner. He didn't even have to coax her into ordering dessert. The hard part was deciding which one. They decided to get two different ones and share.

On the way home, she told him how much she enjoyed the date. "I hope you don't think this is our only one. I hope we can do it again soon. I really enjoy being with you Lily and I hope you enjoyed my company as much as where we went and what we did. And I said, *I hope,* a lot didn't I. So you can see how important it is to me."

"Of course I enjoyed being with you Danny. I'm sorry if I didn't tell you that. I really did have a great time with you and with what we did tonight. I would like to do it again too."

He parked by the curb and walked her to the door. Once they reached the porch, he leaned over and kissed her on the lips. He felt the same jolt as before running through his body. She jumped too, as if she was feeling the same thing. He looked at her face and saw surprise written all over it. "We're not bad together, are we Lily?"

She grinned and said "I don't think so."

Chapter 19

Saturday was here. Finally, the day of the Bazaar had arrived. Excitement ran thru the house. Even Max who had spent the entire evening decorating and setting up tables was caught up in the emotions. He was loading all the crafts and baked goods in his car to deliver to the church. He could only fit Madge in the car because the car was packed so tightly with what they were taking for the sale. He promised to come back and pick up Lily and Rosie as soon as they unloaded the car. Since it was raining out, they did not want to walk over to the church and spend the day in wet clothes and shoes.

Lily and Rosie finally arrived at the church and headed over to Madge to help her finish setting out the items they had made. Once they were finished, Madge told Lily and Rosie to walk around and check out the items other people had made. This was the time to make their selection because once the doors opened to the public, there would not be another opportunity.

Rosie selected a handmade doll. Lily picked out a coffee cup for Danny that said, *"It's the Law"*, a crochet hat for Rosie, a pin for Madge and a welcome sign for Max to hang in his shop. She paid for everything and they quickly hurried back to help out Madge. When they got to their table, they saw Danny in Uniform.

"Are you working?"

"Not really, but I think showing up in uniform may discourage anyone from trying to get away with something. What do you think Junior Deputy?"

Rosie giggled and said, "I'll watch out too."

"Just promise me, if you see anything, you won't do anything but let me know. Remember I'm the real Deputy. You will be my lookout."

"Ok, but what does a Junior Deputy do then?"

Lily said, "You get the Deputy in trouble. See what you got yourself into Mr. Danny Deputy. Never try to outsmart a girl."

"Point taken. Rosie, a Junior Deputy is a law-abiding citizen and just alerts the Deputy to something that needs to be checked out. They cannot do the same thing as a real grown up Deputy. Ok?"

"Ok. Maybe when I grow up I can be a real Deputy."

"Maybe so, if you still want to then. Well ladies, I came over to buy Madge's fudge, at least what's left after Lily bought some."

"Ha! Ha! I haven't bought any fudge yet. But thanks for reminding me. Soon Danny and Lily had bought most of Madge's fudge and Danny took it out to the police car for safekeeping. Madge said, "Enjoy it now while you are young. When you get to my age it goes right to the hips."

The doors opened and immediately the room was crowded with shoppers. Lily was amazed at how many people came and how much they bought. She occasionally caught sight of Danny watching the crowd. Max had come to take them to lunch but Madge and Lily sent Rosie off with him and decided to stay with their table. Neither one of them was very hungry. They were both excited to have so much fun they didn't want to give up a minute of it.

The older church members were manning the lunch counter. They were assisted by some teenagers mostly their grandchildren. The menu consisted of Hot Dogs, Corn Dogs and Pizza Slices. This was easy to prepare and made eating in a confined space manageable. Shoppers from out of town and even the merchants found this a satisfactory arrangement. Many people from other towns made this an annual outing for their family because they appreciated the quality of the crafts and food and the reasonable prices. Because food was available in the same building, people tended to stay and shop longer without being persuaded to leave when hungry youngsters complained. The men often took the children over to get something to eat and relieved the women of keeping an eye on them. This way the women were able to spend more time choosing the perfect gift without distractions.

By four o'clock, almost everything was sold out. Madge said, "This is the most fun I have had in many years. You and Rosie have made my life so much richer. It was so much fun this year having us do our crafts as a family. I hope we can continue the tradition for many years to come. Thank you Lily!"

"Madge, I enjoyed as much if not more than you did. And did you see our Rosie con the lady with grey hair into buying her ornaments by telling her '*that I made with my little hands*'?" They both laughed so hard the tears were running down their faces.

Max walked over with Rosie. "What's going on with you two? What did we miss?"

"Just have Rosie tell you how she managed to sell all of her decorations. Not one is left over!"

Rosie had the decency to blush.

"Go ahead and tell your father. You are not in trouble. You did it for the church, right?"

Rosie told her father how she managed to convince the grandmotherly looking ladies to buy from her. Pretty soon, Max too, was doubled over in laughter.

"I guess I should give her a summer job in the store."

Madge said "Please don't give her any more ideas. Plus the only reason she is not being talked to about taking unfair advantage, is because it is for the church and I know God will forgive her."

Maybe because of the rainy weather or the amount of crafts for sale this year the crowd was the biggest Madge had seen in many years. As she surveyed the other tables, she noticed they were quickly selling out. This was good because no one liked to feel their crafts were not desired and have to lug them home wondering why.

It was well after six when Max picked up Madge, Lily and Rosie. Luckily they all fit into the car, so only one trip was necessary. Madge was happy that she had very little left over and would donate it to the Church for the Nursing Home Patients. This was the tradition adopted by the Ladies for Christ committee and Madge was proud to have been the one credited with the idea many years ago.

Soon Lily was at home soaking in the tub, Madge was lying down and Rosie was fast asleep after an exhausting day. Unfortunately, Danny was just starting on an emergency call. The dispatcher had taken a call from Mrs. Brown reporting her daughter was missing and specifically asked for Danny to come out to her house. As Danny drove up to the address, he remembered the '*peeping tom*' boys.

He was met outside by Mrs. Brown. "My daughter hasn't come home. I've called all her friends. Her girlfriend said she left her after they went to the Church Bazaar. She said they left right after lunch. They were supposed to meet later but my daughter never showed up. It looks like she has been missing for over six hours how. I didn't start to worry until it got dark out. She knows she has to let me know where she is if she is out after it gets dark out". She started to cry.

Danny asked what she was wearing, how old she was and if he could have a recent picture. He promised to alert the Sherriff and look for her right away. He also asked for the names of her girlfriends so he could question them too.

"Sometimes they are afraid to tell parents things they will tell the police if they know how serious it is once the police are involved."

He left and decided to pay a visit to the boys first, then follow up with the girlfriends. As he drove up to the house, he noticed the boys standing outside. He got out of the car and walked up to them. "Anything you boys want to tell me?"

The boys all looked at each other. The tallest boy said "No sir".

"Well it looks like we either have a prank or a situation. I'm kinda hoping this is a prank. Then we can get it resolved quickly and I can go home. I got a call from Mrs. Brown. I'm sure you gentlemen remember her. Well, your peep show is missing. Do you know where I can find Karen?"

He could tell from looking at their faced that they had no idea. The taller one spoke again. "We haven't been anywhere near that house since you caught us."

"Well any idea where she could be?"

"She's not someone we hang out with. We really never talked to her. Just looked that one time you caught us."

The smallest of the boys grinned sheepishly and added, "Well, maybe a couple of times before that, but I swear, not after you caught us."

Danny looked at the boys and his instinct told him they were telling the truth."Ok, if you hear anything about her, call me."

He got in his car and looked at the address for the girlfriends.

The first girlfriend repeated the facts she had told Karen's mother. They went to the church, more to check out the boys than the crafts. Very few boys were working this year so after they ate lunch there, they decided to head home.

"Karen and I lived in different directions from the church. We decided to meet later because I had some homework to finish up. The plan was for her to come over to my house around four- thirty and we'd decide what to do that evening. We said good-bye and the last I saw her, she was walking away."

"Was there any other girls with you?"

"No, because it was raining, the other girls didn't think it was worth going out in the rain, for a stupid craft thing. Once we got there, we kinda agreed it was a dumb idea ourselves."

"Did you notice any strangers hanging around?"

"Hey, I saw nothing but strangers. This was a Church Bazaar remember."

"How was her demeanor? Was anything going on with her that you noticed or she mentioned to you?"

"Listen, I don't like to rat out on a friend but Karen was different. Kinda wild. Nothing scared her. She loved attention and excitement. Not much into school. I probably would have skipped the whole thing if I had known the others were going to back out. But, I felt sorry for Karen when I realized that she would have been left alone at the last minute. To be honest, my parents didn't like me hanging out with her."

"So why did you?"

"I guess because she is funny and I guess because we are so different we get along. I never really thought about it."

"Any boyfriends?"

"She wished............No one really seemed interested in her. She seemed to scare them off."

"If you hear anything, make sure you call the Station. Ok."

"I will. I hope you find her soon. She is probably just having fun somewhere."

Danny hoped that was true, but his gut told him otherwise.

He called Mrs. Brown and told her he had checked out Karen's friend and she had confirmed the story. He would keep looking and check with her tomorrow but if Karen showed up to let him know right away. Then he drove to the station to fill out a report and let the dispatcher and other officers know. When he was filling out the paperwork, he took the photo out of his book and looked at it. He immediately felt his heart beat fast. My God, she was Lily. On closer inspection, he noticed her eyes were not as innocent or warm looking and there was tightness around her mouth. Plus, Lily never wore that much make up or had a fancy hairstyle. If you knew Lily, you would see the difference. At first glance though, you could mistake her for Lily.

He told the Dispatcher to call him if there was any news on the girl. He decided to catch a few hours sleep and see if she came home in the morning. If not, they would start a manhunt for her. He would arrange to have volunteers meet and comb the area.

Danny checked in with Mrs. Brown early Sunday morning. Karen has not returned. She had searched her room for any notes but found nothing. She was crying, convinced that Karen had not run away from home, but that something terrible had happened to her. He told her he was going to arrange a search party for her. Since it was Sunday, he would have the Pastor make the announcement at the end of the service today.

True to his word, Danny arranged for the Pastor to announce there would be a meeting in the Church Hall immediately after the service to organize a search party to try to locate the missing sixteen-year-old, Karen Brown.

Almost all the men and women came to the meeting. Danny spoke about his plans.

"I think the best thing for us to do is break into groups of drivers and walkers. This will be our meeting place. I'll need some to volunteer to ride around the streets and back roads to see if you notice anything suspicious. We will also have a group to canvas the area around town. The park and the woods. I want to remind everyone that your only job is to search and report back to us. Do not put yourself in danger. Call it in. The Sheriff will be in the Station and will respond to any sightings you have. Also, I want to remind everyone to think back to yesterday. We had a lot of strangers in town. Did you notice anyone suspicious? Did you see anyone looking at any of our young girls? I know all of you are parishioners and probably working; but go home and talk to your neighbors who are not members of this Church, but may have come to the Bazaar. Ask anyone you see if they noticed anything. Anything at all, may be a help in locating Karen. I have several copies of her picture. Each group will have one. Note her description when you talk to your neighbors. Now any questions?"

Several of the elderly people raised their hands. He nodded for the gentleman in the front of them to speak. "We cannot join the search party but we will make coffee and hot chocolate for the search party so when they come back they will have something to warm them up."

"Thank you all for your help. Hopefully we will have good news at the end of the day." As Danny spoke these words, he doubted that would be the case.

114

Madge called Bea and explained the situation. Max would go with the men, but Bea and Lily would get together with her and make some sandwiches for the search party. Lily wanted to join Max but they convinced her they needed her more here since she was not as familiar with the outlying areas as the others were.

By the end of the day, everyone was cold and damp because freezing rain had started to fall. No one had discovered anything that would point to where the girl was, or what might have happened to her. Danny decided to talk to the Sheriff about seeing if they could bring in some search dogs from the city. No reports were called in. Not even crank calls. He was beginning to think, if she was found, she would not be found alive. He shook his head and told himself to think positive, but he knew from experience that the longer a child was missing, the higher the odds that it would not turn out well.

Danny continued his search. He spent his days going over and over the surrounding area. The dogs were not available until the next weekend because they were sent to another town to search for missing boy scouts. Another setback. The townspeople interrupted their Christmas conversations to talk about poor missing Karen Brown and how awful it must be for a mother to endure. The town took on a sorrow no one had experienced before. For the first time, no one felt safe. This was a new feeling in a town where everyone looked out for each other. There was almost a feeling that they had failed to protect each other. They wondered how someone could invade their town. Was that person still out there? There was a fear of the unknown. They didn't know how to defend themselves because they didn't know what or who was responsible. They began to look at each other with suspicion. Danny knew he had to get this case resolved or it could affect this town in a way it would never recover. Things would never be able to return the way it was before the disappearance of Karen Brown.

A week had gone by and there was no news. They were no closer to finding the missing girl. At church, they all prayed for her and her mother. The pastor reminded everyone to think back to the day of the Bazaar and if they remembered anything to contact the Sheriff or Deputy Danny.

After church, Mrs. Jacobs went up to Danny.

"I've been away. Saturday night after the Bazaar, I got a call from my sister asking me to come out and help her for a few days as she was having minor surgery. I just got back in town last night and did not hear about the poor missing child until during the service today. I did see a girl who looked like the picture of Karen Brown. The reason I remembered is, because at first, I thought it was Lily from the diner. They look alike, don't you think?"

"I see the resemblance. Go on please, Mrs. Jacobs."

"Well anyway, I was helping out at the Bazaar and I had to run home after lunch because I forgot to take my blood pressure medicine that morning. I guess in my excitement to get there early to help out, I missed my morning dose."

"I understand." Danny wanted to choke her. Why couldn't she get it out?

"I cut across the parking lot and up the side street toward Main Street. Then there is that street that cuts off to the left. I don't think anyone uses it much but it is a short cut to my house. I saw a car pull over and a man sitting in the driver's seat. At first I thought he was lost and looking for the Bazaar. I thought about walking over to give him directions. Then I saw this girl stop and talk to him. At first, I thought it was the waitress from the diner. Lily, what a pretty name."

"So what happened then?" Danny had to control his aggregation. *God, this woman could talk.* He wanted to shake her, to get her to speed up what she had to say.

"Well then I noticed it wasn't Lily. This girl had a lot of makeup on, kinda fast looking if they still use that term today. Lily is so sweet, just like her name. That why I stopped and watched. The man did not look like the type that would interest Lily. The only men I have even seen Lily with are you and Max."

"Please Mrs. Jacobs. Enough on Lily. What about the girl."

"Well I'm just trying to explain why I watched them. I don't want you to get the impression I am a nosey old biddy."

"Never crossed my mind."

"The girl looked like she was flirting. You know how they say things with their bodies? Sort of tempting the fellow. Well, just as I was about to turn away and leave them to their own mischief, the girl walked around and got into the car with the man. You know Lily would never do that!"

"Can you describe the car and the man for me?"

"Well the car was kinda beat up. Some dents and paint missing. Mostly grey."

"What make, model or year? Did you notice?"

"No, I was honestly looking at the girl and the man in the car."

"OK, can you tell me what he looked like?"

"Well, he was sitting down so I don't know if he was short or tall or fat or thin. His face was rather ugly. Scars and kinda unshaven. That why I couldn't imagine Lily even stopping to talk to anyone who looked like that."

"Ok, so far we have an unshaven face with scars. What about his hair. Color? Length? "

"Well, he looked like he needed a haircut. I hate the styles nowadays. It was brownish, and he sent chills through me, now that I think about it. Like a wanted poster in the post office. You know like a gangster."

"Ok. How about you stop in the police station tomorrow and look at some mug shots?"

"I'll be there in the morning."

"Thanks for your help Mrs. Jacobs."

Danny had never had so much trouble getting information out of anyone like that before. He would be sure to tell Lily she had a friend in Mrs. Jacobs. But when he thought about it, I bet all the customers feel that way about her. She brings out the protective feelings in all of us. He hoped that by waiting until tomorrow, Mrs. Jacobs would have a chance to remember more. Other Law Enforcement people may disagree, but Danny thought the witness had not known about the incident until today, so chances were she was in shock at what she realized she had seen. Best to give her time to go over this in her mind. Not have her get confused with faces in a mug book. Remember what it was she saw. Yes, he was sure that was the best decision.

The next day Mrs. Jacobs did come to the station. Luckily, Danny was there. He decided to speak with her, to see if she could describe the man any better or remembered any more details. She gave him the same information. Then he asked her if she thought the car looked like any car someone else in town drove. She said she'd think about it some more and let him know. He had the mug books brought out for her and told her to let the dispatcher know if she had any luck.

He left to see if there was any place he had missed in previous searches. As he was driving, he started to go over all the information in his mind. Nothing could explain what happened to the victim. Nothing lead them to believe she got unwillingly in the car. If she knew the man, why didn't she at least call her mother to let her know she was all right? Besides, wouldn't she at least tell one of her friends? It was looking more like foul play than a teenager running off with a boyfriend. Then something started to nag him. He called Max, Madge and Bea.

117

"We need to meet tonight. There is something we need to discuss about Lily. Can we meet at Madge's house, say around six?" He repeated the same conversation to all three and all three agreed. They tried to get more information out of him but he wanted to talk about it when they were all together.

They all met at Madge's house and were anxious to hear what Danny had to discuss. Lily was also there and Rosie was playing upstairs.

"You all know about Karen Brown's disappearance. I know Lily, Max and I are relatively new to town. What I need from you, Madge and Bea, is to fill us in on anything that has happened like this before."

Madge and Bea looked at each other to see if anything sparked a memory for either of them. Bea was the first to speak. "The only thing I remember is the time Marylou Ottoman ran off with what's his name. I can't remember his name anymore. But she was nineteen and they had been dating. Her dad wanted her to go to college. Remember Madge, she came home after her first year and they ran off to get married? Boy that sure made her Dad angry. He finally talked her into an annulment and she finished college, moved away and married a college sweetheart. That must be over ten years ago now. Hear she is happy, so I guess it worked out alright."

"Yeah, I remember that. I thought Mr. Ottoman would never get over it. But that really wasn't the same as this disappearance now was it?"

"No, but that's all I can think about."

Danny asked them if they could tell him anything about Karen Brown.

"Tell me about the girl. I really didn't know much of her before now. What was she like?"

Bea spoke up. "Well, I saw her sashaying down the street. That girl always looked like she liked the wild side, if you know what I mean. Always flirting with anything in pants. She came in the diner a few times to check out the single men eating there but I scooted her out real fast. I don't put up with that nonsense."

Madge said "I've seen her around town but I never really paid any more attention to her than I did the other teenagers."

"Did anyone remember seeing her at the Church Bazaar?"

No one did.

"It was so busy said Madge; I think most of us were busy watching over our tables. I know she didn't buy anything from us, did she Lily?"

"No, not that I remember."

"Ok, now I want you to look at this picture I have of her."

They huddled together and looked at the picture.

"Does she resemble anyone to you?"

He could tell they were all trying to decide.

"Let me make it easier for you. Look at her and try to picture her without all that make-up and with a different hairstyle."

They all looked hard at the picture. Suddenly, there was an exclamation from everyone.

"Oh, my God." from Madge

"I didn't see that before." from Max

"This is unreal" from Bea

"I can't believe it. It looks like me!" from Lily.

"This is why I wanted us all together. Mrs. Jacobs brought this to my attention. I must admit when I first looked at this picture Mrs. Brown gave me, I had a fleeting thought of Lily but as you can see, if you know Lily like we do, there are many differences. But Mrs. Jacobs only knows Lily from the diner. Now, what I am going to tell you must remain confidential. I have to trust you to keep this among yourselves. Do I have your word?"

They all looked at him and agreed.

"Mrs. Jacobs claims she left the Bazaar after lunchtime to take some medicine. On her way she saw someone who she thought was Lily talking to a man in a car. What causes her to stop and watch was the fact that the man didn't look like someone Lily would associate with. She then said the girl got in the car and they drove off. Now I started thinking, what if he was looking for Lily. Maybe he mistook Karen for Lily."

They all looked at Lily.

"Now Lily, I know you haven't told us much about your past. I don't think any of us really cares, unless it puts you in harm's way. Do you think I am on the right track here?"

The color drained from Lily's face and Madge put her arm around her shoulder.

"Lily, I'm not trying to scare you. I care very much for you. Right now, I have to look at this from the law enforcement side, along with the personal side. I have a young girl missing. We have not been able to find her. Number two, if you are in danger, I am going to do my damndest to protect you and I can guarantee everyone here will do the same. I can tell you another thing too. The only reason Mrs. Jacobs paid any attention to the man in the car was because she likes you Lily, and was going to see if you were in danger. Believe it or not, you are loved for who you are now. Your past means nothing."

Bea, Max and Madge all started to talk at once. "Danny is right." "Let us help you."

Lily ran from the room. She went up to her room. God she was scared. Why did she have to have her happiness end? She started to pray. In Church, she had learned that God never gives us more than we can handle. Bet she was starting to doubt that she could handle this.

Downstairs, the four of them discussed what to do.

"Danny, I don't know how we can get her to tell us anything. She had something bad happen and Lily is definitely scared", said Madge.

Max said, "Right now we have to band together to make sure Lily is safe at all times. If that means we all go where she goes. So be it!"

"I agree. We have to find some way of gaining her trust. It doesn't look like she's ever had much of that before we met her," said Bea.

Madge said, "Here is what I know. You all must not say a word to Lily and I'm only telling you all, so you know how fragile she is, and will keep that in mind and not pressure her. When she first came here, she had nothing but some money. I took her shopping once I realized how pathetic her wardrobe was when we did laundry. She didn't even have the basic undergarments. I found out when we went to pay for the clothes, she kept all her money on her at all times. I convinced her to open a bank account. I doubt that she rarely spends even a small amount of what she makes. Then there was that time that drunk groped her at the diner, remember Bea? How hysterical she became? Then, there was a man in town asking questions about her. According to Mr. Ottoman (who I found out later told Lily), he told the man she stopped here briefly but was headed to California. Hank also alerted his bus driver friends to steer any inquiries to California. One thing I know for certain, that man scared Lily so much she wanted to leave town."

Max said, "The only thing I remember is when Rosie turned four she wanted to know how old Lily was and Lily didn't know. That always struck me as odd because she is certainly young enough not to worry about telling her age."

Bea said, "All I know from working with her is that the girl doesn't know trouble. She steers away from uncomfortable situations, is easily taken advantage of by the other waitresses, and doesn't even realize they are doing it. She doesn't have a mean bone in that body. She has the soul of an angel."

Danny looked at all of them. He thought he loved Lily before but now he was even more in love with her. He swore an oath to himself that he would not rest until he was sure Lily was safe, once and for all.

"Well, I can't say this meeting had the outcome I expected but I'm glad we all agree that we need to protect Lily at all cost. My gut tells me she is going to need us because I do think she is in danger."

Madge said, "Danny I know you went out on a limb to give us this information. I think we all agree it was necessary to hear about that man in order to protect Lily. If there is anything we need to know, please keep us informed. The information will stay with us...." Just then, Rosie ran down the steps. "I'm hungry".

Madge said, "I was just going to put dinner on the table. We are having company tonight so go get Lily and tell her to come and eat with us. She's in her room."

Thursday was Thanksgiving. The town was not as festive this year because of the threat hanging over the town. Was someone out there waiting to strike again? Was it one of our own that was behind this? Would we ever be safe again?

Madge tried to move forward with the family dinner. She baked deserts and bread and prepared the turkey. Even Lily and Rosie, who enjoyed each Holiday and were always excited when each one approached, were less than joyous this year. However, Madge was determined that they would all eat together as a family and observe tradition as they had in the past. Bea and Danny were given orders to attend. Madge told everyone that this is a day of Thanksgiving. They were going to thank God for all their blessings, which she reminded everyone, far outweighed the bad. To ignore the day of Thanksgiving was to ignore God. End of story. Everyone agreed to come to dinner after she made that clear.

Friday the search dogs were due in town. Everyone was hoping the search would be successful but they also feared that if it was it would not be good news. The town just wanted closure to the unknown threat hanging over it. Was it something that could threaten them too or just a onetime tragedy that only affected Karen Brown?

Danny was kept busy organizing the areas to be searched. He had an agreement with the unit to search the entire area within five miles of town. Chances were, if she was not found in that perimeter, then she was far from town and without specific clues, much too difficult to find.

Rosie was excited because today was Friday and the new toys were on the shelves at the department store. She and Lily had decided to stop by on their way home. Once in the store, Rosie let go of Lily's hand and raced to the toy department.

"Come on Lily," she shouted.

"Stay where I can see you! I'm coming," laughed Lily.

Rosie was busy looking at the dolls.

"I don't know which one to ask for. I like the one that giggles. Hand it to me please and I'll show you."

Lily reached up and took the doll down. They looked it over and played with it the best you could, with it still in the box.

"OK, put it back now, I want to look at the other toys."

Rosie took off down the aisle while Lily put the box back on the shelf. As she straightened out, she felt the sensation that someone was watching her. She turned around and surveyed the area around her. No other person was in the aisle. She immediately felt uneasy and went off to find Rosie. As she rounded the corner, she heard Rosie screaming and she noticed a man walking away. She could not see his face because his back was to her. Rosie kept screaming.

She ran to Rosie and said, "What's the matter, Rosie, were you talking to that man?"

"He was asking if you were my Mommy."

"What did you say?"

"I told him I can't talk to strangers, he started toward me and I started screaming and he left."

Lily reached out and hugged Rosie tight.

"You are hurting me Lily, not so tight."

"Sorry, I just got scared for a minute, I am so proud of you." She took hold of Rosie' hand and said, "I want to tell your Daddy about the doll. Let's go see him at the store."

"But I haven't finished looking."

"Maybe Daddy will come back with us. Ok?"

"Yeah, let's get Daddy."

Lily and Rosie left the department store and headed down the block to Max's store. Lily could not shake the uneasy feeling and wanted to protect Rosie. They were not going to walk home alone today. Max was surprised to see Rosie and Lily return to his store and could tell something had upset Lily. Rosie told him they came back to tell him about the doll she liked. She spent the next few minutes excitedly explaining every feature of the doll. Max only half listened because his attention was directed at Lily. Her face was ashen and her eyes were terrified.

Max said, "Tell me what else happened while you were in the store."

Rosie looked at Lily to see if she was going to get in trouble. Lily said, "Tell Daddy how proud I am of what you said to the man in the store."

Lily explained what happened when she was putting the doll back on the shelf and Rosie told him about the man who tried to talk to her and what she said.

"Well, I think we should tell Danny how his Junior Deputy handled herself today, don't you Lily?"

Lily realized what he meant. They should report this to Danny. "Ok. I did promise Rosie that you would go back to the store with us. Is that possible Max?"

"I'll take a few minutes to close up. Not too much business right now anyway, so then we can walk home together. Rosie, please go in the back and make sure your crayons and books are put away."

Max and Lily moved out of hearing of Rosie. Lily explained, "I had a sensation of being watched. Then when Rosie told me what happened with that man, I wanted to get her somewhere safe. I can't let anyone hurt her trying to get to me."

"Lily, we want you both safe. You did the right thing. We can't take any chances right now with any of us."

Max, Lily and Rosie, went back to the toy store and stayed close together. Max and Lily kept looking around the store to see if there was any sign of anyone suspicious. After Rosie decided on three toys to consider, they left the store and headed home for dinner.

Danny had been busy all day and no progress was made. It was now dark and the search was suspended for the day. He got the call from Max and stopped by Madge's on his way home. They were eating leftover turkey for dinner when he arrived and they insisted he join them. After dinner, Madge took Rosie in the kitchen so Max and Lily could explain to Danny what happened in the department store.

Danny was upset but grateful that Lily and Rosie handled it so well. "Max, did Rosie say what the man looked like?"

"No, I didn't want to ask her too many questions until we got home. I didn't want to scare her."

"Do you mind if I talk to her? With you here, of course."

Max called Rosie back into the dining room. "Danny wants to ask you some questions. Ok?"

"Actually, Rosie, I want to tell you how proud I am of you. You are doing a great job as my Junior Deputy. I heard how well you remembered the rules of not talking to strangers. Now I want to test your memory. One of the things a Deputy has to learn is to remember what suspects look like. So I want to see how far your training has come. Don't worry, you won't fail. Now close your eyes and think back to the man in the toy department. Did you look at his face?"

"Yes,"

"What color was his hair?"

"Brown."

"What color were his eyes? Did he have glasses on?"

"Brown eyes. No glasses."

"How about his nose? Was it big?"

"I don't remember."

"OK, what about his face. Was he nice looking?"

"No, scary."

"What do you mean by scary?"

"He had scars on his face and mean looking."

"Good Job. Did he look like anyone you have seen before?"

"No and I don't want to take this test anymore. Daddy can I go play?"

"Junior Deputy Rosie, you passed your first test. Great Job. I think we are both done."

Max said, "Thanks for helping Deputy Danny. Give me a hug and go play."

Lily said she had only seen the back of the man's head; her first instinct was to protect Rosie, so she didn't go after him or watch him leave.

"That's exactly what I wish more people would do. Leave the investigation to the police. Lily you handled that perfectly for you and Rosie."

They talked a few minutes more about the search efforts. Danny asked Lily if he could see her the next evening after work. Maybe go out for dinner. She agreed and he left.

The next evening Danny picked up Lily. Once in the car, he asked her if they could change the plans. Instead of going out of town, he wanted to know if they could either eat at the diner or cook dinner at his place.

"I don't want to make you uncomfortable about going to my place but I'm tired and I could use a friend to talk to, it's been a couple of stressful days with the search party here."

"That's fine. I would enjoy helping you cook."

They got to the apartment and Danny headed into the kitchen. He told Lily to look around. He really liked the apartment and was grateful to Max for renting it to him. She came into the kitchen as he was browning ground beef. "How about chopping the onions and green peppers?" Soon they had the ingredients ready for the sauce and left it on to simmer.

"You know I really love to cook. It relaxes me and it gives me a feeling of accomplishment. The only thing I hate is cooking for myself. It's lonely not having anyone to share dinner with. You are lucky having a family like Madge's to come home to each day. I envy that."

"I like to cook too. You're right, I am so lucky. I never thought I would ever live with this much happiness. Don't you miss your family?"

"Yes I do. I had a great time growing up, although I did give my parents some problems. I think that's why I went into law enforcement. Every time my friends and I got into mischief, my Dad dragged us down to the police station. He made sure we paid for our bad deeds. I think I did more community service than anyone who lived there. In fact, I think my Dad invented community service. He always said if you cause trouble, you are responsible for making it right again. I swear, I raked more leaves, painted more buildings, than someone hired to do it." He started laughing. "I guess that' why I handle the mischief in town with the approach that I do".

Lily laughed. She was enjoying the evening with Danny but she thought to herself. *I always do. He is a nice man.*

"Ok let's get the salad together and then we can sit and relax until the sauce is done."

They prepared the ingredients and then went into the living room to sit down.

"Lily, you never talk about your family. Did you have fun growing up?"

Lily looked at Danny and said "No. My Mother died when I was two and my Father didn't want me, I guess."

"Did you have any brothers or sisters?"

"No, just me. He did say once that I had a sister by his first wife but when she left, she took her with her. I never saw her."

"Is your Dad still alive?"

"I don't know. I never think about him."

"Did you come here to get away from him? Is that who you are scared of?"

"No. Can we talk about something else?"

"Sure, I don't mean to pressure you or make you uncomfortable. I just want to protect you and I need to know what I am protecting you from. Or who?"

"It is hard to talk about what happened before I came here. It is not something I want to remember. Give me time. Ok?"

"Of course, but remember that whatever happened is in the past. I want you to get past that and consider your future. Which, I hope, includes me. I really care for you!"

He reached over and hugged her. She hugged him back. He was starting to think he was gaining her confidence. He kissed her on the cheek and said "Let's eat. I'm starved."

They talked about Rosie and her excitement in picking out the right toys to put on her list to Santa.

"You really love Rosie, don't you, Lily?"

"More than I ever thought possible. She is so enjoyable to be around and smart too."

"I was really proud of how she handled herself in the store with you when that man approached her."

"Me too. But you know now, I'm afraid to have her with me, in case the man tries something, I don't want her hurt."

"Lily, no one including her father wants her in danger. But I think she is pretty smart. If something would happen, she would be able to run for help. She is very good at recognizing trouble. If you feel uneasy about this, just make sure you and Rosie are not walking alone anywhere. Just like you did when you went back to Max's store. As long as you are cautious, you should be ok."

"I'll talk it over with Max. Just to make sure how he feels."

"That's a good idea. I really love having you here for dinner. It has been such a rough week. I can't get that poor missing girl out of my mind. It is so frustrating not to know where she is. I'm afraid if the search dogs do not find anything now, we never will. I appreciate having a friend to talk to. As the Deputy Sheriff, everyone seems to be looking to me to solve this case. Honestly, the Sheriff doesn't seem too interested in anything. Since I've been here, the only time he has really done anything, is when we found that man in the wrecked car with the money. Remember?"

"Yes, I do remember that. Everyone was talking about that in the diner."

"Well that was the only time he got involved but then he backed off real fast and sent the guy packing when we couldn't charge him with anything. Sorry, sometimes I get discouraged. I just need a shoulder to lean on. This is when I really miss having someone in my life to share things with."

"Danny, I don't know much about the law stuff but I love to have you talk about things to me. I do like you. You are a nice man."

"Now you are going to make me blush. But thank you. I do appreciate your friendship." He thought to himself, I hope it can be more soon.

They cleaned the dishes and sat down again on the sofa and talked of trivial things. He decided to keep it light. Soon it was time for her to leave. "How about an ice cream cone or a Sundae to top off our dinner? We can stop at the drugstore on our way to your house. Your choice. We can walk or I can drive you.

"Sounds great! Let's walk. I feel safe with you and it is a nice evening out. Pretty soon, we'll be having snow."

He talked her into a hot fudge sundae. They had settled into a comfortable relationship and enjoyed their time together. Lily was right; it was a perfect evening to walk. Just a perfect fall evening. The leaves rustled as they walked and the air smelt faintly of wood burning in fireplaces to ward off the evening chill. The air was crisp but the breeze blew just enough to swirl around the leaves still attached to the trees waiting to be released to join the ones that had already fallen. She loved the way they swirled in the air thru the light breeze and looked just like they were dancing. The farm had few trees since most of the land was plowed for planting. Living here, trees lined each street and the houses all had a big tree out front. Funny, she never thought of this before. How similar the yards were, when the houses were so different. She stopped a minute and had a fleeting memory of *her tree*. Danny looked at her and she laughed "Just enjoying the trees. Guess you think I'm silly but I love watching them. Sometimes it reminds me as if they are playing a game together."

Danny reached over and kissed her. He never knew anyone like her. She made him thankful to be around her. Her appreciation of everything was contagious. They held hands the rest of the way home.

Once they reached the porch, Danny led her over to sit in the swing. "Let's just sit and enjoy each other before you have to go in."

They sat down and he put his arms around her and moved to swing with his foot. He felt Lily relax against him and lean in tight. "Are you cold?"

"Just a little."

He leaned down and kissed her on her mouth. He felt her stiffen but that passed quickly and soon she was returning his kiss with such feeling that he was getting dizzy. He came up for air and looked at her. "Lily, you know I'm in love with you."

"I think I am feeling the same for you."

"I think it's time we spent more time together. I miss you so much when you are not with me. Let's plan on getting together more often. Is that ok?"

"Yes and we can cook at your house."

They both started laughing and Madge looked out the window. "You two keep on doing what you are doing, I just thought I had some teenagers necking on my porch".

They both laughed and Danny said, "Madge, Lily sure makes me feel like one!"

Chapter 20

Sunday was cold and rainy. They all bundled up for church. As they neared the street where the church was located, they could see past the pond over into the woods. The search dogs were still out and narrowing down the area they had left to search. The service at church today was directed to prayers for the successful end of the long painful search for Karen Brown. Everyone, by now, had little hope of a success but joined in the prayers to bring peace to her and her family.

It was late afternoon when they made the discovery. The shallow grave was found under leaves at the edge of the woods about a mile from town. Volunteers had searched that area earlier but the leaves had cleverly hidden the spot and made it unnoticeable by the previous searchers. The dogs were able to identify the scent. Once the team had started to uncover the debris, the makeshift grave became evident.

This news quickly spread thru town and everyone met back at church to meet with the Sheriff's department and receive more information. Afterwards, there would be a prayer service.

Danny was surprised when the Sheriff actually attended the meeting. Most of the questions could not be answered until the Medical Examiner had a chance to do an autopsy. There was no way to tell what the cause of death had been. They were all advised to still be cautious and report anything suspicious. The police would not rest until the person responsible was apprehended.

Finding the body was expected to bring closure to the town but it had the opposite effect. Now it was real. The realization hit everyone. Karen Brown had not gone off on her own free will. Someone had deliberately ended her life. Grief and fear hung over the town. No one felt safe. Someone had violated one of their own. Danny and the Sheriff were under pressure to solve this crime quickly.

The search team left and the body was moved to the Morgue in the next town. The funeral services could not be held until the body was released to the family. Fundraisers were being planned to help Mrs. Brown with the funeral expenses. The High School held several band concerts and put on a play. Jars lined the counter of every business and the churches took up and extra collection on Sunday.

Nearly the entire town turned out for the funeral that was held two weeks from the discovery of the body. There was no viewing because of the condition of the body. The stores all closed during the service and the church held a reception after the funeral. The Sheriffs' department circulated among the crowds to identify any strangers and anything suspicious. So far, they were coming up empty handed. No direct link to the mysterious man in the car. Danny was getting very frustrated. He felt he missed something but whatever it was, he could not find out what was causing this doubt.

Danny decided to look on the police data base and see if he could find a link to a crime committed somewhere else. Anything to get information on the killer. He contacted all law enforcement agencies asking for any other unsolved kidnappings, abductions, and murders of young girls. He went back and amended the search to include all victims. Then he decided to request information on dead bodies found buried under suspicious circumstances. That should do it, he thought.

He and Lily continued their dates which mostly consisted of cooking dinner together. Danny had insisted Lily take a key to his apartment because he did not want her waiting outside if he was running late. Often, when he did work late, Lily was already starting dinner. She occasionally brought Rosie because Rosie protested that Lily was not spending as much time with her as she was with Danny. She often had to remind Rosie that she did see her every day on their walk home and grownups needed some grownup time together.

Danny came rushing in the door and was glad to see Lily and especially glad she was alone. He kissed her and asked when dinner would be ready. She was about thirty minutes away from finishing so he told her he had just got some answers from his inquiries to other police departments. He brought them home to read because he wanted to be with her instead of down at the police station.

He was reading the reports and nothing struck him as related to his case. Lily asked if there were a lot of crime in other areas. He started reading them off more in the vein of conversation than anything. "Here's an interesting one. A farmer had to dig up outside his house because of a well problem. They found a man's body buried under a vegetable garden. No clues. Not related to our case because it was a male."

Lily quickly turned around to face the sink. She turned on the sink to disguise any sound she may make. She felt faint. She broke out in sweat and was afraid she would fall. She prayed Danny was not noticing anything. Luckily he was still talking, going over the reports. She gathered herself together and headed to the bathroom. Once there, she splashed cold water on her face and sat on the toilet and put her head down. Soon she felt good enough to go out and finish in the kitchen.

"Lily, you don't look so good. Is anything the matter?"

"I just feel kinda sick right now. I think I'll sit down."

He jumped up to get her a glass of cold water. "I'll finish getting the dinner ready. Lay down for a few minutes. I know it was selfish of me bringing home this gruesome stuff. I apologize. This whole thing has got me to the point that I don't think straight anymore. I was so anxious to see you, I just wanted to spend as much time here as possible."

"That's ok. Just felt faint. Sorry."

Soon the aroma of dinner soothed Lily and she got up and set the table. "No more police talk ok?" she said.

He agreed and actually was glad to have someone to talk to about something other than work.

After they cleaned up, they sat in the living room and Danny told her how good she made him feel. He reached over and took her into his arms and she immediately responded by kissing him. It was almost like she was clinging to him and could not get enough of him. She was looking for comfort and to get the image of the body on the farm out of her mind. He was surprised by her new feelings. He wanted so much to make love to her but was taking it slow. He kissed her throat and down to her breast. She shivered but did not pull away. He unbuttoned her blouse and began to caress her breast. God she was beautiful. He felt himself grow hard and did not know how much longer he could control himself. She reached out and lifted his shirt over his head. Soon they were both uncovered. She caressed his chest and kissed him urgently. He sucked on her beautiful breast and felt them grow hard. She arched her body toward him.

"Lily, I want to make love to you but I want you to be ready. I will not force you."

She responded by reaching down to slip off her jeans. He was afraid he would not be able to hold back. Just looking at her almost made him come. He had never felt this way before. He loved her so much, he wanted to possess all of her and make them one. He got up and carried her to the bedroom. She did not seem self- conscious or afraid. He wanted to take his time and caress every part of her body. He was losing control and could no longer wait. He entered her and was surprised how ready her body was to receive him. Their bodies fit so well, it was almost as if it was the reason they were created. To be with each other. Lily did not understand what was happening to her body. She had never felt this way before. The response of her body to Danny's surprised her. He brought her to the peak of ecstasy. She had never experienced an organism and thought she was going to die. Her heart raced but she did not want him to stop. Once he came, he eased off her and drew her into his arms. "Lily you are the most beautiful person inside and out. I never thought anyone could bring me this much happiness."

Lily looked at him but did not reply. Instead she dug deeper in his embrace. They laid there for a few minutes. He realized he had not been the first one to make love to her but it really didn't matter to him. He was glad she was now his. He knew she felt the same way about him but found it difficult to express her feelings. He reached out and said "Lily, I'm sorry if I did not take the time to satisfy you but I have looked forward to this day since I first laid eyes on you. I knew I loved you."

He started to kiss each inch of her body. It was more beautiful than he had ever imagined. He started with her ears, he neck and made his way down to her breast. She held his head and moaned softly. He moved down to her stomach and then into the mounds of yellow fluff between her legs. She stiffened at first but passion overtook her and her need grew. He continued down her legs and feet. By then she felt she would go crazy. She grabbed him and pulled him toward him and said "I need you to love me."

He replied, "Lily, that is never going to be a problem."

They laid quietly for a long time afterward. Satisfied and loved, were the thoughts going through both their minds. She could not get over the beauty of his body. For the first time in her life she knew what it was to make love, not to do the sex thing but to actually have this act serve as an expression of love. The joining of two hearts and souls. And to feel as if someone cared about her needs, not just his.

They got up and took a shower together. He was always surprising her with the intensity of his feelings for her and he was always looking out for her. He made sure she was satisfied and took care of her needs. He had the impression that had never happened to her before and he was glad he could be the first one to bring fulfillment to her.

"Lily, I know this is the first time for us and I didn't think of using protection. Not that I would mind a baby, but I want you to be ready when we do get you pregnant. I'm old fashioned enough to think we should be married before we start a family. But if something happened because of tonight, I want you to know I love you and it wouldn't make any difference to me."

"I guess I never thought of it either. What should we do?"

"Well the easiest thing is to let me handle it. Ok?" Lily agreed because honestly she didn't know how to prevent pregnancies. Maybe she should ask Madge.

Lily and Danny added a new dimension to their relationship. They spent as much time together as possible and people started to think of them as a couple. Danny took care of the protection and Lily still felt uncomfortable asking Madge about sex.

No new leads had come in on the man who was suspected of murdering Karen Brown. Danny no longer discussed any information with Lily that he thought might upset her. Most of their time was spent discovering each other. He had not pushed her for any information about her past but was sure she would confide in him when she was ready.

Now that Thanksgiving was over, Christmas was approaching quickly and most of the activities around town were related to decorating and baking. Lily was really getting excited this year and was looking forward to Santa's visit to Rosie. They still continued to stop by and look at the toys each Friday. She had her list almost completed. Santa was due to make his annual visit to the fire station in two weeks. She told Lily that she had to have her list completed by then because she would not have a chance to change her mind after Santa took the list back to the elves in his workshop.

The big tree by the pond was decorated and the lights were turned on with a ceremony. They all joined in to sing Christmas Carols and drink hot apple cider. The pond had frozen enough so skaters could use it. Max surprised Lily by announcing he knew how to skate and had brought skates for Rosie. It was fun for her to watch them skate around the pond and join other skaters in a merry mood. She loved this time of the year.

Everyone seemed to forget their troubles and she thought it is almost as if the cold air blew in and took the sadness away. It seemed like a long time since the town had an occasion to forget about the murder. She was glad they were moving forward in the healing process. She herself was viewing life differently since Danny had become such a big part of it. She was so happy; she wanted everyone to feel that way.

Danny on the other hand did not feel as optimistic as the rest of the town. It was almost as if he knew this change would not last.

Madge was busy baking cookies and fudge. Lily and Danny were hoping she would include fudge in her Christmas present to each one of them. They dropped hints whenever they were around her. Rosie was in the Christmas Play at the church this year and everyone was busy helping her learn the songs and the speaking part she had. Lily and Danny had gone shopping together to pick out presents for Rosie, Madge, Max and Bea. She didn't know what he was getting her and she was unsure what to get him.

Chapter 21

The man had made a plan. He was going to get his money from the Sheriff and then go after Lily before he left town. It had not been hard to locate where the sheriff lived. It had been harder tracking down Lily. He had made a mistake in picking the wrong girl the first time but before he killed her she was more than willing to talk. He got excited just thinking about the terror in her eyes. She had been more than willing to spill her guts in hopes of saving herself. Even offered him sex. Said she was a virgin. Not that he believed her the way she was dressed and made up. Hell, she had come right up to his car and got right in. He was disappointed to find out she was just a town teenager. But he really didn't have too much information to go on. Did the best he could to narrow it down. He laughed to himself remembering he did take advantage of her offer and was he was right, she was no virgin. It was a shame he thought, that I had to get rid of her. She wasn't that bad once she got started but then he thought of the thrill of killing and couldn't decide if he liked the killing or the sex better. He couldn't wait to try Lily out. Funny how easy it had been to find out Lily's name and where she lived, when the girl was trying to save herself. Good stroke of luck that he thought to ask her about that thieving sheriff too before he killed her. Once he had his money back, he would be free to leave the town for good.

He buried the body and took what money she had on her. Not worth the effort but he wasn't going to bury it with her. He never gave a thought of what a waste of life the victim was. He didn't have much respect for life or anything else.

He decided to leave town for a while. He hadn't planned on getting the wrong girl and knew now the town would be searching for him. Since he was a stranger, there was a good chance that he would be picked up for questioning if he was spotted in town. He wanted to avoid that at all cost. So he left until the heat blew over. Then he would deal with the bitch Lily.

He returned to the town after reading the body had been discovered and the funeral had been held. Then he began to watch the sheriff's house for several days. He soon knew the sheriff never varied his activities. He came home, took a nap in his chair, cooked something in the microwave, sat and watched TV then went to bed. Today he had come by during the day and jimmied the back door. That way, he could surprise the sheriff while he took his nap before dinner. He knew there were no dogs in the house and no alarm system to contend with. He laughed to himself how easy this was going to be.

The sheriff arrived on time and went inside. Then the man crept up to the house and waited outside about fifteen minutes. He looked in the window and saw the sheriff with his mouth partially open and eyes closed. Good, now to be quiet and go in through the back door. He made it into the living room without waking him up. He held the knife at his throat and the sheriff's gun in his hand. He thought "*The dumb shit left his gun out for me right here on the table*" and almost laughed out loud. The sheriff woke up with the pressure of the knife on his throat.

"What the hell?"

"Quiet sheriff and do what I say and no one will get hurt." He tossed the sheriff's handcuff's over to him.

"Put these on and the gun won't be necessary."

The sheriff obeyed and put on the handcuff.

"What do you think you are doing? You are in a lot of trouble son."

"First of all, I am not your son. Second of all, you are thieving bastard. I am here for my money."

The sheriff looked at him. He could see the recognition dawning on him.

"You are that fellow who had the money in the car. I put that money in the bank."

The man laughed. "You may have put some money in the bank but it sure as hell was not what you took out of my car. I had close to twenty-five thousand. I know because I counted it after I stole it. You may have pulled a fast one over everyone else but not me. Now enough talking. Give me the money and I'll walk out of here and leave you handcuffed. Keep lying and I leave you with a bullet in your head. Your choice."

The sheriff could tell he meant what he said. All you had to do is look in his eyes and you could see evil.

"I left it at the station."

"Bullshit, you have it here."

"I swear it is in the station house. In my office."

The man swung the gun and hit the sheriff across the face.

"No I want to know where it is."

"We can go down there and I'll get it for you."

The man swung again and caught the sheriff across the face and nose. He nose was bleeding down the front of his shirt. "Now, one last chance. Where is the money?"

The sheriff looked around the room as if to judge his chances of getting away. He started to stand and the man took his foot and kicked him as hard as he could. They both heard the ribs crack.

"This is it sheriff. I can find it with you dead or alive. I'll tear this place apart and set fire to you chained to your chair."

The sheriff was not a brave man. His refusal to talk was more out of greed than toughness. He now realized he could not bluff his way out of this. He told the man the money was hidden in his freezer in the basement. The man hit him again to immobilize him and went to check. Sure enough, he noted the money was in plastic grocery bags. He went back upstairs and counted it on the kitchen table.

"Looks like most of the money is here. Do you have anymore to make up for what I lost?"

The sheriff shook his head "No". His mouth was swelling and he could not get the words out.

"Don't shit with me. Where is it?" He shot the sheriff in the foot.

The sheriff managed to get out "bedroom" between his screams.

The man left the room and went in search of the money. He found several hundred stuffed in dresser drawers in the bedroom. He came back and looked in the sheriff's wallet. "No use leaving anything behind because you won't be needing it."

He laughed as he turned around and used the sheriff's gun to shoot the sheriff twice in the head and once in his chest. He decided to set the house on fire. He found some gasoline by the lawnmower in the garage; poured it over the sheriff and throughout the house. He threw the gun on the sheriff's lap. As he left, he grabbed a dishtowel, lit it, tossed it on the sheriff, and left by the back door.

He figured he would stop by on his way out of town to pick up Lily. He knew she didn't work at night and decided it was worth a try. If not, he'd have to come back.

He pulled up in front of the house and did not see any cars in the driveway. He noticed that usually there was only one car parked overnight so that meant they were out. But was Lily at home? There were lights inside the house. He decided to wait.

Lily was alone this evening because Danny was working the evening shift. Max had gotten off early and taken Madge and Rosie to the next town for dinner and to see a Christmas movie that Rosie wanted to see. She decided since she had the house to herself, she would wrap the presents she had purchased. After she was done, it was dark outside but still early. She decided she would go to the Department store and look for a gift for Danny. She felt some apprehension about going out alone. Nothing had happened recently and it was actually not that far to walk. She bundled up and locked the door as she headed down the street. She noticed a car parked across the street but it was empty, no one was in it.

He couldn't believe his luck. She was home and she was coming out. He quickly ducked behind the bushes. He saw her hesitate and glance at his car. It was now or never. He came out of the bushes and ran toward her.

As she passed her house, she felt someone rushing at her from the bushes out front. She was knocked to the ground and the man was calling her names. She was caught off guard by the initial attack but it only took her a minute to realize she was in danger. She was easy to subdue. He dragged her to the side of the house. She was so small. He was so full of hate that he just started to beat her. He forgot his original plan to abduct her and make her suffer. He let his rage overtake him. She fought him and reached for his face to claw at him. Her first thought was to get out from under him so she could run for help. That only seemed to make him madder. She raised her feet and arms to push him off. He started to beat her face. She felt like she was going to pass out. She tried to scream but nothing came out. He had his hand on her throat. She finally was able to reach out and try to jab his eyes. He took her arm and she heard it snap. She knew she was going to die. Just then, she heard a car pull up. He apparently heard it too because he turned around to look. That was just enough time for his grip on her neck to relax and she started to scream. He almost didn't hear the brat screaming in the front of the house. He barely had time to run away before getting caught. He hit her one more time in the head and jumped up and ran across the backyard. She was losing conscientiousness but she heard Rosie screaming her name.

He circled back around the yards and just as he suspected, they were so concerned for their precious Lily that they were still outside with her. Chances were they had not even called the cops yet. He eased himself into his car and quietly drove away. As he headed out of town, he heard the distant sound of sirens. He laughed. At least the money is safe. And he thought of another plan for dear Lily.

Chapter 22

When she woke up, she didn't know where she was. She was in a strange room and bed. At first she was afraid that the man had managed to take her somewhere. Then she felt her arm. It was heavy and her face was bandaged. As she became fully awake she saw Danny dosing in a chair close to her bed. She tried to sit up and fell back down. He felt the movement and quickly jumped up and went to her side.

"Well, hi there. How are you feeling?"

"Danny, what happened? I can't remember."

"Well my love, you have been in and out of consciousness for the past two days. You had us all scared. Rosie is beside herself and Max and Madge have been taking turn coming to see you. The Doctor says you are one lucky girl. No bones broken in your face although you got a few nasty punches thrown your way. Your arm was not so lucky, it is broken but they promised me it should heal fine with no permanent damage."

"I remember someone jumped me and pushed me down. I tried to fight but I couldn't get him off me. Did he do anything else?"

He looked at her and then realized what she meant. "No sweetheart, he didn't touch you anywhere but your face and arm. The Doctor and nurse checked just to be sure."

"Did you catch him?"

"Not yet. But I will. Can you tell me what happened? Why were you outside?"

"I can't remember right now. I'm so tired and I ache all over."

"I'm not surprised. That man really roughed you up." His voice started to crack with emotion and she could see tears forming in his eyes."

140

She saw the love in his eyes and said, "I'll be fine in a few days. Don't worry."

As she fell back to sleep, she felt him kiss her and smiled.

When she woke up again, Danny was gone and Madge was sitting in the chair.

"Where is Danny?"

"He had to leave. He has been here since they brought you in and hasn't left your side. Once he was sure you would be ok, he called me and told me he had to take care of some police business and for me to come see you. I've been here about three hours now so my guess is he'll be back soon."

"I'm sorry I'm such a bother to everyone."

"Shush. Don't you even think that. We love you, Lily. Rosie is frantic. I have to ask if Max can bring her in if that is ok with you. She thinks you are going away like her mother did."

"Of course, I want to see her. In fact I remember her screaming."

"Yes she was the one who actually spotted the man. At first, we didn't realize he had you, but Rosie's screams scared him off."

"Danny said he got away."

"It was our fault. We were so concerned about you we couldn't think fast enough. By the time Max ran into the house to call for an ambulance, he noticed a car speeding away."

"I'm just glad he didn't try to hurt any of you."

"Do you know why he attacked you?"

"No, he was saying hateful things and calling me names. I don't know who he was."

"Ok, enough questions for now. I'll leave the rest for Danny to ask. Thank goodness we were too late for the movie and came home early. The food took so long to be served to us in the restaurant. We didn't think far enough ahead to remember there would be a lot of people besides us in town because of Christmas. Since we were so long, Max figured the movie was probably sold out so we decided to go back this weekend just to see the movie. Surprisingly, Rosie did not put up a fuss. It was almost as if she knew you needed her."

"I will be forever grateful that you found me in time. I really thought he was going to kill me and I had no idea what I had done to him."

"Well, put him out of your mind right now. The police are doing all they can to catch him. Do you mind if I check with the nurse and call Max, so Rosie can come see you?"

"No, of course not. I miss her too."

Madge went out to check if Rosie could come for a short visit. She explained the anxiety the child was feeling over Lily's attack and needed to see for herself that she was not going to die. The nurse told her Lily was in a private room and if they kept the visit short, they had no objections to her coming. She went back and called Max. He apparently was asking Madge questions that made her uncomfortable because she became short with him and said "Those things we will discuss at the appropriate time."

"What was that about?"

"Never mind, just some silly stuff that I will take care of later."

"Are you supposed to do something that being here is keeping you from getting done?"

"Not at all! You know men, they worry about the silliest things."

Lily didn't know. She was confused at Madge's conversation and did not want to cause problems between her and her son.

The phone rang a few minutes later. Madge answered it and smiled "You can ask her yourself. She seems somewhat rested and I'm hoping I can get her something to eat."

Madge handed the phone to Lily. She laughed when she heard his voice. He always made her feel so safe. "I'm afraid I slept after you left and have not been much company for Madge but guess what? Rosie is coming up to see me. Madge got special permission."

"That's great. You do need your rest, so don't feel bad about that. I wanted to see if you needed anything?"

"Just you."

"I have some loose ends to clear up here and then I'll be over. I have to work out the schedule for the next couple days to make sure everything runs ok without me and the Sheriff. See you soon. I love you."

After she hung up Lily got a worried look on her face. "What's the matter honey? Something he said upset you?"

Lily thought a few minutes. "He said without him and the Sheriff, what did he mean?"

Madge looked uncomfortable but hoped she covered it quickly enough. "I think he is sick or something. I really didn't pay attention."

They chatted about everyday things. Then, Madge left the room to get the nurse and to see if Lily could have something to eat. She stepped out of the room while the nurse checked Lily's vitals and changed her bed. While she was waiting in the hall, her son and Rosie came around the corner.

"Let's go down to the waiting room at the end of the hall while they get Lily ready for visitors." She explained that Lily had been asleep for so long, they had to do an examination to make sure everything was ok and then she could eat. She left word at the nurse's station to let them know when they could go back in to see Lily.

Max asked if she knew about the Sheriff. Madge gave him a look that conveyed her message to change the subject. "What about the Sheriff, Daddy?" asked Rosie.

Madge quickly said, "He is on vacation, I think. Danny is working extra hard since he is gone."

Max looked guilty at bringing it up and changed the subject.

Once they were in Lily's room, Rosie ran to her and flung herself into Lily's arms. She had tears in her eyes and said "Lily, that mean man hurt you!"

"I know. But something else I know is that my Junior Deputy saved me from getting hurt even worse. You were great!" She hugged her close and showed her the cast.

"I may need some help when I get home. Do you know anyone who can help me brush my hair and help me butter my bread?"

Rosie giggled and said, "Yep, me!"

They all laughed. It was the first time since Lily was attacked that anyone of them felt like they could relax. She would get better. They had all been so scared.

The food arrived for Lily and although she wasn't that hungry, she knew she should eat so she could get out of the hospital. Rosie helped her and they managed to spill as much as she ate. Luckily, Madge had put towels over Lily's chest and lap so it absorbed most of the spills. She and Rosie took turns tasting the food and decided what they liked best and what they decided was the worse. Madge and Max watched them enjoy themselves and each other. Both gave a silent prayer of thanks that Lily had come into their life and that God had decided this was not the time to take her away from them.

After dinner, they talked about Christmas and Rosie talked about her list. They were laughing and having a good time when Danny walked in carrying white roses. He came over and took Lily in his arms and gave her a deep kiss. "I missed you. Looks like I have competition for your attention. I think I'll bribe the competition." He took out a rose and gave it to Rosie. "Can I borrow Lily for a little while?"

"Rosie laughed and said, "Silly, you are her boyfriend aren't you?"

They all laughed and Danny said, "Yes mam, I sure am!"

Madge and Max said they had to leave anyway since it was getting late. They all kissed Lily goodnight and Rosie climbed up on the bed and whispered in her ear.

Lily gave her a big hug and said "Me too!"

After they left, Danny asked what she had said.

"She told me she was glad I didn't have to go to heaven with her Mommy."

Danny sat on the bed and took her in his arms and said, "Me three". They laughed and talked at the same time. They both realized how much they hated being apart.

The nurse popped into the room and looked at Danny and Lily. "I can see how hard it must be for you to be here and away from that hunk." She winked at Lily and said she would see what the Doctor thought about sending her home. "Of course I have to promise him you are going to receive a lot of TLC."

Danny said, "Nurse, that's the least of her problems. Getting her to accept it, is the big problem but I promise you she will be treated with all the love we can heap on her!"

The nurse and Lily laughed and the nurse said, "I'm sure you will."

Lily had to stay in the Hospital for a few more days because she had been unconscious and they wanted to make sure she had no lingering effects from the beating. Madge, Max and Danny took turns coming to see her and the time passed quickly. Finally the day arrived for her to go home. Danny wanted her to stay with him but Madge was determined that Lily return to her house. She pointed out to Danny that he had to work and would not always be with Lily and around to protect her. He gave into that plan once he realized that she was right about leaving Lily alone.

Danny picked her up from the hospital and drove her home. He had missed her more than he could put in words. She was excited to come home and Madge had a homecoming planned for her. Max, Rosie and Bea were waiting for her at home and there was a home cooked meal with roast beef, mashed potatoes and several of Lily's favorite vegetables. Madge thought she needed to have a good meal since she had been confined to hospital food for over a week now.

As Lily and Danny arrived at the house, she was overwhelmed with emotion. It was heartwarming to see the greetings she got and the love she felt from them and for them. It always surprised Lily to know people in this world did love each other. How long ago it seemed now, that she had endured a lonely life. She thanked God everyday for her blessings.

Rosie had made a picture for her and could not wait to give it to her. The picture was quite good and showed a little girl with her arms around a bigger girl. She had the color of hair right and she wrote I LOVE YOU on the bottom. Lily gave her a hug and told her she was going to have Danny frame it for her so she could keep it forever. After much catching up, Madge told everyone it was time to eat because she wanted Lily to get some rest.

Everyone talked through dinner. Bea kept them entertained about some of the customers at the diner and told Lily she was missed. Every day the customers asked about her. "I told them you never had a vacation since working for me and you deserved one, so suck it up, and let the other girls wait on you for a change." Everyone laughed at her description. Lily told Bea she was anxious to come back to work but she wasn't sure if her face would scare the diners away and her cast presented a problem too.

Bea told her that when she did come back it would only be for partial days because she didn't want her best waitress to come back too soon and suffer a relapse. She told her if anyone thought she was overworking her, the customers would boycott her diner. It made Lily feel good about her job but she still felt like she was letting Bea down during the busy holiday season. More people tended to eat out instead of cooking at home so they had more time to shop and get ready for the holidays.

Once dinner was over, Madge told Danny to take Lily up to her room and get her settled in. "I know you two missed each other but tonight Lily needs her rest so I am giving you one hour tops and that means Lily must be lying down and not sitting up talking. I'll be up to shoo you out if you run over that time. Understood?"

"Yes, mam" they both said in unison.

Lily walked into her room and thought at first she was in the wrong room. "What is this?"

"Madge has been busy. She had Max and I paint. Max supplied the new furniture. Madge and Bea picked out the curtains and bed stuff. Rosie picked out the rug. Do you like their surprise?"

"I absolutely love it!" The walls were a pale yellow; the curtains were a combination of yellow, pink and green. The area rug was bright green with some pink abstract designs scattered through. The furniture was white with wood tops. It was the most beautiful room Lily had ever seen. She started to cry. "Don't let Madge and Rosie see you cry, they would be crushed. They spent a lot of time planning this. It was supposed to be your Christmas present. They felt it would cheer you up and you needed it now instead of waiting for Christmas."

Just then, Lily looked up and there stood Max, Madge, Bea and Rosie. They were all grinning and waiting to see Lily's reaction. She ran over and hugged them all. "I may never want to leave my room now. You all did such a wonderful job giving me the perfect bedroom. I don't know how I can ever thank you!"

Madge said, "You are welcome. We all helped out with this and we each had a hand in decorating. We're glad you like it. The important thing is that you are back home with us. Well, we are not trying to use up Danny's time, so we'll let you two talk. We'll be up later to say goodnight."

Danny helped Lily change into a warm nightgown and took time to kiss each part of her body as he did. She laughed and hugged him tight. "Lily, I think we better wait before we do anything more that kiss but I want you to know it is hard not to snatch you away forever."

Lily felt the joy of being with Danny. She missed him too.

They talked and hugged for a while and pretty soon Rosie knocked on the door. "Grandma said Danny's time is up and now it is my turn." They laughed and Danny went to open the door for Rosie. He picked her up and sat her down on the bed with Lily and then reached down to kiss them both goodnight.

Chapter 23

As Danny came downstairs, Madge, Max and Bea were waiting for him. "Did you tell her about the sheriff?" asked Madge.

"No, let her have at least one night at home before we tell her. Nothing is going to change if we wait until tomorrow."

"That's probably best. Poor thing has been through enough. Do you think she'll be able to give you any information on her attacker?"

"I'll try and talk her either tomorrow or the next day. Everyone is on the lookout for the guy. We all think it is the same one that attacked Lily."

Lily slept late the next morning. When she came downstairs she found Madge in the kitchen. No one else was home. "Good morning sunshine. What can I get you to eat?"

"Where is everyone?"

"Rosie had a play date with her little friend from Sunday School. You know the one with pigtails and the baby brother. Max and Danny are at work. But of course, they all called to check on you and find out how you are this morning. So you have to eat breakfast or I'll be in trouble with them."

"How about some cream of wheat? That's Rosie's favorite."

"Sounds good. I want to take a shower and dress in my own clothes after I eat. If it's warm enough, I'd like to sit on the porch for a little while."

"That would be good for you. I always think fresh air is a good cure for being cooped up."

Madge was right, thought Lily. A nice breakfast, shower and fresh air is just what I need to get myself back to normal."

Lily sat on the porch swing and Madge came out to join her. "Lily, I hate to ask but I need to know why you were out alone on the night you were attacked."

"I know I shouldn't have gone out but it was early in the evening. Since everyone was gone I wrapped my Christmas presents. I realized I didn't have Danny's so I wanted to look around the department store without him. It's really not that far to walk. I really feel foolish now that I have caused you so much trouble."

"Don't feel that way honey. It was probably better that it happened outside instead of having him break into the house. Hard to tell what he could have done to you once he got in the house. In a few days we can go down to the store together to look for his present. What did you have in mind?"

"Well, I've had a hard time deciding what to get. I finally thought of a watch. One of those that glows in the dark for when he works nights."

"Well, how about we check out Pete's jewelry store. I was in there looking at their display of sale merchandise and he told me he got in a big selection of watches for Christmas. I didn't want or need one so I really didn't look at them, but it's a place to start."

"I would love that. I feel so scared now. That man said such hateful things to me. I don't know why. I don't know him so I can't understand why he hates me so."

"Well, I'm glad to hear you are scared. Not that I want you scared. But I want you safe. If you're scared, you will be less tempted to take chances. We all want you to stay close to someone and not have you alone by yourself anymore. As far as that man hating you, he is just an evil man. He is full of hate for everyone."

"But Madge, he called me Lily! At least I think he did. It is all blurry now. I was so scared and he was hurting me so bad and I couldn't protect myself." Tears rolled down Lily's cheeks and Madge went over and held her in her arms.

"Lily, I don't want to make you sad. I just want you to talk about it and not hold it in. We are all so concerned for you. We want this man caught."

Lily now had a headache. Said she was going back inside and lay down for an hour. Madge gave her a hug and told her she would bring her a mug of tea up to her room. Once she had her tucked in for her nap, she and Madge talked about her room. Lily told her she still cannot believe it is the same room. "Well, you are family now. Not a border, so you should have a room fit for your status with us. Look at it this way; you are the daughter I never had until now, a sister to Max and a wonderful Aunt and Substitute Mother to Rosie. I think we came out well ahead of you in the thankful department. You have given way more that you have received." She leaned over and kissed Lily on the cheek and told her to get some rest because once Rosie came home, she would want to make up for lost time. They both laughed as Madge closed the bedroom door.

Lily slept badly. She kept having bad dreams. She was being chased. The man caught her and started to beat her. Then he started to rape her. She cried and screamed but no one helped her. The town looked on and laughed. "She deserves it" they shouted. She couldn't find Danny, where was he? Where is Madge? Where is Bea? Max help me! Still no one came to help her. She felt a fist beat her face. He was saying nasty things to her and she thought she recognized the voice. Who was the man? She looked into his eyes. Why was Clyde doing this to me? Try to scream for Danny, he has to hear you. Finally the scream came out.

She felt someone shaking her. She lashed out to stop the pain. She opened her eyes and saw Danny holding her shoulders."Honey, it's ok. You had a bad dream. I just came to check on you and heard you scream. I ran up the steps so fast I thought you were being attacked. You are safe now. Come downstairs with me."

"Danny it was awful. I couldn't find you. No one would help. Why would Clyde hurt me like that? Please just hold me. I need you, don't let me go."

Danny wanted to ask her who Clyde was. He had a lot of questions he wanted answers to, but now was not the time. Lily was so upset, he was afraid she would go into shock. He glanced up and saw Madge looking worried. He said "Just a bad dream. She needs a few minutes to get over it. We'll be down when Lily calms down. I've got her now."

Madge went back downstairs and Lily reached out to Danny. "Make love to me. I need you so bad. I felt so alone and I was so scared that you would not find me." She started kissing him. He stood up and locked her door. "Can't have Rosie getting an education." They laughed and he took his clothes off, then reached out and helped her out of hers. He had missed her so much; she was such a part of his life now he could not bear to leave her. They made slow and sensual love. It was better each time. They knew each other's bodies so well now that they could pace themselves and make sure every desire was satisfied. They laid together afterwards each feeling totally content. It was if it had always been planned for them to find each other. They were a perfect match.

Danny told Lily that he was taking her to his house for the evening and would pick her up as soon as he got off work. As he left, he told Madge he would talk to Lily tonight and about his plans for the evening.

Danny arranged coverage at work so they would be uninterrupted. He also gave instruction that short of a national emergency, he was not to be called at home. He has also arranged for Bea to deliver dinner for them. This is something Bea never did, and even though he was her nephew, he knew she would only do it for Lily. He wanted to make sure everything was in place. He had a lot to discuss and did not want anything to take their attention from what he had to discuss with her.

He picked her up after he got off work and told Madge that Lily would be staying overnight. He told Lily to pack whatever she needed and she went back upstairs to get her things. Once she was out of the room, Danny told Madge he was going to talk to her tonight.

"I know she will be going to church and we can't keep her confined to the house much longer. She needs to know what has happened before someone else tells her, or talks about it in front of her, and she finds out that way. Don't you agree?"

"Yes, you're right. I'm surprised she hasn't found out already."

"I think it is best if she stays overnight in case she has a hard time taking all of this in."

"I'm sure that is not the only reason." Madge laughed.

"Well, you could be right about that. At least I hope so." Then Danny laughed.

"What's so funny you two?" Lily asked as she walked back downstairs.

"Madge was just giving me a hard time about my motives for having you spend the night." He winked at her and Lily blushed.

Danny got Lily's bag and they headed to his car.

"It feels good to be going out. I wish we could walk to your place."

"Not just yet. Soon, but we are going to make sure you get better and then you'll wish for a ride." They both laughed. It was so nice to be going out, thought Lily. She felt almost like things were back to normal.

Bea arrived shortly after they did with their dinner. She gave the food to Danny and sat on the couch with Lily. She looked at her face and couldn't help feeling anger at the man who had caused Lily so much pain. They talked about the diner and menu changes Bea was considering and soon Danny had everything set up at the table.

"Well I best be going. I didn't go to all this trouble to have you sit down to cold food." She kissed Lily and gave Danny a hug before leaving.

"Don't forget to lock the door after I leave."

Danny laughed. "Who is the policeman in the family?"

After they ate, Danny took Lily into the living room and told her to lay down on the couch while he cleaned up the kitchen. He covered her with a throw and she watched him work.

Once Danny finished, he came in to join Lily. He pulled up a chair close to her.

"How are you feeling?"

"Fine, now that I'm here. I missed you. We haven't had much time together since ...... well you know."

"I know. I've missed you more than you could imagine. Like part of me isn't here. There are some things I need to tell you. I wanted us to have a quiet place to talk. Are you up to it?"

"Danny, what's the matter?" Lily was immediately scared that something was wrong. She searched his face and only saw love and concern.

"Well, I need to tell you a few things. Do you know Sheriff Bates?"

"Not too well. He came into the diner once in a while but never talked to me."

"On the night you were attacked, so was he."

"By the same man?"

"We think so."

"What happened?"

"From what we can tell, the man went there to rob him. His place was ransacked and his wallet was empty. The autopsy showed that he was beaten up and then shot. The man then set his house on fire to cover his tracks. The fire must have taken a while for it to be discovered because the call came in just about the same time as the call about you. It was a busy night."

"So he killed the sheriff?"

"Yea, what we can't figure out is why he went after him. As far as anyone knows the sheriff did not have a lot of money. Why him and not someone else, like the banker? We haven't been able to work through that yet."

"Danny, what did you tell me about the sheriff and the banker Mr. Ottoman? Something sounds connected somehow."

Danny thought for a few minutes. Something had been nagging him about the connection but he couldn't put his finger on it.

"The only thing I can think of that connects the two that I may have told you about was when that man had a car wreck and we found money in his car. Remember, the sheriff and I counted it and I had the banker open up the bank to keep the money until we determined what to do with it? As far as I know it is still there."

They both thought about it. Danny was the first to speak. "Do you mind if I call Mr. Ottoman to make sure it is still there?"

"No, go ahead. That's a good idea."

Danny called information and asked for the number of the Ottoman's residence. He was relieved when the banker himself answered the phone.

"This is Sheriff Mc Cain. I need your help. You remember the money Sheriff Bates turned over to you from that fellow who wrecked his car? Do you still have that money in the bank?"

"Yes, of course. In fact, I wondered what was going to happen to it since he died. I figured he was trying to trace it so it got back to whoever was missing it or tracking it to an unsolved crime. Do you have new information, Sheriff?"

"Actually, no. I just am trying to go through some old information and I thought about that money in connection to Sheriff Bates. Sorry to bother you."

The banker told Danny to keep him informed as to what to do with the money and they hung up.

"Sheriff Mc Cain?" asked Lily,

"Sorry honey, I hadn't gotten that far. It seems like when you are around, I do my best thinking. I got ahead of myself. When the Sheriff died, they appointed me as acting sheriff until his term runs out. Then they have an election to vote for a new sheriff. Of course, unless his murder gets solved, I may have a short time as Sheriff."

"Danny, that's great. I know that's what you wanted. Not under these circumstances but that's what you were working toward. I know from what I heard in the diner, you are well liked by the people in this town. More than Sheriff Bates, that's for sure."

"You always make me feel so good when you are around. That why I love being with you." He leaned over to kiss her and she reached up and started to unbutton his shirt.

"Lily, you drive me crazy. I can never get enough of you."

Soon all else was forgotten. They were naked and enjoying each other like it was the first time. Better, he thought, because they knew each other's body so well. She was so thin. He could feel her ribs under her breast. He kissed every part of her body and felt the heat rise in her. "Hurry, I need you

Danny, I can't wait. He found it hard to control himself. He did not have protection ready. He told her he was sorry but he could not stop now.

"I don't want you to. It's alright. I love you".

They lay wrapped in each other's arms. Lily was the first to stir. "Let' go to bed. I can tell it will be a night to remember." Danny laughed and carried her into the bedroom.

They made love again and then fell asleep. Danny awoke with a nagging feeling that he forgot something. He looked at Lily. Something she said. He knew it was something he had missed before. He laid thinking back over their conversation and then it hit him, *the money.* He went over that day when he found the money in the car. He remembered how anxious the sheriff was to help count the money. How often he went to the bathroom. How he sent Danny out for drinks. How he got the guy out of town. He remembered thinking how little money there actually was, once it was counted. In fact, he was surprised when Mr. Ottoman recounted the money and voiced his concern of why it was so important to open the bank after hours for that small amount of money. Could the man in the accident have been the same man who came back to get his money? Could that have been the man that attacked Lily? He got out of bed and went into the kitchen to write all this down.

He was drinking coffee and finishing up his notes when Lily came in wearing his shirt and he hoped nothing else. He got up and gave her a kiss.

"I could get used to waking up to this every morning!" He muzzled her neck with kisses and ran his hands under her shirt. God her breast fit so good in his hands. He reached down and kissed her. She instantly felt the juices flow and her stomach tighten. He led her to the sofa and continued exploring her body. Soon all else was forgotten except the need to satisfy and be satisfied.

Afterwards, they went in and took a shower together. Danny washed her so her cast was kept dry. "Should we stay naked all day? I can't imagine how many times I'll take your clothes off again. Seems like a waste of time." Lily laughed.

"So you have plans for the rest of the day?"

"Only to eat and ravish you."

"Let's eat first. Did you finish telling me everything last night?"

"Well, I'll fix some eggs and fill you in on what woke me up this morning."

As they ate breakfast, Danny told her of his theory about the money. He went over it step by step and said "It's the only thing that makes sense. Why would someone randomly rob the sheriff? Who knew he had money? This all comes back to the money recovered from the car."

Lily thought about it.

"Don't you have a picture of the man? Do the police take pictures when you arrest someone?"

"Yes, you're right. I'll check the station. Would you recognize the man who attacked you if you saw a picture?"

"I think so, I remember his eyes. So cold, so mean, so evil."

"I just thought of something else. The sheriff said he left the room so much because of his prostrate problem. I'll check with the Medical Examiner to see if that showed up in the autopsy report."

"I hope so. I want this man caught."

"Me too, Lily, me too."

Danny was anxious to check out the information but first he had to get Lily back to Madge. Now was not the time to take any chances on leaving her alone. He made up his mind to work unceasingly until this man was behind bars. Until then, Lily was not safe. But why was he after her? He needed to find an answer from her. Until he did, he could not be entirely sure what he was up against.

"Lily, I want you to think about what I am going to ask you. Do you have any idea why that man attacked you? Don't answer yet. Do you know Karen Brown had a strong resemblance to you? I feel this is personal and only you hold the key. Once we can figure that out, we will be a lot closer to catching this guy and you will finally be safe."

He looked at her and waited.

"I don't honestly know. I think it was personal too because he used my name. But I never saw him before that night. I'd tell you if I knew."

"Could he be someone from your past? When you had the nightmare, you said something about Clyde. Who is he, Lily?"

"He's dead. At least I think he is. I heard he was."

"You have to tell me Lily. I love you. Nothing you can tell me will change that."

Lily turned pale. He hated himself for causing her pain. He almost told her it wasn't important but he couldn't because damn it, it was important.

"Take your time Lily. We can work through this together."

"I hate going back to the time before I moved here. Danny, it was not a good time in my life. I guess I'll start at the beginning. I was an only child. My mother died when I was young. I can remember some things but not a lot about her. I remember sitting in her lap and brief moments with her. I know she had long blond hair and a soft voice. At least I think that is what I remember about her. I don't know how she died. One day she just wasn't there." Lily stopped and thought about what she had said.

Danny reached out and took her hand. He raised it to his lips and kissed it and said, "You are doing good. Take your time."

Lilly looked at him and continued. "I don't think my father loved me. As a child I never thought much about it because I never really knew what love was. I just existed. In his mind I guess that's how it was. Like a plant. It's there; you water it and ignore it for the most part. As long as I kept out of his way, everything was ok. I did go to school for a while and that was my happiest time. The other kids were mean to me because I didn't have much. My clothes where old and dirty. I was often dirty. But my teacher was good to me. She helped me learn and shared her lunch with me. We had little food in the house and what we ate was out of cans. I was always hungry. But the knowledge I learned in school was like food to me. I couldn't get enough. Which, now that I think about it, didn't help me to win any friends in school either. The teacher gave me soap and showed me how to wash myself and she often brought me clothes. She would have me stay after school so the other kids were gone when she did things for me." Lily paused again. He could see this was taking a lot out of her.

"Do you want to stop for a while?"

"No, let me tell you a little more. Then one day my father told me I was getting married. Clyde came to the house and gave him some money. He told me to tell everyone I was sixteen. He took me away in his truck and we went to a place called Justice of the Peace and they gave me a piece of paper. Then we went to Clyde's farm. Although, I hated the sex thing, it was the first time I had a bed to sleep in, a bathroom in the house and enough food to eat. I loved the animals and I learned to cook and help out on the farm. Clyde was good to me. I guess I was content. I never knew love like I do now." She stopped again and tears spilled down her cheeks.

Danny reached out and held her in his arms. He kissed the top of her head.

"Lily you have been through so much. I will spend the rest of my life making your life a better one. Let's stop for now. You have said enough.

Lay on the sofa and rest. I want to make a few phone calls and then I have to take you back to Madge. I'll pick you up again after work. I just don't want to leave you alone but I have to go into work for a while. Ok?"

She nodded and lay down on the sofa. He covered her up and soon she drifted off.

Danny called the Medical Examiners' office. He was unable to reach the person who did the autopsy but left his name and number to have them call him back. When he returned to the station, he would check for robberies that occurred around the time he and the sheriff found the money. Maybe he could find out how much the sheriff hid in his house. He needed to get this case resolved if he and Lily wanted to put all this behind them. He was still convinced it was tied into her in some way.

The next few days Danny was busy looking through robbery reports that occurred during the time the money was discovered in the wrecked car. He continued to pick up Lily when he got off work and they cooked dinner together. She was regaining her strength and her bruises were fading on her face. They had faded from black to green and were now yellow. If she were the type to wear makeup, she could easily cover the remaining traces of the attack. She talked about going back to work. Everyone was encouraging her to give herself time to get her strength back. Her job required constant movement and little time to sit down. She reluctantly agreed with the promise she could start back three days a week beginning next week.

Danny decided that Friday he would bring home the mug shots of the man who had been found with the money in his car. He needed Lily to see if it was the man who attacked her. Maybe, he thought, we can continue talking about her past and see if there could be any connection. The Medical Examiner had called him back and confirmed that Sheriff Bates had no underlying medical condition other than some plaque in his arteries that may have needed attention down the road. He had no prostrate problems. That confirmed Danny's suspicion that the sheriff had most of the stolen money and the man came back to recover what he felt was his.

Lily was helping Madge around the house and playing with Rosie. Her life had gotten almost back to normal. She knew she would need to tell Danny the rest of her story. Her only concern was that it may cause him to feel differently about her. In fact her new family will probably be shocked when her life was laid open to them. But she knew she had to confide in them. It was no longer possible to remain silent. Too many people had been hurt and she could not take the chance that anymore people may suffer because she kept her secrets to herself. She was afraid that something from her past may threaten Danny, Rosie, Madge, Bea or even Max.

Danny brought home the mug shots and asked Lily if she wanted to see them first or continue where they left off about her life before coming here. Lily thought a few minutes and decided to continue with the story. She was afraid that looking at the picture may bring up such bad memories that she could not continue if she recognized the man.

"Relax, Lily. Nothing you can tell me will affect how I feel about you. That was the past. We will make a future together. I want you to talk about it and then we can let it go."

Lily looked at Danny and saw the truth of what he said reflected in his face. She also was overcome with the love that was expressed in his eyes. She said a silent prayer for God to give her strength and guide her so she could tell the events as she remembered them. "The last time I told you I was married right?"

"Yes. You moved to a farm."

"Well, there was a lot of work to do. I had my own vegetable garden and grew vegetables for us to eat. Clyde grew corn and hay. He hired people to help plant in the spring and harvest in the fall. I guess that is how he made his money. We did the rest by ourselves. There were a few milk cows and beef cows and pigs. He sold a pig each year to the butcher and in turn, we got some meat to eat. I don't know too much about how that worked because he didn't talk to me about that stuff. I just had chores to do and he gave me the food to fix. I did love swimming in the pond on the farm and I had a special tree."

Lily stopped and was quiet for a few minutes. The tears ran down her cheek. She knew the next part of the story was coming and that was the most painful part.

Danny suggested they take a break and he went to fix coffee. When he came back, he put his arms around her and held her tight.

"How old were you when you got married Lily?"

"I don't know. Clyde told me to tell everyone I was sixteen."

Danny took a deep breath. My God, she was probably much younger. It broke his heart to think of the things she had endured as a child. He looked at her. "Lily, how old are you, now?"

"Danny, I don't know. I don't know when my Birthday is. Clyde had me pick a month and day and I picked July sixteenth."

"Ok, we will go over that later. How long were you married to Clyde?"

"I don't know for sure."

"How many Harvest do you remember?"

Lily thought hard then said "I think about six."

Danny thought to himself. That should make her between twenty-two and twenty-four. But who knows?

"Are you ready to go on?" He looked at her face to see how she was holding up.

"One day after harvest, Clyde sent me into the barn. A man drove up and went into the house with him. They were in there a long time and I fell asleep. The man came in and found me. He beat me up bad and did other things to me."

"Did he rape you, Lily?"

"Yes."

"I am so sorry. I wish I could take it all away from you. If you don't want to continue right now I understand."

Lily sat still. "Right now I need you to hold me. I feel so dirty."

"Lily, I want you to know I love you. Whatever happened to you, you had no control over. You did not cause anything bad to happen to you. It just happened because of bad men. With me, you are making your own choices. You can choose to be with me, choose to love me, and choose to make love with me. I would never force you to do anything you didn't want to do. Do you understand the difference? It pains me to know what you went through. But if anything, I love you more because of it."

Lily started to cry. How could she be so lucky to find someone like Danny? How could she ever be good enough for him?

Danny wiped the tears from her eyes. He kissed her and held her tight. She was overcome with love for him. She kissed him and immediately wanted him inside her. He was quick to realize that she needed to wipe away all the bad memories that had flooded her mind. Soon they were caught up in lovemaking that was so intense that neither one could think of anything else except giving and receiving pleasure.

After Lily fell asleep, Danny thought back over what he had learned. Was the mug shot going to confirm that the man was the same one that had raped her? How was that connected to the money? What happened to Clyde? Was he a threat to their happiness? Was she still married? He was going crazy with both love for Lily and fear of what could happen to come between them. I know how painful it is for her but I have to know everything. How can we get the strength to get through this for both of our sakes?

In the morning, Danny suggested they go to the diner for breakfast. It was time she got back to a normal life. As long as someone was watching out for her, she should be safe. When they entered the diner, Lily was overwhelmed with the greeting she received from the customers and the employees. Everyone came over to her, asked her how she was doing, and when she would be back to work. She received hugs and kisses even from the grumpiest old men. She laughed and told everyone how happy she was to see them too. She caught up on family news and looked at pictures of new grandchildren.

Danny looked at her and realized this was a good decision. She needed to know how much people cared about her. Then he thought sadly, she had never known this type of life existed before coming here to town. He was glad God led her here to him and the people of the town.

Chapter 24

Christmas was fast approaching. It seemed a long time since Thanksgiving and the attack on Lily. Actually, it was not that long ago. They took a walk around town before heading back to Danny's apartment. It was great to see the Christmas decorations and to enjoy the air. To Lily, it seemed like so long ago that she actually felt the freedom to walk safely around town and have Danny at her side. She reminded herself that she still had to buy Danny's present. Monday, she would ask Madge to go shopping with her.

Once they were back inside, they sat down together on Danny's couch.

"Will you look at the mug shot now so we will know if this is the man I am looking for?"

"Yes, I think I am ready."

He got up and went over to his desk and removed a folder. He brought it over and handed it to her. She looked down and gave a gasp. How could this be the same man? He was dead. She and Clyde had buried him. She suddenly felt dizzy. She started to stand up and fainted.

Danny was beside himself. Why did he show her the damn picture? Why couldn't he just leave her alone? He realized he was torn between being the Sheriff and being her friend and lover. He hated himself. He laid her on the sofa and went to get her a drink. She stirred and looked at him with wide eyes.

"What happened? "

"Well Lily, I think you answered my question. This is the man who attacked you. Now I'm putting the picture away and getting us both a stiff drink."

He came back with two glasses of whiskey. "Now drink this. I think we can both use it right now regardless of what time it is."

Lily took a sip and memories came back to her of when Clyde insisted they have a drink. She looked at Danny. How to separate the past from the present without anyone getting hurt? She didn't have an answer.

Once they finished their drink, Danny took her in his arms. "Just relax. You have had a busy day. You don't need to do anything else."

Lily and Danny sat there in silence and enjoyed the comfort of each other. When the phone rang, it startled them both. It was Madge wanting to know if they could eat dinner over there. Rosie is out of sorts missing Lily. So I told her I would ask you if you could come over for dinner. Danny glanced over at Lily and said, "I think that is just what Lily needs too. We will be there about six, ok?"

After he hung up, he told Lily about the call.

"I guess I haven't been much company for Rosie lately. I don't ever want her to think I don't care about her."

"Lily, she would never think that. She is just a little girl and doesn't understand sometimes that you have a life of your own. She is like the rest of us, she wants you to be around her because you are the type of person that people love to be with. You make everyone feel special in their own way. That's a gift not many people have. Don't always think you are doing something wrong. Realize the fact that you always do something right." He kissed her. "Got that?"

"Yes sir!" and she laughed.

"Lily, one more question. I have to know. What happened to Clyde? Are you still married?"

"No, Clyde died. He sent me out of town when he found out he didn't have long to live. He wanted to make sure I was safe from his son."

Danny set out a yell. "Yahoo!"

Lily looked at him.

"Honey, this means nothing can stand in our way. No husband, no marriage. Nothing! Do you understand how happy and relieved this makes me?" He kissed her and showered her face with kisses.

She laughed. "I should have told you sooner."

"You weren't ready then. But now I know."

They went over for dinner and Rosie was happy to have Lily back.

"I missed you! I hate boyfriends!"

Lily laughed and hugged her tight.

"One of these days, when you get a boyfriend, I'll be the one complaining you never have time for me!"

"Do you think I'll ever have a boyfriend like Danny?"

"Well maybe not just like Danny, but of course you will have a boyfriend. But not for a long time. For now, I want you to stay a little girl. "

Danny listened to the exchange and was again amazed at how Lily touched everyone's life and brought such joy to each one.

"Hey, Junior Deputy have you been keeping an eye on Lily when I'm not here?"

Rosie looked at Danny and said "Yes, Sheriff, I have."

He looked at her and said

"Then I made a good choice when I picked you to help me out."

Rosie went over and hugged Danny.

"I don't hate you, just boyfriends."

Danny laughed, and told Rosie he really was a boyfriend because he loved Lily but Lily had enough love for all of them.

Sunday, Danny had to work so Lily spent the night at home. She went to church the next morning with the family and the Pastor made the announcement from the pulpit that Lily was recovering nicely and was back to join them at the service this morning. Everyone turned to look at her and send warm wishes.

On Monday, Lily approached Madge to go into town to get Danny's Christmas present. She had everyone's wrapped so she only needed this one last gift. Madge asked her if she was still thinking of getting Danny a watch because Pete was having a sale this week. Lily thought that was a great idea and suggested they have lunch while they were out.

Lily and Madge walked into Pete's Jewelry Store and Pete was behind the counter.

"Well, you came in to get it sized, did you?"

Madge glared daggers at him and said

"You old fool; we came to get a watch. How many watches do you size?"

Pete had the decency to blush and turn toward the case holding an array of watches.

"Sorry ladies, old age catching up with me. I thought you were someone else. What kind of watch are we looking for?"

"You are not looking for a watch, we are." Madge was really mad at this man and Lily could not figure out why.

"Sir, I'd like to see a watch that allows you to see time in the dark. One that glows and the face is visible even when it is dark outside."

Pete reached into the case and brought out several watches. He explained the different features.

"This one, the numbers glow in the dark, this one, you push a button to light up the entire face plus, we have watches with leather and metal bands."

Lily spent some time looking at each one. Madge asked if anyone of them was waterproof and that narrowed the selection down. Lily spent another five minutes trying to decide.

"Can you write something on the back of any of these?"

Pete turned them over and they decided upon the one that had a flat back and did not require a battery. He called it kinetic which means it runs on solar power and not batteries.

"What do you want engraved on it? Since this has been a good season for me, I'll do the engraving for free."

He winked at Madge and she immediately glared at him again.

How about "Yours forever, love Lily. Will that fit?"

"No problem. I can have it ready in two hours, ok?"

Lily paid for the watch and she and Madge left the store.

"Why don't you like him? He seems nice to me?"

Madge said "Humph, you don't know him well enough."

Lily looked at Madge and wondered if they had feelings for each other and she didn't want to admit it?

"Is he married?"

"No, why do you ask?"

Lily said "Just trying to get to know everyone. No reason."

They walked over to Max's store and visited with him for a while.

"Glad to see you out and about, Lily."

"Madge and I are going to eat lunch. Do you want to join us?"

"That would be great. Rosie is still in preschool for a couple of hours yet. An early lunch would be fine because I am hungry."

They walked down to the diner looking in windows along the way. Madge told Lily she wanted to stop in the department store on the way home. Lily reminded her of the many trips she had made with Rosie and they all laughed.

Max said, "Thank goodness she already gave her list to Santa."

After they ate and Max headed back to his store, Madge made a few last minute purchases in the department store and they stopped by to pick up the watch.

"Now I'm ready for Christmas," said Lily.

This would be Lily's second Christmas with Rosie and Max. And her first with Danny. Life was good. She was in love and loved. She had a family for the first time and felt like she belonged. She was going back to work at the diner and her life was back on track. Little did she know how fragile her life actually was.

Lily always enjoyed the preparations for Christmas as much as the actual day. She loved helping decorate the tree. This year they all bundled up and drove ten miles out of town to a tree farm. Lily and Rosie were in charge of picking out the right tree. After several negotiations with Max, they decided on a Douglas fir. He explained that the first tree Rosie picked out would be too tall for the Angel. They all laughed because the tree she wanted was twelve feet tall. He told her the tree they finally chose would be perfect for the Living Room and it would look much bigger once it was inside the house. They cut down their own tree and had apple cider before heading back into town.

After dinner, Max went to the attic for the lights and decorations. Everyone divided in groups. Max decorated the top half of the tree, Madge and Lily did the middle and Rosie hung ornaments on the bottom. Soon all the decorations were done and Max held Rosie up to place the Angel on top. Madge brought out eggnog and they all sat down and admired the tree. Lily looked around the room and said a silent prayer for all the blessings she was given this year.

Danny told Lily that he was working Christmas and Christmas Eve this year. He explained that he felt his duty as Sheriff was to give time off to his Deputies who had small children. Since he was single, he could manage the calls that came in and only call on additional help if it was needed. They had Rosie's Christmas play at the church on Christmas Eve and Danny promised to attend if he was not out on a call. He would also come over on Christmas morning to be there when Rosie opened her gifts from Santa.

Rosie was so excited it was hard to keep her calm. Lily suggested they bake some cookies for Santa and his reindeer. They ate as many as they made and Rosie was reciting her lines for the play over and over. Soon it was hard for anyone not to join in her excitement. Once the cookies were done, they had a quick supper since no one was very hungry from all the cookies they ate. They all went upstairs to bathe and get ready for the Church play and Christmas Eve services.

The Pastor had a short service and reminded everyone the true meaning of Christmas. The play started right after the service and was held in the

Community Center. Everyone was anxious to see their little ones perform. This year Rosie had the part of the Angel who announced the Birth of Baby Jesus. She had been so excited to wear her costume and have wings Madge and Lily held their breath hoping she did not forget her lines or lose her wings. Suddenly the room became silent. Madge looked around for Max.

"Now where is he? He is going to miss his daughter's first play."

She looked at Lily in frustration. Then the Choir Director opened the curtains and announced that they had a surprise for the audience before the play began. To Lily and Madge's amazement, Max and Bea came out in choir robes and sang "Hark! The Herald, Angels Sing." No one had any idea they had this much talent and even stranger still, no one knew they were going to sing together. Lily looked around for Danny. She spotted him coming in and was glad he could get the chance to hear his Aunt sing the song. It sent chills down her spine just hearing their voices praising God in such wonderful harmony.

They left the stage and the children came out to perform their play. All the practice the parents endured at home and in church paid off. The play was done well and not one child made a mistake or forgot any of their lines.

After the play, the congregation gathered for refreshments and to extend Christmas greetings to each other. The parents of the little children were anxious to get home so the children could be tucked in and last minute preparations completed. The older ones without young children at home were glad to spend an evening with their church family and took their time talking to each other. Max and Bea were enjoying the praises they received and confessed they practiced in the back of Max's store so no one would know of their surprise. They wanted to give back something for all the blessings they had received during the past year. Max and Madge left before Lily, so Rosie could go to bed. Lily stayed with Bea to clean up after everyone left.

Danny had left after the play to make sure nothing required his attention and told Lily and Bea he would be back to take them home and to wait for him. He checked into the station to see if there were any issues, and rode around town. He was satisfied that all was well. He thought, usually people are home on Christmas Eve and stay out of trouble, hopefully this will be the case this year.

He came back to take Lily and Bea home. Lily was staying at Madge's so she could be there in the morning for Rosie. Since Danny was on call, he was actually glad she would be safe but he missed having her sleep beside him.

The next morning Rosie came running in to wake Lily. "It's Christmas. Hurry up and let's go see what Santa brought us! Hurry, Hurry!"

"Ok, just give me a minute to get my robe and use the bathroom."

As Lily walked out of the bathroom, Max and Rosie were waiting for her at the top of the steps.

"Ok, said Max, let's see what Santa left."

They all scrambled down the steps and were greeted by a beautiful tree with lots of packages underneath it. Madge came out of the kitchen and said "I put some cinnamon rolls in the oven and coffee is made if anyone is interested. And guess what, Rosie? It snowed last night and we have a white Christmas!"

Rosie's attention right then was focused only on the presents. She was anxious to see if Santa filled her list. She looked pleadingly at Max and he laughed.

"Mom, right now I think we have a little more pressing issue than food or snow. Rosie is anxious to see her presents."

"Well, let's not wait any longer."

Rosie was very excited because this was the first year she had actually put so much time in choosing the toys she requested from Santa and the first time she had written her own list. Everyone was as excited as Rosie to see her gifts. She patiently removed the paper and examined each gift. She then took it around the room and explained why she had asked for this present instead of other ones she saw in the store.

Madge said to Max, "I think we may have a research analyst among our mist. Where did she learn all of this?"

"I don't know Mom, but let's hope it continues." They all laughed with appreciation for Rosie's enthusiasm.

Madge and Max gave Rosie and Lily ice skates for Christmas.

"Rosie has outgrown her skates and pestering us to let her go ice skating and we thought you might enjoy it too."

Lily was excited to try them out with Rosie.

Max gave Madge clothes dryer.

"It will be delivered later because I wanted to keep it a secret. Now that Lily is occupied with other things, I thought this would benefit both of you. No need to hang clothes outside anymore."

Lily blushed and Madge laughed out loud.

"You are just afraid I may recruit you, and you would have to hang out the clothes, and have the neighbors make fun of you."

Max kissed Madge on the cheek and said

"That, too."

Soon it was time to eat breakfast and get ready for church. Lily quickly helped clean up the mess left from the wrapping paper. Once it was done, they ate and went to get dressed. Madge put the Turkey and Ham in the oven to bake while they were gone. Bea and Danny were coming to dinner. Max casually mentioned that he had invited someone to join them for dinner. Madge looked at him.

"I didn't know you were interested in dating anyone."

"I'm not. Who said it was a woman?"

"Well, not that it matters but who is it?"

Max laughed and looked at her. "Pete." He said.

"Why did you invite that old fart?"

"Because you are both single and I thought he might be lonely for a family."

"Well, Max don't be getting any ideas on my account. I like my life just fine, thank you!"

After church, Lily and Madge got the rest of the dinner started and then Bea arrived. She joined them in the kitchen and Madge told her that Pete was joining them this year.

"About time you noticed how he feels about you. It's written all over his face. You must be the only one in town that doesn't see it."

Madge swatted at Bea and said

"Not only do I have a meddling old biddy for my best friend but now I find out I have one for a son too." They all laughed.

Pete arrived carrying a big basket of fruit and a bottle of wine. Rosie met him at the door and told him to come in and see her presents. He was truly grateful to have been invited to a family Christmas. His wife had died many years ago and they never had children. He took off his coat and then handed Rosie a gift.

"I sold these in the store and thought it would be perfect for you."

She thanked him and opened up the gift. Inside was a music box covered with jewels that played music when it wound up with the key attached to the bottom. She reached up and gave him a hug.

"This is perfect. I have one with a ballerina and now I have this one. I love it." She ran off to show it off to everyone.

Dinner was ready and Danny had not arrived. Bea suggested they set a place at the table anyway because she was sure he would make it if he could.

Half way through dinner, he rushed in and explained that he may not be able to stay long. There had been several traffic accidents, due to the snow and Christmas cheer, not going well together. He was working alone. He left this phone number with the dispatcher, if he got a call. He apologized for not making it in time to see Rosie open her presents.

If he was surprised to see Pete at the table, he did not let on. He sat next to Lily and gave her a kiss. Rosie responded with "Yuk."

He got up and went over and kissed Rosie on the cheek.

"You are just jealous. I know you want me as your boyfriend but my heart belongs to Lily."

They all laughed. Rosie then told him all about her presents and promised to show him each one once dinner was over.

Danny and Rosie were in the Living Room together looking at her toys.

"Rosie, can I tell you a secret?"

"Sure."

"I bought Lily a ring and I want to ask her to marry me. What do you think she will say?"

"I think she will say, Yes."

"Do you think I can be alone with her for a while when I ask her?"

"You can go..............I can't think where you can go. Maybe the bedroom or bathroom?" "

"Well, I don't think the bathroom silly. Maybe we can have the living room by ourselves. Can you keep everyone in the kitchen or dining room for a while and send her out here?"

Rosie ran out of the room and came back holding Lily's hand.

"Call me when you are done asking."

Lily said, "Done asking what?"

Rosie looked guilty and ran off into the kitchen. She shut the kitchen door once she was inside, and told everyone they have to stay hidden, because Danny was giving Lily a ring and asking her to marry him.

Danny had Lily sit on the sofa beside the tree. He stood in front of her and got down on his knee.

"You know by now that you meant everything to me. I want to spend the rest of my life with you. I promise you that if you marry me I will do everything to make you safe and happy. I cannot live without you and the thought of losing you scares the hell out of me. I want us to be together forever. Please say you will marry me and be my wife."

Lily looked at Danny and saw the love in his eyes. She wanted him so much. Could she say yes? There were still things she had not told him. Could she become his wife and still keep this from him? She was torn by her heart. He stood up and took her in his arms.

"Lily, I know you feel the same way for me. I want you to get past whatever happened before and look to our future together. That is what is important. That is the only thing important. Just go with your heart."

She knew at that moment that she would risk everything for him. He was right. The most important thing that ever happened to her, was now holding her safely in his arms. "Yes, Danny I love you. I will marry you."

Danny let out a loud shout of joy and everyone ran into the room. They gave hugs and congratulations and were glad they could be a part of the event. Danny said, "I almost forgot the ring."

He handed Lily a small box. She opened it and was surprised to see the Diamond surrounded by a Ruby on each side.

"The diamond from my heart and the birthstone of your birthday." And he slipped the ring on her finger.

Pete put his arm around Madge and said ,"Am I now forgiven?"

They all laughed and Max said, "This calls for a drink."

Just then, the telephone rang and Danny was summoned to return to the sheriff's office to handle a call.

Chapter 25

After Danny left, Madge and Bea started talking about planning the wedding. Lily must have looked confused because Max stepped in and said, "Ladies. Give the girl a chance to be engaged for a while. Don't rush her. Let's enjoy the rest of Christmas first before we start on the wedding."

The look of gratitude that filled Lily's eyes made Max feel he had done the right thing.

He winked at her and said, "Goodness the poor girl never gets a minute to herself or a chance to absorb what is happening without the whole family taking over and butting in and yes, myself included. I'll give you away. Walk you down the aisle. Whatever you want."

Now they all laughed, including Lily.

The rest of the evening was spent playing with Rosie's toys and talking about things in general. Lily was so distracted by the ring, she found it hard to follow any conversation and was grateful for the chance to play with Rosie and get her mind off everything else.

A few days after Christmas, the dispatcher called Danny on the radio. Sheriff, I have a police department from out of state trying to reach you. He has called three times. I left notes on your desk but he is so persistent, I thought I should let you know in case you want to come in and call him back.

"Did he say what he wanted?"

"He has an unsolved murder and received information that the person of interest may live in our town."

"That's the craziest thing I ever heard of. I'll come in and see what information he has."

He thought a minute. Then he realized it may be related to the two deaths still under investigation, not necessarily that the person lived here in town.

Danny headed back into work. Funny, for a small town, there was always something, that managed to keep things stirred up. He reflected over the past year, the murders of Sheriff Bates and Karen Brown, the attack on Lily and fact that nothing had been solved. He felt some discouragement over those facts and could understand the frustration connected with unsolved crimes. This is why he stopped what he was doing and headed back to the office. The sooner he reassured the out of town police that no one in his town was responsible for their crime, the sooner they could concentrate on finding the right suspect. He knew how that went.

He made the call as soon as he retrieved the messages on his desk.

"This is Sheriff McCain from Colorado. I understand that you wanted to speak to me."

"Thanks for calling me back Sheriff. I need to check out a lead I have on an unsolved murder. We found a body on a farm sometime ago. It was found by accident when the farmer had to dig up the ground due to a problem with his well."

"I saw that come across the police alert, now that you mention it."

"Well, the farm belonged to Clyde Hill. He's dead now and the farm is rented out. He arranged all that before he died. I guess I am getting off track."

"If he is dead, was his the body you found?" Danny hoped the fear he suddenly felt did not betray him in his voice. He tried to keep it steady.

"No, Clyde died a natural death. He is buried on the farm in the family plot."

"So how does that relate to my town?"

"We had Clyde's son come in and claim that the body is that of his brother. He claims his father had a…. ahem, sorry to put it this way but he said he had a whore living with him. Thinks the whore killed him to keep him off the farm. He has been pestering us off and on since we found the body. We couldn't follow up on anything because he had no proof of the woman or the identity of the woman. Nothing for us to go on. Couldn't find anyone to confirm his story."

"So why call me?"

"Well I'm getting to that. The son came in and said he found the woman. She was living in your town. He saw her there."

"So did he tell you who she was?" Danny was now rubbing his forehead. He was getting a killer of a headache. He knew it was about to get worse.

"Said she was going by the name of Lily. Could be using the name Lily Hill. Do you know of anyone who lives there by that name?"

Danny was momentarily stunned. No, it can't be. This cannot happen to us.

"If I find her, what do you want me to do?"

"I need to follow up on all leads as I know you do, Sheriff. She will need to be questioned. Depends on how that goes. If she is not the right person, no harm no fowl as they say. If she is guilty, I'll have to bring her in and charge her."

"Ok, let me check around. Do you have a description of her?"

The Sheriff read off the description. Danny did not have to write anything down. He knew her features so well. His stomach was in knots and he told the sheriff he would call him back the next day after he checked out a few things. He took down his name and telephone number and shoved it in his drawer.

Danny immediately felt anger, fear and most of all a denial that this was happening. What was he going to do? He loved Lily. He told her nothing else in her past mattered. How could he arrest the woman he loved? Then he realized he was just plain mad at himself. Now, he was doubting her. How could he carry out his duties and still uphold his oath of office when he was so conflicted? For the first time in his life, he hated his job.

He left the office and told the dispatcher he needed some personal time and was leaving for the day.

"So what was so important with the phone call?"

"Just anxious to check out a lead. Don't think it will pan out. I have to take something for this headache. See you in the morning."

Danny did not want to confront Lily right now. He needed to think. What could he do? They could chuck everything and run off together. That sounded good in theory but what would they do for income? He knew they would be hunted down. Not only that, but they would hurt a lot of people. They had roots here now. How could he protect Lily? He went into the kitchen and poured a large glass of whiskey and thought maybe my old friend Jim will help me decide as he looked at the label on the bottle.

Danny sat for over an hour killing the contents of the bottle. Nothing helped. No new ideas came to him and the drink was not working to numb his pain. He started to cry. After he sobbed, he got up and took a shower. *How long has it been since I drank so much and how long since I actually cried?*

The next morning he went down to the diner for something to eat. He had put on jeans and a jacket after his shower. It was strange to see him in during the day without his uniform. He sat in a booth by himself and noticed Lily was helping out. He didn't realize this was the day she was starting back to work part time. It looked like she was doing fine with the cast still on her arm.

She glanced over and he immediately noticed the surprise on her face. Then she noticed his clothes and came over. "Hey, handsome, looking for good food?" and laughed.

The tears threatened to come back. "I want coffee and the breakfast special. You know how I like my eggs."

She looked at him strangely but quickly left to place his order and return with the coffee."Danny, what's wrong?" *You look terrible.*

"Bad day at the office. I need food and then I need to see you. What time do you get off today?"

"I'm only here for four hours. I will be getting off at one. Should I come up to your apartment?"

"Yeah, do that. I'll eat and then meet you there."

Lily was puzzled. She had never seen Danny act like this. What had happened? Something must be terribly wrong. Did he regret his decision to marry her? She suddenly felt the beginning of fear creeping through her body.

She delivered his food and left his check on the table. She then hurried off to wait on other customers. She told herself to calm down. He is entitled to a bad day. But when she glanced back over at him, she had her doubts.

Danny left the diner before Lily got off work. He was more upset now more than ever. After seeing her, it made it all real. How much he could lose. How much they could all lose. He headed back to the apartment. His fear had now turned to anger. He needed time to think this out.

Lily arrived after work. She walked in and went over and gave him a kiss. He could not respond. He was too angry to return her kiss. Maybe not at her, but the fact that everything had been going so good, and was now spinning out of control. He who always felt in control; now was helpless.

Lily looked at him. She saw the pain reflected in his face. "What's wrong?"

"I don't know where to start Lily. It seems there is a lot I don't know about you. I am in a very tough situation right now. I feel like my world had ended. I am a police officer and am now faced with the toughest challenge of my life. Do you have any idea how this is tearing me apart?"

Lily immediately felt her muscles tighten. She knew her world was about to come crashing down. "Tell me what it is."

"I got a phone call from a sheriff in another state. Do you know a Sheriff Axelrod? He said he got a lead in an unsolved murder case they had in Greenwood and traced the suspect here to Relay. They are looking for a Lily Hill. Anyone you know?"

All the color drained from her face. She knew this day would come. Just not now. What could she do or say to take away or explain that awful day so many years ago?

"I know there are a lot of things in my past that I could not share with anyone. Not that I was trying to hold them back but I was so ashamed and afraid that I would destroy everything."

Danny's face reflected his pain. His mouth was held so tight his lips seemed to disappear. The eyes that looked at her were almost cold. For the first time since she met him, she felt fear and anger radiating from his body. "Murder is definitely enough to be ashamed of and it does destroy lives."

Lily looked at him. She knew she had done the one thing Danny could not condone. She knew what they had would never exist again. There was nothing she could do to take away what was happening. She stiffened. Her whole body felt like it was betraying her. She could not let him see how he hurt her. "Ok. You can arrest me. I can't go on anymore. You seem to have your mind made up. I'm not going to try and change it".

"Damn Lily, that's the problem, I can't arrest you. I cannot do what is required of me. I can't bear to look at you now."

"I'm going home now. I'll wait at Madge's for you to come for me." She straightened up, handed him back the apartment key he had given her and left.

He sat there numb. How could he arrest Lily? How could he go on with his life? He had no idea what to do. For now, he would do nothing. He had about twenty-four hours to come up with a plan before he had to call the Sheriff back.

Lily left Danny's. She knew in her heart that he would do the right thing. How could she put him through such pain? Oh my God, there were so many people that would be hurt. Rosie, sweet Rosie. Madge the mother she never had. Bea and Max. How could she hurt these people?

As she walked home she passed the bank. She stopped and walked inside. How much money could she take out without causing suspicion? "I need to take out some money. How much is the limit?"

The teller looked up her account and told her there was no penalty for withdrawing and she could take the full amount. Lily decided to take just enough to get where she had to go.

She walked home and was surprised to find the house was empty. Max's car was in the driveway and she thought he might be there. He must have walked to work today. She saw a note in the kitchen. Madge was helping a friend make curtains and would be home for dinner. She gave instructions for Lily on the dinner preparations. Lily stifled a sob. How we take life for granted. How fast it can change.

Lily went upstairs and wrote a note to leave on her bed. She laid her engagement ring on her pillow and threw a few things in a bag. She took out her passbook and laid it on the bed. She doubted she would need it anymore. She looked around the room and took in everything for one last time. How happy she had been here. This was the first time she had lived in a house with love. Nothing had been expected of her. She was accepted without any stipulations.

Now it was time to go. She shut the door and went down stairs. She stood on the porch deciding what to do. She noticed Max's car. He kept the keys in the kitchen. She decided the quickest way out of town was to drive. She had only driven the truck once but decided she could do it if she was careful.

Once she started the car, she carefully backed out of the driveway. Good so far. Then she decided she could not chance driving past the diner or Max's store so she took the long way out of town. Everything was coming together. She would drive to the next town and catch a bus out of there. Leave the car so Max could find it.

Lily made it to the town without incident. She parked the car in front of the police station and headed to the bus terminal. She purchased a one-way ticket to California. That was the original plan with Clyde, so she would go there and then decide what to do next. She hadn't had time to think anything thru. So only knew she had to leave before she hurt anyone any more than she had already.

Once on the bus she kept to herself. She decided she would look at each town they stopped at to see where to get off. She had purchased a ticket to the farthest town in California, but she knew she would not go that far. The important thing now, is to use the time on the bus to think about and plan, her next step. Again, she was alone. *No one to lean on. Back to self-survival. Well no time for pity now.* She thought to herself. I knew the risk and I still took the chance. How hard it was to leave Danny. She had never thought she would have such happiness. Her new family, Madge, Max, Rosie and Bea. She would never see them again. Tears suddenly rolled down her cheeks and she realized that she would give up anything to spare them pain.

Lily slept off and on for most of the day. She decided tomorrow, she would look for a place to get off the bus.

Josie

Chapter 26

The next day Lily was ready to get off the bus. She had decided to avoid the small towns and get off the bus when it stopped at a larger one. More chance of getting lost and go unnoticed that way. Around two in the afternoon, she got her wish. The bus had a layover and everyone got off the bus. Since she did not have any luggage, she didn't have to notify the bus driver. She went over and sat in the terminal and tried to decide what to do. There was a newspaper box sitting there so she went over and put the necessary coins in to buy one. The first thing was to get a job and place to live.

Most of the jobs stated experience needed. How to get past that without needing a reference? She decided to leave the terminal and walk around town. She noticed a man watching her and felt uneasy. Best to move on. As she left, he followed her. She picked up her pace and walked fast but soon he was beside her on the sidewalk. He said, "I couldn't help noticing you back there. Are you looking for a job?"

She looked at him. He was dressed in a leather coat and although she didn't know a lot about clothes, she knew his were expensive. She didn't say anything.

"Miss, it's you I'm talking to. Looking for a job?"

"Sorry, I just got here. Why do you ask?"

"Well, I always have jobs for pretty girls like you."

"What kinda job?"

"Let's say as a companion to older men. They always like em young and fresh and you look like you fit the bill."

Lily shuttered. Although she didn't know exactly what he meant, she knew enough to know it was not good. She had read stories about this kinda thing and did not want to do what he suggested.

"No, I'm not interested."

"You think you are too good for me, huh? Well I'll let you in on a little secret. You will come looking for me soon enough. Here is my number, you'll need it. I give you just a few days and you'll find out you need protection. A lot of young girls just like yourself, come here looking for work and don't find anything. You won't be any different."

Lily took the piece of paper he handed her. She just wanted him to leave her alone. She decided to duck into the first restaurant she came to and get out of his way.

Once they approached a Denny's, she told him she had to go.

She sat down in a booth and ordered coffee. She had to calm herself down. The waitress was not busy and tried to talk to Lily. She was about Lily's age and asked her if she lived or worked around here. Lily told her she was new to town. She decided to confide in her about what happened at the bus station.

"Honey, consider yourself lucky. That must have been Big Jim. He hangs out there and tries to lure the innocent ones who have no place to go. He is a bad dude. Good for you for breaking away. What are you doing here anyway?"

Lily decided to alter the truth. Something she rarely did but there were a lot of things she did now that surprised her.

"I broke up with my boyfriend and needed a fresh start."

"I don't know how fresh this city is. I came here two years ago myself. I got tired of my dear old stepdad using me as a punching bag, among other things."

"I'm sorry."

"Yeah, just goes that way to some of us, I guess. Do you want anything to eat or don't you have any money?"

"No, I have some money. I will take a Cheeseburger and fries."

"Good choice. Real comfort food." She laughed and went to put the order in.

Lily had never had a girlfriend her age but she like this girl right away.

When her food was delivered, Lily was busy reading the paper looking for jobs. The waitress sat down the plate of food and said, "I'm Josie, what is your name?"

"I'm Lily."

"Just like the flower? I like that. I think my Dad wanted a boy so he named me Joe but I go by Josie."

Lily laughed. "Maybe my Dad wanted me to stay in the fields so he named me after a flower."

They both laughed but were struck by the bond they immediately had. Funny, it seemed like neither one was wanted by their Dad.

"Find anything in the paper?"

"Most everything wants references. I don't have any."

"Never worked before?"

"Yes but I don't want anyone to find me. Or know where I went."

"You didn't rob anyone or do anything illegal did you?"

Lily laughed. "No, nothing like that."

"We're not hiring here right now. Are you looking to waitress?"

"Doesn't matter really what I do. Just need a job."

"Well I get off soon. How about you sit here and wait for me? As you can see we aren't exactly busy. Once I get off, I'll show you around town. Ok?"

"Thanks, Josie."

Just then, a group of people came in and Josie headed off to seat them. She kept glancing at Lily while she worked. Not sure why but they had sort of connected right off. But it wouldn't surprise her if Lily took off and didn't wait. She seemed like…. what was the word she was looking for? Yeah, seemed sort of scared. If she was running away from her boyfriend, he must have treated her real bad.

It surprised both Lily and Josie that Lily had not left but waited for Josie to get off work.

"Lily, I'm glad you waited. I wasn't sure you would."

"I really wasn't sure I would either."

"So let me change in the back and we can go explore the town."

Josie came out wearing jeans and a sweatshirt. She had pinned her hair up and looked older than Lily had first thought.

Josie looked at Lily and decided she looked younger that she first guessed but that only intensified her desire to help her if she could. She remembered when she was new in town and had a few close calls. Men were always looking out for fresh ones to step off the bus and scare them into the wrong line of work. She herself had made a mistake in trusting someone who approached her and had a tough time getting away from them. She didn't want any other girl going through what she did. She still got scared, just thinking about it.

The streets were busy, but no one seemed to know each other. Just people going from one place to another. Not like my town, thought Lily. Everyone stops to say Hello. Then it hit her. It was no longer her town. Isn't this what she wanted when she decided to get off the bus?

Josie looked at the sky. "It is clear out. Hopefully, it will stay that way and not rain. Let's head into the center of town. We can look in the windows and just maybe there will be a *Help Wanted* sign. Although, don't get your hopes up too high."

Lily enjoyed looking at the area. It was all new to her and so different from what she had left. So many more stores. So many more places to eat and so many more people. She even saw two Movie Theaters.

Just then, they spotted a store called *Millie's Treasure Chest*. Josie said, "Let's go in. Millie is a neat lady and her store is fantastic."

They went inside and Lily immediately saw what she meant. She had never seen so many treasures. Small trinkets up to large pieces of unusual furniture. It was breathtaking. Like nothing Lily had ever seen before. She examined each piece being careful not to touch anything for fear of breaking it. Soon a lady approached them. She was dressed just as exquisitely as the things she sold. Not a hair was out of place and her subtle makeup was artfully applied Lily was fascinated with her. Her tall thin figure looked almost regal. Her face was set in a smile that seemed to glow. Lily immediately felt small and shabby in comparison. If the woman noticed Lily's discomfort, she didn't comment.

"Millie, you always have the most wonderful selection. You must sell a lot to keep rotating your stock. Every time I come in, some new merchandise is on display. This is my friend, Lily. Lily, this is my favorite customer Millie. She loves our pumpkin pancakes."

Millie laughed. Lily had never heard such a musical laugh. "It's a good thing you don't serve them every day or I wouldn't fit in the store!"

Josie spoke to Lily, "Millie does come in every day in the fall when we have them. I miss not seeing her every day."

"So what are you two doing today?"

"Lily is looking for a job. As we were walking by, I told her we had to stop and see you. I wanted her to look at all your wonderful things. They are fantastic, aren't they Lily?"

"Yes, they sure are."

Millie told them to take their time and look around. She had a few things she needed to do but to call her if they wanted anything.

"I've never seen anything like this. It is all so beautiful. Thank you for bringing me in."

"I thought you would like it. It's my favorite store. I don't buy anything because I don't really have any room to keep it, but I just like to imagine how I could decorate a house with it."

Several customers came in and made purchases. Millie appeared again and seemed frazzled. "I just got a big order from a store in New York. I'm trying to get it all together and I keep getting interrupted. Sorry about that. I don't mean to ignore you."

"That's ok. We have to move on now anyway. Lily is looking for a job and I didn't mean to get her off tract."

"Wait a minute." Millie shook her head as if to clear it. "Lily are you really looking for a job?"

"Yes, I am."

"What kind of job?"

"Either as a waitress or working in a department store, I guess."

"Listen, I need some temporary help right now. I can't promise a permanent job, but it you are agreeable to working part time for a while; we can see where it leads. You can take time off if you need to go on another job interview. It's getting late now, but come in tomorrow around nine in the morning and we can talk."

Lily didn't know what to say. She looked at Josie. Josie nudged her. "Now is the time to say great, I'll be here."

They all laughed and Lily could not believe what she heard. She looked at Millie and said "Great, I'll be here."

Josie and Lily left the store and Josie put her arm around Lily.

"How is that for your first day? Not bad, huh?"

"Josie, did you know she was looking to hire someone?"

"Actually, no. I really do like her store and I just wanted to go in. Plus, I really like Millie. She is a nice lady and a great customer."

They continued down the street and looked in the windows of the stores they passed.

"Josie, I just remembered. I don't have any of my nice clothes with me. I just took a few things before I left. How can I work there without nice clothes? You saw how she was dressed."

"Not to worry. I have something you can wear tomorrow. If you get the job, we can go to the second hand store. I get great stuff in there myself. Unless you are too high and mighty to wear used clothes."

Lily laughed. "You should have seen some of the things I used to wear to school."

"Hey, it's getting dark soon. Why don't you stay with me for a few days? I have a small place but it's clean. You can sleep on the couch or in the bed with me. Whatever you want."

"Are you serious? Why would you want a stranger in your apartment?"

"Listen, as a waitress you kinda get a feel for people. You are a troubled girl but not a bad girl. I trust my instinct."

"Only for the night then. Tomorrow I'll look for a room somewhere."

Lily slept on the couch and slept remarkably well. When she woke up in the morning, Josie was dressed and in the kitchen drinking coffee. Her place was small but efficient. She had been right about it being clean. Josie did not have much but her place was clean and she had a knack for decorating. Everything looked so homey. Very welcoming. Just like Josie.

"Good morning Lily. Looks like you slept ok."

"Oh, I did. You have really done a great job decorating your apartment. I really like it."

"Well I had to live in dirt and grime all my childhood. I made up my mind that if I ever got out of there I would be clean and make a place look like a home even if it was only me who lived there."

"I'd say you succeeded."

"So let's get you coffee, a shower and pick out an outfit to wear on your interview today."

They headed out the door together. Lily had to try on several outfits before they found one that fit good enough over her chest. They were close to the same size but Lily definitely had fuller breast than Josie.

"Are you sure those suckers are real?"

Lily blushed. She never knew they were any different from other women. She never paid any attention. They were just there. Danny often complimented her on them but he also liked other parts of her body. She scolded herself about thinking of that now. That was in the past.

Lily knocked on the door to Millie's shop. It was still closed and the sign said it opened at nine-thirty. Millie looked out through the blinds and let her in.

"Lily, come have a cup of tea. I wanted to meet with you before the customers started to come in."

She took Lily back thru the store into a small kitchen area.

"I keep this here so I can have a place to regain my sanity. I could really use this for floor space but I decided I need it for me more than for the merchandise. I lost my husband at a young age. We never had children so I needed something to occupy my life. So this essentially has become my life. Since this is not a full time job, I don't need a formal interview, just time to fill out employment papers and an informal chat about what you have done before. Just a condensed work history. There are security cameras all over the place and I have a security firm that monitors them. So if you plan on robbing me. Don't. You don't have a chance in Hell of getting away with it."

Lily felt her face begin to burn. Did she look like a criminal? Did Millie think she came here to steal? "I would never take anything." is all she could get out.

Millie smiled. "I really didn't think so, dear. I just have to protect myself. I think you passed that test. But just so you know, there are cameras everywhere. So if you notice anyone taking anything I'll show you what to do. No piece of merchandise is worth losing a life over."

Lily smiled and nodded her head.

Millie poured the tea. Lily had never seen someone make tea from loose tea and use a fancy teapot. Millie saw the surprised look in Lily's face and laughed.

"This is the one indulgence I won't give up. It makes me feel like a lady, just like I will not give up dressing fashionable each day. Some of my customers don't understand why I dress like this since I do so much packing and shipping but old habits are hard to break."

Lily smiled and thought *I really admire her. It should be interesting working with her.*

Millie talked for another fifteen minutes and then told Lily she could start today if she wanted to. Lily was surprised how much information Millie was able to get out of her in such a short time. She had stuck to her story about running away from a boyfriend but blended enough truth in with her past to be believable. Millie told Lily that her main concern today was getting the shipments ready. She explained how to read the inventory sheet and order sheet. How items were stocked and how they needed to be packed and subtracted from inventory on hand. Soon, Lily was so engrossed in doing everything right; she did not notice Millie checking on her or even what time it was.

"Lily, it's after one o'clock. Let's break for lunch."

Lily jumped. "You startled me. I'm sorry, what did you say?"

"Lunch time. Meet me in the kitchen."

Millie had made a salad and had French bread on the table. She complimented Lily on the job she was doing and how quickly she had caught on.

"I think I did everything right. If you don't mind after lunch, can you please check to make sure? I don't want to get anything wrong."

Millie was impressed. She usually had to keep after employees to work. That's why she rarely hired anyone. She managed to do it herself unless she got an unusually large order like this one. Usually, by the time the order was filled and shipped, she and the employee had had enough of each other and parted ways. *Well time will tell with this one, it always does,* she thought.

Lily asked Millie to explain the store merchandise to her. They were so many interesting things that Lily wanted to see and learn about. Never had she seen so many different items all in one store. She particularly liked the fairy collection. Millie explained that they were her best sellers. All were made by hand. The original pieces were created by an artist who then made a mold and limited the reproductions to just ten. The mold was then destroyed. Each piece was then hand painted but the artist chose different colors for each piece so no two were ever alike. She explained the details that were incorporated into each piece.

"This one has the fairy bending over a treasure chest. See if you can spot the same mold used for all ten. I even have trouble because with the different way they are painted, it gives them all a unique look."

Lily examined the display and could only detect seven of the same mold. Millie laughed and pointed out the other three.

"This is amazing. You are so lucky to be able to have a store with so many interesting things. I cannot imagine being able to sell them once you see them."

"I'm lucky that I found the artist and that she actually lets me sell them for her. I don't get much walk in business but this store is comfortable. Most of my customers are in New York and some in California. I have picked up a few in other cities too. Therefore, it really doesn't matter where I am located, as long as I have access to a reliable shipping company. I've built a good reputation over the years and have been able to attract only the best artist. My entire inventory is top quality and not something you find anywhere else. I'm so happy to find someone who shares my enthusiasm for the pieces. Lily, you are as rare as the merchandise. Thank you for taking the job. That was also one of my better decisions. Hiring you."

Josie walked in right before closing time. She was glad to see Lily was working hard and seemed to be enjoying herself.

Millie heard the door chime and came out. "Hello, dear. Lily is just finishing up."

"It looks like she is doing ok. I hope?"

Millie laughed. "Yes, you are not in trouble. You referred a good one. So far."

"Good. I'm glad. I think the kid needs a break."

"Josie, you are a nice person. Really one of the few I've met in my lifetime."

"Thank you, ah I guess."

"How is school coming along?"

Just then, Lily came out of the storeroom and overheard the question.

"Josie, I didn't know you went to school. That is terrific."

"Tell me that after I graduate. Which, by the way, is in two months."

Both Millie and Lily said "Congratulations!"

"Not yet. I still have to pass. Let's stop and pick up some dinner on the way home and I'll show you that store I talked about yesterday. Ok?"

"Great. But I don't know what time I get off." She looked at Millie.

"Go ahead. You have done more than I would have thought possible for today. And did it right too. Tomorrow, just dress in casual clothes. No need to dress up and lug dirty boxes around in the storeroom. Jeans are fine. Now run along you two."

Again as they left, Josie put her arm around Lily. "I am so proud of you. You know I took a big chance of losing a good friend of mine if you screwed up on the job today. Looks like you are both satisfied with the arrangements, so now I have two friends instead of one."

Josie told her they could skip the second hand store today if she wanted to since she could wear jeans to work tomorrow. Lily suggested they go in and check out the store anyway because she would need clothes eventually. Once in the store, Lily and Josie were like teenagers picking out and trying on clothes. Soon they both walked out with bags of clothes. Pleased with the price, fit and the selection.

"I love this time of the year. So many people get rid of the stuff they got for Christmas and hated, others just clean out the old stuff to make room for the new things. Works for me! I'll never pay retail again. Unless of course, I meet a rich man. But maybe not even then."

Lily agreed this was the way to go. But mostly she had fun sharing the experience with her first real friend.

After a stop at the grocery store, they headed back to Josie's apartment.

"You know, I can't keep staying with you. It's too much to ask. I promise I'll look for a place tomorrow."

"Forget it. You and I work tomorrow. Plus, I have school after work so I'll be home late. I need to give you a key. The weekend is soon enough. Let's enjoy each other's company before you become a pain in my ass!"

Lily grinned. She had never heard anyone talk like Josie before. She said what was on her mind and was so honest in what she said. Yes, she thought, I like being with her. The weekend is fine.

They made spaghetti and meatballs. Lily asked Josie about school. Josie told her not to get too excited. She wasn't becoming a nurse or doctor. Just a hairdresser. She explained she was getting too close to thirty. She didn't want to be a waitress the rest of her life. She had always been good fixing hair and decided to go to school and maybe someday she could have her own business. At least it gave her something to work for.

Lily thought that was a wonderful idea and told her so. Lily had always wanted to continue going to school to learn more. She admired Josie for actually doing it.

Lily and Josie got along well. Lily with her calm sweet nature and Josie with her take charge, no holding back, approach to things complemented each other. Both thought on several occasions, *If I had a sister, I would have wanted her to be like her.*

Soon the weeks passed. They had gone out looking for apartments for Lily but found most were too expensive for the little money she made working for Millie. They decided Lily would stay until something cheaper became available. Neither admitted it to each other but they both hoped nothing did. For they both dreaded the loneliness they would feel when Lily moved out.

Chapter 27

Madge arrived home and noticed Max's car was missing from the driveway. Funny, he must have come home for lunch and picked up his car then, because he walked to work this morning. As she entered the house, she had another surprise. No aroma of food cooking reached her nose. Again, she was confused. Lily always started dinner when she left her a note.

She went into the kitchen and started dinner wondering what was going on. She was not a superstitious woman but she suddenly had a chill run down her spine. She thought of the old saying of her mother's, *Like someone just stepped on my grave.* Now where did that come from? God, I'm getting dotty in my old age.

Soon Max and Rosie came in. Max headed into the kitchen ."Mom, did someone borrow my car?"

"Not that I know of. I thought you came home at lunch and drove it back to the store."

"Well, Lily doesn't drive. Where is it?"

"Honey, if I knew I'd tell you. Call Danny and see if Lily is with him. Then you can mention the car."

Max came back into the kitchen. Rosie was sitting at the table drawing. "Rosie, can you please go upstairs and wash up for dinner?"

Rosie grumbled her reluctance but Max said, "Now." And she took off.

Madge turned to him. "What was that all about? I never heard you talk that way to Rosie."

Max told her that Lily was not with Danny. "Apparently, they had some problem between them today and she left his place after she got off work to come here. He was upset to learn she wasn't here now and is on his way over."

189

"It's not like them to have a disagreement. In fact not like Lily at all. What did Danny do to her?"

"Mom, I don't know. It is strange. Yes, not normal for them at all."

Madge ran up to Lily's room. The light was out and the door shut. She called out to Lily but got no response. She eased open the door and saw the bed was empty. She reached out and turned on the light, and then discovered the ring and notes on the bed. She called down the stairs, "Max, come here please."

Just then, the doorbell rang. Max opened the door and let Danny in before heading upstairs. Danny and Max went upstairs to see what Madge had discovered. They saw her holding Lily's letters and tears running down her cheeks. Danny reached out and took the letters from her. He read first the one addressed to him and then the one addressed to Madge.

Max was the next one to read the letters. They looked and saw the passbook from the bank and the engagement ring on her pillow. They were all soon overcome with grief.

Dear Danny,

I love you with all my heart. I cannot imagine ever loving anyone again after you have been in my life. I know now that I have to leave. I cannot make you or even expect you to carry this burden because of me.

I'm not sure where I am going. I have not made any plans to leave. I knew when I left you today, I had no other choice.

Please forgive me. Do not look for me. I know what I must do. I just need to gain the courage to do it. Eventually, I know the path will take me home to face what I deserve.

I hope you give me the time to do this. If not, I will understand.

Love Always,
Lily

The letter to Madge included the entire family.

Madge,

I can never thank you enough for all you have done for me. I never had a woman in my life before you. I figure God was saving that for you. I have gained so much by knowing you. Rosie and Max have brought me more joy than I ever thought possible. I want you to know I have been as honest with you as I could be. I'm sorry there are things that happened before I met you that cannot be forgiven. I am forever sorry that you may suffer because of anything I did. The last thing you deserve is pain for taking me in and teaching me how to love. Tell Bea I love her too.

Please tell Rosie I would never leave her if I had any other choice. I love her very much. Tell Max I am grateful to him for sharing you with me.

Love,
Your Lily

"Danny, what does this mean? What burden? What did she do that was so terrible? Why did she think she had to leave? What could be so terrible that she couldn't trust us to stand beside her and get through it?"

At that moment, Rosie decided to run in.

"Lily, Lily, where are you?"

"Honey, Lily had to take a trip out of town."

"She'll be back soon, won't she?"

"We hope so."

"Can we eat now? My hands are clean."

Max was the first to recover.

"Sure, let's go. Mom, I'll take care of Rosie. You and Danny talk it over."

Danny looked at Madge. This was all his fault. He loved Lily unconditionally, yet he did not handle the situation well when she needed him. He should have been more prepared. He knew something may come up one of these days. Lily was so reluctant to speak about her past; he had to have known there was a reason. A good reason. He hadn't even let her explain. Could he ever make it up to her? Could he ever find her?

He told Madge about the call he received from the sheriff in another state looking for Lily Hill. He left nothing out. He told her how badly he had handled it with Lily. How he never gave Lily a chance. How his goddamn job got in the way.

"Danny, you know Lily does not hold this against you. You know she said in her letter, you did what she expected you to do. Now we just have to find her and get this all straightened out. Lily could never kill anyone. You and I both know that."

They decided they had to do everything possible to find her. He would leave right away and alert the police to look out for Max's car. They were sure that must be the way she left town.

Danny went to the station and put out a missing person's report and gave the details of the car she left in. Less than an hour later, he got a call from the police station in the next town reporting the car parked in the police station lot.

"We thought it was strange that the car had been here all day. It didn't belong to anyone who worked here. It was parked so it would be noticed, not out of the way as if to hide it."

Danny thanked him and said he would bring the owner right over to pick it up.

Danny and Max headed out with a spare key.

"I didn't know Lily knew how to drive, come to think of it" said Max.

"Well, she must have driven before because the car wasn't damaged and she parked it in a safe spot."

Danny told Max that while they were there, he was going to check out the bus stations. He doubted if she would rent a car but if they had no luck with the bus terminal, they would check that out too.

Once they arrived at the police station, Max signed a release for his car. As he went out to check on it, he noticed the keys under the floor mat. She had thought of everything. Strange how she always tried to make life easier on everyone, he thought to himself.

Danny told Max to head on home and he would stop by when he finished up in town. He then headed over to the bus station. It wasn't too busy and he went up to the counter. After showing his identification, he asked to speak to the clerks on duty in the afternoon. Only three were still working. The first two had no memory of anyone resembling Lily's description buying a ticket. The third person he interviewed did seem to remember someone that looked like her, buying a ticket to somewhere in California. He couldn't remember where. Danny asked him to check his records and the clerk said if it was a cash sale he could not trace it. Danny then told him he wanted a printout of all ticket sales he had that day.

"Man, give me a break. Do you know how long that will take?"

"I'm not going anywhere until I have that information so you better get going or it will be a long night."

"I can only give you destinations, not names of passengers. Besides, the cash payers only get a ticket. They can sell it to someone else for all we care. This isn't an airline for God's sake."

"Fine, fine. Cool your heels. Just give me the list of stops. What tickets you sell and where they stop. Good enough?"

"Well why didn't you say that in the first place?"

Danny was losing patience but realized he had no legal grounds to stand on just now. He only hoped he could persuade the clerk to give him at least that much.

Danny sat in the station keeping his eyes on the clerk hoping to get him motivated enough to hurry up. After about twenty-five minutes, he saw the clerk wave to him. He approached the counter and got a print out of all the California stops from buses leaving from this station. He handed the clerk a twenty-dollar bill and left.

Once he got to Madge's, Rosie was in bed and it made it easier to talk. They went in the kitchen and Madge had coffee and sandwiches made. Of course, she had called Bea and she was also waiting for him.

Danny decided to call his Dad and ask him to check with his fellow drivers. He gave him a list of the towns and he agreed to check and get back to him.

"What do we do now?" asked Bea.

"I am in shock right now Aunt Bea. Give me a few minutes to get my head together."

They drank coffee and each tried to think what to do. Madge and Bea made a futile effort at holding back their tears.

Danny then said the first thing he had to do was to call the Sheriff back about Lily, and head him off. Tell him she moved on. Buy some time for her. Then maybe take the bus and get off at every stop or drive thru the towns the bus stops at and look around. If he rode the bus, he may have a better chance in talking to each driver. He wasn't sure what the best approach would be.

Bea spoke up. "I know I'll be a little short without Lily at the diner but I can manage. How about I buy a bus ticket, and take it through to the farthest city in California? That way I can talk to each bus driver. They may open up more to me. I can say I am her Mother and she ran away for some reason. We can make something up. Then if I get a lead, I go right to a phone and call you. As Sheriff, I know you can't take that much time off right now."

"That's the problem Aunt Bea; I am always putting the job before Lily."

"She wouldn't expect anything else from you. Give us a chance to help you. We all love Lily, it not just about you. We are all suffering a loss right now."

The next day Danny made the dreaded call to the Sheriff about Lily. He explained that they did have someone with that name, but after checking, he found out she had moved away. He then asked for details of the murder and if he was certain the person named Lily was responsible.

"Like I said. We are at a dead end here. The body was found by accident by a fellow renting old Clyde's place. The rent does get deposited into a bank account for a Lily Hill, which we believe was his wife. According to the Doc here in town, Clyde knew he was dying and wanted to get the girl out of town. Didn't feel she could handle the planting and harvesting by herself. Told him she was too innocent and pretty to leave her alone out there. She left before Clyde died. According to the Doc., it was Clyde's decision, not hers. Years ago, there was someone looking for Clyde's son and I went out to the farm to check. Clyde said he had been around looking for money, he gave him what he had and he left. His sons were good for nothing and frankly, I was glad when they left town because they were always in trouble and up to no good. Come to think of it, I never did see the girl that was supposed to be his wife. Never thought much about it really. Old Clyde never caused any trouble and tended to keep to himself."

He paused, as if lost in thought.

"Sheriff, you said Clyde had two sons?"

"Yeah. That's where I was going. The youngest son shows up. The one that was rumored to have been in the Army. He goes out to the farm and finds out his Daddy is dead and someone is living in the house. He came to see me. Nothing I could do. Old Clyde had made sure of that. The will left everything to Lily Hill, his wife. Nothing to his sons. Never even mentioned them in the will."

"So what about the Murder?"

Danny was getting a lot of information but it was trying his patience on how long it took the Sheriff to spit it out.

"Well couple years go by and the farmer has well problems out at old Clyde's place. Has to dig in the yard. Finds the body. They have a graveyard out there, can't figure why they didn't use that. No one would have ever known. Funny, huh? Well somehow the son finds out and comes in to see me. Swears it was his brother, and insisted the girl killed him. Well, by then, old Clyde is dead. The only one left is the wife and she is gone. No other leads. The son gives us enough information to ID the body. The rent money sits in the bank. Never touched. Can't trace the girl through that. We pretty much didn't have anything to go on. Then the son comes in and says he has tracked down the girl; she is living in your town. That's why I called. To be honest, I don't much trust the son, but the law is the law, and I have to follow up. Sorry she wasn't there, I'd like to get this resolved, one way or the other. If nothing else, to get the son out of my hair. As I said, he is a mean son of a bitch. Well now I've talked your ear off. Do you have any questions because if not, I got to go get me some lunch?"

"No Sheriff, you have been more than helpful. I'll let you know if I come across anything that can help you. Been nice chatting with you."

Danny was surprised to learn all that he had. So this Clyde had two sons? Could one of them been the one who attacked Lily? Is that how he knew where she was? A lot to think about alright!

That evening he met everyone at Madge's after Rosie was asleep. They decided that Lily was probably not in any immediate danger at least from being arrested. The main thing was to find her and bring her home. They could take care of everything else once she was home.

"Dad called me today. No luck with the bus drivers so far. He is still checking. Aunt Bea, are you still interested on taking a bus trip?"

Once she agreed, they decided on the story she was to use on the bus drivers. Her daughter was running away from her abusive husband. He was now arrested and facing jail time. She needed to find her and let her know so she could testify. If she didn't, chances were, the husband would get off. Bea was also taking cookies and Madge's fudge to use as bribes if necessary. She would leave in two days. The trip would take about a week if she went the whole way round trip. It was agreed that she would call every day.

Bea boarded the bus in the same station as Lily had left from. They figured the time frame of when Lily left. She worked four hours at the diner, stopped by to see Danny, went to the bank, went home to write the notes (no clothes were missing so she didn't take time to pack) drove to the next town. So Bea left on the three-thirty afternoon bus. Danny dropped her off and checked in with the local sheriff to see if they had any news.

No one expected to hear from Bea until the next day. They all agreed that Lily would have stayed on the bus at least that long. Bea grabbed the front seat so she would have better access to the driver. She gave him an hour to settle into his route and for the other passengers to get distracted by sleep or by listening to their music. She started out with small talk and he seemed friendly enough. She decided to try the cookie route before hitting on the daughter issue.

This leg of the trip did not produce any results for Bea. She stayed on the bus as the bus drivers changed and again she questioned each driver. She got off once a day to get a hot meal and wash up. This was the time she called home. They decided she would stay on until the end, just in case Lily did stay on the bus the entire way. The last day of the trip she made her final call.

"Danny, I have talked to every driver. I honestly don't think any of them noticed Lily. You know she could have sat in the back part of the bus and kept to herself. I noticed some people doing that myself. In fact, after some of them got off the bus, I commented on them and the driver said he didn't notice. I repeated this to several different drivers and got the same response. I guess they only notice the ones like me who keep up a conversation with them. I'm heading home unless there is something else I should do."

"No, you did great. Come home and we will plan our next step."

Madge and Max went about their days as well as they could. Rosie was fretful and out of sorts. She missed Lily and in her childish way, only expressed the depth of her sorrow through disruptive behavior. They tried to reassure her that Lily would return, but she could see in their faces, they were not entirely sure that would happen.

Danny continued to work each day and devoted most of his day searching for answers. He read every report posted on crimes in California. Any mugging, rape and even murder he checked out to make sure it wasn't Lily. His Deputies handled most of the disturbances called in and tried to leave him alone. They all were aware of how much he was suffering.

Now that Bea had admitted defeat with their first plan, it was time to decide what to do next. Once she got back home, he decided he would make the trip in his car and stop at each town and personally talk to the town police.

It was two weeks now since Lily had left. They were no closer to locating her now than when she left. Danny felt in his heart that she was ok because she was a survivor, but he would give all that he had, to make sure. Even if she could never forgive him for his lack of faith in her, he needed to try and win her back. Most of all, to make sure she was safe and help resolve the issue that drove her away.

Rosie was taking Lily's absence hard. She insisted that she sleep with both of the dolls they had gotten for Christmas. She couldn't understand why Lily left without telling her and often woke up at night crying for her.

Madge often went into Lily's room to try and feel her presence. The first time she had sat on the bed and looked around the room. It was neat and clean. She thought to herself, no one coming into this room for the first time would ever get a feel for Lily. There were no photographs, no little mementos or souvenirs that people tend to collect and display. Didn't I touch her life in any way? Why did she feel she could not confide in me? She was consumed in guilt but then shook her head. She knew that Lily had loved her. She knew that Lily had never felt confident that love could last and can get you through the bad times. Lily never experienced those feelings before coming here. When she comes back, I will do everything in my power to make it up to her. Madge never doubted that Lily would return.

Chapter 28

Lily was working full time helping out Millie. Although Millie had only hired her for a part time position, she soon discovered that Lily was a hardworking and honest employee. She found she was able to send her shipments out much faster and increased her buyer's orders. She also was able to get other things done that she normally had to do after the store closed. Therefore, she asked Lily to work as much as she wanted to. Lily was happy to work because she had nothing else to do. Josie was working full time and going to school and it was lonely without her. Lily had become accustomed to the active life she had living with Madge and missed being part of a family. All she had now was Josie so when she wasn't home with her, she often ended up crying over all that she had lost.

Lily did not earn much money but she insisted when she got paid that she and Josie share her check. She argued that she would not have the job or a place to stay if it wasn't for Josie. This way they were both profiting from Josie's generosity in sharing her life with Lily. With the extra money, Josie was able to work less hours and spend more time in school so she could finish sooner that she had planned.

One day after school, she ran all the way to the store to see Lily.

"Guess what! We are having a test this week on make-up and hair styling. One of the owners was able to get one of the Cosmetic Companies to send someone out here to be the judge. I need a model. If I don't bring in my own, the school assigns one to me. I need you Lily. Please say yes."

Lily was stunned. She didn't know what to say. She had never worn make-up and never had anyone do her hair for her.

"Hey, you gotta do this! You are so beautiful, I can't lose. We won't have to color your hair. Just maybe trim and style it. The make-up will wash off. You should see some of the ugly customers I get in the shop. My luck, the school will assign one of those hags."

Lily laughed. "I wasn't going to say no. You just surprised me. If I can get off work, I'll be your guinea pig."

Millie heard the exchange between the two girls.

""When is this Josie?"

"Friday night at the school."

"Can I come and watch?"

"Are you serious? I would love it!"

"Then we will both be there!"

Lily was actually excited that she could help Josie. She had done so much for her it would be nice to help her for a change. To be honest, she was even looking forward to the makeover. They talked about what colors would look best on Lily and decided on a hairstyle.

Finally the evening arrived. There was excitement running thru the crowd because of their special guest and also because this demonstration of their ability was one third of the final exam needed for graduation. Josie had already taken the written test and scored ninety-eight percent. The final test was hair color. She knew Lily would never agree to that. Plus she thought, Lily's hair color is already perfect.

Millie took a seat in one of the chairs set up for parents. Funny, she almost felt like one tonight. She had become so attached to the two girls in such a short time. They reminded her of sisters. She laughed to herself *except I haven't seen them fight yet* thinking of her brother when they were younger.

Soon all the models and stylist were seated at their station. The instructor introduced each one of them and explained the grading system and what was required in this test. Hair style including cut, shampoo, blow dry and curling iron. The facial part included waxing and makeup.

Soon everyone was busy. The instructor inspected each step the stylist performed on their models. Lily was excited for Josie. They talked as she worked. She had her eyebrows waxed and could not understand why anyone would choose to go through that pain. She was careful not to move or make a sound because she didn't want the instructor to think Josie was hurting her. After her hair was shampooed and wrapped in a towel, Josie started on her make-up. She made sure the chair was turned away from the mirror so Lily would not see anything she was doing. She knew Lily never wore anything on her face. In fact, she didn't even own any cosmetics.

Next she cut her hair and started the final step of styling. She chose a simple style to enhance her facial features rather than distract from them.

She would do an upsweep hair style on the model chosen for the coloring part of the exam. But for Lily she would layer her hair and keep it natural. She stepped back and inspected her work. Even Josie was amazed at how much this changed Lily's looks. She was still beautiful but in a more sophisticated way. It took the edge off her innocent look and enhanced the maturity that had gone unnoticed. She turned the chair to face the mirror so Lily could see the transformation herself. Lily did a quick intake of breath. "Is that really me?"

"Yes, honey. Beautiful, exquisite and enchanting you."

"You did magic."

"No, I just brought it out. It was always there. You are the magic."

The instructor approached them. She spent a long time looking over Lily's make-up and hair style. She told Josie she had definitely demonstrated the art of a good stylist. The cut and the application of make-up captured the best of the client. Not overdone.

"Most students make the mistake of assuming more is better. They think they have to impress the instructor with fancy hairstyles and heavy make-up. What they forget is that when they graduate and get a job in a salon, they will be working on customers and customers want an easy style that they can duplicate at home. My philosophy is that clients want make-up that creates compliments not disapproval when they leave the chair. Josie, you definitely captured all of that on this model."

Josie and Lily hugged each other.

"I think you are going to get a good grade on this."

"I hope so. I don't know how the cosmetic judge feels though."

"Is there prize money for the winner?"

"No, just a possibility of a job offer. But to be honest, I don't want to just work with cosmetics. I like doing the hair part best."

Lily said "Good because I am more likely to get my hair cut than the eyebrow plucking again."

"It's called waxing. You are such a woose. They look nice by the way."

The instructor thanked everyone in the audience for coming and cheering on their student.

"As you can see we have completed the exam. I will not announce the final grades but I will stop at each station and give an overall summation of what is done right and what is done wrong. This gives students a chance to see how work is judged and hopefully they will learn from each other and bring that knowledge with them when they start their career."

Lily and Josie both found the summation very informative and not one student was embarrassed by the comments and suggestions presented to them. Josie, however, did experience some discomfort at the praise lavished on her work. The final part of the evening was the cosmetic award. Lily was disappointed that Josie did not win but was glad she did not have all the make-up on her face that the winner's model did.

"See, I didn't think I'd win. I think they have to give it to the person who uses the most of their product on their model's face regardless of how they look."

Lily laughed, "I see what you mean now. I am grateful that you did not win!"

They were both laughing when Millie came over to them.

"I'm sorry you didn't win the contest for the make-up".

"We were laughing about that!"

Josie told her about the contest and how she really didn't want to win so it was ok. They chatted and she complimented Josie on how great Lily's hair and make- up suited her. Millie suggested a late supper to celebrate and they all agreed it would be nice to unwind and have something good to eat.

Lily was starting a new life and was grateful for the friendship she had with Josie and Millie but she missed her real family as she came to think of Madge, Max, Rosie and Bea. She often caught a glimpse of a little girl on the street and her heart skipped a beat. The longing for Danny was the most unbearable thing she had to endure. She often thought how different it was from what she had with Clyde. With Clyde, it was like drifting through life. Doing what needed to be done. Enjoying what she could, but never the intense love she found with Danny or the love and caring she had with *her family.*

Josie was making progress in school. With the additional hours she had now that Lily shared expenses, she was able to use them in school instead of working. She only had two weeks left until she completed the course. Josie was so busy studying and preparing for the final requirements they rarely had time together. Lily was becoming increasingly homesick and lonely. She found it hard to concentrate sometimes. In fact, Millie mentioned it to her one day.

"Are you getting tired of working here? You are not as focused as you were and don't seem the same as you did when you first came here."

Lily looked at Millie. "I'm sorry. I am missing my family. Sometimes I wonder if I made the right decision to leave regardless what the problems were."

"Well honey, I can understand that. Let me know if I can help you out. Sometimes talking about it helps."

"Thanks! I'll try to do better."

"I didn't say you were doing badly. Just not like you used to be. I know I cannot replace your family but I do care for you and am here for you if you need to talk. You know Lily, you and Josie are now such a part of my life I don't know what I did before I had you both in it. So, I don't want to find out. It would probably break my heart."

She reached out and gave Lily a hug.

Lily was again amazed at life. How different it was from her childhood. She had never realized how much she had missed and the love that had been denied her was now overflowing. How lucky she was.

Just then the door opened and the delivery man came into the store.

"Not your usual large order today, Millie. Just a small package."

Millie thanked him and signed for the package. Once he left she opened it and laughed.

"Well, just what we need right now. A gift from one of my customers with a note telling me how pleased he was with our last shipment. Since you helped with his order, what do you say we open it?"

Inside the box was a box of Ceylon blackberry tea and some Russian Tea Cookies. They headed to the back room and Millie told Lily to sit down and she would prepare the tea and then they would indulge themselves in fat calories.

"I always find the best way to lift my spirits is to indulge in fattening food."

Once they were seated at the table enjoying their unexpected treat, Millie started talking to Lily.

"You know honey; I have grown quite fond of you. I haven't talked much about myself just as you haven't talked much about yourself. I tend to keep things inside myself and I see that trend in you. I grew up poor and never had much. Luckily I had great parents and they gave us plenty of love. I had a brother but he died when he was ten of a ruptured appendix. That about destroyed my parents because they thought it was just stomach flu. I finished high school and started going to what they called Secretarial School back then. I guess that was what my parents were waiting for. Me to grow up. Missing my brother was too hard on them and they never got over it. They died within six months of each other of what I always thought was a broken heart."

"I'm so sorry."

"No need to be. I know they are happy now reunited with Jimmy. Well anyway, I got out of school and knew I had to find a job. As luck would have it, I walked into the first place I saw with a sign in the window *"Help Wanted"*. That's how it was before computers and all the new fangled things that are out there now to find a job. Anyway, it was a small business that supplied restaurants with all the non-food items like pots and pans down to sugar holders and bud vases. Back then, it was all mail order through a catalogue. We did get some phone in orders but very few. I guess that's how I got interested what I do today. Although my merchandise is more interesting, don't you think?" she laughed.

Lily agreed. She was hanging on to every word that Millie said and from the look on her face, Millie could tell she wasn't bored so she continued on with her story.

"Well, one day the son of the owner came into the store. He was in Law School and just home on break. He was so good looking and charming. All the women were soon vying for his attention. Believe it or not, I was actually shy back in those days, so I just kept on working. I listened to the women talk about him and learned that he was just as nice as he was handsome. He was not dating anyone and was committed to making good grades. He had one more year to go until he graduated and he was planning on setting up his own Law Practice. I never heard that he took any of the office staff out on a date. He went back to school and then one day about six month later, he shows up again. I had been on the job almost two years by that time and was moving up in my position. That may have been because the job was my life by then. I had no family and did not date. I spent very little and worked as many hours as I could. I had nothing to distract me. I was focused on a career. The other young girls were working until they found a man to marry. They were more interested in clothes and a good time, than moving into a career job. That's how it was back then. Now women work through marriage and child rearing. Women want a career. Times have changed for the better for women. I know you are too young to remember. Way before your time."

Lily grinned and told Millie she was enjoying hearing about her younger days.

"What about the son of the owner? Did he come back after graduation?"

Millie laughed "I'm still at the beginning of the story. Well, as I said, he comes in again. By then my desk was moved closer to the boss's office because he had come to depend on me for a lot of things and he didn't want me far away from his beck and call. Anyway, I'm getting off track.

The son comes in this time and notices me because of where I'm sitting. He stops to chat, made some small talk, and of course, I'm tongue tied and made a fool of myself. He goes into to talk to his father and I see them both looking at me. Now I know I'm in trouble. I'm sure he told his father just how stupid I am, and is right at that moment, suggesting he fire me. I feel my face start to burn. Then I start to sweat because I'm scared to death. What will I do without my job? How can I afford to live?"

"Millie, you really thought that?"

"Yes, I did. I had no self-confidence and was scared of my own shadow. You would never think that was the same person you know today, huh?"

"You are so different now. I can't believe you are actually talking about yourself."

"I am and it only gets better. On the way out of the office, the son stops and says goodbye to me. Now I know I'm being fired. Goodbye means he will never see me again because I won't be here. A little while later, the boss calls me into his office. I take a deep breath because I know what is coming. He tells me to sit down and closes his door. He sits at his desk and looks at me for a minute. Then he starts talking. He tells me how much his son means to him and how he would do anything for him. I stand up and he looks at me funny and asked if he has offended me. Then he says that his son wants to go against company rules and ask me out. I fainted dead away."

Lily starts to laugh so hard the tears are running down her face. Millie joins in and soon her makeup is in desperate need of repair. The buzzer sounds because the front door has opened.

"Lily, can you see who that is so I can repair my face. I cannot let anyone see me in this state. I'll ruin my reputation."

The delivery man has returned and now is delivering a regular order. There are five large boxes on his dolly and he rolls them into the workroom while Lily signs for them.

Millie comes into the room and surveys the boxes and looks at the invoice.

"Just in time, I have had so many requests for this artist. She is really making a name for herself. We better leave my storytelling for another day and get these unpacked and inventoried. So much for leisure time but thanks Lily for listening to an old lady ramble on."

"Millie, I enjoyed every minute of it. I can't wait for you to continue."

"Tomorrow, then."

Chapter 29

Danny looked at the calendar. God, it was almost six weeks since Lily left. He rubbed his face. When was the last time he shaved? He knew he had lost weight. His pants were baggie and his belt was moved back a few notches. The atmosphere in the station was deteriorating. He had worked so hard to raise morale and now he was causing it to plummet. Soon they would think this happened to anyone in his position. Just like Sheriff Bates. He knew he had to shape up. It was so hard to cope with the pain that was constantly a part of him.

He finally decided he was taking a leave of absence. He was going to find Lily.

Danny met with Madge, Bea and Max and explained what he was going to do. He would find Lily and get the best lawyer to defend her. He doubted if they could convict her of anything because from what the sheriff had told him, the case was circumstantial, at best. He seriously doubted, if she had a good lawyer, that she would even be charged. He had to get her to go in for questioning and get her cleared as a suspect once and for all.

He made arrangements for his Deputy Sheriff to cover for him. He would still be available by phone but any personnel issues would be handled by his deputy.

The next day he left after lunch to time his arrival at each bus station around the time the bus did. Although he was driving his own car, he planned to stop at each bus station. He was sure he could gain some information by going in person. Bea certainly didn't have any luck with the runaway daughter approach.

He went to the town that she had left Max's car and checked in with the police station. They had no information. He could tell from the sheriff's mannerisms that he doubted the story Danny told him about why he was still tracking Lily's disappearance. He then went to the bus station and looked around. Maybe something would come to him. He sat there a few minutes and observed passengers getting on an off the buses. He decided to move on. The next stop was at least two hundred miles away which meant he would drive all night.

The first stop was a small town and really not much to see. He checked with the sheriff to see if they had any new people in town and the sheriff said, "No one moves here, they just move out." Danny could see what he meant because it was a dead town. One gas station that served as a bus stop and a general store. He decided to move on to the next stop.

It was late in the afternoon of the second day. He came to a fair size town. Much larger than his. Now this looked like a possibility. He doubted if a stranger would be easily recognized here. He decided to sit in the terminal and get a feel for the clientele. It didn't take long for him to notice that every time a young girl got off the bus, she was approached by a big dude hanging around in the terminal. He pegged him right away as trouble. He wondered if Lily got off here and got into trouble with him. He watched a young girl being approached as she got off the bus. You could tell she was not waiting for anyone and was not familiar with the place by watching how she looked around and held herself. No confidence there, that was easy to see. Soon she was engaged in conversation with the man and was shaking her head as if to say "No". He could tell the conversation was not going the right way. She exited the terminal carrying her suitcase and the man followed. Danny decided to see what was happening once he got her outside.

The man tried to put his arm around the young girl and she tried to shake him off. She looked at him and Danny could tell she was weakening. Whatever he was telling her, she was thinking about it. Danny decided to check her out. He called out

"Hey, Sue is that you?"

They both stopped and looked at Danny. The man grabbed the girl and tried to hurry her down the street. She dropped the handle of her suitcase and he ignored it and continued to push her toward a car. She tried to stop but he had a firm grip on her arm. Danny increased his pace and yelled

"Stop".

The girl froze and the man pushed her down and jumped in a car and drove off.

"Are you ok?"

"Yeah, I guess."

Danny showed her his badge. No need for her to think she got away from one bad situation just to get into another.

"How about a cup of coffee or a coke and you can tell me what was going on."

"Ok."

Danny spotted a Denny's up the street and thought that would be a safe place to take the girl. They went in and sat in a booth. The waitress came over and took their order.

"Can you tell me what they big guy wanted? Didn't look like you were sure you wanted to go with him."

"I just got in town. I was going to look for a place to stay for a while. He came up to me before I had a chance to think which direction to go in and tried to talk me into a job offer."

"What kinda job?"

"We never got that far. Once you called out he got mean and grabbed my arm and started pulling me."

"Well little lady, I don't know that guy but I know guys like him. They prey on bus stations looking for innocent girls. You should be glad you got out of there."

The waitress sat down their drinks.

"Couldn't help overhearing. Were you talking about a big ugly dude in fancy clothes?"

The girl's eyes got wide. "Yes, that was him."

"Honey, that was Big Jim. You are lucky to get away from him. He went after me and my roommate. Some are not so lucky to get away easy like you did." She laughed, "We should call this place Denny's Safe House because we seem to be the place some of the girls come after he goes after them."

Danny asked her why the police didn't do anything to stop him. She told him no one complains. The ones who get away are just glad to be safe and the ones that don't, can't.

Danny asked if she ever remembered a girl coming in by the name of Lily. He gave her a description of her and showed her his badge.

Josie stiffened. She thought, *what are the chances I would be working today? What are the chances I would over hear the conversation and butt in on their conversation? Shit, shit, shit. Is this the guy Lily ran away from? Don't open your mouth. Don't ask any questions. Calm down and don't give anything away.*

Josie shrugged her shoulders and said, "We get a lot of girls in here. But I don't remember a Lily or a girl that matches that description."

Danny looked at her. He felt that she was not telling the truth. She recovered well but her initial reaction has indicated she knew something.

"Can we talk in private?" He rose and put money on the table and told the girl to be safe. He didn't wait for an answer but went across the room and sat down.

Josie followed and said "This is not my table."

Danny looked at her "I don't give a damn whose table it is. I need answers and you are going to give them to me."

Josie was suddenly fearful. Did he abuse Lily? Surely he wouldn't hit her here in front of everyone if she didn't answer her.

"What do you mean?"

"Look, we got off to a bad start. I am beside myself. My fiancé ran away. I'm trying to find her and bring her back home. Everyone misses her. If you know anything at all, please tell me."

"I don't remember this girl in particular. Honest. We get so many girls in here because we are close to the bus station. She could have come in and again she might not have. You scared me because you are a cop is all. Besides. I only work part- time. I go to school. So if she did come in, I wasn't the one to see her."

Danny did not fully believe her but he could tell she wouldn't tell him anything more. He decided he would hang around this town for a while.

Josie could not wait for her shift to end. She had to get out of here. She had school tonight but maybe that was better anyway. If the guy followed her, she didn't want to lead him to Lily. If he followed her home, Lily would probably already be asleep.

Danny hung around across the street and watched for Josie to leave. An hour later, she came out dressed in street clothes. It was a good thing he paid attention because at first he was expecting to see her leave in her uniform. She looked around as if expecting Danny to be watching for her. Luckily, he had gone inside a store and was looking out the window. He watched what direction she took and waited a few minutes before following. The streets were not busy so he stayed back and kept close to the storefronts. He saw her hesitate a few times but maybe just window shopping. She soon increased her pace and he saw her go into a tall building. He waited outside and looked through the glass entrance door until he saw her get on the elevator. He then entered the building. He looked at the list of businesses listed on the directory and saw the sign for the Beauty School. That must be the school she was talking about. He decided to wait fifteen minutes before going up.

Once the doors opened on the floor where the school was located, he could see the customers sitting in the waiting room. He casually walked over and looked in the door hoping they would think he was waiting on his wife. He looked around and spotted the waitress combing someone's hair. He quickly ducked out of sight so she did not spot him. Now what? He looked for a sign. It was on the door. It closed at nine this evening. Chances were, she would be here until then. It was now close to five. He would come back by eight and wait until she left. He had to move his car and get something to eat.

He was crossing the parking lot thinking about Lily. Please let her be safe. He was so deep in thought that he did not notice the man watching him. Suddenly, he felt immense pain shoot through his head. He lost his sight and then fell unconscious to the pavement.

He woke up in the ambulance. He was confused and unclear as why he was there. The paramedic was talking to him. He had a hard time focusing on what was being said. His head hurt so bad. Had he been shot?

"Sheriff, Sheriff Mc Cain, can you hear me?"

"Am I shot?"

"No, but you sure took a whack on the head."

"Where am I?"

They told him and explained how he had been found in the parking lot at the bus terminal. It didn't look like he was robbed because he still had his badge, wallet, and money. His watch was still on his arm.

Danny was treated at the Hospital and it was determined that he had a concussion so would be required to stay for at least twenty-four hours for observation. The town Sheriff would be in to talk to him tomorrow. They gave him something for pain and ask if there was anyone he wanted to notify that he was here.

"Lily" he said

"Lily who? Is that your wife?"

"Did I say Lily? Sorry, It's hard to think right now."

They told him they would come back later when the pain medicine had time to take effect and try to bring a phone in for him to use.

Danny dozed off and on and the staff kept waking him up to make sure he was ok. The pain had started to ease and he was starting to remember the events of the day. Thank God, he had his gun locked up in his car. At least the person who attacked him did not have a chance to steal it. Now he had lost his opportunity to follow the waitress home and see if he could locate Lily. Now that he thought about it, he didn't even know the name of the waitress and she said she was only working there part- time. How could he have been so stupid and let himself get mugged like that. He started thinking..........I wasn't robbed. Chances are, it was Big Jim getting back at me for interfering in his business. Well, I won't be afraid to tell the sheriff about his activities.

The nurse appeared carrying in a telephone. She plugged it in the outlet and asked if he wanted her to dial a number for him.

"I'm afraid it is long distance. Is there any way you can make the call for me? I left my phone in the car. Just leave this number for them to call me back?"

"Sure, I have a cell phone in my purse. I'll take a quick break and step outside. Just give me the number and tell me what you want me to say."

Danny gave her Madge's home number. "Just tell her I need to speak to her at this number and I will explain everything."

Soon the phone rang and Madge was on the phone. He told her about arriving in town and went through the entire day for her. She was upset that he had been attacked and promised to call Bea. She was also hopeful that Lily was there and that he had a chance of tracking her down. He heard her talking to Max in the background and Danny told her he was tired and he would call them back in the morning.

Madge and Max were busy discussing what to do. Max felt he should go out to get Danny incase he could not drive home himself. Madge thought they should both go. Then there was Rosie. What to do with her? Finally, she called Bea and told her to come over. She heard from Danny.

Bea was soon there. They sat at the kitchen table drinking coffee and trying to decide what to do. Who should go, who should stay? Finally, it was decided Madge and Max would both go. They would have Bea stay with Rosie. Since Rosie had pre- school and play dates, Bea and Rosie would be fine with that arrangement. Max would drive until he got tired and then Madge could drive until they got there. If they left tonight, they should be there by the time Danny got out of the hospital. Rosie was actually excited with the news of her Dad and Grandmother leaving for a few days and leaving her with Aunt Bea. Since Lily had left, she did not have much one- on- one time with anyone anymore. Now it would be just her and Aunt Bea.

Max and Madge made good time. He tried to keep to the speed limit but often went over it when the road was clear. He did not want to chance a ticket, or worse an accident, but they were determined to get there as soon as possible. They stopped once for a fast food burger and coffee along with a bathroom break. Otherwise, they kept to the road.

Madge was taking her turn at driving so Max could take a break. He soon fell asleep.

The sheriff came in to see Danny the first thing in the morning. He told Danny that he wasn't sure how long he had been lying in the parking lot before he was found. One of the employees discovered him when they went to get their car after work. He explained to the sheriff why he was in town and told him about the man in the bus terminal. How he noticed him harassing the girl who got off the bus. How he had followed them and when she broke away, he took the girl in to Denny's. Relayed his conversation with the waitress. He said he felt that the man the waitress said was Big Jim, must have felt he would teach him a lesson for interfering with business. The sheriff listened with interest but Danny wasn't sure he got through to him on Big Jim.

"Sheriff, I'm not trying to run your town, I have enough trying to keep things straight in mine. You have a larger area to cover than I do. I understand it is difficult to know what goes on sometimes. Plus, the waitress said the girls either don't or won't complain. I'm just advising you of what I saw. Since I wasn't robbed, I think it was a warning to butt out. You can take it or leave it. My concern is finding Lily and leaving town."

After that, the sheriff seemed more agreeable. He took what information Danny could supply. As far as his attacker there was not much of anything, he could supply. He hadn't notice anyone approach him.

The nurse came in and told Danny he was doing well and may be discharged after lunch. The doctor had to make the final decision but according to the test results nothing appeared abnormal.

"You will have to be careful for a while and follow up with your doctor to make sure there are no further complications that arise from the concussion."

Danny decided to rest before he was discharged so he would be ready to begin his search for Lily once he got out.

Madge glanced at the clock in the car. Almost two in the afternoon and still fifty miles away from their destination.

"Wake up Max. Max, call the hospital and make sure Danny stays there until we get there in less than an hour."

Max shook himself awake and they pull off the road to use the phone.

Chapter 30

Josie thought she would never finish class. She needed to see Lily. She almost stopped in to see her before class but had second thoughts in case she was being followed. She hadn't known Lily long but she felt a fierce loyalty toward her. Together they would decide what to do. She had only a few more days of school left until she fulfilled the requirements to graduate. She had already passed all the test. If they had to, they would leave town together.

The lights were still on in the apartment when Josie came home. She had been careful when she left school to make sure she wasn't followed. She ducked in several doorways and stores to make sure no one was waiting for her. She felt sure no one had followed her home.

Lily had a pizza in the oven.

"Good, I think I timed this right. I thought you might be hungry because you had a long day today."

She looked at Josie. "What's wrong? You look terrible? Are you ok?"

Josie looked at Lily and said "We need to talk. Let's eat first."

Lily felt that old feeling of fear creep into her. She knew from looking at Josie it would not be good news.

They sat down and each took a piece of pizza. Suddenly, neither one had any desire to eat. "Please tell me what is wrong, Josie? Did I do something to upset you?"

"Oh Honey, of course not. But I have to tell you what happened today at work."

Josie explained about the young girl coming in to the diner just like Lily had, to get away from Big Jim. She explained that she was brought in by the most handsome man she had ever seen. He apparently rescued her outside Denny's and because of her big mouth she butted in on their conversation and said it was not unusual for Big Jim to go after young girls at the bus station and that it happened to me and my roommate.

Apparently, that got his attention; he showed me his badge and said he was looking for his girlfriend, Lily. Somehow I knew it was you. I think I covered my reaction well enough that he didn't know for sure that I recognized it was you he was looking for. But he seemed to question me a lot and seemed suspicious that I was holding something back from him.

Lily looked at Josie and tears rolled down her face.

"Listen to me Lily. I am your friend through thick and thin. Whatever is going on, we will get through this together. You have to tell me. You have become my family in the short time we have known each other. I have never had anyone in my life until now and I'll be damn if I'm going to let you go. We'll move away together if we have to leave here. Now damn it, tell me!"

Lily was overcome with emotion. She knew just what Josie felt because she felt it herself. She has never had a girlfriend or sister and Josie filled both descriptions. She decided to tell her everything from as far back as she remembered as a child.

They sat together on the sofa while Lily began her story. They both had tears running down their cheeks but Lily did not stop. She went through all the painful things as well as the happy ones. It felt good to finally be able to be completely honest about her past without fear. She believed Josie when she said she would be with her no matter what.

It was almost morning when she finished. She explained that she ran away to protect Danny. The discovery happened so sudden she didn't have time to plan what to do. Her first thought was to run away and find someplace safe so she could figure out what to do. She knew she would go back and face the charges, but needed time to build her nerve up, to plan how to do it.

Josie told Lily they needed to decide what to do together. She didn't think Lily could be charged with murder. How could they prove anything? She wished she could talk to Danny again and find out more of what he thought. She had school again in the morning and was working the dinner shift at Denny's. Maybe he would be back. Now that she knew the story, she wouldn't be unprepared as she was before. She asked Lily to trust her.

"I trust you completely or I would not have told you everything."

"I will protect you. I just have to know what we are facing here. Of course since it's you, I can be more objective than you and Danny, at least I hope so."

"Ok. I'm tired of hiding and not living without fear all the time. You find out what I should do and I'll do it. But only if you are there with me."

"I'll be there sister, I promise!"

Danny agreed to wait in the hospital until Max and Madge arrived. He questioned his ability to drive and felt he would have more luck in locating Lily with their help. The doctor was delayed in getting the paperwork completed. He and the nurse were just getting off the elevator in the Lobby where the nurse was going to leave him to wait, when Madge walked through the front door. After fussing over him, she helped him outside where Max was waiting in the pickup lane.

"Where to Danny? You don't look so good."

"Let's go back to the beginning. I don't have a clue what to do or where to look. Our only lead may be the waitress at Denny's. Find the Bus Terminal and go past it until you reach the first light and then take a left. You should see the sign for Denny's about a block or two up that street."

Max pulled up in front of the restaurant in about twenty minutes. He found metered parking a half block up the street. He pulled in and looked in his rearview mirror. Danny was dozing. He told Madge to let him sleep and he got out to put money in the meter. As he came back to the car, Danny woke up.

"We have two hours on the meter. Do you want me to run down and see if any waitress matches the description of the girl you told us about? She may not be working. If she isn't here, we can get a Hotel room and you can rest."

"No, we all should go in. You must be hungry and I think if I get some decent food and caffeine, I'll feel better myself."

They went into the restaurant. As it was the last time, it was almost empty. Danny described the waitress to the hostess and asked if she was working. To avoid suspicion, he told her he forgot her name but his mother insisted she wait on them because she was so pleasant to them their last time in.

"Sounds like Josie. She is due in later. You have about an hour to wait."

Danny looked around the room and noticed a booth in the corner. He could see who came in, but once they were in the door, no one would notice him. Since she had never seen Max or Madge, she would not recognize them and be scared off. He asked the Hostess to seat them there as they also needed to discuss some family business over dinner.

Danny pulled out a baseball cap he had found in the back seat of Max's car and put it on. He thought it would help disguise him. He didn't want her spotting him and running off. He doubted if he could give chase, let alone catch her, in the shape he was in today.

The waitress came over and Max ordered coffee for everyone. When she brought it to the table, he gave her a ten dollar tip and told her to check back for refills but for now they were just going to drink coffee and talk.

By the time Josie came in the front door, they were starting on their third cup of coffee and Danny was feeling much better. As he had hoped, she was passed him before she glanced over at their table.

As their waitress returned to fill their coffee cups, Madge asked her if she would ask Josie to stop by so she could say "Hello".

Madge saw Josie approaching the table. She could tell from her expression that she was trying to remember her and didn't succeed.

Once she reached the table she said "I'm sorry I don't..................."

At that moment, Danny reached out and grabbed her wrist. She didn't finish her sentence and had a look of shock on her face.

"Sit down Josie. This is Madge and her son Max. I'm sure Lily told you about them."

"Yes she did."

Just then she realized she had betrayed Lily. How dare they do that to her? Grab her and get her off guard like that? Now she got mad. "What do you want?"

"We want to find Lily."

"Seems to me, you should have treated her better when you had her."

Danny said "You don't know anything about it."

"Like hell, I don't, Lily told me everything."

Max looked at Danny and could tell they were not connecting. Danny was about to lose his temper and Josie was getting so defensive; he doubted they would get anything out of her, even at gunpoint. Not that they would actually use a gun, he thought, but he could see that Josie was the type of friend that would stand up for Lily. He decided he and Madge may have better luck.

"I'm sorry if we are scaring you or getting you upset. We all love Lily very much and want her to know we need her back in our lives. I know we must have made mistakes with Lily but if we did, they were unintentional."

"Well, I'm taking care of Lily now, so you can leave and go home."

Danny's face turned red and Max glared at him to show his displeasure and make sure he keep quiet.

"Josie, is their anyway we can talk to Lily? I need to see for myself that she is ok?" Madge's voice broke and tears flooded her eyes.

Josie's boss signaled to her and she got up to see what he wanted. They saw them exchange words and she headed back to their table.

"Sorry if we are causing you any trouble with your Boss. We can meet you later."

"Well, I guess, I quit. He told me to get back to work and I told him this is family business and I wouldn't be working until I finished over here. His decision, when we finish, if I still have a job. We'll see."

They waited for her to speak again.

"Where did I leave off? Oh, yeah I know. Lily told me what she has been through as far back as she can remember. She had a hard life. So did I. So I can understand where she is coming from and why she is ashamed of some things. Unless you have been through certain things yourself, you can't possibly understand how hard it is to share these things. Well anyway, we hit it off as soon as she got into town. I think you already know she had a run in with Big Jim. We ended up as roommates and get along great. I love her like a sister. I have one more day of school left and then I will leave with Lily or stay here. Whatever she decides. You can see why I don't trust you. How could you judge Lily and turn your back on her? I don't understand. If I ever loved someone enough to ask them to marry me, I'd sure as shit know it was for better or worse. All you've shown her, is that you only want the better part. Now as far as I'm concerned that is not love Sheriff Danny Mc Cain."

Madge and Max started to speak but Josie raised her hand.

"You two are unfortunate to be here and hear what I have to say because my quarrel is not with you. From what Lily tells me, you have been nothing but supportive to her. He on the other hand, has hurt her terribly. Lily is a survivor but not a fighter. Me, on the other hand, I am both a survivor and a fighter so I will fight for Lily's happiness. You have a long way to go to convince me that you can provide that. From what I'd heard, you only think one way and cannot consider there are circumstances that can often affect an outcome in different ways."

Danny has sat quietly and listened to what she had to say. He knew she was right and he had failed Lily. God, he thought of nothing else since she left.

"Josie everything you are saying, I have said to myself. I reacted badly and would do anything to make it up to Lily. I need a chance to tell her and explain it to her. Won't you let me see her?"

She talked to them for a while and explained how Lily had been trying to come to grips with what was facing her and that she was close to turning herself in. Josie wanted to know what evidence they felt the police had to tie Lily into the murder of the body found on the farm.

Danny had told Max and Madge the reason Lily had left so suddenly so they were not surprised by her question. Danny asked permission to speak and Josie told him to go ahead because she needed to know where they stood legally.

"I know the sheriff doesn't have any strong proof but Lily is the only lead they have. Apparently, the brother of the victim pointed the sheriff in Lily's direction. He needs her to come in for questioning. We have decided to hire the best lawyer to represent her and see if we can find out more facts. That way we can get the suspicion against Lily dropped. Right now, as far as I could find out, they just want to question her, not arrest her. The safest thing to do is to get a lawyer before she goes and admits to anything we can't take back."

"Well, thank you for that. I'll make sure Lily is aware of what you told me. In the meantime, I suggest you order something to eat. I am leaving and I will try to get in touch with Lily. It will be up to her to decide. But I warn you, if any of you even try to follow me, I will not tell her about this conversation and I promise you, you will never find her. Do you understand?"

Danny looked defeated. Madge explained that Danny had been in the Hospital because he was mugged after he left here. The hospital had contacted Max and Madge and they had driven down to help him. He was still weak after the beating he received and none of them wanted any harm to come to Danny or Lily.

"If you would just give us a chance to see Lily, we will go home if that's what she tells us she wants us to do. Please let her be the one to tell us." Madge pleaded.

Max told Josie he admired her courage and he appreciated her friendship with Lily. They were not going to discourage that. But, she must understand what a special person Lily was to them. She had touched their lives in such a way, that they could never leave her unless that was her decision.

Josie said she may be gone an hour or more. She would bring Lily back with her. If Lily decided not to come, she would call the restaurant and let them know. She wasn't sure what Lily would decide but she would not try to influence her. It would be Lily's decision about what she did.

Josie spoke to her boss again, picked up her purse and headed out the door. It took everything for Danny not to get up and run after her. They were all afraid that she would not tell Lily and they would never see her again. They decided to order dinner but no one was really hungry or had an appetite but it was a way to pass the time. Max went over to a pay phone and called Bea to check on Rosie. He filled her in on what had happened so far. Then he went to add more money to the parking meter.

Josie did not trust them not to follow her. She made frequent stops and detours until she was satisfied that they had kept their word. She arrived at Millie's store and quickly ducked inside. She told Millie she had to speak to Lily immediately. She asked her to let them know if anyone came in and appeared as if they were looking for either one of them. She and Lily went into the back room where no one would see them from out front. Josie told her about meeting Max, Madge and Danny. She told her Danny had been in the hospital and just got discharged and Max and Madge came down to help him look for her.

Lily was glad they had come for her but was not sure she should see them. She wanted to make sure Danny was ok and had no permanent damage but was unsure just what to do.

"I don't know what to do. I'm happy and scared at the same time. Plus, I don't want to drag them through what I have to do and cause them any more unhappiness than I already have."

"Well I wish you had fallen for Max instead of Danny."

"Why do you say that?"

"He seems more level headed. I liked him actually."

"Well you did say Danny was attacked. He was probably in pain. I'm sure he feels bad and it really wasn't his fault I left. I did it to save him from trouble. He is the Sheriff and doesn't need to have this to deal with. He is actually the nicest person I know. And he does love me, no matter what you think."

"What I think isn't important right now. It's your decision. You need to decide what you want to do."

"I can't make a decision right now. I just told you last night and reliving my past was exhausting. I don't know if I can go through this again today."

"I'll call them and tell them you need another day. They can get a hotel room and give you the extra time to decide. If you want to see them tomorrow, we can meet somewhere. If not, we can call them and tell them to go back home."

"Do you think they will understand?"

"They will have to understand. Listen, it's your life and your decision. You haven't had much chance to make your own decisions and now you can. You are in control. I just want you to be sure what you decide is what you want. Agreed?"

Lily reached out and gave her a hug. "Agreed."

Josie told Millie they had to leave for the day that something came up. Millie was concerned but it was almost time to leave for the day anyway. Lily had made excellent progress and the orders were almost up to date with the requested shipping schedule.

Once Josie got Lily safely back in their apartment, she left and used a pay phone to call Max at the restaurant. She decided she did not like Danny and would only deal with Max. She called the restaurant and asked to speak to Max. The manager was not happy to have his phone used for personal calls. He decided to make an exception for Josie because he secretly hoped she would not quit, as she had threatened to do.

Once Max came to the phone, Josie told him she had met Lily and told her of their wish to see her. "Frankly, I think Lily wants to see you but is scared right now. She needs to think about it and needs some time. Are you staying in town tonight?"

"If we can't see Lily tonight, we will stay. I have to tell you, I cannot leave my daughter Rosie too long. Right now, Mom and I can stay another day. I'm sure Danny will stay as long as he needs to. Tonight, I think he needs his rest too. Tomorrow may be better for everyone. Although I'm sure he doesn't agree, he needs the time to get himself together. It hasn't been easy on him either. He really does love Lily. I know you have your doubts but I have seen them together for some time now so I think you need to trust me on this."

"Right now, you are right. I don't like him and I certainly don't trust him. That's why I will only speak to you. The only reason I trust you is because of what Lily feels for you and Rosie."

Max glanced over and noticed Danny and Madge were watching him. If he gave any indication who he was talking to just now, he knew Danny would rip the phone out of his hand. Knowing how rocky the situation was with Jodie, he could not chance getting her riled up and hang up on them.

"Ok, how can I get in touch with you tomorrow?"

"I'll get in touch with you. Give me a phone number. Doesn't Danny have a cell phone?"

"I have to ask him if he brought the department phone with him. Will you promise not to hang up?"

"You only have a few minutes. And I don't want to talk to him."

Max went over and asked Danny if he had the department phone with him. Danny confirmed he had left it in the car with his gun. He immediately asked why and wanted to know who was on the phone. Max told him not to ask questions right now, just to give him the number. He would explain everything once he was finished with the call.

"Josie, I'm going to give you the cell phone number and hope you call us tomorrow morning one way or another. We have to find a hotel room so I don't know where we are going to be staying." He gave her the phone number.

"Ok, we'll be in touch tomorrow."

Max hung up and went back to the table.

"Well Danny, you sure have alienated Lily's new friend. Now she will only talk to me. She said Lily needs some time to get herself prepared to see us. I explained that Madge and I have to get back to Rosie but would stay overnight and she agreed to call in the morning. I think you need a good night's rest and work on your demeanor. I know you have been through a lot but so has Lily. You need to let up. In fact I don't even recognize you today myself."

Madge reached out and patted Danny's arm. "We know you love Lily. We know how this is affecting you. But Josie doesn't. Her only concern is for Lily. You have to understand she is our only link to her now. I need you to get a good night's sleep and get your thoughts together. Lily is scared. We have to show her we are there for her. No temper, no police attitude. Got that? Just remember she is the woman you love. Josie did make a valid point."

Danny hung his head. It was throbbing and they were right. He was not himself. He needed the time to get it together. "I know you are right. Let's leave and get a place to sleep tonight. I need a hot shower and some Tylenol."

Lily and Josie talked about what to do. Max had agreed to stay until tomorrow. Lily knew she could not go on with her life until she turned herself in for the death of Clyde's son. She didn't even know his name. All she could remember was the attack on her and Clyde. She wanted to get it over with. Even if she had to go to jail.

"Lily, I think we have to trust Danny. He doesn't feel the sheriff has any proof. Just wants to question you. He wants to get you a lawyer to go in with you. This way you can be protected from saying the wrong thing."

"But I am guilty. I helped bury the body. I was there."

"Listen to me. I know what you told me about what happened. It didn't sound like Clyde had any other choice. The only mistake he made was not reporting the incident and burying the body."

Lily and Josie talked back and forth for another hour and they both started to yawn.

"Neither one of us got any sleep last night. We need to try and get some tonight. I want you to be able to decide what to do tomorrow. Maybe by sleeping on your decision, you will get your answer when you wake up."

Lily doubted it but they both lay down and soon were asleep. She was screaming in the middle of the night. She was having a nightmare and reliving the rape in the barn. Josie jumped out of bed and ran to the sofa where Lily was sleeping. She reached out to wake Lily and found she was covered in sweat and shaking.

"Wake up. You are having a dream." She shook her and Lily reached out, punched, and fought her.

"Lily you are having a dream. Wake up."

After a few minutes she was able to arouse her from her sleep. By now blood was running out her nose when she was punched. When Lily woke up and saw her she screamed.

"Is he here? Did he hurt you? Where is Clyde?"

"Lily, you are safe. It is just us here. You just had a bad dream. You caused my nose to bleed when you punched me. It must have been a doozie of a nightmare."

"I am so sorry. I did that to you? I was having a dream and I was being attacked."

"It's not surprising. We brought all that back to you by talking about it last night and today. You are ok now. Do you want a drink? Let me get you some water."

Lily was breathing hard. She was still shaking "It seemed so real."

"Bad things are difficult to escape. Doesn't seem fair that you have to keep reliving it, but it happens. I used to get them too."

"You did?"

Yes, that's why I understand."

"What would I ever do without you?"

"I hope you never will. I plan to be around for a while. Even if you marry that Sheriff that I don't like."

They both laughed and Lily felt better being with such a good friend.

"Let's try to go back to sleep. We both need it. I'll be in the next room if you need me."

Soon they both were sleeping peacefully. Both were by now exhausted and neither dreamed.

The next morning Lily woke up and told Josie she had made a decision. She was going back to where she started from. She wanted to go alone.

"I don't want anyone else involved. I want to do this by myself. I was alone when it happened and it is not right to bring anymore pain to the people I love."

"Well, I'm going with you. You are not facing this alone. You need someone to be there for you. Let's face it; until we met each other, we were both alone. That seems to be the best plan as far as I'm concerned. Who knows, after they hear your story they probably will not even go any further in pursuing this thing."

"No, I want to do this on my own."

"Well, that's not going to happen. I will follow you so we may as well make the journey together instead of separately."

"I don't know what I did to deserve you. You trust me; you are really the sister I never had."

"Well, that's more like it. You know I will stand beside you no matter what."

"Ok, but what do we do about Danny?"

"I'll call Max and tell him you need more time. I won't tell them what you are planning to do right now. We may have to tell them once you get back there but for now we don't have to tell them anything."

"I feel bad about treating them like this."

"Well don't. I think they half expect it anyway. I'll tell Max we will keep in touch with him if you want me too. He can tell the others. He is the only one I feel comfortable talking to but if you want me to talk to your Sheriff, I'll do that for you too."

"No, Max is fine. I'm afraid if I hear Danny's voice; I will break down and lose my nerve. Better we just let Max talk to them for now."

"Ok, then I'll go call Max. What do you want me to say?"

"Just what you said, I need more time and I will contact them when I'm ready."

Josie left and found a pay phone. She called Max and told him she was sorry but Lily did not want to see them just yet. She could hear the pain and disappointment in Max's voice and felt sorry for him. Funny, she liked talking to him and wished again that this was the man Lily had fallen in love with. She felt he would have stood beside her and not let her get away.

"Max, you have to understand Lily is hurting right now. She needs more time to get over Danny's rejection of her and decide what to do."

"Josie, listen, Danny did not reject her. You have to understand he is a police officer. He was torn between a personal decision and a professional one."

"Bullshit. I don't know you that well but I think if it had been you, you would have known what decision you would have made. Tell me I'm wrong but I have a feeling you would have known Lily could not have done what they said she did. You would have moved heaven and earth to prove it. Just like I would. That's the difference."

"Ok, ok, let's not fight right now. You know I have to get back to Rosie. This is affecting her too. She feels she has lost Lily. We all need to know Lily is alright. We need her to know we all love her. I know you don't want to hear this, but Danny is really hurting. He loves her so much he can't function."

"I'll let Lily know. She wants you all to go back home and she will get in touch with you when she is ready. She is not ready right now. You have to trust her. She is safe and coping as best as she can right now. She just needs some time and space to do it."

"Will you promise me that you will keep in touch with us?"

"Yes, I did tell Lily that I would call you and let you know how she is doing and you can tell the others."

Max gave her his home and work phone numbers. He told her how much it meant to him that she trusted him.

"I'm a pretty good judge of character and you passed the test right away. That's why I promised Lily I would call you and keep you updated about her."

She hung up and walked back to the apartment. Lily was getting ready for work. She told her how the conversation went and told Lily how lucky she was that so many people cared about her.

Max and Madge returned home. They were exhausted and discouraged. They waited until Rosie was asleep before they had a chance to tell Bea about their trip. How disappointed they were because they not been able to actually see Lily. They told her about her friend Josie.

"Do you think Lily is safe or do you think she is in trouble? I don't like the sounds of this. Do you think this Josie is hiding something from us?"

Max spoke up, "I was the one Josie contacted. We all met her in the restaurant. Unfortunately, she and Danny butted heads. I think if anything, she is protecting Lily. She would only talk to me on the phone. Since I talked to her a few times, I can honestly say that I think she was looking out for Lily, protecting her, not causing her any harm".

Bea looked at Madge for confirmation.

"I agree with Max. She did get quite miffed at Danny but she was very protective of Lily."

"What is Danny doing now?"

"He promised us that he would head back. I think he is stubborn enough to try and hang around for a while but I got the impression, not that she actually said anything, but Josie and Lily may be leaving there soon. I told this to Danny but you know him. He is not about to give up without a fight."

"Yes, I know. I hope he does decide to come home soon. I'd feel better if we are all together if she decides to contact one of us."

Chapter 31

"I've decided I'm going to work another week for Millie. I know she has one or two more big orders due to ship out. I want to stay and help her. She may be able to hire someone during that time to help once I leave. She has been so good to me, I owe her at least that much. Plus, you my friend, have some unfinished business to attend to before we can leave."

"Huh, what are you talking about?"

"Your school and graduation. I want you to finish everything you need to before we leave. You may want to get a job someday and have your license. Isn't that what you have been telling me?"

"Yeah, with everything else, I almost forgot about that."

"Well, let's make sure we have everything in order and then we will leave."

Lily went to work and told Millie that she had to leave and go back home to take care of some unfinished business. She felt bad lying to Millie. But saying that, seemed to make the most sense. She never felt at home where she was going and the unfinished business was a far stretch from what she knew she had to face.

Millie was having a hard time accepting her resignation. She tried to get her to just take some time off but Lily couldn't do that to Millie. She knew in her heart that she would not be coming back.

"Lily, I know this sounds crazy but I really have become quite fond of you in the short time you have been here. You are almost like a daughter to me." She laughed, "Well maybe a granddaughter but you know what I mean."

"Yes I do Millie because I feel the same way about you. But I have to leave. I really don't have a choice. Until I get this behind me, I will never be able to feel settled."

"Well promise me you will not forget me. Please keep in touch and let me know how you are doing. You can always come back and I will have a job for you."

They embraced and again Lily was surprised at the affection she was given. She had never had this as a child. It continued to amaze her how freely it was given by those she had met as an adult. She knew if she was ever lucky enough to have a child, she would make sure they knew they were loved and valued. She reminded Millie that she wanted to hear the rest of her story before she left. Josie was finishing up her classes for night school. As soon as she had her diploma, she was going with her, so she would not be alone. Millie made a mental note to make sure she talked to Josie before they left.

Lily got right to work and checked the inventory to make sure the orders could be filled with the stock on hand. She didn't want to leave Millie with any backorders. Fortunately, she discovered it was all in stock items. Once she started packing the merchandise, she lost track of the time. Soon Millie reminded her it was time to take a break for lunch.

"Good. Maybe while we eat you can tell me the rest of the story. I am anxious to know what happened after you fainted in your boss's office."

Millie laughed "If you're sure it won't bore you to death."

"Never. Please. I hated to think I would leave before you finished telling me. It is so interesting."

"You flatter me, but here goes. I'll talk while you make the tea and microwave the casserole I made for us to eat. I have been meaning to tell you that I think you have mastered the art of making tea with fresh tea leaves. Almost as good as I make it. Let's see...........Well, of course I was embarrassed when I came to. The boss was frantic. I blurted out and ask if I was fired. He looked at me like I was out of my mind. He told me I wasn't fired. He went on to tell me what a great employee I was and that he didn't want to lose me. That's why he discouraged his son from asking me out. You see, he thought if I didn't like his son, I would feel uncomfortable working for him, and leave. I told him I loved my job and was not interested in dating anyone right now."

"Then what?" Lily asked as she set the food on the table.

"Well, apparently the boss told his son and he never came in again before he went back to school."

"So was that the end of it?"

Millie laughed. "No, he finished Law School and showed up at my desk one day with a bouquet of roses and told me he was taking me to lunch."

"And.............."

"Well we got along great. He was a gentleman and a scholar as we used to say. We fell in love and were married within nine months. He stayed in town and got a job in a law firm and I continued working for his father. He wanted to work for a law firm for a year to gain experience. Then move to another town to set up his own small practice. We planned to save as much money as we could before we moved. He wasn't sure where we would go, but he wanted warm weather. He had rheumatoid arthritis and the cold really affected his movements."

"Is that why you moved to Arizona?"

"Not at first. We decided to travel first and check out the warmer climates. Before the internet, that was the best way to research. Experience it. Now you can do so much on-line that you don't have to move from your computer" she laughed. "Anyway we went to Florida first and we were not really fond of that area. One morning he woke me up and said he wanted to head out to Arizona. Of course, I agreed. We had one on those silver top campers that his parents bought us as a going away present so we could take our home with us. Those were the days............"

So you came here? Yes we did end up here. He set up a small practice and wanted to keep it small. He was not really interested in money. He was more interested in helping people and enjoying life. We traveled every chance we got. We even made a few trips overseas. I didn't work at first. Soon the years passed. Once we were married over five years, we began to wonder if we would have any children. During the next two years, I did get pregnant two times. One was miscarried at six months and the second one was born dead. After the last pregnancy, I almost bled to death and had to have a hysterectomy. That was the end of children for us. That's when he suggested I find something to do. He told me to look around and decide. I had enjoyed the job I had working for his father and I knew that I would look into doing something similar. But, I wanted to supply my customers with something more interesting than pots and pans. That's when I thought of creating an eclectic inventory of decorative and collectable pieces. I had quite a collection of treasures myself from our various travels."

"How lucky you were to have such a lovely things that you could turn into a business." said Lily.

"Yes I was lucky, very lucky. And I'm almost to the end of the story. Do you want dessert? I made chocolate chip cookies last night."

"That would be great. You keep on talking and I'll make more tea and set out the cookies."

"After I decided what I wanted to do, we began contacting various artists hoping to gain accounts, and convince then to allow me to be their agent in selling their inventory. It was convenient having a Lawyer for a husband. Anyway, as we were finalizing our plans, we received a call that my father-in-law had died. We left for the funeral. While we were home, I was approached about taking over the business. I knew the weather there was hard on my husband. I had really lost interest the restaurant supply business. I was so excited about handling a more interesting inventory. We both agreed to turn the offer down. No other family members wanted to take on running the business so it was sold. Within a few months, we received a very generous check from the sale and when the estate was settled we were further surprised at how large the inheritance was. We would not have any financial worries for a very long time."

"So what did you do next?"

"Well, we had all the paperwork in place for my business and I was looking for property to work out of. I had originally thought I would rent warehouse space. Since I was just starting the business, I was going to work alone. Unfortunately, my husband's health was starting to fail. Maybe because of the death of his father. Anyway, one day he went to his office and had a heart attack at his desk. They said he died instantly. I was devastated and did not leave our house for six months. Then one day I was walking through our house looking at everything and I saw my collectables. I realized that I had to go on with life. I owed it to him and myself. I showered, left the house and went to his office. I decided I would make that my store. I set up the business just as you see it now. I needed to be around people and not stuck in a dark warehouse. So here I am."

"Let me guess, you decided to call your business Millie's Treasures because that is how you felt about your collection."

"That's absolutely correct!"

"You were very brave to do that on your own."

"No, I was a coward. I lost six months of my life that I can never gain back. I cannot imagine my life any different now. I have something to do, I love what I do and I am very lucky. I wanted to share this story with you

Lily. You are very brave. I don't want you to be afraid to do what you want. Sometimes we think we have lost everything, but if we give life a chance, it's surprising what opportunities are still waiting for us."

"I see what you mean but I don't think I am as strong or capable as you were."

"You will surprise yourself one day with what you can do. Don't sell yourself short. Now let's get back to work before I start getting blubbery about your leaving me."

They both laughed and hugged before heading back into the shop area.

The Return

Chapter 32

Josie worked hard to make sure all her school requirements were satisfied so that she would be certified and eligible to take the licensing exam in any state she wanted to work in. One thing she had decided was, she would follow Lily to the ends of the earth. She finally felt like she had family. Judging from Lily, who had acquired a lot of new family, she hoped she could follow in her footsteps. It was not a bad feeling to let someone into your life after being alone for so long and not trusting anyone but yourself.

Josie and Lily went to the bus station and purchased their tickets. They were packed and ready to leave in two days. Josie had finished up with school and Lily had finished the two big shipments for Millie. Josie was giving up her apartment. They decided if they came back here, they would get a two-bedroom place anyway. Millie had gotten in touch with Josie and made her promise to keep in touch with her. She had also offered to store anything Josie wanted to keep. That way she was sure she would eventually hear from Josie when she needed her things back. Josie stopped by and dropped off a few boxes of household items. Millie gave her a cell phone and an envelope with some money in it. She made her promise she would use if it she and Lily needed it.

"Besides, Lily gave me more help than I have ever gotten out of any employee. I'd feel better if I knew you two had a little extra money in case no one else is there to help you out."

"And to think we would never have met if you didn't like pumpkin pancakes", laughed Josie. "Seriously, I cannot imagine not knowing you. You have been a good friend to me and Lily."

Millie reached out and gave her a hug.

"You girls brought more into my life than I can ever repay you for. I want you to promise to keep in touch. No matter what happens, call me and I will help you out anyway I can."

Josie hugged her back and knew Millie spoke the truth. She would be able to depend on her if she and Lily ran into any problems.

"That means more than I can tell you." Josie and Millie both had tears threatening to spill out of their eyes. Josie mumbled that she had to leave now.

They decided to take very little for the trip. Hopefully, it would not require them to stay long in the town and then they could decide what they wanted to do with their future. Lily did not say anything but Josie knew Lily still had some unfinished business with Danny. And that she would return to see him, Max, Madge and of course Rosie when this was all behind her. Josie was actually hoping to see Max again herself. Then she thought, "*Where did that come from?*"

She started to laugh and Lily looked at her. "What?"

"Nothing just a stupid thought."

"Tell me."

"Well it sounds stupid but I was actually thinking I wouldn't mind seeing Max again."

"It isn't stupid. He is a nice man."

They both laughed and if anyone had noticed them, they would think they were two carefree young girls enjoying life.

The bus ride took several days and although Lily was determined to follow this through, it was tempting to get off and start over again. But, she knew she had to get it all behind her, regardless of the outcome. She was grateful for Josie because she knew she would not be facing this alone.

Josie kept watch on Lily and could sense the apprehension in her. She was tempted several times to suggest they get off the bus at the next stop. She stopped herself each time though, because she knew Lily had to finish whatever business she had left undone.

Lily relayed the story Millie had told her of starting her own business and the loss of her husband. They both agreed that she was a special lady and they both wanted to keep in touch with her. Josie shook her head and said, "Sometime life sucks. Here we are without a family and so is Millie. Why couldn't we have been her kids?"

Lily looked at Josie and realized she was just as lost as Lily had been before Madge, Max, Rosie and especially Danny had come into her life.

"Please God, get me through this so Josie and I can start over together. I know they will all love her the way I do."

Finally the bus pulled into town. Lily heard the driver announce the destination but when she and Josie got off and collected their bags, she had no feeling of coming home. Josie suggested they store the bags in the hotel and get lunch.

"Where did you eat when you lived here?"

"I never ate in a restaurant the whole time I was here."

You are kidding me."

"No, I had ice cream twice but no food."

"Well, let's just go get something to eat and take our time. Thank goodness the bus ride is over and we don't have to rush through eating anymore." Josie wanted to give Lily time to get used to being back before they rushed into the next step of her plan.

Both ordered comfort food. Lily chose the Hot Turkey Sandwich with Gravy and Mashed Potatoes and Josie chose the Hot Beef Sandwich.

"Let's order a Sundae for dessert." Josie laughed. "We may as well ruin our diets all the way."

Lily agreed, "I always love eating like this on bad days. Leave the salad and healthy choices for the good ones."

After they ate, Josie suggested they take a walk through town. Lily was able to identify the places she had gone with Clyde. The General Store and the Second Hand Store were still there but Lily had no desire to go inside either one on them.

Josie suggested that they head back to the hotel and get some rest. Tomorrow would be soon enough to go to the police station.

"Remember, we are going to say I am your sister. Even though we don't look alike, we can tell them we had different fathers. Otherwise, they may not let me in with you."

Lily agreed to both suggestions and they headed to the hotel.

Chapter 33

Danny did not return home right away. He could not shake the feeling that if he tried hard enough, he would find Lily. His only thoughts were of her. He was a man obsessed. He could not let go. He knew he had driven her away and it was up to him to bring her back. He roamed the streets both night and day. He rarely slept. He survived on sheer determination. He only ate and slept when he could no longer walk.

Max kept calling him each day to convince him to return home. Danny would say, "Just one more day. I know I'll find her."

Finally he was exhausted. He knew he had lost. Nothing he had done had helped to locate her. He went into the Denny's restaurant where Josie worked. The manager told him she had left a couple weeks ago. Danny figured it was about the time he had last seen her. Now he knew he had lost his last lead to Lily's whereabouts. He decided to order a large breakfast to fortify himself and make one last attempt in looking for Lily. Tomorrow he would return home.

After he ate, he started out on foot. He would go in each store again and make sure he had not missed anyone of them. He would check out the employees to see if anyone recognized Lily.

He had no success and it was after two o'clock. He decided to take home a gift for Rosie. Max had told him how sad she was, so maybe he could find something to cheer her up. He spotted the sign as he was deciding what to get her. *Millie's Treasures.* The window displayed a variety of collectables. He especially liked the fairies. He decided to go in and see what else they had.

Millie heard the door buzz as a customer arrived. She called out that she would be there in a minute. She hastily set down the inventory sheet she was checking and walked out to the front of the store. She was immediately concerned because this man looked unkempt and well, scruffy. Not like someone who could afford her merchandise. As she came closer, she thought to herself, *"If he would clean himself up, he would be a handsome young man."*

Danny looked at the lady approaching him and was struck by her elegance. This was one classy lady. Once she was close enough, he noticed she had a kind face but he also saw hesitation in her. Then he thought to himself, how he must look.

"I'm sorry. I don't mean to alarm you. I am leaving to go home and wanted to take something back to the daughter of a friend of mine. I saw your sign and was drawn inside by your fairy collection. I know I must look unsavory but I promise I'm not. Here, let me show you my identification."

As he reached into his jacket pocket, Millie saw the look on his face.

"That's alright, I'm glad you stopped in. No need to prove yourself. How old is the daughter of your friend?"

"Well, Rosie is in kindergarten. So I think that makes her five."

Millie felt her heart skip a beat. "Did you say Rosie?"

"Yes, why?"

Millie caught herself. "Just an unusual name that isn't used much anymore."

Danny looked at her. Was she holding something back? *"Now I know I'm losing it, suspecting an old lady"*, he said to himself.

"Does she have any special interest? She is kinda of young for my collection. I'm not sure children her age would enjoy something that is not meant to be played with."

"Well, Lily gave her a music box for Christmas and she takes good care of that so I think she would be thrilled with one of the fairies."

Millie swallowed, "Is Lily her mother?"

"No, just a good friend. As a matter of fact, that is why I am in town. I'm looking for her?"

"Who? Rosie?"

"No, Lily."

"Is she lost?"

"Listen, lady I don't want to talk about it. I've spent almost a month in town trying to find her and tell her I love her. I made a stupid mistake and now I can't find her to fix it."

"Who are you anyway?"

Danny wasn't sure why he answered her. Something was nagging at him. But he decided to tell her.

"I'm Sheriff McCain. Danny McCain."

"I think you and I need to talk. Come into my back room. I'll fix you something to eat. You look like something the cat dragged in."

Danny laughed at her choice of words.

"You don't by any chance know my Aunt Bea or Madge do you? You sound just like them."

She settled Danny down in the chair and poured him a glass of port wine. "I don't think you are officially working today and I think we both need this before we talk. Just a minute, I'm going to run out front and put the *Closed* sign on the door. We don't need any interruptions."

Once she came back, she set out a platter of assorted cheeses, crackers and some chicken salad she had made for lunch.

"Now, tell me your story. Once I hear it, I may or may not decide to tell you what I know. So it better be the truth."

Danny looked at her. He saw the determination in her eyes and he knew she would be honest with him, if he was honest with her.

Danny was not sure where to begin. But he decided to start at the beginning. Once he got started, he was surprised how good it felt to get it all off his chest. He didn't leave anything out. He told her about Lily's attack, the death of the Sheriff and his worry for her over the mysterious death in the town she had come from. He told of all the people who loved her. How she had touched so many lives since she had come to their town. He finished with the engagement ring and promises they both made. Then his doubts over his job and the problem hanging over them that threatened their life together. Could he handle them both without sacrificing one for the other? His discovery of how little anything else mattered to him once she left. Too late, he realized what mattered most to him. Lily.

When he finished he was surprised to discover how much food he had eaten. It felt good to finally talk about Lily to someone besides Max and Madge. He looked at his watch and discovered he had been talking almost two hours.

"Well, I believe you. I can tell you just made a dumb mistake so I'll let you know what I can. You see, Lily worked for me here in the store. I also realized soon after I met her, what a special person she was. She was troubled and missed her boyfriend and family. There was something she said she had to do so she could get on with her life. That's the reason she gave me for leaving. I'm just glad she didn't leave town alone. As least I know she has someone with her, to look out for her."

Danny's heart sunk. He was afraid to ask but needed to know.

"Who went with her?"

'Why, Josie of course."

Danny laughed with relief. At least it was not another man. He told Millie he knew Josie but was sure she did not like him. She had made that clear.

"Well, you don't really know Josie. She is like a mother lion looking after her cubs. She will defend Lily to the death, if you get my drift. I'm sure she took you as a threat to Lily's happiness. Honestly, anyone would be lucky to have a friend like Josie. She is strong like Lily but with toughness to her that Lily doesn't have."

Danny told Millie he was going back home to decide what to do next. Since Lily had left this town, there was nothing left for him to do here. He promised to keep in touch and let Millie know what he found out. Millie promised to call if she heard from Josie or Lily. They picked out a fairy statue for Rosie. Millie suggested one with blond hair peeking under an opening in a tree that was hiding a pot of emeralds. She told Danny to tell Rosie that Lily is like a jewel; she will be returning as soon as she gets her shine back.

Danny laughed and said he would have to run that by Max. They may find Rosie out in the yard polishing all the rocks. Millie agreed and told Danny she never had any children so she hadn't thought of that.

Danny headed back to his hotel and was anxious to get back home. He called Max and told him what he had learned from Millie. He was relieved to learn Lily had been well taken care of and was not traveling alone. For some reason Max laughed and said, "Fancy that." Danny didn't ask what he meant, just wanted to get started home.

Chapter 34

The next day, Lily and Josie headed to the police station. Neither one had much appetite but stopped on the way to eat a light breakfast. Lily found she was too nervous to eat and could only drink her tea. The bagel she ordered was not touched. Josie drank coffee and managed to eat half of the blueberry muffin before, she too, gave up.

"Are you sure you want to go through with this? It's not too late to leave. You say the word and we are out of here!"

"No. I've put it off long enough and I came this far, I can't turn back. I'm tired of running."

"Ok, Sis I'm with you all the way."

They headed out and made their way to see the sheriff.

As they entered the door, Lilly asked to see the sheriff. The person at the counter asks what they needed. He looked at the two young girls and wondered what brought them in. It was not often they had anything serious happen in this town and figured it was just something that he could take care of instead of bothering the sheriff.

Lily was the first to speak. "I understand he is looking for me."

"Looking for you? Not that I know of. Do you know why?"

Lily spoke softly "About a body found on Clyde's farm."

The man looked surprised. He was trying to remember what it was. Then it came to him. "Take a seat and I'll get the sheriff."

As he entered the sheriff's office he said "You'll never guess who just walked in."

"Well, unless it is the governor, I have no idea."

"Remember you were looking for the girl Clyde had out at his place? The one who left before he died? The one you were looking for question about that body we found?"

The sheriff had a shocked look on his face. "You mean she just walked in? Did she say anything?"

"Not really, I wanted to let you know she was here before I questioned her."

"Well, send her in."

He returned and told Lily the sheriff would see her now. He asked Josie to remain in the lobby but she made it clear they would both walk out the door if they could not be seen together. They were not going to be separated.

The sheriff looked up as they entered. His face registered surprise at the two young girls in front of him.

"Well, ladies please sit down and tell me what brings you here."

Lily spoke but her voice betrayed her. It revealed her fear.

"I understand you are looking for me in regards to the death of a man buried out at Clyde's farm."

She stammered out the last words and her face registered panic. The sheriff studied her for a minute before speaking.

"Tell me what you know?"

Lily sat back in her chair and took a deep breath. She wasn't sure how to begin. She leaned forward and took Josie's hand.

"I know the man that we killed was Clyde's son. We buried him in my vegetable garden."

Josie did not realize it but she was squeezing Lily's hand so tight her fingers cracked. She immediately let go and looked at the sheriff.

"Does Lily need a lawyer?"

The sheriff sat there a minute and went over his options. He thought the girl knew something but found it hard to believe she had acted alone. However, Clyde was dead and it only left her to face the charges. It was an election year and this may be just what he needs to get reelected. He looked at Lily and said

"Well, that's up to you. You can give me a full statement or I can read you your rights and put you in jail until your lawyer shows up. That's up to you."

Josie spoke first. "Yes, we want a lawyer."

For the first time she wondered why they had thought they could just walk in, tell the story, and walk out again. Why hadn't either one thought this through?

Lily said "I'll tell you everything."

Josie jumped up and said "No she won't." She looked at Lily. "We have to get a lawyer first before you say the wrong thing."

The sheriff looked at Josie. "The way I see it you have no legal right to be here. I'm asking you to leave."

"You are wrong sheriff; I am not leaving her alone."

The sheriff picked up the phone and called the officer back in the room.

"Please escort this lady out of my office and take Lily here into the interrogation room for questioning."

For the first time, Lily actually realized she was going to jail. She knew this had been hanging over her head for years but she had not really thought about the outcome of her confession. Now it became a reality.

Josie left the police station and walked across the street. She felt sick to her stomach. She should have been better prepared. She decided she had to call Max and let him know.

Max actually answered the phone on the first ring. He was waiting to hear from Danny because he expected him home today.

"Max, it's me Josie."

"Hi, Josie. What's going on? Where are you?"

"Well, I'm in deep shit and I need your help if it isn't too late."

"What do you mean?"

"Lily got it in her head to come back to her old town and turn herself in. They locked her up and kicked me out. I'm afraid she'll never get out of there. She doesn't have a lawyer and the sheriff seemed more than happy to charge her. I don't know what to do now. I need your help. I'm not sure who else to turn to and I guess Danny should know. At least he has some police background. He may have an idea."

"Josie, slow down. Start from the beginning."

Josie told him about Lily's decision to come back and get this situation behind her so she could live without looking over her shoulder all the time. She said she had convinced her to let her come along. Now she felt she had let her down because she was sitting in jail right now and Josie not allowed to be with her.

"Danny is on his way home right now. He should be here anytime. In fact, I thought it was him who was calling me. Do you have a place to stay?"

"Yes, I'm in the only hotel here. The *"Outsider Inn"*. I guess it would be funny, the name I mean, if things were not so serious."

"Well go back there and I'll call your room when I hear from Danny. Give me your room number."

After he hung up, he immediately called Madge and Bea and told them to come to his store immediately. He also called Danny to see where he was. He thought it best not to tell Danny anything about Lily right now. No need him getting fired up. He would either have an accident or decide to head to Lily without stopping home first. Better, they all talked this through before making a rash decision. Danny can't seem to think straight where Lily is concerned.

Once Madge and Bea arrived, he told them what he had learned from Josie. They decided that when Danny got there they would have him call the sheriff and find out what the charges were and then get a lawyer for Lily. They needed one that practiced in that state. He may be able to find out the best one to get for her.

Danny arrived less than an hour later. He could tell from their faces that something was wrong. He felt his chest tighten. He knew it had to do with Lily. He was anxious to find out what it was, but dreaded hearing it, if it was bad news. Somehow he knew it was.

"Ok, who is going to tell me what is going on?"

"How was your trip?" asked Max trying to delay the news for a few minutes.

"Fine, now what's up? I know it's about Lily so you better cut to the chase and spit it out."

"Well, apparently Josie and Lily decided to go back to Greenwood and get this mess straightened out. Actually, Lily decided to go back and Josie insisted she go with her. When she went to the sheriff, he put her in jail. Now before you run off half-cocked, let's figure out what we need to do. We talked about it while we were waiting for you, and decided we need to get her a lawyer. Before we do, you should call the sheriff and find out what the charges are. What he is planning to do."

"Ok. I see what you mean. I'll go over to the station and make a call to him. Then I'll come back here and we can decide what comes next."

"We will be here, now hurry up" said Madge "I cannot stand the thought of Lily being caged up. She must be scared to death."

Danny went right into the station and headed to his office without speaking to anyone. They all looked surprised at his manner but lately he had changed so no one thought much of it. This was starting to be the norm.

Danny dialed the number to Sheriff Axelrod. He had written it down when he had talked to him before and shoved it into his top desk drawer.

"Sheriff Axelrod, I understand that you found the girl you were looking for. Lily Hill? Is that right?"

"Why yes I did."

"Well do you mind telling me what she is charged with?"

"Can't see that's it any of your business. Frankly, I'm kinda glad this case is finally getting solved. She is being held on murder, fleeing a crime scene and failure to report a crime. No bail. She has proven she is a flight risk."

"Does she have an attorney?"

"Didn't seem to want one. Said she was guilty. That's enough for me."

Danny felt himself beginning to lose control. He took a deep breath.

"Sheriff there are some people who care for Lily and have asked me to see if you can recommend a lawyer for her. Do you have anyone qualified in your town."

"What do you mean qualified? Our town has a lawyer and just as good as big city ones."

"Now don't get offended, Sheriff, I meant do they specialize in criminal law?"

The sheriff laughed. "I guess if they did, they'd starve. Not enough criminals here to support them full time."

"Can you give me a name so I can pass it along?"

"Wasting your time. There is only one lawyer in town now. The one we did have died and his niece is working at taking over his practice." He read the name and phone number to Danny and hung up.

He headed back over to speak to Max about what he had learned. Again, leaving without a word to anyone in the station.

He walked in and found Madge, Bea and Max waiting for him. He told them what he had found out.

"She has to have an attorney. We can't let her go this alone without anyone helping her out. She doesn't realize what she has gotten herself into and frankly the sheriff could care less as long as he has someone confessing to an unsolved crime." said Danny.

Max looked at everyone and said "That's pretty much what Josie said. They won't even let her see Lily now."

"Well, I am heading there."

"Danny, Josie doesn't really relate to you and you get yourself into trouble by yourself when Lily is concerned. You are not going alone. I will have to go with you if we can ever hope to get this sorted out. Mom, can you and Bea watch after Rosie again?"

Danny said "I almost forgot. I found out where Lily was working and I brought back a present for Rosie from there. Maybe I should give it to her and tell her we are leaving to go help Lily."

Chapter 35

Josie headed back to her room. She was uncertain she had done the right thing but realized she didn't have much choice. She had come with Lily to protect her. So far, she was doing a bad job. She was unable to see her and unable to come up with a plan to help her. Yes, she definitely needed assistance on deciding what to do. She would wait for Max to call her back with advice.

Danny went to see Rosie. He gave her the gift he had brought back for her. She looked at him and said, "I want Lily to come home. Why didn't you bring her back?"

He looked in those sad eyes and knew he had let everyone down. "I'm going to do everything in my power to bring her back to us. I'm borrowing your Daddy to help me. See this fairy. She is looking into the bottom of the tree to find her treasure. Well, we are going to look for our treasure. You know who that is?"

"Yes, Lily."

"Well, I want to ask your permission to borrow your Daddy to take with me to get Lily back. I need you to be strong as my Junior Deputy and wait here and follow all the instructions your Grandma and Aunt Bea give you. They need your help now too. Is that ok with you?"

"Yes Danny. I'll be good. We'll make a Welcome Home banner for Lily."

Danny looked at her eyes. So full of trust and belief that Lily would return. He only hoped he would not let her down. "Ok, we are going to leave soon."

Max called Josie and told her they were on their way and asked her to get them a room close to hers if possible. He told her they were driving straight through and should arrive sometime tomorrow.

Josie sat in her room but could not rest. She needed to do something. She went over to the Sheriff's office again but was stopped at the front desk. She was told Lily could not have any visitors and she needed to leave. She immediately felt despair. They were not giving Lily any breaks here. She was frustrated, mad and scared; all at the same time. In truth, she had never felt so helpless. Not sure what to do, she decided to take a walk through town. She had gone down the street and was turning across to the other side when she suddenly felt as if someone was watching her. She tried to shake off the feeling but it was so strong she started to realize *it was happening*. She ducked in the first store and pretended to look at the items displayed by the window. She kept an eye on the street. Luckily, it was not busy today. Not many people were on the street. The salesgirl came up and asked if she could help her. Josie told her she was just looking at ………. and she glanced down and she was standing beside some hole diggers and tools. Josie realized she looked foolish. She had entered a hardware store. She looked at the girl's face. The girl was looking at her but her face was friendly. She decided she needed to talk to someone.

"Listen, I know I look like Looney Tunes but I was just taking a walk and I had this feeling someone was watching me. It was creepy, so I just ducked in here to see if I could catch a glimpse of who it was."

The girl looked out the window and could not see anyone.

"We have a back door for employees. I can let you out that way if you want. No one will see you leave. Once you come to the end of the alley, you will be close to the diner."

Josie thanked her and followed her to the exit. Once she was outside, she followed the directions the girl had given her. She decided she would get something to eat. That way, she could sit down and try to get herself together.

The man who had been watching Josie lingered down the street from the Hardware Store. He waited twenty minutes and did not see her come back out. He walked toward the store and decided to go in. As he walked up and down the aisle, the same girl who had talked to Josie approached him.

"Can I help you find anything?"

"I thought my niece came in here and I was hoping to catch up with her and take her to lunch."

The girl looked at the man and suddenly felt afraid.

"Sorry, I didn't see any women in here. I just got here myself and she may have been gone by then. I can ask my boss if you want me to."

"Nah, I'll catch up with her later." He left and walked up the street.

The clerk looked after him as he left. She was glad she had helped the girl escape. Somehow she knew he was not her uncle.

Josie usually did not drink coffee but decided to get a cup today. She knew that the customers who came into the diner and ordered coffee were not harassed by the waitress as much as someone who ordered a coke or ice tea. She could never figure that out. Maybe because drinking coffee was a slower process and viewed as a ritual instead of just having a drink. Kinda like sitting at a bar having an alcoholic drink. No one expected you to just gulp that down. Anyway, it would bide her time. She figured she could waste a good hour. She would drink her coffee and then order lunch. As she glanced at the clock on the wall, she realized it was late afternoon and she would have either a late lunch or early dinner. Her mind was going in all directions. She laughed to herself. *I'm losing it. I am talking to myself. Thinking of the most ridiculous things and imagining that someone is watching me. No wonder I am no use to Lily. Snap out of it girl.*

As Josie was berating herself, the man continued looking for her. He stopped at each store wondering if he had made a mistake about which doorway she had entered.

Josie had three coffee refills. She was starting to feel like her insides were swimming. She ordered something to eat and went to the bathroom while her food was being prepared.

Once she finished, she looked at the clock. Good she thought to herself, I have filled ninety minutes sitting her. Now what to do? She decided to head for the drugstore and look for a magazine to take back to the hotel room. As she wandered up and down the aisles, she noticed a bank of payphones. She chuckled to herself and thought that is not something you see much of anymore. As she stood there, she thought of Millie. She debated what to do. She was so lonely. The thought took her by surprise. Before she met Lily she never thought of being lonely. She liked being by herself with no one to worry about except herself. Now she realized how much her life had changed. She no longer enjoyed being by herself. She needed the comfort of friends who were a family to her. She made a quick decision to call Millie before she lost her nerve.

She went to the counter and got change for the phone. Once she dialed the number for Millie she felt better. As the phone was answered tears filled her eyes.

"Millie, its Josie."

Millie could hear Josie's voice. She was immediately afraid. In all the time she had known Josie, she had been tough and in control. Now she was far from sounding that way."Josie honey, what's wrong?"

"It's Lily. She is in jail and they won't let me see her. I don't know what to do."

"Calm down. I'm here for you. Just start at the beginning and we'll figure something out."

Josie explained what has happened after they arrived in town. She didn't leave out any detail. Even the feeling that she was being followed. Millie listened to every word and was suddenly afraid for them. She had to do something. "Where are you staying? I'm coming out there."

Josie felt bad that she was causing Millie to worry but secretly glad that she would come out to help. She told her where she was and where she was staying.

After Millie hung up, she called in a few favors. Soon she had plans to fly up to Greenwood. She had an offer of a small plane which could land close to the town. Since there were no commercial airlines that flew there, and the bus would take too long, she had no other choice. She hated to fly especially in a small plane. She knew she would do all she could for those two girls. She closed her shop and alerted her security company so it could be guarded while she was gone. She was not too concerned about her store because it didn't generate that much walk- in income and her orders were current and nothing needed packed and shipped right now.

Josie went back to the motel and decided to sit in the lobby for a while. Soon she grew bored and headed up to her room.

Chapter 36

Danny and Max decided to drive straight through. They took turns driving and sleeping. They only stopped for gas and that's when they grabbed something quick to eat. Usually a sandwich or hot dog inside the gas station. Danny was quiet for most of the trip. Max was concerned for him and didn't know what to say. He knew the situation wasn't good and he wasn't sure what they were going to do. Only that they had to get there as soon as possible. He had heard and read too much, about how the law worked in some small towns, to even feel comfortable that Lily was being treated fairly. From what Josie said, she wasn't even given a public defender to talk to.

Millie arrived that evening. She registered in the hotel after finding out which room Josie was in, slipped the clerk some money and insisted on an adjoining room. Once she was in her room, she knocked on Josie's door.

"Josie, it's me, Millie."

Josie was so surprised to hear her voice. She pulled the door open and leaped in her arms. Millie guided her into the room and locked the door behind them. Josie looked at her kind face and started to cry. Millie held her tight and told her she was here and they would get this straightened out. She let Josie cry. She knew she needed to. It was best to get that out before they planned what to do next. As Millie held Josie, they both realized how much they loved each other and how lonely life had been for both of them.

Millie was the first to speak. "Do you realize how much I love you? You are the daughter I never had. For all the pain we are going through now, it is worth it to have you?"

Josie looked at her through tear stained eyes. "Do you know, when I saw the telephone, I knew I could call you and you would come. I never felt that trust before. Especially with my family. Once I met you and Lily, I felt like I had a family for the first time in my life." She laughed. "I even forgot I had the cell phone you gave me. I just reached for the nearest phone available."

Millie had Josie go over everything that had happened one more time to make sure she knew where they stood with the law.

"Is it too late for me to go to the police station?"

"We can try. They haven't let me back in since Lily first got there. I haven't been able to see her or talk to her."

Millie and Josie walked over to the police station together. Josie knew if anyone could get in to see Lily, it would be Millie.

"Good evening officer. I am Millie Rosen and I am here to see Lily whom I understand is being questioned in this facility."

The deputy looked at the lady before him and laughed. She was the most well dressed woman he had ever seen. She held herself like royalty and talked like that too. So out of place in this town. Well regardless, he had strict orders to keep all visitors away from the prisoner. No way he was risking his job. "Sorry lady. You may look like the Queen of England, but you are not getting any special privileges here. She is not allowed any visitors. If you have a problem with that, come back in the morning and speak with the sheriff."

Millie tried to persuade him but he was not budging. Well they would be back tomorrow and she would look in town for an attorney.

"Let's go back to the hotel and plan what we are doing tomorrow. Did you eat?"

"Yes, but I'm sure you are hungry, so I can get something to drink and maybe a dessert."

Millie laughed. "I know you are feeling better if you want dessert."

The next morning they had breakfast and then headed to the only law office in town. The receptionist told them the lawyer, Ms. Adams, was not in. She expected her back after lunch. They made an appointment for two o'clock and decided to take a walk around town.

Millie looked around the town and was struck how meager the offerings and impoverished the town seemed in comparison to where she lived. She did not express her thoughts because she did not want to appear judgmental to Josie. She felt uneasy now with the justice system here. Clearly, they did not believe, *innocent until proven guilty*. She hoped the lawyer would be able to help.

They decided to go back to the hotel to wait until the time of their appointment. As they sat in the lobby, Josie was telling Millie that Danny and Max were also on their way.

Around one o'clock, Josie was getting impatient and could not sit still. She walked around the small lobby and tried to get herself prepared for the afternoon. Suddenly she turned and ran into Max. She forgot herself and threw herself into his arms. He had a surprised look on his face and felt a jolt run down his body when Josie touched him. She suddenly realized what she had done and felt herself blush. "I'm sorry. I'm so scared for Lily. I'm glad you are here to help her."

Millie watched the exchanged and felt herself smile. She knew they had feelings for each other, even if they didn't realize it yet.

Max looked at Josie and suddenly saw her in a different light. She was very pretty and he felt something he had not felt in a long time. Lust? Is it possible to feel that way about a woman again? He shook his head to clear his thoughts. "We drove straight through. It's a wonder we kept the car on the road, we drove so fast. We are going to check into our room and then Danny is going over to talk to Sheriff Axelrod."

"Millie is here. I want you to meet her. We'll wait for you in the bar."

Josie ran over to Millie. She told Millie what the plan was and that they would meet up in the bar.

"I could do with a drink myself but I don't want to smell like liquor when we meet the lawyer "laughed Josie.

Millie said "I agree. I could use one too but we want to make sure we appear at our best. Who was that handsome man you were talking to, dear?"

"That was Max. Did you see Danny? He was at the desk checking in."

"Actually, I met Danny. He came into the shop after you two left town. I rather liked him."

"I wish Lily liked Max instead of Danny. He's much nicer." Josie said with feeling.

Millie looked at her and could not help laughing.

"I'm glad it's not Max, he seems more suited to you instead of Lily."

Josie looked at Millie. "Surely, you're kidding. We are just friends. He's a very nice man. Besides, he's not interested in anyone. He was married once and has a child. But he would still be better for Lily than Danny."

Millie did not pursue the conversation. Unless she was mistaken, Josie and Max would discover each other soon enough without her help because the chemistry appeared to be there.

Soon Danny and Max entered to the bar. Josie introduced Millie and they decided that it would be best if Danny went over to the Sheriff and found out the charges before they met with the lawyer. They would wait in the lobby. If he wasn't back by the time of their appointment, they would meet him in the law office.

Chapter 37

Danny headed over to the jail. He was met by the Deputy and asked him if he could talk to the sheriff. He explained that he was there about the prisoner, Lily Hill.

"Now that's a popular young lady we have there. The sheriff is not letting anyone see her."

"Well, tell him Sheriff McCain is here and not leaving until we talk."

Danny set his face in a scowl and gave his best impression of being ready to become violent if his request was not granted. It must have worked because the Deputy got up and went into the sheriff's office and shut the door.

He returned after a few minutes and said, "The sheriff will give you five minutes. Have a seat until he is ready for you."

Danny pulled himself up straight and set his face. Outwardly, no one would recognize him as the easy going person he usually was. After closer to fifteen minutes, Danny was led into the Sheriff's office. He skipped the formalities and started right in with what brought him here. "Sheriff, I need to know what is going on with your prisoner. What she is being charged with and why she does not have legal representation."

He stood there, crossed his arms and glared at the sheriff.

"No need to get your dandruff up young man. As a sheriff yourself, you know the criminals often look innocent. Hell, she admitted to what she did and refused a lawyer."

"Mind if I talk to her myself?"

"For what reason?"

"First to determine if what you said is true, and second because I don't believe you for one minute."

"Now hold on, I don't like your tone. You have no authority here."

"Now, we can work together, or it's going to get nasty."

"I don't owe you anything."

"Yes, you owe me the opportunity to see her. She lived in my town and there are a lot of people concerned about her. Including me."

"I should have guessed. Had a little on the side, huh, Sheriff?"

Danny reached out and grabbed him by his shirt. "You sack of shit. You are off base on that one. If you are trying to railroad her, you will be very sorry. If you as much as touch one hair on her head, you will find yourself in sorry shape. Do I make myself clear?"

"More than clear. I may put you in jail for threatening a police officer. You are no better than she is."

"Try and prove it."

The sheriff looked in Danny's face and knew he had pushed him as far as he could right now. But his time would come. "Get a lawyer and then come back. Right now, your time is up."

Danny slammed the door on his way out. He was fuming and realized Max was right. He could not act sane where Lily was concerned.

He glanced at his watch. Everyone should be on their way to the lawyer's office. He was angry with himself, the sheriff and in fact the whole world right now. He better calm himself down or the lawyer will probably kick him out too. Why couldn't he control himself better? Why does he get so irrational when he needs to be professional? Lily, of course, sweet Lily. He loses his heart and brain over her.

As he entered the law office he saw Millie, Max and Josie sitting in the reception area. He sat down in an empty chair next to Max.

"What did you find out?"

"Nothing."

Max looked at him. "Tell me you didn't lose your temper."

Danny's face was set in anger. Max knew that had happened.

Josie jumped in "Well, Mr. Danny from what I can see you are not showing anyone that you care for Lily. I think if you really cared, you would put your stupid feelings aside and think what is important for her. All you do is mess everything up. What she sees in you, I'll never understand." She glared at him.

255

He sunk down in his seat and knew she was right.

Max was the next one to speak. "I suggest we let Millie and I talk to the lawyer. Josie can give her facts too but I want you to keep quiet. So far, you have not been able to help us with the sheriff. As far as I see it right now, our only shot left to help Lily, is with this lawyer. Now if you come in with us, can you keep your mouth shut? If not, stay in the waiting room."

Danny looked at everyone and knew they were right. They also looked like they agreed with Max. He couldn't just sit there.

"I promise. I'll just listen. I know you and Josie are right. I am too close to this to think straight. All I can think about is how Lily must be feeling right now locked up in that jail unable to see anyone."

They all breathed a sigh of relief. But they were all cautious. Hopefully, he would keep his word.

The lawyer was younger than they expected. She introduced herself and gave them a brief rundown on her education and experience. "My father wanted to name me T. J. Adams for Thomas Jefferson since our last name was Adams. Sort of a twist on history, since he was a History Professor at the University. My mother inserted the rest of my name to conform to the initials T.J. so I became Tyler for John Tyler and Julia for his wife although my family always called me TJ. Not sure why I'm telling you all this. I wanted you to know about me since you are giving me a chance to help with your case. I want you to feel comfortable. Although I am new in town, I do come with some experience. I graduated from Law School and worked for a large practice. My Uncle died and left this practice to me. Unfortunately, he died unexpectedly. I have not had time to get his office in order. He left me with the mess you must have noticed in the front office."

Once they were seated in her office, they explained why they were there. As planned, Max started the conversation and gave what details they had so far.

"Once Lily made the mistake of turning herself in without legal advice, no one has been able to see her. The sheriff also stated she does not want an attorney. Since none of us can speak to her, we cannot know if that is true or not."

"Please tell me the relationship each of you has with the accused and how long you have known her. I need some background on you too, so I'm clear about what I can expect from each of you".

Each one gave a brief introduction of themselves, how they had met Lily, and what their relationship was with her.

Ms. Adams was busy taking notes and did not interrupt to ask any questions. Once they were all done answering her question, Max gave a more specific background of what had transpired with Lily during the past few years. Danny helped fill in some of the blanks. When they were finished, Max sat back in his chair. She looked at each one of them to try and read their expressions. The girl called Josie was clearly scared, the older lady Millie appeared calm on the outside but her eyes betrayed her. She could see sadness. Max was calm and outwardly in control but she saw pleading in his eyes. Finally, she looked at Danny. He appeared to be angry but she could also feel deep sorrow coming from his face. She realized that this Lily was one lucky person to have so many people fighting for her. Finally, she spoke. "I'm going to go to the jail and try and see Lily. I doubt if I will have any problems since I am now her attorney. Then I will get her side of the story and try to find out the charges against her. With any luck, I'll be able to find out what kind of case they have against her and try to arrange bail. Are you going to stay in town long or should I call you?"

They all spoke at once as if she was speaking directly to them. They all confirmed that they were not leaving until Lily was safe.

Ms. Adams explained her fee. She wanted to know who would be capable of posting bond for Lily's release. Millie was the first to speak up. She told the attorney she was willing to assume all expenses. She left the office to make financial arrangements with the office assistant in the reception area.

They all filed out of the office and decided to go and get lunch so they could discuss what to do next. The attorney had advised then to resist visiting the jail again until she had a chance to talk to the sheriff.

She said "You don't live here but I do. I know the best way to get the sheriff mad is to question his judgment. I know how to deal with him after a few unfortunate encounters."

They were seated in the diner and trying to decide what to do next. Josie looked at Max and said "I want to drive out to the farm where Lily lived when this happened. Can you take me?"

Millie and Danny both thought it was a good idea and wanted to go along.

Max looked at them and said, "One of us needs to stay here in case the lawyer needs us. I think if Josie and I went alone we could look like a couple who got lost and took the wrong road. It will be less suspicious that way."

Max could tell from Danny's face he wasn't pleased to be left out. Millie immediately saw the reasoning behind it.

"Tell you what Danny, if we see anything that may help, I'll bring Josie back and you and I can go back together, deal?"

Danny nodded his head. Max and Josie headed outside and stopped. Josie said "I want to go there but I honestly don't know where it is."

"Think back to anything Lily might have said that would give us an idea. Or maybe someone in town may have known where they lived."

"She did mention the General Store a lot. I think they shopped there and sold some of their pigs. Let's go there first. You do the talking and ask where the farm is."

They headed down the street and entered the store. Josie looked around and could see most of the store clerks were older as if they had worked there a long time. Max decided to start his inquiries in the grocery part of the store. Most farmers need to get some supplies no matter what they grow on their farm.

Max approached a man behind the meat counter. He had a bloody apron on and appeared to be the butcher. He explained that he was in town looking to buy a farm. Someone had told him the farm of Clyde Hill might be available and by any chance did he know where it was. The man thought a minute and said, "He, he died a long time ago. We bought some hogs from him back when he was alive but as far as I know the farm is rented to the Nalley family. Don't know if it is for sale."

"Well as long as I'm in town, I'd at least like to ride out and check for myself."

The butcher told them to wait while he checked his records to see if he could find out where it was. "Never been there myself."

Josie and Max waited unaware that they were being watched. The man was behind a row of produce and could hear everything being said. He smiled to himself. *This is easier than I thought.* He left to wait for them to head out to the farm.

The butcher returned and gave Max a description of the area. Although he didn't know how visible it was from the road, he knew the general area and tried to explain the directions to Max.

They got in the car and headed out of town. Since the man following them knew the way himself, he felt no need to follow too closely. Once they were out of town, they turned onto the country road and realized the need to slow down because it was in poor condition. There were ruts and holes and looked as if it had been a long time since it was paved. Max looked at the clock in the car and told Josie it would be dark soon and he was having second thoughts about starting out so late in the day.

Josie said "It doesn't look like we can turn around here. It's too narrow and unsafe. Let's just follow it for a while and see if it gets any better. There may be other houses down the road."

Max looked at her. He was surprised at how comfortable he felt with her. It had been a long time since he had thought about having a relationship with someone. He wondered what it would be like to kiss her lips. He shook his head and tried to dismiss those thought. Now, of all times, he needed to stay focused. As they approached a rise in the road he glanced in his rear view mirror and was surprised to see a car speeding down the road behind him.

"What the............." He didn't have time to finish. The car was directly behind them and not slowing down. He had nowhere to pull over out of the way. He yelled to Josie to hold on, he knew they were going to be hit from behind. Just as he got the words out, the car ran directly into the back of their car. Max struggled to keep the car under control. The car started to swerve and the other car continued to try and hit them again. The trunk popped up blocking his view. He looked in the side mirror and saw the car beginning to approach again. He stomped on the gas to try and gain speed. He didn't know where they were or what was going on. The only thing he knew is that they were in trouble. He looked in the mirror again and realized the car had dropped back. It appeared to be smoking. Maybe the radiator was damaged. He could only hope. Anything to get away from it. Just as Max was starting to think they had outrun the other car, it appeared behind them again. Suddenly another shock went thru the car. It had been hit again. Max held tight onto the wheel. He swerved in and out of the field beside the road. The other car seemed to be backing off.

"I'm not sure if he is still able to drive. If so, you can count on being attacked again. That is one scary dude."

Josie was shaking and afraid to speak. Max was doing a great job so far. At least they were still alive. She was afraid to speak and have her voice betray her fear to Max. He had enough worry right now trying to get away. She looked out the side windows and tried to spot a house where they could seek help. The road was deserted. Just farmland. No mailboxes or roads leading off this road. Nothing to indicate anyone lived here. She wondered if all this land belonged to Clyde. Lily had never said how big it was. They rode for another five minutes and the car suddenly stalled. Max cursed.

"Just when we thought we were safe. Now what?" He asked more to think for himself that to expect and answer from Josie. He started to laugh and laugh. Josie was getting scared.

Then Max spoke "Sorry, guess nervous energy. The car reminded me of a horse in an old western. It gets shot and keeps running. Then all the sudden it drops to the ground. You know, as if it just realizes it was shot a while ago?"

Josie looked at Max, reached over and kissed him. This surprised both of them.

"Sorry, I am grateful that you saved our lives and I thought you needed something to relieve the tension."

Max looked at Josie "Funny, I was thinking of doing the same thing myself. But for now, let get the heck out of here. I feel like we are a sitting target and that guy seemed pretty determined. We need to move as far away from the car as we can and be quick about it. He may be on his way to find us. I doubt that we lost him for long. He didn't act like someone who gave up easily."

They decided to head back into town. They were not sure if there were any other houses out here. Prospects of getting help seemed slim. Better to return to town than chance going further into the unknown. It was already dusk and they were in unfamiliar territory.

"We will need to get well over toward the field, off the road as far as possible, so we can keep hidden. We also need to make sure we follow the road back and be careful we don't keep heading in circles. I'll watch out for anyone coming our way and you watch the distance from the road. That might help us from getting confused. Keep your ears open for any sound. We don't want to run into anyone in this field. Now I wish we had let Danny come. He would have had a gun."

He looked at her and grinned "But then I might have missed out on that kiss."

Josie smiled to herself. She reached out and took his hand and they started back to town. They walked for close to thirty minutes and it was now totally dark. Max suggested they sit down for a few minutes and Josie was grateful for the offer. They were not sure how far they had come or how far they had to go. They also had not seen the other car either damaged or running. If it was broken down, where did the guy leave it? They were both pretty sure they had passed the area of the last impact. Neither one wanted to go over to the road to check. They decide to stay as far off the road as possible to avoid discovery just in case he was laying in wait for them.

They walked for another hour and decided they may be lost. Although they had tried to follow the road, they may have misjudged a turn because they were in the field well off the road. It was almost too dark to see much in front of them.

"I know you probably won't relish the idea but I think we need to stop and wait for daylight. I'm afraid we are getting too far off track and we need the light to continue. Plus I cannot see the ground anymore and we increase our chance of getting injured by tripping on the uneven ground."

Josie was thinking the same thing. She told Max that was fine and they chose a place behind a large rock to give them a measure of protection. They sat down and leaned against the rock. Max put his arm around her to ward off the chill that had set in. After a short while she fell asleep. She started to dream. She was running toward Max and things kept getting in her way. First Lily was looking out behind bars, Danny was standing out in the road blocking her off and Max kept calling to her. She kept running faster and could not reach him. She heard Max calling her name. She yelled to him to let him know she was coming. Suddenly, she felt someone holding her arms, and shaking her awake. She flew open her eyes and looked right into Max's eyes. She instinctively reached out and threw her arms around his neck and kissed him long and hard.

He returned her kiss. Finally she pulled away confused. "Sorry again. I was having a dream I lost you and could not get to you because someone was always blocking my way. You must think I'm a sex maniac."

Max laughed so hard he though he may pass out. He looked at Josie and said "You are the most wonderful person I have ever met. You say exactly what you think and you mean what you say. And as a matter of fact, I like it when you act like a sex maniac."

He leaned over and gave her a long kiss. As she responded, he felt himself grow hard. He was drunk with desire. It had been so long and Josie shook him to the core. He ran his hands over her breast and kissed her throat. She gasped and reached out to unzip his pants. Suddenly they both stopped. They were so in tuned to each other they knew they would both consent to whatever the other one wanted. They also both knew they wanted this to mean something and not a hurried satisfying of sexual desires. Max was the first to speak.

"I want to make love to you more than anything I have wanted to do in a long time. But I want to make love to you, not just have sex. I want you to remember it and for it to mean something to both of us."

Josie was secretly disappointed. It had been a long time since she had had sex. When she thought about it, she had never had anyone make love to her. She looked into Max's eyes and saw raw desire that matched her own. She also saw someone who would care about her. She gave him a kiss and told him she would see him that night in her bed. They both laughed and knew it would be a long night.

Once the dawn broke, they both stood up and looked around. Still no houses in view. They decide to take a chance and walk toward the road. They had a good view of the road in both directions and could not see any sign of an abandoned car.

"I think we have enough distance each way to see if a car approaches in either direction. If we spot anything we will have enough time to run into the field, lie down and hide. So let's continue on the road."

After an hour, they came to the fork in the road where they had left the paved road the night before. Max said, "It seems so long ago, I can't remember if we passed anything before we turned off, do you?"

Josie shook her head. "I was too busy enjoying your company." She squeezed his arm. "I'd give almost anything for a cup of coffee and I don't really like coffee that much."

He laughed and put his arm around her. Funny, he thought to himself, she feels like she belongs right here in my arms.

Soon the road curved and they noticed a small store and gas station. "Let's hope it is open."

Once they arrived there, they discovered it was open and did have a pot of coffee. Max went to use the pay phone to call the hotel and Lily poured two cups of coffee. When Max returned, he told her Danny was on his way and paid the man for the coffee.

"I'm surprised Danny didn't have the National Guard out looking for you. He seems to think a lot of you."

Max looked at Josie. "I know you and he have rubbed each other the wrong way but you have only seen him at his worst. He loves Lily more that life itself. He is also one of the best friends I have ever had. He is very loyal and a fair person. Believe it or not, he is one hell of a sheriff. He is well respected in the town. He brings out the best in everyone."

Josie laughed "Except me."

"Well, I know that's how you feel now but promise me you will give him a chance. You will be surprised. Remember you love Lily and he loves Lily. He is really scared shitless for her right now."

"Ok, for you, I'll try my best." He bent down and kissed her.

Chapter 38

On the way back to town, Max and Josie went over in detail all that had happen the night before, leaving out the private parts. Danny told them he was sorry he was not able to find them but no one took him seriously. The sheriff thought it was a big joke. In fact he implied that you two were off having sex somewhere.

Josie blushed and was glad Danny was in the front seat driving and could not see her face. Max said, "That shows you what a prick he is. Josie and I are more than capable of making love right there in the hotel instead of out in a field somewhere."

He surprised himself at the words he had spoken but Danny seemed unaware of anything between Max and Josie. His thoughts were currently only on Lily.

"I'll stop and get you two something to eat, drop Josie off, and then I'll take you back to find your car. After we find out how bad the damage is, we will arrange to get it towed so we can get it repaired. I also need to rent a car. I borrowed this one from the hotel clerk and have to get it back."

They stopped by the hotel, returned the car and found Millie in her room. She hugged Josie and tears filled her eyes.

"I was so scared. So was Danny. You can't imagine what he went through to try to find you. No one would help us. I can't tell you how glad I am that you both are ok."

They left and went out to get breakfast. Once they finished, Danny and Max left to find a rental car. Millie and Josie headed back to the hotel.

"Now Josie, you look exhausted. My goodness, spending the night out in that field, I know you were terrified. Go up to your room and take a long bath or a nice hot shower and try to get a little sleep. I'll come wake you when the men return or if I hear from the lawyer. Just in case she calls before they get back, I'll be in my room making some business calls."

Josie decided on the shower because she was afraid she would fall asleep in the tub. It seemed like she had just laid down in bed when there was a knock on her door.

"Just a minute." She hurried out of bed and opened the door.

Max slipped into the room and immediately took her into his arms.

"How long until we can safely go to bed?"

Josie laughed and grabbed her clothes and ran into the bathroom to dress. Once she came back out, Max was sitting in a chair looking exhausted himself. She sat on his lap and cuddled with him. Both were amazed at how quickly they had become comfortable with each other.

Max told her the car was not damaged too badly, other than the appearance. Just the back tires and rear end work, which could be fixed here. It should be drivable until they got it home to get it checked out by his mechanic. Danny had rented a car to use. The lawyer had called for them to meet her at two o'clock this afternoon.

"How did she sound?"

"Actually, Millie talked to her. She seemed to think we may have some good news. In fact, she sent me up to wake you. I get the feeling she suspects something?"

Josie laughed "I get the feeling she knew before we did."

They all met back in the hotel lobby and caught up on what was going on. Josie explained the feeling she had that she was being followed before everyone arrived in town. She thought the accident may be directed more at her that at Max. Danny asked her some questions to try and figure out why. Josie had never been here before so it was unlikely that anyone knew her. Suddenly, he had a strange feeling that maybe it was directed back to Lily. After all, they had arrived in town together and someone definitely sounded like they didn't want Josie anywhere near her. Although they all listened to his theory, no one really thought that was the case. However, Max insisted they all be on guard and not leave Josie alone.

Josie looked at Max and hoped he meant inside her room too. He glanced at her and she saw the beginning of a smile as if he had the same thought.

As they entered the law office the first thing they all noticed as they sat in the waiting room, were the files sitting everywhere. The law assistant looked overwhelmed.

Mille asked "Do you have this much business in such a small town?"

The girl looked up and replied, "Actually since Ms. Adams took over the practice from her uncle, we have been going over his files. Some are so old everything is handwritten. I'm overwhelmed with the amount of paperwork that is here."

Millie silently hoped that they were devoting enough time to new cases. Her first thought centered on the doubt that they had chosen the best lawyer for Lily but realized there was not much other choice in this town. She needed to discuss that with Ms. Adams as soon as they were able to talk with her.

"Sorry you have to wait. We are running behind today but I know she wants to see you", the girl informed them.

Honestly, she did look overwhelmed, answering the phones, typing and trying to make some order in the vast paperwork in front of her. Millie felt sorry for her but remembered she had to put that aside right now and assert herself for Lily's sake.

After more than twenty minutes, the door opened and Ms. Adams called them into her office.

They sat down and were offered coffee, which they all declined. Millie was the first to speak, "I trust you realize how important it is to us to get Lilly out of jail immediately. I couldn't help noticing how bogged down your assistant is right now. I want to make sure we are not lost somewhere in all your paperwork."

The lawyer's face clouded over then relaxed. "Sorry, I can understand what you must think. Honestly, I was not expecting to be so busy. I just took over the practice from my uncle and his filing was atrocious. Luckily, I don't have too many new cases right now, but I assure you, they are my first priority. Tracy is doing a good job out front. But I'm really going to have to consider getting someone in here to help her, at least temporarily, in order to get the old files straightened out."

Millie felt bad for being so blunt but was pleased that she had made her point. "Well, now that we are here, we hope you have some good news for us."

"I do have some news. Not sure if you will think it is good or not. I was able to meet with Lily. She is adamant that she take the blame. She wanted to protect all of you, especially Danny, from any further worry. She worded it ....*she did not want Danny subject to any conflicts with his job.* After I spoke to the sheriff, I realized why, since you yourself are a Sheriff, Mr. McCain. Now, from what I could find out from Sheriff Axelrod, he wants to charge her with leaving the scene of a crime, failure to report a crime, accessory to murder, and whatever else he can come up with. He is waiting for the Prosecutor to come in from the county seat. Meanwhile, he said she is a flight risk and is going to fight her posting bail. I don't think they have much of a case against her as far as evidence is concerned. However, she did willingly come in and confess. That's my biggest problem right now. Also, unfortunately, it is an election year and I get the impression that this will be the major factor in his reelection. Solving this case will get him votes. He does not want to chance losing this publicity right now."

"How was Lily? Was she being treated ok?" asked Josie.

"Yes, as far as I could tell she seemed frightened but not scared if you know what I mean. Obviously, she is sorry she caused you all so much pain and she is not sure what is going to happen to her. I can tell she did not think this through. She just had this need to confess and get it behind her. I agree with you, she did not realize that once you confess, it is over with. She is naïve in that sense. She can't just say she's sorry and get a slap on the hand or community service. This is serious...."

"I want to see her." Danny broke in.

"Honestly Danny, you made a very bad impression with the Sheriff. I did ask him and he is not receptive to the idea. However, I told him I would not take no for an answer and I would guarantee your cooperation. Now I need you to promise me that you will behave and focus strictly on helping Lily. So far you have not presented yourself well."

Danny hung his head. He knew she was right. Everyone had been saying the same thing. Josie, Max, even Millie and the lawyer. He knew he had to get himself together.

"Ok. I know I have acted like an ass. I feel so helpless I can't think or control myself. Now I understand why doctors do not treat their family members. It makes you forget who you really are."

Josie surprised both herself and Danny by leaning over, giving him a hug, and said, "I know it's hard, but you have to be strong for Lily and help the best way you can."

Danny found it difficult to speak but said, "Thank you. That means a lot to me."

Max glanced at the exchange. He knew it took a lot for Josie to say that and he realized he was falling deeper in love with her the more he was around her.

Ms. Adams watched them and thought Lily was lucky to have such support behind her. She only hoped she could help them. This was going to be a tough case to handle with the defendant confessing to the crime. She prayed she was good enough to defend Lily.

"Ok, now I need to go with you Danny. That's the only way you can get into see Lily. Unfortunately, you are the only one I can take. But I'll work on getting her more visitors, if it goes all right with your visit. So you see Danny, you have a lot riding on your visit." She smiled and added, "I know you'll do fine."

Danny agreed to meet at nine o'clock in the morning to head over. They realized there was no more to be discussed today and they headed out.

Max told them to head into the bar for an afternoon drink and he would meet them there. He wanted to call home and make sure Rosie was ok and let his mother know what was happening.

"Don't tell her about the car accident", said Danny.

"Do you think I'm nuts? You know she would be on the next bus out of town and Rosie would find out I'm sure. No, I'll just fill her in on Lily for now."

Max spent the next few minutes reassuring Rosie and Madge that everything was going well. He told her Danny would see Lily in the morning. He tried to keep the concern out of his voice. Even though Madge could hear it, she was determined not to let him know she too, was afraid for Lily.

Josie ordered a coke, Millie and Madge hot tea and both Max and Danny decided they needed a beer. Each one tried to be brave for each other but not one believed they were succeeding. Max looked at Danny, "How about you and I ride out to the farm? I think I know the way now. I'd feel safer if you took your gun. I don't want Josie in danger again. I'm starting to wonder if there is something we are not supposed to find out. We need to pursue that."

Danny looked at Max. It was better than sitting around. "But what about Josie? We need to make sure she is safe and of course Millie too."

Max replied, "We shouldn't be too long. We have a different car now. Millie and Josie should sit here in the bar in plain sight of the bartender and waitress. The after work crowd should be coming in soon. Then they will be surrounded by people. We'll be back for dinner. What do you say girls?"

"Well, it's been a long time since anyone called me a girl but I think Josie and I will be fine in here," laughed Millie.

After they left Millie decided to question Josie.

"Have you given any thought about how long you are going to stay here?"

"No. Not really. I haven't thought that far ahead. I don't have anything to get back to anyway."

"Well, you must be running out of money. I'm sure Danny and especially Max have to leave soon. I worry about you staying here by yourself. I don't mean to interfere. You don't owe me an explanation but I worry about these things."

"No that's ok. I guess I should think about it. I have been so focused on Lily, I really haven't thought ahead."

"I've noticed that you have thought of one other thing" Millie teased her.

"Is it obvious?"

"Only to me but I wouldn't be surprised if Danny wasn't going to start noticing anytime soon".

"I'm sorry. I know it's a bad time but the more I'm around Max, the more I think he could be the one."

"No need to apologize to me. I'm happy for you. For Lily too. Both Max and Danny seem like nice boys."

Now Josie laughed, "Boys?"

"Well to me, you are all kids", Millie laughed.

They sat there for a while in silence, both lost in their own thoughts.

"Millie, what about you? You have a business to get back to. You must be close to the time you need to leave. I've been selfish, only thinking about myself and Lily. I'm sorry."

"That isn't why I asked. But yes, soon I have to leave. I really don't want to. But there is no one else to help me out with the shipments since Lily left. I should think about retiring."

"No you shouldn't, you love what you do. You should think about hiring some employees to help you out more. You never seemed so happy, as when Lily was there."

"Honey, she did help out. In fact a lot but it was her that I enjoyed. I doubt if I'll ever find that again, no matter who I hire."

They both became silent again. The cocktail waitress came over and asked if they needed anything. Millie felt guilty taking up a booth in a prime location but felt safe sitting there. "Yes, we will both take a refill and do you by chance have any appetizers we can order?"

The waitress left and returned with a menu. Millie urges Josie to order something so they could continue sitting in the booth without people looking at them and wanting them to move on. They ordered the things that Millie thought would take the longest to prepare and the waitress went away satisfied. She apologized for bothering them but several customers had asked her how long she thought it would be until they vacated the booth. She explained that once they ordered, she knew the questions would stop.

"I had that same problem at Denny's especially on Sunday. When we were busy customers did not like to wait on a table."

They continued to sit there long after the appetizers appeared on the table. Neither one was hungry and knew they wanted to be able to eat something when Max and Danny returned for dinner. No one bothered them again and soon the bar emptied out as the after work crowd headed home.

Chapter 39

Danny and Max headed out the way Max had remembered from the last trip with Josie. Danny drove and Max kept a lookout for anyone following them that may look familiar. Cars were on the road but none appeared to be interested in them. Most only were behind them for a short time and then turned off. Not one had continued the same distance for very long.

Once they turned onto the unpaved road, Danny decreased his speed.

"See if you can see any signs of where the other car hit you. We may be able to pick up some debris and trace it."

They traveled for several miles and Danny stopped suddenly.

"Look over there. Is that something on the side of the road?"

Max hopped out but left the door open in case the needed to move quickly. Danny kept an eye out on the road in both directions. So far they had not passed anyone or anything for that matter. Max returned holding a metal piece.

"Not sure if this is new or not. Could have been there a long time. There are no tire marks or signs of any other pieces. Let's move on." He tossed it on the floor in the back seat.

Danny commented on the fields as they drove up the road. "I'm not a farmer but this sure doesn't looks like farmland. Look at all the rocks there and some large boulders. Now I see how you were able to hide. It would be tough to plow. I doubt if it was ever farmed."

They drove about thirty minutes up the road until they spotted a house and barn. Danny eased up even more on the gas pedal so they could approach it without causing suspicion. He knew from experience, if he drove up fast, it would alert the owners to danger. If they drove slow, it would appear that they were in no hurry.

As Danny suspected, as they approached, a man stepped into the road.

The man appeared to be in his late fifties, beard and hair, more grey than brown, and wearing bib overalls. His appearance indicated he did not leave the farm often. There were traces of hay on his pant legs.

He asked, "You lost?"

Danny answered, since he was driving, as the man was approaching the driver side of the car. "We are looking for Clyde Hill. Heard this is his farm."

"Well you are a little late for Clyde", he pointed past the house. "He is buried over there but this is, or I should say was, his farm."

"Did you buy it from him?"

"Didn't buy it, just renting from the bank."

"Do you mind if we look around? We came all the way out here and I'd appreciate if you would give us a little tour. I'll make it worth your while". Danny took out his wallet and handed the man twenty dollars.

"Well, not much to see but for twenty dollars I'll show you what I can."

They started out in the barn and walked around the house. Danny and Max stopped to read the tombstones. Then Max asked, "Did we hear about finding a body buried somewhere here?"

"Yeah, come this way I'll show you. Right under the kitchen window. Funny thing that. We had to dig up the plumbing under the window. The pipes got clogged up. Found the bones. With a graveyard here, why would anyone bury a body there? My wife's the one that though I should call the sheriff. They took the body away. Never heard who it was."

They stopped and looked at the spot. They looked at each other as if to say *that is very strange since there was a graveyard on the property.*

The man wanted to know if they wanted to see the inside of the house. Danny looked at Max. For some reason he was reluctant to intrude on Lily's past almost like an invasion of privacy but yet he wanted to know all about her.

"Yes, we would be grateful if it is no trouble", said Max, as if he read Danny's thoughts.

"Not really much to see, nothing has changes since I started renting the place right after Clyde died. Did replace the sink and part of the kitchen floor to repair the damage. Place came furnished. It's pretty much like Clyde left it."

They walked through the rooms and Danny was overcome with sadness. He realized this was Lily's life before he met her. As he got to the bedroom, he was overcome with jealousy at the thought of Lily belonging to someone else and now he realized she may never belong to him. He may never be able to hold her in his arms, make love to her or tell her all the things he should have told her.

Max felt badly for Danny. He could see how hard this was on him. Maybe it was not a good idea to come inside.

"Guess we have held you up long enough. Thanks for being so helpful and showing us around."

"Not much to do anymore. Since my wife died, I don't have company and don't go out much. Actually, thinking about leaving here myself. Not sure what to do."

"Well good luck on whatever you decide."

As they approached the car Danny's attention was drawn to the tree by the house. He stopped to look at it. Max reached into his pocket and withdrew another twenty. He felt guilty for intruding on this man and he seemed like he could use the money.

"You gave us more than the twenty dollar tour. I'd appreciate it if you would accept this from me" he shook the man's hand and opened the car door. He could tell the man was embarrassed at accepting the money but grateful for the offer.

Danny shook his head as if trying to clear it. Then he turned and came over and got in the car without saying anything.

Max thanked the man again, turned the car around and drove back to town. He kept glancing at Danny but he did not seem interested in talking. Max focused his attention on the road. He was grateful Danny did not put up any objections to letting him drive but he could tell Danny was too preoccupied to pay attention to the road right now.

Chapter 40

Josie saw them enter the hotel and waved to them to get their attention. Max nudged Danny to follow him into the bar.

"Well, is everything alright? I see you ordered some food. Didn't know they had a dining room in here."

"We have been here since you two left. We were getting some glares from the after work crowd so Millie ordered appetizers so we could stake our claim here. Smart, huh?" laughed Josie.

Max looked at the cold appetizers and realized he was hungry.

"Hope we weren't gone too long. To tell you the truth I could eat the biggest steak I can buy. I am suddenly famished. How about we go get something to eat and turn in early. We'll fill you in about our trip at dinner."

Josie blushed and hoped no one noticed. Millie agreed that they all must be tired and dinner then, rest, sounded good to her. Danny just shrugged his shoulders and followed them out.

Once the waitress came over to take their orders, Max found there was a large steak available. Millie ordered a Cobb Salad, Josie Pasta Primavera and Danny just ordered a Cheeseburger. Max filled Millie and Josie in on the visit to the farm and what they had learned.

"It does seem strange that there was a graveyard and yet the body was buried by the house. If it had been in the graveyard, there probably would have not been any chance of finding it", said Millie.

"Really strange", said Josie. "I wonder why?"

No one really had an answer. Danny hardly ate and did not join in on the discussion. Once the check arrived they paid and headed back to the hotel. Max was yawning from the amount of food he ate and his lack of sleep. He told Millie he would walk Josie back to her room.

Max dropped Josie off outside her room and kissed her goodnight. He whispered in her ear "I'll be right back." He and Danny headed back to their room and Josie told Millie goodnight. Millie winked at her and smiled.

Once Max got back to the room he shared with Danny, he told him he was spending the night with Josie to protect her. Danny looked at him but did not seem to understand the real reason. He looked so lost that Max felt sorry for him.

"Now promise you will get some sleep so you can see Lily tomorrow. She will need you rested and your mind clear." Danny nodded and went over and lay on the bed. Max hoped he would be tired enough to sleep.

Max had brought his overnight bag so he could shower and shave in Josie's room. As he knocked on the door, he heard the shower running. He used the key Josie had slipped in his hand when he kissed her outside the door. He removed his clothes and stepped inside the shower with her. He was immediately hard. God she was beautiful. He reached for her and enveloped her into a kiss.

She laughed "You don't waste any time, do you buster?"

Max ran his hands down her back and then came up and cupped each breast in his hands. He was amazed at how well they fit into his hands like they were molded just to fit there. He kissed her and sucked on her lower lip.

"You don't know how hard it has been not to do this in front of everyone. I have wanted to taste and devour every inch of your body. Do you know what you do to me?"

Josie's voice grew husky, "Nothing more than I have wanted to do to you."

They continued to explore each other's body, yet each was surprised at the ease in which they knew where to touch and how to satisfy. It was as if they had been there before. It was the realization that nothing had come before or would come after. Their bodies made a commitment to each other long before their hearts and minds did. They recognized the reason they were created and why they found each other. Both were close to the edge of passion. Max lifted her up and carried her to the bed. Both were dripping wet and yet unaware of anything except the animal instinct to bring each other to fulfillment. Once he entered her, there was no holding back. Both climaxed at once. Both were satisfied and clung to each other. Neither felt the cool air touching their wet bodies. Neither wanted to ever part. Max remained inside of her. Josie contracted her muscles to hold him there.

Finally Max spoke, "Josie, I never want to leave you."

Josie murmured, "Mummm, I agree."

Immediately, Max felt himself growing hard again. He wanted to make this last. He kissed her hard on the lips and ran his tongue over her teeth, then he moved down to her neck and nuzzled her throat. He sucked on her earlobes and moved down to her breast. They were firm and erect. He sucked on her nipples and heard her groan. He continued to move down her body stopping to explore each new place. He ran his tongue around her belly button. He continued down into the silkiness of her womanhood then he parted her and began to explore with his lips and tongue. She shook in ecstasy and grabbed his hair as she began to climax. Max immediately withdrew and moved back up to her breast. He did not want this to end too quickly. He wanted to raise her to the peak and bring her back. He wanted her to beg for him to enter her. He wanted this to be the best she had ever had. He wanted her to remember their first time together. He wanted to possess her and never let her go. Soon they were covered in sweat. The air was no longer cold in the room. Their scents mingled in the sheets under them and their bodies were wrapped so tight it was hard to remember that they had never been this way before. They climaxed at the same time. How could something be so right? How could they ever go about their daily lives apart after this? Both were thinking the same question.

Both exclaimed at the same time, "I love you."

Max propped himself up on his elbow and played with her nipple.

"Josie, I cannot even think of being without you. I can't imagine how my life can ever be the same now that I found you. Even though I was married before, I never knew this type of happiness could exist. You have to come home with me. You have to marry me."

Josie looked at his face and reached up and ran her hand across his furrowed brow. She felt the same way, but knew they had other people to consider right now.

"We have to remember why we are here. Lily needs me. Needs us. You also have Rosie to think about. You can't just bring me into her life and say this is my new wife."

Max knew she was right. He was consumed in need. He needed her. He never realized it was possible to need anyone this much.

"I can't let you go. What can we do? This is not a one night stand. This is forever. Hell, I didn't even think of protection. Did you? I just knew it was right and that I was making a commitment as soon as I touched you. This is forever."

Josie reached over and kissed him. She felt herself begin to moisten and thought *will we ever get satisfied?* As soon as she deepened her kiss, she felt him grow and cover her body. Satisfied again, they fell asleep wrapped in each other's arms. Soon it was getting light out. Max awoke and looked at the clock on the nightstand. He ran his hand between Josie's legs and realized she was ready to receive him. "Are you awake?"

She laughed and said, "I felt you move", as she reached out and enveloped his swollen penis in her hand.

Once they were sated, Max told her they needed to get up and dress. She persuaded him to take a shower together and then they would get ready for the day. She was surprised at his stamina and her desire. But she was too engrossed in touching his body and his exploration of hers to hurry the shower. They finally felt waterlogged and were content with drying each other.

"I feel like a teenager having sex for the first time. Is this for real at my age?"

Josie told him she was glad he wasn't a teenager because then he wouldn't know what places satisfied her. They both laughed and got dressed to face whatever the day brought.

She called Millie's room and asked if she was ready for breakfast and Max left to check on Danny. They agreed to meet downstairs.

Once they were eating breakfast, they all felt rested and satisfied. Danny looked like he had slept and was not as pensive as he was yesterday.

"Have you decided what you are going to say to Lily? Well, after the personal things", Max asked. "We need to know what we can do. So we are counting on you to let us know."

"I hope she tells me more than just that's she guilty. I hope to find out why the body was buried where it was. And that tree seemed to be calling out to me. Funny, huh?"

Danny left to meet the lawyer and head to jail to visit Lily. Millie decided to walk back with Danny to the Hotel. She had some business calls to make and it was close to where Danny was going. Josie and Max decided to linger in the diner and talk. Neither thought they could go back to the hotel. It was hard to concentrate on anything when they were alone together. They both knew they would end up in bed again. Best to stay in a public place.

"I need to know what you are going to do, Josie. I have to get back home soon and I do not feel comfortable leaving you here alone. I'm sure Millie is going to leave soon too. Danny doesn't want to, but he does have a responsibility to the people in our town, so he will have to go back and catch up on his work." Max looked at Josie and decided to wait for her thoughts, before he voiced his opinion on what he wanted her to do.

She looked at him but did not speak for a few minutes. He could see she was thinking about his question.

"I don't know how I can leave her here alone. She had no one to look out for her. I know you all have to get back to work and right now, I'm the only one without a job so it is up to me to stay."

"But can you afford to stay here? We have no friends that you could stay with, no one to look out for you. Don't forget, there is someone out there that may be dangerous. Someone has been watching you. I'm afraid that as soon as we leave, he will try something. I trust the sheriff here about as much as I trust a car with no brakes."

Josie laughed at his analogy. She knew he was right, but now, she wasn't sure just what to do. She looked at her cooling coffee and thought about her options. Max was right; she really could not afford to stay. She had no job and very little money left. This town did not appear to have any opportunity for finding a job. From what she had observed since she had been here, most of the businesses had long term employees and not an overabundance of those.

"Are you ok? Did I say something wrong?" Max sounded worried.

She looked up and noticed his face. His eyebrows were drawn together and caused his forehead to look like the letter *H.* How much she was learning about him. She knew when he had that look on his face. It indicated that he was concerned about something. Very concerned.

"No what you said was true. I do need to have a plan. I can't just camp out on the jail steps." She laughed to ease the tension but her laugh fell flat. "I really don't know what to do. I guess Lily and I did not think any of this through before we acted. Now I see how foolish that was. Maybe once Danny gets back, he may have some information and that might make it easier to decide." She shook her head and deep down doubted it would.

They decided to take a walk around town to pass the time. Max was hoping to get a glimpse of whoever had followed Josie but did not want her to know. Max put his arm around Josie's shoulder and they decided to explore the entire town. So far, they had only ventured into the streets that were part of the business area, and had not seen any of the residential streets.

The town bore out Josie's impression that it had stopped growing long ago and had done little to renew itself. No signs of any new businesses or anything that appeared to have been modernized since it opened. Josie looked at Max and laughed. "Do you think they ever get new stuff in the store? I bet we would find new clothes on racks that we now see in second-hand stores in other cities."

Max laughed. "You know, I bet you are right. Want to check it out?"

They entered several stores and had fun going through the merchandise. Josie had been right. Max had to admit it was a sorry selection.

"If you see anything decent that I can buy to take back to Rosie, let me know. She loves little surprises and I hate to disappoint her. I have had to leave her so much lately."

"Ok, we'll see what we can find." Max and Josie both enjoyed the break from worrying about Lily and their first experience shopping together. Neither one bought anything, but the merchandise was interesting and elicited some funny comments between them. Anyone observing them, would mistake them for a couple enjoying each other's company without a care in the world.

At the last store, Josie saw an old place setting made for a child. She examined it and found it to be in excellent condition. The price was more than reasonable and she decided to buy it. Max agreed it would be a good idea.

"She'll feel like a real grown up with her own china dishes. I doubt if we can find a toy here that I would feel is safe. They all look so dated; they probably missed any recall if there was one."

Next they headed down the residential streets. Just like the stores, the houses looked aged. Most were kept up. Lawns were mowed and paint was not visibly peeling but far from fresh looking. They both agreed if they peeked into any windows, they were certain the original kitchens and most likely the furniture would still be there.

"Funny how different towns can be. I don't know why, but I would not want to live here if I had a choice." Josie said more to herself than to Max. She shivered and felt a sadness hanging over this town.

Soon they had been walking for an hour and were surprised at how fast the time had flown since they left the diner. Most of the houses they passed appeared to be occupied. Very few indicated children were living in them. Very few had bikes, wagons or toys in the yard and the school they passed looked very small. Now Josie realized why she felt the sadness. The town had lost its most valuable resource. For some reason, the town could not renew itself through the next generation because there simply weren't enough young people to carry the town. How sad, she thought. Do they even realize what is happening?

When they reached the hotel, Millie was sitting in a chair reading. They asked if Danny had returned and she stated she had not seen him but she had been in her room catching up on business matters. Max decided to go up and check his room to see if Danny had returned. If so, they would be right down to go over his visit with Lily.

Chapter 41

Danny walked over to the lawyer's office to meet with her before their visit with Lily. The office had no one else waiting. The assistant was busy with files. Danny surveyed the clutter of paper and wondered how they could find anything if they needed to. He hoped Lily's paperwork was not mixed in with the other papers. You hear all the time about important papers being lost or misfiled. He knew he was getting paranoid but just thinking about Lily's chances of getting out of jail, caused him to focus on everything that may make a difference. He was about to say something, when the door to the office opened and the lawyer walked out into the reception area.

"Hi, Danny I'm glad you are on time. Come in for a few minutes so we can discuss our visit."

Danny scowled at her, "I know how to act. No lectures."

"I'm not going to lecture you. I just want you to understand that we are at the mercy of the sheriff. If you piss him off, you will be in and out before you have a chance to sit down, let alone be able to speak to Lily. I need your cooperation here. Just humor me and tell me you can handle this."

Danny nodded his head. "Yes, I understand and I will put my personal feelings aside."

"I'll be watching you. If I think you are getting yourself in trouble, I'm going to step in before the sheriff does. Now let's get going".

They walked over to the jail side by side and as soon as they approached the door, Ms. Adams patted his arm. "You ok?"

Danny opened the door for her and said, "Yes," without much conviction.

The lawyer told the Deputy at the front desk who she was and that she was there to meet with her client Ms. Hill. She him that Danny was accompanying her to the meeting and it had been cleared with Sheriff Axelrod.

The Deputy left the desk after telling them to wait. He returned shortly and told Danny he would have to be searched before they were allowed in. The lawyer could bring in a briefcase but all her personal effect would need to be left with him. TJ had no personal effects because she knew the procedure .She had left her purse in the office. Danny was searched and his pockets emptied. Once that was done, they went to meet Lily.

They were escorted to Lily's cell. Danny immediately felt his cheeks start to burn. He was furious at how they were being treated. Not even allowed to meet in an office somewhere. He stepped in and immediately felt his heart break. Poor Lily. He glanced at her face. She was so pale. Her face had lost all its innocence. Now it was replaced with sadness and resignation.

Their eyes met at the same time. If he lived to be a hundred, he would never forget what he saw there. Hurt and despair. Had he hurt her that much? Could he ever make it up to her? Could he ever forgive himself? God, how could I have been such a fool? So many thoughts ran thru his mind that he could not speak. Suddenly, Ms. Adams nudged his arm. He cleared his thoughts and knew he had to say the right thing now if he was ever going to get back Lily's trust.

He moved toward her. He enveloped her in a hug and said, "Lily, I am here for you. We will get through this together. I'm sorry if I hurt you."

Suddenly she began to cry. "Danny, thank you for coming. I have been so scared and alone. I didn't think anyone would care about me anymore after they knew what I had done."

Ms. Adams coughed. "I'm afraid you two need to sit down. You are not allowed physical contact."

Lily looked around her small cell. "I guess we can sit on the bed. There is a chair here too."

Lily and her attorney sat on the bed and Danny pulled the chair over so he was facing Lily. The attorney spoke to both of them. "I don't know how much time we will have together so let's get started on what we know and what we don't know. First, the paperwork has come thru to charge you with murder. I think they want to scare you into pleading to a lesser offense. They don't have any proof other than your confession. We need to discuss everything that happened. No matter how bad. Now is not the time to hold anything back. I need to know the whole story. And the true story. No matter how bad you think it is, we cannot fight this without knowing what we are dealing with. Now, Lily, if you want to talk to me in private, that's understandable. Danny will do anything to help you get out of here. He will understand if there is something you want to tell me in private. Isn't that right, Danny?"

Danny reached out and took Lily's hand in his. "Please don't let my actions in the past influence your decision now. I want you to do whatever you can to get out of here. If you are uncomfortable speaking in front of me, I'll understand. I just want you to know that I have had a lot of time to think about us. I know I never want to live without you again. The time you were gone was the worst time of my life up to now. I won't lose you again."

Lily looked at Danny and realized he was telling her the truth. She saw the love and also the pain reflected in his eyes. She looked at his face and noticed how drawn he looked. She was sure he meant everything he said.

"Ok, I want to tell you both everything. I need to be free of the ghost that sit on my shoulders and pierce my heart. I don't think I will ever be free of them. When I tell you everything, I'm sure you will know why."

Ms. Adams got out her yellow legal pad to begin taking notes. Danny sat back in his chair to give Lily room to begin. She started her story back as far as she remembered growing up and did not stop until she returned to this town. During the story, Danny had many emotions, anger, fear, pity and total love for this girl that had suffered so much and yet she had retained her innocence and goodness. How was it possible for someone to survive such a life?

The attorney did not interrupt to ask any questions. She made notes to go over and clarify but did not want to stop Lily until she was done. The story was so riveting that she felt at times as though someone was telling her of a movie they had seen. Nothing could be like this in real life, she thought. She listened so intently at times, she did not notice the tears that ran down her face. She was totally engrossed in hearing all that Lily was saying.

Once Lily was finished, neither Danny nor Ms. Adams, could speak. She reached into her briefcase and removed a box of tissues.

The Sheriff appeared at the door to the cell, "You all have used up your time. I need to get the prisoner fed her dinner before the night staff comes on duty. You have five minutes to finish up."

T.J. Adams looked at her watch. They had been listening to Lily's story for over ninety minutes. She was surprised at how fast the time had flown but also by the fact that the sheriff had actually given them so much time. Also, she was glad neither Danny or herself had interrupted Lily to ask questions. If they had, chances were Lily would not have had the time to finish her story.

"Your hearing is scheduled in two days. I doubt if I can get bail. First of all, because you turned yourself in, and second of all because you do not have any roots in this town. They will see it as a chance to walk away again. Nothing to hold you here. I'm going to try and get the judge to hold you in this jail here in town instead of putting you in a county prison. You will be closer to me and I feel you will be safer than locked up with other prisoners. That's the best I can offer now. Once you are charged, I'll have a better idea of what I am facing so we can start on you defense."

Lily and Danny looked at her as if seeing her for the first time. Now that the words were spoken it was real. Both felt a cold shiver run through their body.

The Deputy appeared to escort them out and lock the cell door. T.J. Adams left the cell with Danny. She made a point of sending Danny outside and she went into speak with the sheriff.

"I know I'm new in town. I appreciate all you have done to allow me time with the defendant. I want to let you know ahead of time that I am asking that Lily to be held in your jail instead of the County Jail. I realize this may be an imposition on you, but I am asking you for your help by not opposing my request. I need to be close to her to help with her case. Because I am new in town, I'm not real sure if this is possible, but I want to try. I also may need to talk to you about my Uncle. You realize I took over his practice but I really know little about him."

She could see the sheriff was initially against her request for Lily but once she asked for his help she saw a shift in his attitude. She would have to build a relationship with him if she had any hope of being successful in this town. That much she was sure of.

Chapter 42

Max came downstairs and found Millie and Josie in the bar waiting for him. He noticed that Millie was having hot tea and Josie a Coke. He decided to grab a beer while they waited for Danny.

When Danny returned, they could see from his face that the visit had not gone well. Max was the first to speak. "Well, Danny, tell us what you found out. How was Lily holding up?"

Danny looked at them and let out a sigh. "She is being formally charged in two days. At the hearing, they will decide what happens to her before the trial. I didn't realize there was a possibility that she could be transferred to another jail. The lawyer is going to ask that she be kept here. She doesn't think we have much chance of getting her out on bail. So I guess there's not much I can do until after the hearing. I'll decide then. Lily is holding up pretty good considering the situation. She told us the story of her life before I met her. Believe me, she handled situations that no one should, or for that manner could have, endured and survived."

No one spoke for a few minutes. They all thought back to the Lily they knew. What they each had been privileged to share with her, by having her in their life.

Millie said, "I am staying here until after the hearing. Then I must get back to my business and handle some orders. I guess we should discuss what we are all going to do so we have a plan."

Max said, "I too, have to leave soon. I have Rosie to take care of. I know Lily will understand. I can return if I need to."

Josie stated that she had no place to go and nothing holding her to any other obligation, so she would stay in town. Danny lamented that he did need to get back to his job too. "It's killing me but I know I have to leave or resign. Lily does not want me to do that."

Josie suddenly realized how desperate the situation was. She had little money on which to survive on her own. She would be left alone in this strange town. She would do anything for Lily but suddenly she was frightened for both herself and Lily.

The morning of the hearing, everyone was up early and attempted to eat breakfast before they headed out of town. No one had much of an appetite. They had decided that Max and Millie would return home directly from the hearing. Danny and Josie hoped to be able to talk to Lily and her lawyer after the hearing to plan their next step. Until then, they were unsure what they would do next.

They all sat in the courtroom and listened to the attorneys present their case. Josie had a difficult time following the arguments and looked at Max's face to see if it was going ok. He was intent on the proceedings and leaned forward in his seat. She reached out and grasp his hand. He squeezed back.

Suddenly it was over. They all filed out of the courtroom.

"Tell me what happened? I couldn't understand anything." Josie looked at Max then at Danny.

"Well, they are charging Lily with manslaughter and obstruction of justice. That tells me they do not have enough to charge her with murder. Which is a good thing. The lawyer was right; they are holding her without bail because she is considered a flight risk. The judge did agree to let her stay in the town jail."

Max put his arm around Josie. "Now you and Danny need to decide what you two are going to do. Millie and I agreed to wait around until you have a chance to meet with Lily and her lawyer."

Just then, Ms. Adams emerged from the courtroom and headed over to them. "I have arranged to meet with Lily and she has permission for a short visit with Danny and Josie. I hope the rest of you understand that I was pushing my luck for two visitors. They are arranging a room for us. She will be handcuffed. A deputy will be standing guard while you are in the room with her. So keep that in mind when you talk to her. It will not be a private conversation."

Soon they were summoned to the conference room. Max and Millie took a seat on a bench in the hallway. Danny entered the room followed by Josie and the lawyer. Lily was seated at a table and the guard stood in the corner. Danny rushed over to Lily and the guard immediately advised him he needed to take a seat. He was not allowed any physical contact. Danny felt his heart constrict looking at his Lily in handcuffs. He would give anything to make this all go away.

"Well, Lily I think Ms. Adams did a good job for you. We are sure she will be able to prove your innocence. Just hang in there. Ok? We are all here for you. Max and Millie are waiting outside even though they were not allowed to come in".

Lily looked at Danny and then at Josie. "I love you both more than I could ever say. Right now you have to go back to your job and your life. I have to wait until my trial to find out what happens to me but I want you both to go. Please don't hang around town and put your job or life on hold for me. I need to know you are both ok. Staying here won't help me."

Josie spoke up. "Lily I don't have a job or a life without you. I'm staying".

"Josie, I want you and Danny to both leave. In fact, I want you to stay with Madge. You can use my old room. Promise me?"

Josie looked at Danny. Danny shook his head to indicate it would be alright with Madge.

"Ok, but I will be back."

"Now you two, I want a few word with my client in private. The guard will escort you out and I'll meet you in a few minutes."

As Danny and Josie emerged from the room, they walked over to Max and Millie and told them what had happened during their visit.

Max grinned and said, "I think that is an excellent idea, Josie. I'm anxious for you to meet my Mom and Rosie. I know they will love you and it will help them cope not having Lily back right now."

The lawyer soon came to join them.

"I'm glad you are all leaving. It is the best thing for Lily right now. She is so worried about all of you; she is not focusing on herself. I need her totally committed to getting her facts together and helping me win this case. I have all your phone numbers and will call you with any updates or if I have questions. And of course, you can call me and check on Lily when you want."

They all left for the drive back in Max's car. All lost in their own thoughts. All saying a silent prayer for Lily.

They arrived home and were greeted by Madge, Bea and Rosie. As soon as they arrived they were led into the dining room.

"I know you need a good home cooked meal after all you have been through. Come and eat before you tell us what happened."

Rosie looked at them and said "Where is Lily?"

Josie saw the pain in Max's face and knew he was struggling with what to say. "Rosie, I'm Josie. Lily told me all about you. She said what a brave girl you are and that you are even a Junior Deputy."

Rosie got a big grin on her face. "Yes, I am."

"Well Lily couldn't come back right now so she asked me to come and meet you. She told me I could stay in her room and that you would show me around. Is that ok with you?"

Rosie smiled and took hold of Josie's hand. "We have to go upstairs to get to Lily's room."

Max looked at Josie and at that moment the look on his face betrayed his feelings for her. It was apparent that Max was in love with her. He said to Rosie, "Let's eat first sweetheart and then I promise you and Josie can spend time getting to know each other."

As soon as dinner was over, Rosie again urged Josie to follow her upstairs. Once they were gone, Madge looked at Max. "Is there something you want to tell us?"

Max misunderstood and said, "Danny was the one to see Lily; he should tell you what is going on."

Madge laughed. "Honey, of course I want to hear about Lily but I'm your mother. I want to know what's going on with my son. If I'm not mistaken, you seem to have fallen in love."

Millie spoke up, "I would say they have fallen in love with each other."

Soon Millie, Bea and Madge were acting like old friends. They were getting to know each other and found they enjoyed talking to each other. Each relayed their story of how they met Lily and shared their concern for her situation. Danny excused himself and left as soon as he was done eating. Max left with Danny to check on his store and said he would only be gone for a short time.

In the morning, Rosie headed out to school. Max suggested Josie come downtown and see his store and get acquainted with the town. On the drive in, Max made several detours and pointed out the various businesses and the general layout of the town. Josie was glad to see where Lily had spent the last few years and realized she must have been happy here. She recognized some of the things Lily had described to her and felt closer to Lily by seeing them for herself. Max parked in back of his store. As they walked around to the front street, Max pointed out the stairs leading to the second floor.

"That is where Danny lives. I fixed it up and rented it out. My store is downstairs facing the street."

Josie followed him into the store. It was large and filled with Furniture, Accessories and Appliances. He showed her how he had sectioned off the areas to create rooms so the furniture and accessories could be more appealing. The appliances were displayed in an area separate from the furniture.

"When I first took over the store, the previous owner had refrigerators sitting next to chairs and washing machines next to sofas. I didn't know how anyone could picture them in their house. I know I couldn't." He laughed and added, "The furniture was so old, I donated most of it to charity. I could not justify selling it as new furniture to any one shopping here. So everything you see, is new and worth the price."

Josie laughed. "Well I'd say you did a good job. Although I've never bought much furniture for myself but if I needed any, I'd come here."

Max looked at her and leaned over and kissed her. It surprised them both at how the kiss awakened such feelings. Once they pulled away, Max said, "I can't go on like this much longer. I'm not made to have casual affairs. I want you more than I've ever wanted anything in my life."

Josie looked at Max. Her eyes betrayed the passion just brought to the surface. "I know. But I can't make any commitments until Lily is free."

Max hoped she was right. Somehow, he was worried that she would not be free and if she was, it would not be soon enough.

Danny eased back into his workload and at least while he was on duty, he gave it his all. The staff was relieved to have him back and even more amazed at how he took back control. No one asked about Lily. Not that they didn't care, but they didn't want him to lose his focus now that he appeared to have it back. It was important to his Deputies that he continue as Sheriff. They all remembered the previous sheriff and did not want someone else stepping in ruining all of the positive changes that Danny had made.

Millie left after a few days with a promise to return soon. She and Madge formed a deep friendship, which she felt would last a lifetime. She laughed to herself at the term. *Well, at least what time I have left.*

Madge was amazed at life herself. Funny how just a few short years ago she was leading what she felt was a happy life. She had her Boarding House and was content. Now she realized what happiness really was. She had her son and granddaughter living with her. Lily had come into her life and now Josie and Millie. She smiled at thoughts of Josie. *I've never seen Max so in love, not even with my daughter-in-law, God rest her soul.*

Lily continued to be confined to her cell. Her lawyer continued to work on her defense.

Chapter 43

Josie loved Max and enjoyed being around Madge and Rosie but she was getting frustrated, just sitting around waiting for something to happen. Although she helped at the store when Max needed her, and at the diner when Bea had someone call out sick, she felt she needed to do more to help Lily. One day when she was alone, an idea came to her and she called the lawyer, TJ Adams. When Max came home, she told him what she had decided to do and ask him to drive her to Greenwood.

Max was reluctant to let her go. She reminded him that he had no hold over her and could not stop her. She looked at his face and realized that she had hurt him. "Max, you know I cannot go on with anything else until Lily is free. She needs me. She needs someone with absolute conviction that she is innocent. I have to be there for her." She put her arms around his waist and held him tight. "This is not about you and me right now and it cannot be about us until I'm sure Lily is safe."

He agreed to drive her back. She outlined her plan. She had called TJ and asked about the files in her office. If she was still thinking about hiring someone to help her sort and organize them. If so, she would do it. All she wanted in return was a place to stay. The lawyer had finally gotten back to her in just a few hours and told her she had found her a place to stay and that she would take her up on the offer.

Max checked into the hotel they had stayed at before. It was decided that he and Josie would spend one night together before he headed home. They had been very discreet because of Madge and Rosie and had only shared a few brief kisses and were both longing for more. Once they entered the hotel, they did not leave their room even to eat. They both knew this was the only time they would have alone together for a while.

They next morning they were both reluctant to leave each other. Max held her tight and made her promise to be careful. He handed her the cell phone and told her his number was now programmed in, so she must promise to call him every day. She looked at him and could not believe that she had found someone as wonderful as him.

They ate breakfast and then walked over to the law office together. Max wanted to be sure Josie would be taken care of, and did in fact, have a safe place to stay. Ms. Adams insisted they call her TJ. She explained that Josie was going to stay in her spare bedroom because had also inherited her uncle's house, along with his law practice, so she had plenty of room. She told them she would welcome the company and more importantly, the help in sorting the files. Her current assistant was reaching the breaking point. She was afraid she was going to quit soon if she didn't have help. It was getting to be too much taking care of new business and doing the thankless job of getting the old files in order. TJ said, "I cannot believe my Uncle could ever find anything in this mess. I don't know how he functioned."

Max left and Josie started right in on sorting files. TJ suggested they sort the files into cases instead of alphabetically for now. She needed the wills, court cases and other miscellaneous cases sorted out. They went back so far, she didn't even know what was still relevant. Josie got the files off the desk of the assistant, Tracy, and began there. "At least Tracy will feel some relief if she does not have to work around the clutter on her desk", said Josie.

Within two days, Josie had most of the files that had been sitting in the Reception Area sorted and stacked for TJ. They had agreed to continue that system before creating any permanent arrangement for the files. When TJ was out of her office, Josie retrieved the files stored in there. Tracy was now only holding the current files so they were not intermingled with the older ones.

Josie was sitting on the floor in TJ's office on the fourth day. She was checking dates on the files and writing this information on the front of the file. She reached up to push her hair out of her face. Her hand brushed her earring and she felt it fall out. She did not see which way it rolled, so she got on her hands and knees to look. Still not finding anything, she laid down on the floor to see if she could notice a rise in the floor to indicate its location. An old trick she learned when she lost one at home. As she looked under the chairs along the wall, she noticed what appeared to be a part of a door. She got up and moved the chairs. Sure enough there was a low door that was hidden by the chairs. She stooped down and tried the doorknob. Surprising it swung inward to a hidden room.

She noticed steps leading down into the room. The door was recessed into an area that allowed her to step down to a landing before taking a few steps to another level. The door was actually full size once it was opened. How clever it was disguised. She took a hesitant step inside and felt along the wall for a light switch. She was rewarded immediately as her hand touched it. The room was full of files. Some arranged in bookcases, some in boxes but none in file cabinets. She eased down the steps into the room and pulled some out of the bookcase. They were over thirty years old. She decided to wait until TJ returned before she disturbed anything. She estimated the room was probably twelve by fifteen. There was a table in the middle that indicated someone had worked in this room at some time in the past. It looked old and dusty and carried the lingering odor of stale cigarettes and cigars.

Josie closed the door and put the chairs back again to hide the location. She decided it was up to TJ to determine what to do about this room and who to tell that it existed. Not that she didn't trust Tracy, but TJ may want to keep this information private for now.

As she put the chairs back, she stepped on her earring. *Well at least it wasn't a total waste of time.* She returned to the outer office to finish up there.

It was several days before Josie was able to talk to TJ alone.

Josie was getting familiar with the town and often took a walk at lunchtime. She enjoyed the weather and even though it was a small town, she always found something different each time she explored the different streets. She could see that it was never a prosperous town but the residence seemed to try and keep their homes and businesses in good repair. Nothing appeared new. It was as if the town stood still and just continued on as it always had. Josie could not imagine staying here after Lily was free but it would do for now. She wondered why TJ. chose to come here, but decided she must like having the independence her law practice afforded her. She did travel often, which was why Josie had not been able to tell her about the room she discovered. She decided she would definitely do it today since TJ had plans to return to the office this afternoon.

Once Tracy had left for the day, and TJ was alone in her office, Josie went into TJ's office and shut the door. "Did you realize there is a secret room off your office?"

TJ looked at her as if she was speaking a foreign language.

"I found one. You never mentioned it to me so I wasn't sure if you knew. If you were keeping it a secret, I didn't want to say anything in front of Tracy. Did you know?"

"No. I'm not sure what you are talking about? Explain to me what you found."

Josie went across the room and moved the two tall overstuffed chairs and the half door was exposed.

"Mother of God! Don't tell me my uncle hid something in there?"

Josie laughed. "I didn't see any dead bodies but a lot of dead files. Come in and take a look."

Josie showed her how to maneuver herself over the doorway how to the step down onto the landing.

"Not sure why it was designed this way. I would have thought a trap door would have made more sense."

They both entered the room and Josie showed her how to turn on the light. "I take it, you didn't know about this?"

"I had no idea. But I have to admit, since I came here, the files in this office have taken all my attention. That and the new clients I have. I haven't really looked that hard around the office. I wonder what other surprises there are here?"

"I didn't tell Tracy, just in case you didn't want to share this discovery. Let me know what you want me to do. I guess you should go through these files too. May be something you need to be aware of. I pulled a few out and they were pretty old. Your Uncle may have used this room to store old files. Although it seems funny how he concealed this room. It has a smell too. Like pipe tobacco, do you smell it?"

"You have a point there. Yes, we need to see what is here. I'll work with you each evening for a couple hours if you are agreeable. Then I will be able to make a decision. For now, it is best that we don't let anyone but the two of us in on the existence of this room. And yes, I do notice an odor. We may want to air it out."

TJ had some things she needed to attend to right away, so she didn't want to start until that was finished. She told Josie she could start without her. Just let her know what she found. Josie decided to start sorting through the room after Tracy left then next day.

Josie had been granted permission to visit Lily three times a week. She was allotted thirty minutes each time. Although she wished for more, she was grateful that TJ had been able to arrange for that much time. Usually she talked about her work and what she had discovered in town. She was surprised that Lily didn't know many of the places Josie found during her walks around the town. If anything, she was sad at the existence Lily must have endured when she lived here. But Lily was always excited to see Josie, and looked forward to hearing whatever she had to say. It was as if she was living her life through Josie and that both angered Josie and saddened her.

Lily was becoming complacent in her situation. She needed her to fight and prove herself innocent. What she needed most was to believe in herself. Believe that she was innocent. Lily seemed to have lost the enthusiasm that made her Lily. Danny was coming out to visit her in a few days and Josie decided she would try to talk to him. She had not told Lily about her feelings for Max. She felt bad withholding the information. She felt guilty at how lucky she was and how unlucky Lily was right now.

Chapter 44

Josie started coming into work after lunch. She had made great headway in getting the old office files sorted, organized, stored or refilled. TJ decided they would tell Tracy the shorter workdays were because the Josie was almost finished. TJ need to conserve the amount of hours she paid for Josie's time. That way, Josie would stay and work through the evening on files in the secret room and Tracy would not become suspicious. It was not unusual for TJ to work late, so if any lights were on in the building, it would be assumed it was because she was still there.

Once they had spent an evening together looking at the dates of the files and getting an idea of what they contained, Josie was able to work independently. It was decided that she would sort the files initially according to what services were rendered. The court cases would be set aside until last. TJ wanted to know if any of the material may be related to current situations such as wills, deeds or outstanding trusts.

Josie was amazed at how far back the files went. She was enjoying her work. Also, she felt she was helping pay back some of the debt she owed TJ for allowing her a place to stay and arranging visits to Lily.

She had started to explore the outreaches of the town. Since she now had the mornings off, she had decided to get in shape. Initially she walked and then was able to build up her stamina to start running. Once she was running, she found the stress was reduced. She was amazed at how far she could go by running and was seeing parts of the town she had not seen before. She rarely met anyone on her outings and was glad for the solitude. *Funny,* she thought to herself, *I used to enjoy talking to people when I worked in the restaurant, now I just want to keep to myself.*

Danny arrived in town and she was disappointed to see he was alone. Although Josie talked to Max every day, she still missed having him there to hold her. She was secretly hoping he would surprise her with a visit. She met Danny at the hotel and told him of her concern for Lily. "We have got to get her to fight. She is becoming content to stay in jail. I can't seem to get her to understand. She can beat this if she helps us in proving her innocence. I need you to get through to her!"

"I intend to try my best. I want to tell you how grateful I am that you are staying here with her, and not giving up."

"Danny, giving up is not an option for me. You should know that by now."

Danny gave her a hug and said he was heading over to the jail to try and see Lily. "I'll kiss the damn sheriff's feet if that's what it takes to get his cooperation. I realize that now. I was a real pain before."

As Danny entered the police station he stopped to look around. He realized just how small and outdated the facility was. Not that his town was overrun with crime, but his station was much newer, and from what he observed, more organized. The Deputy sitting at the desk had several cans of coke and opened snacks littering his workspace. He reminded himself not to comment on what he saw.

"Good morning Deputy. I'd like to have permission to see Lily Hill, if it is convenient for you." Danny almost chocked on his words but secretly smiled when he saw the deputy's manner relax. It was apparent the deputy recognized him and was bracing himself for a confrontation.

He got up from the desk and told Danny to have a seat and he would be right back. Soon he returned alone and asked Danny to follow him. He was led down the hall to the same cell he had been in before. No one else seemed to be in any other of the six cells he passed. As they approached her cell, the deputy told Danny he was granting him a thirty minute visit. First, he had to make sure he was not carrying anything into her. Once he was cleared, the deputy opened the cell. He told Danny he would check back on them, locked them in the cell and left.

Danny and Lily looked at each other. They knew not to make a move toward each other until the deputy left. Once they heard his footsteps retreating, Danny gathered Lily in his arms and kissed her. Both realized how much they had missed the physical part of their relationship.

"Lily, Josie tells me you are not putting any effort in getting yourself out of here. Listen to me. A lot of people are hurting right now. Not just me…. but Rosie, Max, Madge, Bea, Millie, and especially Josie. We need you back in our lives. You have to help us come up with your defense. It's not just punishing yourself. You are punishing us. Now I expect you to think about what I'm saying and start helping us."

They heard the deputy walking down the hall to check on them. Danny called to him and said to Lily, "I'm not staying the thirty minutes; I'm leaving when he gets here. I said what I needed to say and I want you to think about it. I'll be back tomorrow for your decision." He looked up and nodded to the deputy. "I'm ready to go."

He followed the deputy back out of the jail. He thanked him for his time and asked if he could return the next day. The deputy looked him over and decided he had no problem with another visit.

Danny met Josie for dinner. They discussed his visit with Lily.

"I know it hurt you to do it, but it had to be done. We need to knock some sense into her. She can be so stubborn sometimes. Why does she have to feel so guilty?"

"I guess it is just because she is such an honest person. She feels she has to be punished, even if it is not her fault. We need to convince her that sometimes things happen and she is not to blame. Sometimes events cannot be controlled. They just happen."

Danny visited with Lily two more times before he had to head home. He could see he was making headway in getting her to think about her freedom. He felt Josie could start to get more information from her now. He would bring Madge with him next time. He wished Rosie could visit but they had all agreed that no one wanted Rosie to see Lily behind bars.

Chapter 45

Danny arrived home and immediately was thrown back into work. He had budget and administrative items that were sitting on his desk that needed prompt attention. He soon was engrossed in getting his department back on track. Although the day to day matters had been handled well enough by his deputies, there were still a lot of things that needed his direct attention. Not much crime had occurred. The mundane paperwork had just sat waiting for his return. He was surprised sometimes at the amount of non- law enforcement duties that came with his job.

He preferred the hands- on aspects of his job and hated spending so much time in the office away from people. That was one of the qualities that endeared him to so many of the townspeople. He decided to spend the next two days getting everything in order in case he had to leave again. The other duties could be handled by his Deputies for now.

His hard work paid off and within the next few days he was confident all the paperwork was current. He decided to explore the town and see what had happened since he had left. His first stop was for breakfast with Bea.

"Well, look who just walked in." He knew he would get a lot of razzing and as soon as Bea started in on him, the other regulars started. "Do we know him?"

"He wouldn't be impersonating an officer of the law now, would he?"

"Kinda reminds me of a sheriff we used to have."

"Naw, he's left town a long time ago."

Danny looked around the diner and grinned. "You guys just won't give up, now will you? I'm glad to tell you I'm back and not above hauling in your sorry asses for disturbing the peace of a police officer."

Soon everyone joined in on the laughter. Danny realized how much he had become a part of this town. He only wished they could get Lily's problem behind them so he could get his life back to normal. This is where he wanted to spend the rest of his life. With Lily and the children they hoped to have.

After leaving the diner, he decided to walk around town and burn off the calories he had eaten. He stopped in and chatted with Pete at the Jewelry Store. Nothing new there. He wanted to ask if he was still seeing Madge but he didn't volunteer any information and Danny decided not to ask. He made his way through town, stopping to chat with the salespeople and owners. He was glad to see nothing was troubling them. He said a silent prayer that he did not have any immediate problems to worry about. He decided to get into his cruiser and cover the outlying streets. He was surprised to see it was getting late. He noticed the schools letting out and pulled over to check for speeders.

He was just heading back to the station when his phone rang.

"Sorry Sheriff, I didn't want to use the radio. We just got a report of what sounds like an attempted kidnapping of a ten year old girl just outside of town. I dispatched the deputy that was here but thought you may need to go too.

"You got that right. Thanks for calling. Give me the location and I'm on my way."

When Danny heard the location, he did a U-turn and headed out to the crime scene. He started thinking it sounded familiar. He then remembered the young girl who had been raped soon after his arrival in town. That guy had never been caught. Danny was still upset over the outcome of that case. He drove fast and soon spotted his Deputy's car on the side of the road. As he pulled over he noticed two teenagers. A boy about sixteen and a girl about the same age. He walked over and saw the young girl about ten years old, in the back of the Deputy's police car. She was crying. Her clothes looked torn and muddy, but thank God, she was dressed.

The Deputy was the first to speak. "This is Brian Rawlings and Jennifer Beatty. They heard the little girl scream and went to see what was going on. I put her in the car. Should I call for an ambulance?"

Danny told the Deputy to call now. They also needed to get in touch with the parents. He leaned down into the car and spoke to the little girl. "Hi. I'm Sheriff Danny. Can you tell me your name?"

The girl swallowed a big hiccup and said, "Bri."

"Ok, Bri, I want to know if you are hurt. Can you tell me what happened to make you cry?"

"I fell. The man grabbed me and tore my shirt. Mommy will be mad. He was mean and scared me."

"Do you have any pain anywhere?"

"Just my arm."

"Well, let's call your Mom and have a Doctor look at you, Ok? Do you know your phone number?"

Bri gave Danny her phone number and he called her mother. The Deputy had already called for an ambulance. Danny told the Mother briefly what happened and ask her to meet them at the Hospital.

Danny asked Brian and Jennifer to ride to the police station and give their statement. He wanted to catch this man and needed to get as much information as he could. He would question Bri, after she was checked by a Doctor and her Mother was with her.

The paramedics arrived just as Danny was hanging up with Bri's mother and he said the two teenagers would ride back to the station with him. He told his Deputy to follow the ambulance to the Hospital and make sure he kept Bri and her parents there until he could talk to them.

Once he had the teenagers in his patrol car, he could tell from their faces they were torn between the excitement of riding in the cruiser and fear that someone would see them and think they had done something wrong.

"Thank you for coming with me. Bri was lucky that you two were close by."

"Yeah, she was scared."

"Where were you in relation to where Bri was?"

"Not far away."

Danny thought he should wait until he got them back to the station before going into detail. He wanted to see their faces when he talked to them.

He escorted them into the station and told them to have a seat. He asked them if they wanted to call their parents before he talked to them. Both shook their head, "No".

Danny explained that he wanted to talk to them individually. That way he could be sure of their description. "Often people are influenced by what they hear someone else say and that other person is not always correct. I want to stress to you both that you are not in trouble. In fact, if anything, you two should be commended for helping Bri. You are just here to help us find this pervert. Are you both ok with this? If you want your parents to come in before you talk to me, we can wait for them. But since you are not accused of any misdemeanor, I am legally able to talk to you without your parent's permission."

He looked at them and they both said, "We're cool."

Danny decided to talk to Brian first and led him into his office. He wanted to put the kids at ease and did not think an interview room would be the best way to accomplish that. "Ok Brian, how old are you?"

"Seventeen, sir."

"Can you tell me what you and Jennifer were doing in that area? Do you live close by?"

Brian's face turned red. He looked as if he was unsure what to say.

"Hey guy. I was young once. If that is what is making you uncomfortable. Just spit it out."

"My parents will kill me."

Danny laughed. "I doubt that but no need for them to know right now. I'm not going to call them if that is what you are afraid of."

"Me and Jennifer sorta like each other. We dated and got really serious. My parents threw a fit because they said I was too young. They really feel Jennifer is not good enough for me. Her parents are kinda poor and she won't be able to go away to college."

"That does happen Brian. Parents do want the best for their kids. At least what they think is best. So what happened?"

"Well, we hadn't seen each other for a couple of weeks. We thought if we cooled it for a while, it would all blow over with Mom and Dad. We ran into each other today and needed to talk. We wanted to meet where no one would see us." He blushed again and looked as sheepishly at Danny.

Danny laughed. "And to get a little lovin tossed in?"

"Yeah."

"Ok, go on."

"Well we were not there long. We kissed for a while, and then all of a sudden we heard a kid scream. It scared us both. Jennifer told me we had to help and started running toward the scream. I caught up with her and saw the old man had his hands on the little girl. I didn't think, I just started yelling at him. He was kinda fat and I knew I was stronger than he was. I know it was stupid, because I didn't know if he had a knife or gun. I just thought of my little sister and got really mad. When he ran, I didn't run after him. Our first thought was to get to the little girl and make sure she was ok."

301

"Well I'm not supposed to encourage citizens taking chances like you did. But it was lucky for Bri you did what you did. And you should never chase a criminal running away."

"Yeah, I was just mad. Didn't think much about what to do. Just did it."

Danny asked some questions about the man's appearance took notes and thanked him for his cooperation. Especially for his help is rescuing Bri. He told Brian he would see what Jennifer remembered and then they were free to go.

Jennifer confirmed what Brian had told Danny and he walked out to the waiting area with her. "You kids need a ride home?"

"Nah, we're good said Brian."

Danny looked at Jennifer and she nodded.

"I don't have a problem with my parents by being seen with Brian."

Danny realized the tension growing between them.

"Well you two have been very helpful. Call me if you think of anything else that might help."

Danny headed to the hospital and met Bri's mother. He called her out into the hallway and explained to her that he had to talk to her daughter while everything was fresh in her mind. "I will be as gentle as I can. I need you to let her talk and not interrupt. I want to catch this man as soon as possible. Do I have your cooperation?"

"If she gets too upset, I'll have to tell you to stop."

"Agreed, let's go in now."

Bri looked so tiny in the bed that Danny's heart ached for her and her Mother but he knew he had to act fast.

"Hi, Bri. Remember me? I'm Sheriff Danny. I want to ask you some questions. You are not in trouble. In fact, you are a hero in my book. I want you to answer me honestly. You are not in trouble. You did nothing wrong. Don't even think you did. I know you were concerned about your torn clothes and I know your Mom is not upset about that. In fact I'm sure she is grateful if that is what helped you to get away. Now close your eyes and try and tell me what the man looked like. Hair and eye color. Fat or thin. Stuff like that. Ok?"

Bri looked at Danny then at her Mother. "It's ok honey. Do what Sheriff Danny said."

"We want to catch this man before he hurts you or any other children. So don't be afraid. You are safe now with your Mom and me to watch over you."

Bri closed her eyes. "Grey hair. Brown eyes. Kinda fat. Old. Smelly." She opened her eyes and Danny saw the fear in them.

"Good job, Bri. Tell me how he found you."

Bri had two tears suddenly run down her cheek. She looked anxiously at her Mother.

"Bri, you are not in trouble. Your Mom loves you very much and wants you to be honest so we can find him." Danny glanced at her mother to get confirmation.

"The Sheriff is right, honey. Just tell us what happened. We will understand."

"Well, I was walking home with Abby as I always do. She was in a bad mood and we had a fight. With words not fist." She again looked at her Mom.

"That's ok. Girls do have disagreements sometimes. Tell Sheriff Danny what happened next."

"Well, I told her I didn't want to be her friend anymore. We split up. I went a different way. I was thinking about dumb Abby and wasn't looking at where I was going. Sorry, Mom."

"That's ok, honey. It happens sometimes to all of us."

"I heard something at the edge of the woods. I thought it might be a deer. I stopped and walked closer. That man came out and grabbed me."

She started to sob. Her mother put her arms around her. "It's ok, you are safe now. Can you tell us what happened next?"

"I screamed. Then I heard someone running. Two teenagers came over and started yelling at the man to let me go. I can't remember anymore."

"Bri, you did a wonderful job. On behalf of the Sheriff's department I want to thank you." Danny smiled at her and thanked her mom for her cooperation.

They walked out into the hallway together. Bri could still see them through the glass door, but she was not able to hear their conversation. She said, "I never met you before Sheriff but I guarantee you will get my vote at the next election. I never saw anyone handle a child with such compassion. Thank You."

"No problem. You have a great little girl in there. I'm going to do my best to catch the bastard. Sorry for the language but I won't rest until he is locked up."

He left and headed back to the station to complete the paperwork.

Danny knew he had to act fast before panic seized the town. He made a call and sat back to work out his plan.

Chapter 46

Danny met with his new Deputy. Garrett was young looking and on the small side. Danny had reservations about hiring him, but once he interviewed him, his intelligence and his convictions more than made up for his size. Although he was thirty-one, he looked more like twenty. He was built solid for his five foot -six height. With his clear complexion and light hair worn short, he had an innocent look that made him appear much younger than he actually was. . Underneath his outward look, Danny saw a character that could be *hard as nails,* as Dad always described someone like Garrett.

Garrett listened as Danny laid out his plan. A slow smile formed on Garrett's face as he realized he was to be directly involved in Danny's plan. He was glad he had applied for the Deputy's job. He admired Danny as a boss. He knew Danny would give him a chance to prove himself. He had a way of encouraging his Deputies to do their best and succeed. Although he was new to his job, he had heard the talk that Danny was having personal problems that did not always keep him focused and devoted to the job. He often had to leave town to attend to them. Garrett hoped they would get this crime solved and allow Danny to show everyone he was back in full force. The election would soon be looming over his head and Garrett knew he would do everything in his power to support Danny and help him overcome the skepticism felt by some of the other officers to get him re-elected.

They decided to meet after an early lunch. Garrett was to dress as a teenager and Danny was to be disguised as a bum.

Garrett and Danny walked over to the woods where Bri had been attacked. They split up. It was necessary for them not to be seen together.

Danny stumbled and weaved to give the appearance of someone who had been drinking. They had both been over the area many times after Bri's attack and knew the area well. The plan was for Danny to appear as non- threatening as possible, just drunk. And for Garrett to look like a kid hooking school, to anyone watching them.

Once they decided no one was watching them, Garrett scooted up a tree to get a good view of the surrounding area. Danny crawled into a group of bushes to conceal himself and listened for any sounds. They knew they would not be so lucky to catch the old man today, but both would do this as long as necessary. The afternoon wore on and Garrett had not seen a single person pass by. Soon it would be time for the school to let out. Hopefully, he would be able to observe how the kids used the woods. That would help him to determine where the best observation point would be in the future. Danny was out in the bushes listening for sounds that may not have been heard by Garrett. They had agreed on no contact and it was difficult for each one to know the other's exact location. They only knew that they were both out here and would back each other up if necessary.

The school let out and very few students used the path in the woods. No doubt their parents had lectured them on staying away from here, even if they have to walk the long way home. Human nature being what it is, and knowing how kids thought they were invincible, he was sure some would not be deterred from using the woods. Boys more than girls. But they needed to be careful in case the old man was watching. He hoped they would remember that.

As Garrett suspected, several boys entered the woods and immediately lit up cigarettes. They joked and talked about girls as if danger did not exist for them. They may be right thought Garrett; the girl was the target of the attack. No one noticed him but as he knew, teenage boys were more interested in what they were doing. Not in being cautious. He noticed two girls walking along the outer edge of the wooded area with two boys. The girls appeared nervous and were shaking their heads in disagreement. He could tell from their body language they were fighting the suggestion of entering the woods. He allowed himself a smile. He knew the hormones were raging in the boys and they were hoping to *get lucky* in the woods if they could convince the girls to enter. Funny, he thought, little has changed in the years since he was in school.

The girls appeared to win the debate and they walked off, away from the woods. Garrett had not seen anyone else approach the woods. He stayed there for another hour, carefully slid down the tree. He listened for any sound of leaves moving, before coming out of the cover of the tree. He walked slowly as if he had no set place to go. Once he was past the school, he quickened his pace and headed to the station to wait for Danny.

Soon Danny entered. He appeared to have stopped home and changed clothes. "I didn't want to blow my cover by walking into the station in my undercover clothes."

"I should have thought of that."

"Well, you're new. Dressed as a teenager will draw less notice than a bum. But let's keep that in mind."

Garrett knew Danny was reprimanding him but he knew he deserved it. He admired the way Danny did it. He felt the full impact of what was said but Danny had a way of keeping your self- esteem intact. That is what made him a good Sheriff. He wondered if Danny realized that is what inspired his men. Probably not, some people were just born leaders and did not look for personal rewards. Just wanted to make a difference in the world.

Danny and Garrett continued their stakeout. They decided to include the morning watch before school and then after school. Both were feeling frustrated at the lack of progress in the investigation. No other information had turned up and the stakeouts had yielded nothing useful. They continued this for two weeks and decided one more week then they would need to try something else. They had noticed recently that the town was settling back to normal and panic over the attack was less evident.

Other things quietly slipped into the lives of the townspeople and took their focus off the attack. Danny knew this was the normal course of life, but was still fearful that once they let their guard down, something might happen again. He and Garrett were going to continue watching the woods. They were not ready to give up on that yet.

Wednesday of the next week, school let out early for a teacher's meeting. Signs were posted in town to alert the parents in case after school care needed to be arranged. The weather was perfect. The sun was shining and a cool breeze kept the temperature from being hot. It was one of those days that just put a spring in your step. This was a perfect day to lure kids where they usually did not go. A false sense that all was right with the world. Danny and Garrett knew they must be on high alert today.

Garrett decided to move to a taller tree to have a wider view. He had dressed in dark brown pants and a forest green shirt in hopes of blending in with the tree. He had not climbed very far up when he noticed the two couples from a few weeks ago approach the edge of the trees. The girls were still hesitant but the boys appeared to be winning the debate. He decided to stay where he was so as not to make any noise. Just as he suspected they walked into the woods. One couple stopped to kiss and it was evident she was more willing than the other girl to let her guard down. They exchanged a few words with each other and they walked away from the other couple.

The other boy tried to kiss his girl but the girl resisted and kept looking around as if she felt someone would see them. The boy reached out and put his arms around her. Garrett could tell from her movements that she was weakening. As the boy put his arm around her shoulder, he directed her farther into the woods. Garrett felt a reluctance to watch, yet he knew he had to protect them. It was obvious they only had one thing on their mind. And, it wasn't their safety.

He started to climb higher into the tree when suddenly the branch gave way. He slipped down and his hands were cut by the bark on the tree in his effort to grab hold of branches. He caught himself on a jutting branch and landed in a sitting position on a lower branch. His groin felt the impact and for a few minutes he felt tears well up in his eyes. Once the pain eased up, he realized how lucky he was. He sat very still and tried to replay it in his mind. Hopefully, no one heard anything. He shook his head as if to clear it and decided to try again. This time he tested each branch with his hands to see how sturdy it was. He managed to climb up to almost the top.

He looked out and saw the first couple. She was blond and was wearing white pants. All he saw now was the legs sticking out underneath the boy. Her shirt had been removed and the boy was fondling her small breasts. He turned away embarrassed and looked for the other couple. She had red hair and had on jeans. It didn't take long to see them. This boy appeared to be having a harder time with his conquest.

Garrett was thinking that they were much too young to be getting into sex. He thought to himself that he must be getting old. He probably felt the same way at that age himself but it's different when you grow up. Funny how you think kids should still be innocent at this age. He reminded himself why he was here, and knew he had to forget what he was seeing and concentrate on why he was doing this. The boy reached out and lifted the girl's shirt over her head. Garrett was shocked at how big her breasts were. Now he was getting very uncomfortable. He glanced away and looked out over the area. No one else was in sight. He looked over at the first couple and they were still involved. At least her pants were still on. He glanced over to the other kids and he saw the boy appeared to want more that his girl was prepared to offer. Goodness man, aren't the boobs enough? He chuckled to himself! I bet the other guy would love to see them. Garrett thought, this job is getting to me. Now who is the pervert? Next time he thought, Danny is getting the tree and I'm getting the bushes. How much can a man endure in the line of duty?

Suddenly the girl jumped up. Her breast bobbed and shook as she made gestures with her arms. She appeared to be upset with the boy. She grabbed her shirt and quickly pulled it over her head. From what he could see, she made that made it clear she was not going to continue what they were doing and that she had enough. The boy appeared to lose interest and get up and walked away leaving the girl by herself. He could see the uncertainty in her face. Her pride appeared to win out over her fear of being alone in the woods. She turned and walked away from the direction of the boy which took her deeper into the woods.

Garrett decided he should follow her to make sure she got out of the woods safely. He knew she would soon be out of his view as the trees became denser and provided cover that would be difficult, if not impossible, to see through.

He cautiously descended the tree. Once he was down, it took him a few minutes to get the feeling back in his legs. They were cramped from sitting and the near fall had made his crotch uncomfortable. Once he was sure he could control his movements, he set off. He knew Danny was out there and would judge his movements. If he made noise, it would get him discovered and not bode well with his boss. This was the first assignment he had been trusted with, he was working with the Sheriff, not another Deputy. He was determined not to disappoint.

It didn't take long for him to hear the girl's footsteps in the woods. From the sounds of the leaves and twigs snapping, she was moving slowly. Garrett thought to himself, probably scarred shitless and afraid to move but forcing herself to get out of there.

Garrett heard an intake of breath. As if the girl was surprised. He stopped to listen, wondering if the boy had found her and wanted to make up. He heard what sounded like a scuffle and then a moan. He decided to break the rules and run toward the noise. He would worry about repercussions later. Just as he spotted the girl, he noticed the person on top of her was not the same boy. She was thrashing around on the ground and the man raised his hand to strike her. He saw Danny rush over and pulled the man off. He tackled the man and the man seemed crazed. He kicked and swung his fist. Danny definitely outweighed him and it was no contest for the man. He quickly had him in handcuffs. Garrett glanced over at the girl. She was cowering on the ground holding her ripped shirt across her chest and sobbing. He could see she was too terrified to move. He walked over to her and sat down. "I'm Deputy Garrett and that man making the arrest is Sheriff Danny McCain"

The girl looked up with terrified eyes.

"Are you hurt?"

Still she did not speak.

Garrett looked at Danny and said, "Let's get her checked out. She may be in shock."

Danny picked up his radio and called the station to request a car and an ambulance.

The girl started sobbing harder. Garrett reached out and put an arm around her. He thought how much she had been through today. First with the supposed boyfriend and then this maniac. He knew she needed someone. "Can I call your parents? Mom? Dad? Someone to be with you?"

"I'm scared they will be mad. God what did I do?"

"Listen to me. I'm sorry what is your name?"

"Amber. Amber Goodbred."

"Ok Amber. I guarantee your parents will only be thankful everything is ok and you are not hurt. You aren't hurt are you?"

"No."

"Good. See parents love their kids. Their safety is their biggest concern. They may get mad at you but they are madder at themselves and the guy who hurt you. Why don't we call them? You can meet them at the hospital. They need to see you are ok."

She smiled weakly and said, "Ok."

The paramedics arrived soon after and took the girl off in the ambulance. Danny told Garrett to ride with her to make sure she felt safe until her parents arrived. The other Deputies arrived right behind the ambulance and took the man off to jail.

Just as Danny was driving back to the station his cell phone rang. "Sheriff here"

"Danny, it's me Max. I need you right away. Mom is sick. I think she is having a heart attack and I am on my way to the hospital. The paramedics just left with her and called me to come right away. I need your help with Rosie until I can get something arranged. She is in the diner with Bea but she needs someone to take her home. I dropped her off on my way to the hospital."

Danny cursed under his breath. Not that he was upset with Max but it couldn't be a worse time. He really needed Lily. How much she had helped out in situations such as this was a reminder to him how much she needed to come home.

"Of course, I'm on my way. Don't worry about a thing. We'll get Rosie taken care of. She must be worried too. You take care of Madge and make sure they get her fixed up."

Max was faced with the thought of losing his mother. He started to choke up but managed to get a "Thank You" out before he broke down. His thoughts went to Josie and how much he needed someone to be with him now.

Danny picked up Rosie and took her home. He decided to call Garrett and explain what was going on and to ask him to handle things the rest of the day. He realized he needed someone in the department he could depend upon in cases just like this. It would be good to give some authority to Garrett. He could always reach him if he ran into any problems.

"Make sure you record both the interview and when you read him his rights. We don't want to have any problems with procedures when he goes to court. Call the D.A. and tell him what we have. I'll meet with him tomorrow. We can hold the scumbag without formal charges until then. Any problems, call me right away."

"Alright Sheriff. You take care and let me know if you need any help tonight. I don't have any plans." He hesitated and added "Thanks for your trust. I won't let you down."

"I know that Garrett or I wouldn't put this responsibility on you. Thanks again."

He smiled as he hung up. Well something good did come out of today, they caught the pervert and Garrett stepped up to the plate. Danny needed some good luck. It was about time.

Danny was helping Rosie with her homework when the phone rang. He thought it was Max and he answered cautiously afraid of what he would hear about Madge.

He was surprised to realize it was Millie on the phone.

"This is Millie calling for Madge. Do I have the wrong number?"

"Sorry, this is Danny. She isn't here right now."

"That's strange. We were talking on the phone today and I got busy. She told me to call back tonight. Do you know when she will be back?"

Danny walked into the kitchen with the phone and shut the door. He told Rosie to finish coloring in the picture and he would be right back.

"Millie, Madge is in the hospital. In fact, I thought it might be him calling. He thought it may be a heart attack and he asked me to stay with Rosie. I hate to be the one to tell you, and not give you more details, but that is all I know for now."

"Oh that poor woman. I hope I didn't upset her today. We were talking about Lily and Josie and I was feeling rather down. I hate to think I said something that could have caused her to get upset. Sometimes, I just don't think."

"Millie, don't feel responsible. I know neither Max nor Madge would want you to worry about that. Now I could kick myself for breaking the news to you this way, but to be honest, I feel helpless here with Rosie and I just needed someone to talk to. Please forgive me."

Millie smiled to herself. She could see now why Lily fell in love with Danny. Such a nice boy. Well actually man. Millie reprimanded herself.

"I'm glad you told me. I want to know. Let me know if you need anything. Please call as soon as you hear from Max. I am not going to sleep until I know what is going on."

"OK, thanks. I will. I promise you will either hear from me or Max as soon as we know anything."

Danny hung up and headed back to Rosie. God, he was lonely. How fragile a family's happiness could be. He said a silent prayer for Madge. He returned to find Rosie smiling and just laying down her crayons. "See Uncle Danny, I stayed in the lines."

Danny reached out for the picture and examined it. "Wow, I have never seen anyone do such a great job of staying in the lines. I think this calls for some ice cream before we get you ready for bed. Maybe we have time to watch one of your favorite cartoons on the T.V. Your choice."

"I'm glad you are babysitting me tonight. When Grandma and Daddy get home, I'm going to tell them I want you to be my babysitter from now on. At least until Lily comes back." She looked at Danny. "She is coming back isn't she?"

Danny looked into her eyes. He knew they would do all they could to get Lily home and he was now sure it would happen. "Yes, Lily will be coming home to us."

Chapter 47

Josie threw herself back into her work. She had gotten into a routine and enjoyed her morning runs even in the rain and her work on the files in the afternoon and evening. She enjoyed the solitude and the sense of accomplishment when she realized she had made headway in the files. She had never worked in an office before but found she had a knack for organization. TJ seemed pleased with her progress. She read over the files Josie set aside for her and spot checked the others. She also realized Josie was right on, when it came to evaluating the information in the files.

One weekend Josie asked TJ if she would ride out to the old farm where Lily had lived. She agreed it may be a good idea for her to see where the crime actually took place.

As TJ drove, Josie relayed the events of her last trip with Max. They had never made it all the way. When Max and Danny went back out together, they had found it was being rented. She was hoping the same man was still there, because he had allowed them to look inside the house. Josie was hoping they could too. She still felt uneasy on the desolate road and kept checking to make sure they were not being followed.

When TJ questioned her, she said, "I have no idea why we were followed that day, but it still has me spooked. Funny that when Max and Danny came back they were not bothered."

"Well, I want you to be cautious. It may be some pervert after you. You be careful when you jog. I don't want to worry about you."

Josie laughed but still had the feeling that TJ might be right. She needed to remember to pay more attention to her surroundings.

They spotted the house at the same time. "Looks like we made it here ok."

As they pulled up next to the house, they noticed a truck. When they got out of the car, they got a closer look. It appeared someone was loading up the truck.

"Hello, is anyone here?" TJ called out.

Soon a man appeared and looked at them. "What can I do for you? Looking for someone?"

TJ introduced herself and Josie to him and explained that they were friends with Max and Danny. "They told us how helpful you were when they visited. Do you mind if we also look around?"

"Go right ahead. I decided to move closer to my son. Now that my wife is gone, I hate the isolation. Never thought I would, but who knows why we change our minds as we get older. As you can see, I am loading up my truck. Don't have much. The house comes furnished. You interested in renting the place?"

"Not really. Just wanted to see where my friend lived years ago."

"Didn't know the previous owners. Heard he died. I rent this from the bank. Come on in and look at whatever you want. I don't have a problem with that."

He shook his head. He had no idea what the fascination was with this old place but heck the women were both easy on the eyes. He was glad for the company.

TJ and Josie walked through the house and noticed the details. Kitchen was old but functional. The fireplace in the living room was made of stone and looked inviting. The house was old but appeared to be in good shape. Small but comfortable was what Josie was thinking. She asked if she could walk around outside. She remembered Lily talking about her tree. For some reason she was uncomfortable inside the house. She hoped the feeling would pass when she went outside.

The old man told them to take their time and look around all they wanted. "Not much to see. I don't farm, but there is a barn and interesting graveyard out back. I'm going to finish packing. I want to try and leave in the morning. Good thing you came today. Otherwise you would have to get the key from the bank."

They walked outside and Josie spotted the tree. It fit the description Lily had given her. She imagined it must have grown even taller since Lily had left but she could see why Lily chose it. The branches were spread out as if reaching to the sky. The leaves were still healthy and looked as if they were painted on. They were as close to perfect as nature would allow. She felt a breeze stir through the leaves as if they were whispering to her. She was overcome with a sense of calm. She eased herself to the ground and leaned against the tree trunk and closed her eyes. She had the feeling if she listened hard enough, it would release its secrets.

TJ came over and shook her shoulder. "Are you falling asleep on me?"

"No. Was I asleep?"

"I walked into the barn and looked around. Couldn't find you at first. Then I spotted you sitting under this old tree and you certainly looked relaxed enough to be asleep. We better finish looking around and get out of here. Leave the old man to his packing. Is there anything else you want to see?"

"No, let's head back."

As they drove back to town they were both lost in their own thoughts. Neither one spoke until they entered the town. "I'm going to the office. Do you want me to drop you off somewhere?"

Josie thought a minute "If you don't mind, I want to work on the files in the room off your office. I still feel we are missing something in there."

They entered the building and both went to work. Josie looked around the room and thought *if only the walls could talk. What is the secret you are holding?*

Josie was surprised when she pulled out an old ledger. She couldn't imagine how difficult it must have been to keep records before computers. She laid it on the table and was relieved to put it down. It was heavy and covered in dust. She decided to leave it until later. Probably just receipts of fees collected and not currently of interest to either her or TJ. Instead she went back to the files. She never realized how tedious, and to tell the truth, downright boring this job turned out to be. She realized she was grateful this was not a career path she had chosen. She liked being more involved with people instead of paper. First the waitress job and hopefully she would soon be doing what she really wanted to do, work as a beautician. Funny she thought to herself, when I started going to Beauty School I had no idea that I would end up here. Hopefully we can get Lily out of here and start our *real life.* She laughed. *And I'll stop talking to myself.*

A file cabinet was hidden behind some boxes. Because of the angle, she had not noticed it on her initial inspection. Now that the boxes were getting emptied, it was easier to see. The bottom drawer of the file cabinet was stuck. She got down on her hands and knees to inspect the drawer.

It didn't look bent or crooked. She tried the lock. It was unlocked. So what was holding it? She opened the drawer above that one and tried to reach behind the drawer once it was fully opened. Nope, nothing felt jammed. She closed that drawer and decided to sit down and brace her feet and pull with all her weight on the drawer handle. She could feel the resistance and muttered to herself. *It's you or me buddy and I'm counting on me.* Still nothing moved. She remembered there was a screwdriver in the outer office. She went to get it. As she passed TJ's office, she noticed she was still here.

"The bottom drawer in the file cabinet is stuck. Do you mind if I jimmy the drawer? I'll be careful but I can't open it without using something to pry it open. It is so old, I suspect it has rusted."

"Sure, whatever. I really do not plan on keeping all that stuff and will probably get rid of most of the file cabinets. Knock yourself out."

She looked at Josie and laughed "Not literally. Please don't hurt yourself."

Josie joined in her laughter and realized she must have sounded like she was asking permission to put down a rabid animal. But heck, she hated to lose to a stupid file drawer.

Once she was back with the screwdriver, so worked on loosening the drawer. She tried to pry the drawer away from the cabinet and realized the task was not as easy as she thought it would be. Good thing TJ was not interested in reusing the cabinet. She could tell she would cause damage when she finally pried it loose. She probably shouldn't bother with it but her determination was stronger than her patience.

She just knew she was going to open it not matter what. Finally she had an opening in the drawer. At least enough to wiggle the drawer. Her first assessment was right. It was rusted. Maybe now she could get enough grip to pull it out. She grabbed the edge of the drawer and used all her strength to pull. Not giving into caution, she sat on the floor again and used her entire weight to force it open. She heard a loud squeak and the drawer released from the track. The force sent her back on the floor and the drawer sat on top of her. She had scratches on her leg from the drawer but did not pay any attention to the discomfort. She was focused on looking at the contents. As she crawled over to look inside the opening the drawer had left once it was removed, she saw papers crammed in the back of the space. She wiggled her hands into the space but could not quite reach it. Now she was really determined to find out what was there. She remembered seeing pliers in the toolbox and went to get them.

As she walked out of the room, TJ glanced up and was shocked at her appearance.

"Hey, do you know your leg is bleeding? And you look like you just fought in a bar fight and lost. Are you ok?"

Josie reached up and smoothed her hair out of her face. She was still mad at the drawer and murmured "Fine. Just fine." And headed to the toolbox.

By the time Josie had removed the paper from the drawer, with the added length of the pliers, her arms were covered in scratches from the sharp edges inside the cabinet. She sat back to appraise the damage. She did not want to get blood on the papers she had worked so hard to retrieve. She looked up and noticed TJ watching her.

"Well, it looks like you won the battle, if not the war. Now go look after those battle scars. The last thing we need is for you to get an infection. Then we are leaving and going home for the night. I'm tired and I know you must be." She laughed "And a shower wouldn't hurt you either".

Josie looked at the pile of papers but knew TJ was right. Better to look at them when she was more rested and could concentrate. Most of the old papers gave her a headache just trying to read the handwriting. Those that were typed, were hard enough.

The next day Josie decided she was definitely going to get to the end of this filing. The first thing she did was look at the ledger. As she was reading the entries, she called out to TJ. "Look at this. I cannot believe what I am reading. No wonder this room smells. Your uncle was using this as a poker room. He kept a ledger of what was lost and not all that was lost was money. There is property listed here."

"Let me see that."

TJ took her time looking as the entries. She turned to Josie

"We better keep this door closed and locked and not let anyone know what we discovered until we know the extent of what we found. Better to keep this secret safe and avoid any nasty repercussions."

"I'll check this ledger against the papers I found in the file drawer yesterday. There may be a reason that drawer was jammed."

TJ left and went back to her own office. Josie was deeply engrossed in her research. When TJ returned shortly to check her progress, Josie immediately let out a scream.

"Josie, what the hell is wrong with you?"

"Sorry, you made me paranoid and I was getting some real interesting facts by comparing these two. The ledger and the papers. I wasn't expecting you to come back so soon."

"So tell me what you found."

"Well.........interesting enough, this town looks like it changes ownership of houses so frequently it makes you wonder how anyone knew where to sleep at the end of the day."

"What are you talking about?"

"The deeds were in the file cabinet. The ledger listed the present owner. It appears to me like your uncle kept track on paper but never filed the transfer of the deeds. My guess is that the property was used instead of money to play cards. So it could change from game to game."

"Are people nuts? I cannot believe this is true."

"Well you are the lawyer so you should know better than me."

TJ took the ledger and papers over to the other table in the room. She sat down and studied them for about thirty minutes. She then turned to Josie and said, "I have to believe you are right about this. It's scary. How many people are living in a house that they think they own and in reality, it was gambled away. Right under them?"

"What are you going to do?"

TJ shook her head. Right now nothing. I cannot make any decision that will have this impact on the town. I need to check what I can before I decide. We need to see if the deeds we have are in the name of the families actually living at that address. It may eliminate some, but this is too complicated for me to make a rash decision."

Chapter 48

Max called to let Danny know Madge was being admitted to the Hospital. They were going to do more test in the morning. For now, it did appear to be her heart but they would have more answers after her test. He would be home soon to tuck Rosie into bed. Not much he could do at the Hospital for now and Madge was given a sedative to get some sleep.

"Max, Bea is coming over soon too, she is spending the night, just in case you need her. I need to go back to the station to check on some things. Since we made an arrest today, I need to make sure the paperwork is in order. Therefore, I may leave when Bea gets here. Oh, and one last thing, Millie called and is very concerned about Madge. She wants you to call her when you get home, no matter what time it is. Make sure you call me if you need anything."

"I can't thank you enough, Danny. I appreciate your help today."

They hung up just as Bea arrived. Danny filled her in on everything and then went back into the living room to kiss Rosie goodbye. "Daddy will be home soon. I have to go do some Sheriff stuff. Can I trust my Junior Deputy to take care of Bea?"

Rosie laughed "Sure, Sheriff Uncle Danny. I know what to do." She reached out and gave him a hug. He looked at her sweet face and realized he wouldn't mind having a child. God, he missed Lily.

Max came in soon afterwards and he got Rosie in bed. He talked to Bea, then headed into the kitchen, to fix a sandwich and to call Millie.

He filled Millie in as best he could. He was surprised to hear that she was coming out to help.

"I'm in a slow period at work right now. My supplier is making new molds and it will be awhile before she ships any new pieces. So for now, I'm free. I know you need to concentrate on Madge right now. I would love to be there to help you out with Rosie and the house. So, that's that. I should be there tomorrow."

Max was surprised and didn't know what to say. How lucky he was to have such caring people in his life. He was quiet and he heard Millie say, "Just say it's ok and I will feel better. I don't want to impose."

Max was caught off guard. "Millie, I'm stunned. It's too much to ask of you but I could really use your help. I can't thank you enough."

"No need for thanks. I want to do this. For you and for me. So thank you. See you tomorrow."

True to her word, Millie arrived early the next morning.

"How did you get here so fast?"

"I had two of my friends drive me. One drove me in my car; the other drove the car they are going back in. I wanted my car here in case I needed it. I dropped them off at the diner and after they eat, they are heading back."

Max reached out and embraced her in a hug, "You never cease to amaze me. Thanks for coming out to help."

"Max I am not getting any younger. I never realized how much family meant to me until I met Lily and Josie. I now view you all as my family. You are giving me more than I ever imagined I was missing in my life. No more talk of that. What do you need me to do? How is your Mother today?"

"I was going to head over to the hospital after I got Rosie ready for school. Come have breakfast with us and we can drop Rosie off together. That way you will know where the school is located. Then we will both go to the hospital together."

"Have you called Josie?"

"No. I thought about it but decided I should have a little more news before I worry her."

"Just don't forget to let her know. That girl will get hurt if she thinks you don't want to tell her."

Max laughed, "I sure don't want any problems between us. I saw how she felt about Danny, although I think she has mellowed some."

Rosie appeared in the doorway of the kitchen. She looked at Millie and then ran over to hug her. "I missed you."

Millie felt her eyes tear up and quickly stopped them. "I missed you too. That's why I told your Daddy I wanted to come and visit."

"I'm glad. Did you know my grandma is sick?"

"Yes honey, your daddy told me she is in the hospital getting fixed up so she will be home soon. Maybe I can watch you after school until she comes home."

Rosie smiled and agreed she would like that.

Once they dropped Rosie off at school, Max and Millie made their way to the Hospital. Traffic in the parking lot was light today and they had no problem finding a spot close to the door.

Madge was asleep when they reached her room. They noticed she had an IV hanging by the top of her bed with fluids dripping into her arm. She also had electrodes running on her chest and the readings appeared on the TV screen above the bed. Millie was unsure what this all meant. Hopefully, it was nothing serious that couldn't be fixed. She examined Madge's face and she had good color and did not look like she was in pain. None of the tell tale signs of that in her face. Millie breathed a sigh of relief and offered up a prayer for a quick recovery. As they were standing there, Madge must have sensed their presence and her eyes opened. She smiled at Max but frowned when she noticed Millie.

"God, am I that bad? They called you here?"

Millie laughed and reached over to kiss Madge on the cheek. "No, as a matter of fact, I came to help out with Rosie. You'll be fine, but I was worried about her."

Madge looked at her to make sure she was telling the truth. Worry lines appeared in her brow. Max was quick to speak up. "Has the Doctor been in? Have you had any more tests today? How did you sleep last night?"

"Whoa, one thing at a time. The tests are scheduled, the doctor will be in when they are done, I cannot eat anything until after they are finished and I slept ok between the times they woke me up to take my vitals. Now don't get your panties in a knot!"

Max and Millie laughed out loud.

"Thank God you are still feisty, that makes me feel better, Mom."

They were all laughing when the nurse came in to wheel her down for the start of her test. Madge introduced them and the nurse informed them that the test would take most of the morning. Then she would likely want to sleep after that. She advised them to go home instead of sitting in the waiting room. She said they could call anytime to check on her. She would leave a note for the hospital to call as soon as she was back in her room.

Madge agreed that was the best thing to do. "Besides, you need to get to work and Millie must need to nap. I'm sure she is tired herself."

Max and Millie left and he dropped her off at the house. Max gave Millie a spare key. "Mom is right, try and work in a nap. I'll be home for lunch and we can call the hospital then."

"And call Josie?"

"That too." He kissed her on the cheek and headed off to work.

Millie had just walked into the house when the phone rang. She answered it and spoke to Danny. She filled him in on what was going on and told him not to worry because she had things covered for Max. She would take care of Rosie.

After she hung up, she walked through the Living Room. The sofa looked inviting and she decided to lay down for a few minutes so she would be fresh for Rosie. Soon she felt someone shaking her. She sat up and experienced a moment of fear. Then she looked in Max's face. "Sorry, I guess I was tired. I forgot where I was for a minute."

Max held up a bag and told her Bea had sent home soup and sandwiches. "Not sure what kind, but she is a great cook."

"How kind of her. I am rather hungry."

After they ate, Millie cleaned up the dishes. Max suggested she stop by the store later and they would pick up Rosie from school together. "Mom often does that. I want Rosie to have things as normal as possible in her life."

"You are a good dad. She is lucky to have you."

"I'm the lucky one. She's been through so much so early in her life, yet she still seems unaffected."

"Much of that is due to you, I'm sure."

"Mom and Lily deserve some of the credit."

Suddenly there was a silence hanging in the house. Both realized how important it was to get Lily back. Then Millie smiled to herself as she looked at Max, *I bet he wants Josie here too. For a much more personal reason.*

Max called the hospital and was told Madge was still waiting for one more test. They expected her to be back in her room by three and then take a nap. The Doctor was not expected to be in to see her until after six. He relayed the information to Millie. They decided to go see her after dinner unless she called them to come in sooner.

"I'll stop by and see if Bea can stay with Rosie for an hour or so. That way you can go to the hospital with me and then Bea can go once you get home."

With their plans made, Max went back to work and Millie decided to unpack. Max had suggested she stay in Lily's room because it was close to the bathroom. She soon got settled and decided to explore the town.

When Millie stopped into see Max, she was amazed at how large his actual showroom was. How much inventory he carried.

"Do you really do that much business in this town to carry such a large inventory? I'm not questioning your business ability, just surprised I guess."

"No offense taken. Yes, I have done quite well. I sell to customers in several of the surrounding towns. I keep my profit margin low and offer very competitive pricing on everything. I think it is better to make a sensible profit on many items instead of a large profit on just a few. I enjoy what I do and I have been able to build a steady client base. Many of my customers come back when they need something. I think they have found me to be fair and that means more to me than anything. "

"I noticed the vacant store next door. Is that for sale?"

"I think so. The store had a small repair shop there. You know for TV's and appliances. I felt sorry for him each time I sold a new appliance. Most people now want to buy new instead of making repairs on the old ones. I have asked a few customers and they said with all the new features on the appliances, they just want to replace the old one. They reminded me that it is more energy efficient too. Guess that about sums up his business demise. He was getting older, and from what I gathered, he was not too sorry to retire."

"Does it have an apartment upstairs too?"

"Why all the interest?"

"Well to be honest I have been thinking about relocating. I am all alone. My customers are mostly in the big cities, New York, Los Angeles, and Chicago. I really do not have to be in any particular place to run my business. My artists are all over and operate by mail order. I miss Josie and Lily. I have the feeling this is where they will end up when everything gets straightened out, so why not entertain the possibility of moving too."

"I'm sure that would make them happy. It's a lot to consider and I don't want to influence you, but we would love to have you in our family and part of the community." He grinned and was surprised at how happy the idea made him.

They entered the hospital and found Madge talking to the Doctor. Madge introduced them to him and told him it was ok to speak in front of her son and good friend.

Dr. Abrams explained that for now, Madge was in good condition. From the test they had performed, they concluded that she did not actually have a heart attack but what is called an abnormal heart rhythm. This caused her heart to slow down to a dangerous level. Luckily, they were able to shock it back in rhythm before any damage was done to her heart. They needed to insure this did not occur again. He was recommending a device that they implant into her chest to handle this condition, if it occurred again. She would be asleep for the procedure. The device would be wired to her heart and would then be capable of pacing her heart back into rhythm, or acting as a defibrillator, if needed. Once this was done, she could go back to her normal activities and lead a generally unrestricted lifestyle. If she decided on this option, he would have the doctor chosen to perform the procedure, meet with her and her family to go into a more lengthy discussion. He advised them to think about it and let him know. For now, he wanted to monitor Madge and keep her in the hospital for a few more days.

After the doctor left, Madge started to cry. Max went to her and tried to comfort her. Millie said, "I have an acquaintance in New York who had this done over five years ago. He is fine and works full time. Do you want me to have him call you and let you know about his experience? Sometimes it helps to know someone who has been through the same thin, than just relying on medical jargon."

Madge wiped her eyes and looked at Millie. "Yes, I'd like that. I'm not ready to pack it in just yet."

Max looked at his mother "God knows, I'm not ready to let you go just yet. You are still needed too much."

They all laughed to cover the tears stinging their eyes. Although, it sounded like the condition could be fixed or corrected, it still brought Madge's mortality into each of their thoughts. All were painfully aware of what danger she had faced.

Madge told them to go home and take care of Rosie. She was going to catch some sleep and talk to Millie's friend tomorrow. Max told her that Bea was probably going to come up after they got home and Madge smiled. "That's fine. Tell her if I'm asleep, do not wake me up."

On the elevator, Millie asked what was with Bea and Madge. He laughed. "They have been friends for so long they fight like sisters. Each one tries to keep the other one from knowing how much they love each other. But, we saw through that a long time ago. I'm sure once Bea gets there, Mom will discuss all the options and come to her decision. She relies on Bea's advice but would never admit it to anyone."

They arrived home and Bea left immediately to make it before the end of visiting hours. Max went up to tuck Rosie in for the night. Millie decided she was going to take a long soaking bubble bath and then go to bed. Max would call Josie as soon as he had Rosie settled in for the night.

Chapter 49

Max placed a call to Josie. Luckily, she heard the phone ring and looked at the number. She was glad to see it was Max. She missed him terribly.

She was so excited to hear from him, she started right in talking a mile a minute. She caught him up to date on her job, explaining about the ledger. The trouble she had getting a drawer open, and started in on their visit to the farm where Lily lived.

"Hey Josie, take a breath honey. You are wearing me out."

"I'm sorry. I just miss you so damn much and I miss talking things over with you."

"Well promise me you will leave that ranch alone. I worry about you and I get a bad feeling thinking about that place."

"The guy who lives on the farm was real nice and besides he is moving out. In fact, he was packing up when we were there."

"Ok, but now it's my turn to talk."

He explained about Madge's condition and Millie's arrival. He also told her about Millie's idea of relocating her business to live close to them.

"I'm so sorry about your Mom. Do you want me to come home?"

"Of course I want you here. But I know you are making progress with TJ and want to be close to Lily. I just want to get this behind us so we can move on. Millie is helping out with Rosie and will be good company when Mom gets home. So we have that covered. My loneliness is what needs to be fixed."

Josie knew she loved this man. God how lucky she was. She wanted this all to be over soon. More than she had ever wanted anything in her life. "I know. I miss you so much I ache all over."

"Me too!"

She laughed. "Now don't go there or I'll jump on the next bus out of here."

"Not a bad idea. I want to come up soon but right now I don't know how I can get away."

"I know. Besides, I need you, but they need you more right now. I've waited for you all my life so I guess I can wait a little bit longer."

They talked some more and Max promised to call her the next day when he knew more about Madge.

Josie was more determined than ever to finish up her job here. She knew if there was anything in the office relating to Lily's earlier years, she would find it. Maybe, then maybe, they could get Lily out of jail.

That evening TJ came down to the file room and surveyed the files sitting around the room. "We need to decide what to do with all this mess. Tell you what, maybe instead of looking through each one too much, look and see what the file contains. Like you did with the newer files you already sorted. Wills, deeds, lawsuits etc. Sort them in piles and then we can start on one thing at a time. Forget the dates; just go with the type of case it involves. That way, I will look at the files by topic and determine if it is active or a retired file. I honestly don't feel up to tackling this myself. Once we get a better system, I can pass some of these on to Tracy. She can determine which ones are still in effect. Some of those deeds may be outdated because the property could have changed hands since then. The wills are also suspect. The person could have made new ones. She can call them and find out. That way, if they want to update it, they can come in."

Josie was glad for the suggestion. The job was getting tedious and she was definitely getting bored. She was afraid she may miss something important. This may give her a new direction and relieve some of the monotony.

Soon the files were getting some direction. The disorder actually looked like it was decreasing in size. Josie finally felt she would be able to realize an end to the job. Not that she regretted it, because it allowed her to stay close to Lily but she was anxious to move onto something else.

Josie had a nagging thought. *"What if there is information about Lily here?"* I better look at the ledger more carefully. She was about half way through when she came upon an entry that made her stop. The name Clyde Hill was listed. It indicated that he obtained the farm from Leroy Ridder over twenty years ago as payment on debt incurred by Mr. Ridder. Nothing mentioned of the amount of the debt. So this is how he came to own the farm. Now I have a direction. I will look for any information filed under Clyde Hill and see if I can find out anything else she said out loud all though no one could hear her. It took another two hours but she did locate two additional files.

Max interrupted her search. He kept her informed about his Mother's condition and told her it looked like Millie was permanently settled into her room at Madge's, at least for now. She still talked of moving into her own place once Madge recovered and was able to return to her normal activities. He was surprised at how much he had come to depend upon her. In fact, now that the surgery was over, Madge would be coming home.

Josie spoke next, "I found some information about Lily's life here. It appears the farm was part of a gambling debt owed to Lily's husband. I've just started looking to see if I can find any other information. I'll let you know if I find anything else of interest."

Max continued to update her on the family and told her how much he missed being with her. She wanted to ask him to come here but knew she was just being selfish. She could not put any more stress on him. He was dealing with his mother and daughter now. They should be his main concern. She told herself to, *suck it up,* and told him she was fine.

After the conversation with Max, Josie was more determined than ever to get through the files. She needed to find anything she could on Clyde Hill. First she decided to check for any files with his name. Nothing was in this room, so she went out front to check the more current files. It was getting frustrating and she was beginning to have doubts that anything else was here.

She glanced up as TJ came into the office. At once, she knew something was terribly wrong. TJ was bleeding and seemed disoriented.

"Oh my God, what happened? Here, sit down and let me check you out".

TJ slumped in the chair and Josie ran to the bathroom to get wet paper towels. She applied them to her face and wiped the blood off. It appeared the blood was coming from her nose and not from a cut.

"Do you want me to call the Doctor, take you to the Hospital, call the police?"

"Give me a minute. I need to get myself together. I need to think."

"Can you tell me what happened?"

TJ's breathing eased and her head started to clear.

"Josie, I think someone is watching us. Not sure why, or if it is you or me that they are after, but we need to be careful. I can't figure this out. I don't want to get the police involved right now."

"But you are hurt. Were you were attacked?"

"I think it's time I told you some things. You see, my Uncle did die. That much is true. But, he may have been murdered. It was never proven, but I still wonder. He was found just inside the front door. He died from hitting his head on the table out there. The conclusion was that he stumbled, hit his head and died from a blunt force to his head. In other words, when he hit the table, he hit it in just the right angle, that it caused his death. I never did buy that theory but I could not disprove it either. My Uncle could have been attacked as he came in, pushed into the table and left there."

"Why didn't anyone investigate that possibility?"

"Well, as you know, this is not the most intuitive Police Department. They took the easy way out. Just assumed he tripped and fell. My feeling, especially now that we discovered the hidden room, is that someone was looking for something. He came in and surprised them; they pushed him causing him to fall. He hit his head and they left him to die. That's why we need to be cautious. Until we find out what we have here.... what someone wants."

"That may be true, but I still think we should report this, get you checked out. It does appear that only your nose was injured but we still should make sure you are ok."

"He didn't touch me. I tripped running up the steps. My heel must have caught on the step and threw me face first into the riser of the step. I'm ok. Just mad at myself."

"Well what happened to scare you?"

"I got out of the car and saw the lights on in here. I knew you were here and I was not being too cautious. Anyway, as I got closer to the steps, I felt someone watching. You know, when you just get that tingle in the back of your neck? I looked around and thought I saw something move. I started to run up the steps and fell. I cannot say for sure that someone was actually there. I didn't really see anyone. I just know what I felt."

"Still sounds scary to me. And from what I know of you, you don't scare easily."

"True. I guess this whole thing with the files, ledger and stuff we found has me on edge. Plus the fact, I am trying to handle so much at once. I never realized how my Uncle ran his practice. I guess I jumped in too soon and took over without giving it much thought. From afar, it looked like the perfect opportunity to escape the rat race I was in, and take over a small town practice. You know, lead a quiet country life. Wills, probate and occasional legal matter. Give me a chance to enjoy life instead of working twenty hours a day. Little did I know!"

"You'll get there. Once we get this all straightened out. Now we really must find out what secrets are hidden in your files. If we can get that resolved, I think we can find out the truth about your Uncle and you can have the life you want."

"You may be right, Josie. But for now, we both need to realize we may be in danger. We need to be very careful. In fact, I don't think either one of us should be here alone at night."

"I hate to be intimated like that. I want to get finished with the files and you cannot always be here when I am."

"I want you to promise me that you will not work alone at night."

"How are we going to finish anytime soon if we do that? You are not always able to come here when I do. Sometimes you have to go out of town. Should we tell Tracy and let her help?"

"I don't want to involve her yet. We need to know who we can trust. Even though I trust her with current matters, I'm not sure what we are sitting on in that back room and I hesitate to involve her. She may slip and tell the wrong person. Unlike us, she has lived here a long time and knows most of the people in town. It may be too tempting for her not to share. We need to make sure no one knows of our discovery. We will be safer, the less people who know, the better off we will be."

"I guess you're right. Well, if you are ok, I'll get back to my files."

"Ok, but we are leaving together. No arguments on that!"

"Yes, Boss!"

Chapter 50

Madge came home much to the relief of Max and Rosie. Millie was staying on, helping out during the day when Max worked. Things were getting back to normal in town, now that Danny had made an arrest in the case of the child molester. After a background check, it was discovered the man had already served time on similar charges and had been released from prison. He had disappeared after his release and no one was able to keep track of his whereabouts. That in itself, made Danny more determined to put him away forever. He made sure he had all the facts lined up and spent all his free time getting the files in order. He was determined not to let this one slip through the system.

Max was planning to go see Josie. He wanted to take Rosie but was discouraged from doing that by Millie and Madge. They were afraid she would find out Lily was in jail. They did not think it was wise to put her, or Lily, in that situation. Max was resigned to going alone.

The day before he left, Danny told him he was going to accompany him. He needed to see Lily. He felt she had enough time to think over what he had said, and wanted to catch up on her case with TJ and the sheriff.

Once they arrived in town, they met up with Josie. They all headed to the diner for dinner. Josie filled them in on what had happened to TJ, about the files in the office, and how she felt she was being watched, at times, herself.

Max looked at Danny and Josie. "Call me crazy, but I think we should help out. I'll talk to TJ and see if she has any objections to us helping you out. Maybe with extra hands and eyes, we can finish up this job sooner for you."

TJ had no problem with the extra help. After all, Danny was a police officer and she would pay Max to help out. They agreed on a fifty-dollar fee. Max said he would take it, so it all remained legal, but he would take them all out to dinner when they finished. He was sure TJ was not getting rich off her practice in this town.

On the second day, Danny was working between his visits with Lily. He had just returned to the office. He noticed Max and Josie deep in work and did not want to disturb them. He walked over to the far end of the room, sat down and started on a box that had been pushed off to the side. Suddenly he started to sweat. His hair stood up on the back of his neck. He forced himself to keep calm. He had a file in his hand that both scared and excited him at the same time. There was no notation on the folder of what it contained inside, but once Danny started to read, he knew he had found something very important. Some instinct told him to remain quiet before he shared his find. He glanced around and was relieved to see that Max and Josie were not paying any attention to him. Good, now he had to get them out of here so he could lay the papers out and look at them more closely.

He called out to them, "Hey, since I'm here now, why don't you two run over and get lunch? I can hold down the fort while you are gone."

Max replied, "I think we should all go. We could all use a break."

"I ate before coming back after seeing Lily." He lied and hoped they didn't notice his stomach rumbling.

"Ok. Sounds like a good idea. I'm getting stiff and I'm sure Josie is too. Maybe we can take a walk while we are out and get rid of the kinks." Max always agreeable, felt Danny had a reason for sending them off. He glanced at Danny to see if he could read anything in his face. Danny remained unreadable.

Once they left, Danny grabbed the folder and went into the conference room and spread all the papers out on the table. He was so excited, he read through the information quickly. Once he absorbed what was in the file, he reread it again more slowly, to make sure he did not miss any pertinent information.

He knew he had to think about what he had discovered before showing it to Josie. He needed to have TJ. look at this first. Yes, he decided that would be the best way to handle this. She must to be the one who determines what needs to be done with the information.

Max and Josie returned and Danny was relieved that he had a chance to hide the file until TJ returned. He was suddenly on edge. He needed to get out of the office. He explained to Max and Josie that he was heading back to the hotel. He needed to check in with his Deputy. Make sure everything was being handled in his absence.

Once he left, Josie said to Max. "Is Danny alright? He sure is acting strange today. Did you notice how on edge he seemed? You know him better than I do but I just sensed something was bothering him. I'm sure he would have told us if it had to do with Lily, don't you?"

Danny did go back to the hotel. He called into the department to check on things, but he was so distracted, he did not talk long. *Funny how it is all starting to come together. I want to keep my head for once. I need to make sure I don't screw up.* He remembered how he had first reacted to Lily's dilemma. *Yeah, I really blew that one!*

Max and Josie finished the pile of files they were working on, had them all sorted and ready for TJ's final decision. They had eaten lunch and had taken a short walk but both wanted to get away for a while, enjoy each other's company. Max would need to leave soon and they had not had much time together since he arrived.

"Hey, let's go for a ride. I'll call the hotel and tell Danny we will be gone for the rest of the afternoon. I won't invite him to go with us; we need some quiet time by ourselves."

Josie leaned over and kissed him. "Sounds good to me."

"Well, where do you want to go?"

"Call me crazy, but I want to go back out to the farm where Lily lived. I want to look around again. The man who lived there has moved so no one should be there."

"Why, do you want to go there of all places?"

"I just feel like it is trying to tell us something. If we are by ourselves, we may be able to figure it out."

"Ok, but we are leaving before it gets dark. I don't want us out there when we can't see our surroundings. It's too dangerous."

"Agreed."

They knew their way now and it seemed less sinister than the last time. Max was very cautious in leaving town and made sure they were not being followed. He pulled off the road several times when he found an opportunity to hide the car among brush or trees. If someone was following them, they could easily spot the tail. After three times, Max felt confident they were not being followed.

Soon the road gave way to the unpaved area and they knew they were getting close to the farm. As Josie had told him, the renter had moved out. The house and driveway was deserted. Josie commented that the house had that empty feeling as if it mourned the passing of life within it walls. "So sad how a house offers you comfort and safety but once you leave, it looks so weak and forlorn. It is as if all the memories are lost."

Max looked at her. He had never heard her talk like this

They walked around the house and tried the doors. They were locked. Josie said she did not really want to go inside anyway. They headed to the graveyard and looked at the headstones.

"This one had Clyde's name but no date of birth or death."

"They all look crude as if they were made by hand, by the survivors. Wonder who made the one for Clyde?"

"Let's go into the barn and look around, enough of this."

Josie grabbed his hand and steered him to the barn. Once inside, they could still smell the scent of hay. Even though it looked like it had not been changed in a long time, it still covered the floor. Josie walked further inside and looked up.

"That must be the hayloft that Lily talked to me about. She told me she used to sit up there and felt at peace when she was by herself. Let's climb up."

Josie and Max found the ladder was still stable. They made their way up to the loft. Josie was surprised at how the loft had the same effect on her. She looked at Max with his broad shoulders, his hair graying at the temples. Maybe the peace and contentment was because she was with him. The love reflected in his eyes. She reached out, put her arms around his waist and gave him a passionate kiss. He returned it and then pulled away to look at her. "Have you ever made love in a hayloft?" His eyes were cloudy with passion.

"No, but it sounds just like were sent here for that reason. Don't spoil it and tell me you have."

Max laughed, "No, you will be the first. Is that a yes?"

Josie reached out and unzipped his pants. "How about a nice long time in the hay and then we will take a swim in Lily's pond before heading back to town? Think we have enough time?"

He looked down at his erection and laughed. As far as I'm concerned, we can start right now."

They made love with such intensity that it surprised them both. Once again, they knew they were meant to be together forever. Max yawned, "Can an old man get a short nap before we head out to swim?"

Josie snuggled closer to him and he wrapped his arms over her. "Sure, I'm rather tired right now myself. But don't think this lets you off the hook on that swim. I am imagining what we can do in the water."

Max groaned, "You drive me crazy woman. But I would not have it any other way." He laughed and fell asleep before she could respond.

Josie woke up and felt the urge to relieve herself. She decided to slip down the ladder and look for a spot in the corner of the barn. She felt strange using the loft where they made love. She gently scooted away from Max. She would give him a few more minutes before waking him. As she descended the ladder, she felt someone grab her. A hand clamped over her mouth. She tried to break free but he had a firm grip on her from behind.

"If you know what is good for you, you will keep your mouth shut and listen to what I say."

Josie was afraid for herself and Max. Who was this man? Did he know Max was here with her? Did he think she was alone? She decided to find out. She bit his fingers that were covering her mouth. He reached out and smacked her across the face and kicked her in the back. She tried to scream but her breath was knocked out of her lungs from where he kicked her. As she fell, he looked at her. "Well it has been a long time since someone naked came my way. Guess I shouldn't miss the opportunity." He opened his zipper and fell on top of her.

Josie was frightened and repulsed. She used all her strength to try and fight him. She managed to get out a short scream. Max came down the ladder and appeared to be so stunned with what he saw, he momentarily froze. Josie then saw the rage in his face as he started toward them. The man quickly sprang at Max, and too late, they noticed the knife in his hand.

It was as if Josie was seeing this from afar. She was so scared; it took her a few seconds to react. By then, the man had managed to cut Max in his arm and it was bleeding. This only seemed to excite the man and he rushed forward to deliver another blow to sink his knife in Max's chest. Josie sprang up and reached out to grab the closest object. Her hands came in contact with an old bucket. She grabbed it and swung it trying to hit the man. Max was trying to fight the man off, but she could tell the injury had weakened him.

Josie heard the sound of feet on the gravel outside. She was now afraid this man had someone with him. They did not stand a chance against two attackers. She glanced at the open door and Danny rushed in. He immediately drew his gun and pointed it at the man. The man did not stop his advance on Max. Max saw Danny approach and used all his remaining strength to throw his body off to the side, away from the attack. Danny used this opportunity to shoot at the man's leg. Once the man dropped, Danny flew at him and got him subdued. He cuffed him and read him his rights.

Danny turned his back on Josie and Max. "I suggest you two lovebirds get dressed. I saw more than I need to see. We need to get back to town."

Danny left with the man in the back of his car. Josie and Max quickly dressed. Josie tore his shirt and bandaged his arm. "We need to get this taken care of pronto. It looks like I stopped the bleeding, but it may need stitches. That knife had to be dirty. It will probably get infected."

Max hugged her. "Did he hurt you? You know what I mean? I'm so sorry I was asleep."

Josie looked at him. "No I was able to keep him from penetrating me, if that's what you mean."

"Honey, I didn't mean it like that. I just want to make sure you are ok. You did nothing wrong."

"Sorry, I have never been this close to being raped. I feel so violated. To think I was naked and walked right into him. He was waiting for us."

"Next time you go exploring, wake me first. Promise?" He hugged her. "Let's get out of here."

Chapter 51

Later that evening, they were all back at the office sitting around the conference room table. Max had four stitches in his arm but it was superficial and should heal without much problem. As Josie suspected, the hospital started him on antibiotics as a precaution against infection. Josie had been checked out and her x-ray did not detect any broken bones or ribs. She would be sore and have bruises but no lasting effects from the punches she endured. They offered her something for pain, but she declined. She would go with Motrin, if she needed anything.

While Max and Josie had been at the farm, Danny had tracked down TJ. He had her look over the file he had discovered. He wanted to do everything by the book so it would hold up in court. He had learned enough from his past mistakes not to let his emotions get in the way and ruin the evidence. Once Danny had discussed everything with TJ, they were pretty sure what was going on.

"Danny had a suspicion that you two would head back out to the farm and we decided he should go check on you." TJ explained, "Good thing he did, huh?"

"You got that right". Max laughed.

Josie blushed. "Guess you found out more than we were ready to let you see."

Danny and Max laughed until tears rolled down their cheeks. TJ looked at them with a puzzled expression on her face. "What are you not telling me?"

Danny looked at Max and Josie. "I'm sworn to secrecy." And TJ just rolled her eyes.

The man who attacked them had been delivered to the Sheriff. Because he had the gunshot wound in his leg, the Sheriff escorted him to the Hospital. It was determined the bullet just grazed the outside of the leg and was not imbedded. The wound was treated in the emergency room with stitches and he was returned to jail. They were holding him for questioning. The Sheriff did not allow Danny in on the interview since he had no actual authority in the town. The sheriff allowed Danny to leave when the prisoner returned to jail. TJ insisted she needed to be with Danny when the Sheriff questioned him. He was told to come in tomorrow for his statement. Max and Josie were determined to accompany him so they could substantiate his story.

Danny explained that he was feeling something was not right about the man that attacked him. "Honestly, I don't understand why? What do we have that he wants? And another thing, I get the feeling that I have seen him before."

"Well the only reason we are even here is because of Lily. Do you think it has something to do with her?"

"Max, I don't know………… Hey, give me a minute….." Danny pulled out his cell phone and dialed. Everyone was looking at him.

"Hello, Garrett, this is Sheriff Danny. I need a favor from you. Look up that guy we held. The one who had the car wreck. Remember, we found the money in his car? His name escapes me right now. Fax over his arrest photo and fingerprints to Sheriff Axelrod. The number is in my desk drawer…..Wait a minute…..the man's name was Hill."

Danny listened for a few minutes and they all noticed beads of sweat forming on his forehead. When he laid down his cell phone, everyone was looking at him. TJ was the first to speak. "Did you say Hill, like in Lily Hill? What the hell is going on? What don't I know?"

Danny rubbed his forehead. He was starting to get the mother of all headaches. He took a few minutes to think before voicing his thoughts. "I arrested a man in town. He had an accident and when we responded, we found quite a stack of unexplained cash in his car. We couldn't hold him. Once we counted the money, the amount was actually smaller that it first appeared. The D.A. felt we didn't have enough reason to charge him because we could not find any reports of a robbery for that amount of money. The Sheriff was anxious to get him out of town. At the time, the Sheriff was handling this case and I was only a Deputy Sheriff. I never thought much of his name. Hill is not such an unusual name and I swear he had no resemblance to Lily. God, now I wish I had checked. Pushed to find out more."

"So now, you are thinking these two men are the same? Surely you would have noticed it when you had him in the car. You must have gotten a good look at him?" TJ was having a hard time understanding.

"To be fair to Danny", Max blushed, "There was a lot of distractions and he was trying to save our life. I really think he had more on his mind at that time. He is probably just getting to the point where he can sort it all out."

"How long do you think it will be before the fax comes in?" she asked.

"Deputy Garrett will call me back when it is sent. I think I need to head over to the station and talk to the Sheriff right now. I want you all to stay here until I get back."

Danny still had to gain the trust and cooperation of the Sheriff. He cursed himself for being so hot headed toward the sheriff but as far as Lily's future was concerned, he would probably do it all over again. Now he had to focus on this new development. He took a deep breath as he headed out the door and walked over to the police department. He knew a lot was at stake and the outcome depended on just how much the sheriff would cooperate, so they could get to the truth.

"Sheriff, I want to apologize for my past behavior. I need your help on making sure we build a case against Mr. Hill."

The Sheriff looked at Danny with contempt in his eyes. "First of all, an apology coming this late is not going to cut it. Second of all, I don't need your help. And third, there is no *we in this case*. At least as far as you're concerned, so you can walk out of my office right now."

Danny stood firm. He relaxed his face to quell the rage he felt building up inside him. He took another deep breath and knew he didn't have much time to persuade the Sheriff. He was certain the sheriff would only give him a few more minutes before he threw him out.

"I know I was wrong. Have you ever loved someone so much, your entire world revolved around them? That's what happened when Lily came back here. I put her before everything else, including common sense. Now can we forget Lily for a minute? Allow me a chance to discuss Mr. Hill."

"You have exactly five minutes, Sheriff McCain. You have no jurisdiction here, no right to be involved."

"You are absolutely correct, I don't. But I do have something that you may be interested in knowing. I've heard that you are up for re-election. Solving a murder certainly will add voters to your campaign. If you just listen and allow me to give you some background information, I'm sure you will agree. I asked my Deputy to fax over an arrest record of the mug shot and fingerprints. We had him in our jail. I'm sure they will match the Mr. Hill in here?"

Danny stopped to gauge the reaction of the sheriff. He noticed his face had lost its edge, the anger appeared to be subsiding and his body leaned forward in his chair as if waiting for information. *Good*, thought Danny, *maybe he will let me finish.*

The sheriff picked up the phone and called his dispatcher and asked him to check if they received a fax of a mug shot and fingerprints. As the deputy went to check, Danny resumed his story.

He explained to Sheriff Axelrod about the man who had the accident and the money they had discovered at the scene. The murder of the sheriff and Karen Brown. He tried to take his time and give the sheriff a chance to take it all in. Danny noticed he now had his full attention. His face only reflected the fact that he was listening to everything Danny was telling him. He decided to continue. "We also have reason to believe this is the man who scared Rosie, Max's daughter, at the store she was shopping in with Lily. We also suspect he is responsible for an attack on Lily that broke her arm and landed her in the hospital. I don't know what his connection is to Lily, Sheriff. But they do have the same last name."

"Yeah, I picked up on that too......" At a knock on the door, the sheriff stopped in midsentence, "Come in."

The dispatcher laid the fax in front of the sheriff. He took a few minutes to read it. He looked up at Danny. "Well there is enough resemblance to connect this to the Mr. Hill in our jail. The hair is longer, he now has hair on his face that may be covering the scars, but definitely enough to be suspicious. We'll know for sure when we compare the fingerprints."

The sheriff leaned back in his chair and put his hands behind his neck as if stretching the kinks out of his shoulders. He thought for a minute and then his voice changed. "Son, I accept your apology. I know it takes two to tango, as they say. And I let you get to me. I didn't appreciate you showing up with a posse and telling me how to run my town." He laughed and shook his head. "You do have gumption, I'll give you that. Let's give Mr. Hill time to cool his heels in the cell overnight. You come in tomorrow. I should get the results of the fingerprints by then, and we can confront him, if there is a match. Meanwhile, I'll check my old files and see if I come up with anything on any *Hill*."

Danny rose and shook his hand. "Sheriff, I appreciate you listening to me. I have been admonished enough already by the *posses* as you refer to them. They told me I was too headstrong to come barging in like I did. I wish I would have been able to listen to them but I guess you understand by now, I know Lily is innocent. If you let me help you on this, I know you will find that out too."

Danny left as soon as he finished. He was afraid to say anymore. He started thinking about Lily and all she had suffered and felt the tears stinging his eye. He dared to let himself hope that the end was near and she could come home.

Chapter 52

Then next morning Danny received a call from the Sheriff. He told him to come over so they could work on their strategy. He wanted them to do the interview before the D.A arrived to consult with them. Try to uncover some solid evidence, maybe get him to slip up and admit to something. He wanted to make sure they had enough to persuade the D.A. to charge him. He then told Danny the man's fingerprints matched the ones Danny's Deputy faxed over the day before.

Danny made a quick call to Max and told him what was happening. "Call TJ and tell her what's going on. I think the Sheriff finally believes me and I think I should go alone to meet with him. You and Josie get something to eat and I will call you once I know something definitive."

"Well, we will be available if we can help. I know Josie is planning to visit with Lily this morning, so she will be in the building if you need her."

"Please caution her not to tell Lily anything right now until we have some firm news. Ok?"

"Yeah, we already discussed that and agreed."

When Danny walked into the police station he noticed the dispatcher glance up. Once he recognized him, he could see his face was no longer hostile looking. "Go on in, the sheriff is expecting you."

Danny thanked him and walked back to the sheriff's office. He laid a bag on the sheriff's desk. "Hope you don't mind, I haven't eaten this morning and took the liberty of stopping by the diner and getting us both a sausage egg and cheese sandwich. Figured we'd need the energy for the interview, Sheriff."

The sheriff laughed. "Now this is a real bribe. My wife doesn't let me have anything with fat in it. This is a real treat and beats the oatmeal I had to eat today. And let's drop the sheriff business. Call me Chuck."

"Only if you call me Danny."

They took a few minutes to eat and he could tell Chuck was really enjoying his sandwich so he decided to let him finish before they began. As the sheriff wiped his mouth, he let out a loud burp. "Sorry about that. That's another thing I can't do at home."

Once the trash was discarded, he pulled out a thick file and slid it toward Danny. "I checked our files on anyone with the last name Hill. This is what I came up with. As you can see, Clyde Hill had two sons. They were always in trouble and caused a lot of problems when they were teenagers. Fights, stealing, all the bad stuff teenagers can get into, they did. I remember them now. As a matter of fact, it jogged my memory. I remember going out to see Clyde because I got a call about one of the sons who had gone missing. I rode out to see if he knew anything about it. Turns out he didn't. I never did see his wife. Heard he had a young one but never saw her. Cannot say if that was your Lily or not."

"How long ago was that?"

"Well Danny, I'd say it was several years ago. Close to five, if my memory is correct."

"Do you know if he was ever found?"

"Not unless he is the body we dug up out on the farm. Don't know which son it was."

"What were their names? I mean first names?"

"It's in the file. Oldest one they called Buck but his given name was Willis. The other one was named Billy Ray. Not a nickname as you would expect for William. Named Billy Ray. They are the only two kids Clyde had. His wife died before the kids became hellions. At least she was spared that. Of maybe she could have prevented it. Who knows? My opinion is they were just born bad."

"So who do we have?"

"Billy Ray, according to the fingerprints. I'm thinking that Buck is the one in the grave we dug up."

Danny spent the next fifteen minutes reading the file and making notes. When he glanced up, Chuck was watching him. "How do you want to handle this? I'd appreciate your thoughts on what is the best approach."

"Well, Danny, how about we go in together. You confront him about what happened in your town; the evidence we say we have tying him to that. Maybe we can scare it out of him. I'll try to be understanding and try to get him to tell us about Lily and his brother." He smiled at Danny. "We both know you can be a hard ass when you get riled up."

Danny looked at the sheriff and laughed, "It does have its advantages sometimes doesn't it?"

They had the prisoner brought down to the interview room. They decided to leave him sit there and wait, hoping to get him mad. Maybe he would lose his patience and get angry enough to lose his temper. He may say some things he might otherwise hold back. Danny and Chuck went over their questions and what they were going to say. The sheriff was going to tape the interview so they could have the D.A. review the tape before making his decision.

Danny and Chuck walked into the room and approached Billy Ray. He was read his rights and informed that the interview was being taped.

"How are you today?" asked Chuck.

Danny immediately assumed a hard stance. "Don't ask that piece of shit about his comfort. Who cares? I sure don't. I'm going to fry his ass."

Billy Ray's face turned angry. You could see the evil lurking there in his eyes. Chuck had to turn away for a few seconds. Danny noticed it too, but he was not intimidated. In fact, he felt they were gaining the edge.

"I'm here to tell you what we have so far. Now, we can make this easy or hard. It's up to you. Myself, I hope you choose hard."

"You cannot hold me. You shot me. You have nothing on me."

Danny stood up and leaned over the table. "How is rape for starters?"

"I never raped her. She came on to me. All naked and wanting a real man. Begged for it. Said the other guy couldn't satisfy her."

Danny reached out and grabbed him by the shirt. Chuck stepped in and said "Let him go, you are overstepping your authority."

Danny slammed his fist down on the table. "You call yourself a police officer? What are you doing, taking up for this piece of scum?"

Chuck told Danny to leave and get some air. As Danny left the room, Chuck leaned over and gave the appearance of confiding to the prisoner.

"Listen here, son, you don't have much of a chance with the evidence we have. I knew your Daddy so I am trying to give you a break and some good advice. Tell us what you know and I'll try and make it as easy as I can on you."

He saw the smirk on Billy Ray's face. It was all he could do to keep his own hands off him. "You think this over. I gotta go to the bathroom." Chuck walked out and went next door to confer with Danny. "You watch all of that?"

"Yeah, I did."

"Piece of shit. I had a hard time acting my part in there. In fact, I thought I would choke on my words. I've seen some bad people in this job, but I tell you, he is so evil, he scares even me."

"Well, we have got to get him to tell us about Sheriff Bates' murder. I'll confront him with the facts and you try to get him to give us something. Then we'll work our way around to Lily. Is that ok? And you keep a lookout for me. I could easily beat the shit out of him. Wipe that smirk off his face. He is not worth the trouble it would cause for me."

Danny entered the room. He looked around the room and said to Billy Ray, "Where is the sheriff?"

Billy Ray just shrugged his shoulders.

Danny looked at him and tried to soften his face. He knew it portrayed the rage he was feeling. "So it's just you and me, I see." He sat down in the chair opposite his and smiled. "How about I take this time to tell you what I found out about you?"

Billy Ray did not say a word, just smiled the most evil smile. Danny felt shivers run down his back. He knew he had to get through this. "Ever been to Relay, Colorado?"

"Can't say that I have."

"Well, that's strange. I arrested a fellow there with your fingerprints."

"Maybe I forgot."

"Sure you did. Just like you forgot you murdered our sheriff."

"Can't prove it. That's a lie."

"We have your fingerprints from his house."

"Not possible. It burnt down."

"Now how do you know that? So you were the one who burnt it down. Don't tell me you are so dumb that you think we still can't get fingerprints? They don't burn up." Danny said a silent prayer that this guy didn't know much about fingerprints."

He looked at Danny and shrugged. "Prove it."

"Oh, I have even more evidence. We have DNA from the girl you raped and buried after you killed her. We have someone who saw you pick her up in your car. We have proof that you attacked someone in their yard and put her in the hospital. You should remember that one. Her name is Lily."

Danny took a few minutes to let this information sink in. He kept his face impassive and waited for Billy Ray to speak. Chuck was watching from the next room and decided Danny was handling this well enough alone. He would stay out here until he felt he was needed. No need for a witness since it was being videotaped. Evidence enough.

Billy Ray started to fidget in his chair. He was starting to show signs of stress. Danny hoped he was just dumb enough to believe everything that he told him. Most of it was true anyway. With the DNA they could tie him to Karen Brown. Ten minutes passed and still he hadn't spoken. Danny abruptly got up and left the room. He went to find Chuck. "Hey, any ideas?"

"Well, I was watching, you did pretty well by yourself. Do you want me to go in now?"

"Yeah, maybe you can see if I got through to him. I find it hard to look at him. He really gets to me. I know I shouldn't feel like this, especially in my job. Does it ever affect you?"

"Yes it does. More that I want it to. Every once in a while, we get a real nasty one."

Chuck returned to the interview room carrying can of Coke. He sat down and pushed the can across the table to Billy Ray. "Sorry I had to run out on you. I got waylaid on my way back from the bathroom. Police business doesn't stop when I'm busy. I had to attend to another matter. How did it go with you and Sheriff McCain?"

Billy Ray looked at him as if he did not believe him but he reached out and drank the coke. He sat there without a word. Chuck waited. "Tell you what. Let's get this over with and get you out of here. Tell me what you know."

Billy Ray continued to sit without response. Chuck noticed his face. It was not as confident as it was. Maybe they were getting somewhere. "Can you tell me why you were out at Clyde's farm?"

"It's my farm now. I have a right to be there."

"Seems to me the last I heard, the bank was renting it out?"

"Nobody lives there now. I'm moving in."

"And the bank is aware of that?"

"Will be. As soon as I get out of here and get it straightened out. My daddy has money hidden somewhere and I intend to get it."

"How do you know that? A lot of time has passed. Could be long gone by now."

"I know how he was. Didn't trust banks. Always said he knew where his money was and how much he had down to the penny. He could get to it at any time and it was safer where it was. He said the bank made it hard for someone to get to their money and didn't have any right to keep his."

"So you think it is on the farm?"

"Yes, that's why it belongs to me. He meant the farm to go to me. That's why he told me about the money."

"Did your Daddy leave it to you? Last I heard on that is he left it to his wife."

"Whore you mean. Don't know as they were married."

"Is this by any chance Lily?"

"Yep".

"Did you ever meet her?"

"Not that I remember."

"Surely you would remember that beautiful girl if you had."

"Slut."

"Why are you so sure?"

"She took the farm away from me and my brother."

"I thought you left the farm. You made that decision on your own, didn't you?"

"Anyone knows the father leaves his property to his sons, not a two bit tramp."

"Well, story around here is that they were married. Legal and binding. Wives do inherit from their husbands. She lived there too."

"Prove it."

"Don't know as I have to prove anything to you on that matter. Seems like the bank is the one you have to convince."

"Yeah, right."

"Well let's get off the farm for a few minutes. Seems like there is more trouble following you than the farm. That should be the least of your worries. Sheriff McCain has pretty strong evidence that you killed the sheriff in Relay. What do you have to say about that?"

"Screw him. I want a Lawyer."

"Sorry you feel that way. If you want a Lawyer, we are going to have to transport you back to Relay. They will charge you there. I won't be able to help you. It will be between you and Sheriff McCain. Tell you the truth, I don't envy you that."

"What do you mean?"

"Well once you leave my jurisdiction, I cannot be involved in helping you. Like I said, I knew your Daddy and would sure like to help you out if I could." He started to rise from his chair. For the first time that day, Chuck notice doubt cross Billy Ray's face.

"Don't go just yet. I need to think."

"Well son, think fast. Sheriff McCain will not wait forever. He wants to get you out of here and away from me."

"What are you offering?"

"Depends on what you have for me. Let's start with Lily. You seem angry with her. What did she do to you? Seems like to me, if you are mad at anyone, it should be your Daddy for marrying her."

"She killed my brother."

"And you know this how?"

"He's dead. She buried him out on the farm. You know. You dug him up."

"You expect me to believe that little thing could overpower a big guy like Buck, haul his dead weight over and put it in a grave she dug herself?" He shook his head as if this was impossible to imagine.

"Well she must have had help."

"So now you are saying she didn't do it by herself. Maybe it was you that helped her."

"No!" he shouted.

"Well, if I am to believe you, you have to do better than that."

"She's a whore. Maybe one of her customers."

"Now Billy Ray, think what you are saying. She's married to your Daddy, she manages to have customers as you call them, without your Daddy knowing, and she kills your brother on a farm where she is living with her husband. Doesn't make sense. He would have to know. Wait a minute.......................... are you accusing your Daddy of murder?"

"Yeah, he could have helped her I guess."

"Kill his own son?"

"He never cared much for us when we were growing up. Yeah, why not?"

"If memory serves me right, he was always bailing you and your brother out of jail. You two were always in trouble growing up. Enough to try any Daddy's patience. But murder? I think not. Better try to come up with something more convincing than that, son."

Billy Ray glared at the Sheriff. His lips were held in a tight line as if he was trying hard to control his temper.

347

Chuck could see he was getting his attention. "How about the sheriff in Relay? Any thoughts on that?"

"Only met him once. He was dishonest, so any number of people could have killed him if you ask me."

The sheriff took his time reading over the papers in the folder in front of him.

"Hmmmm, there is mention of Karen Brown. Tell me about her."

"Don't know any Karen Brown."

"Says here, she was last seen getting into a car with someone who matchers your description. According to reports, she was not so innocent. Now if I was a young strapping guy like you, I could see myself being taken in by someone like her. You know how those loose women get hold of you. They make you do things you don't want to do. Why no one could blame you for a tease like her. Building you up and then leaving you high and dry." He chuckled, "Or stiff and sore".

He used this time to study Billy Ray's face. He felt he was getting through to him. Even though he felt the breakfast sandwich starting to come up, he knew he had to continue and keep his emotions under control. If anyone could get him to come clean, he knew it had to be him. Danny had already alienated him.

"Yeah, she threw herself at me, said she wanted to go somewhere because she was tired of the immature boys here in town and wanted a real man. Gave herself easily enough. Not the first time either. She was experienced."

"So what did she do to you?"

"What do you mean?"

"I've been a sheriff long enough to know how tramps treat decent guys like you. Teased you, didn't she? Caused you to lose your temper. Couldn't blame you if you had to defend yourself. Tell me about it. Maybe we can work it out before Sheriff McCain comes busting in here again."

"Yeah, you're right it was all her fault. I had no choice."

"What happened?"

"She started screaming. She said she was going to tell. She wasn't Lily. She knew who Lily was, and she would tell her what I did to her. I got mad and choked her to shut her up. I had no choice. She made me do it. I had to get rid of her. So I hid her body. Figured no one would miss her. Just another slut out of circulation."

The sheriff felt the bile rise in his throat and his stomach heave. "Good. Thank you. That clears it up. Give me a minute to see how I can help you. I'll be right back."

Chuck passed Danny outside the room. He waved him away and ran to the bathroom. He was right; he lost his breakfast and probably his dinner from last night if there was anything left of that too. He splashed water on his face and leaned over the sink. *God, give me the strength to finish with this monster. I need to get through this so we can lock him away for a long time.*

He met Danny outside the bathroom.

"Pretty rough on you. You look terrible. But you are doing a great job. You got him to confess. Don't stop now."

"You have no idea how rough it is. I tell you, I have never encountered anyone like him. No remorse. No feelings for anything he had done. I am going back in there once I get a coke to settle my stomach."

Danny watched the reaction on Billy Ray's face and knew that Chuck was right in his assessment. This guy did not have human feelings. Nothing seemed to scare or shame him. It was close to thirty minutes before Sheriff Axelrod could get the strength to go back in and talk to him again. Danny stayed out of his way. He realized Chuck was doing a better job than he would, and it was best if he stayed out of the picture for now. He noticed Billy rubbed his leg several times as if in pain. He could not stop the smile from spreading over his face and thinking *At least the bastard is thinking about me each time he rubs that wound.*

"Well Billy Ray, I made some calls and checked some things out. Seems like if you will help resolve the issue with Sheriff Bates and the money, they may look at the charges as manslaughter with Karen Brown. A good lawyer can probably get you off on that. Can you help me with this Sheriff Bates business?"

"What do you mean?"

"They want to clear up the reason for the fire at the sheriff's house. He died in the fire, I take it and there was a matter of some money."

"And I won't get charged?"

"Well seems like you must have an explanation for that. Must have started accidentally, huh?"

"Yeah, I went there to get the money he stole from me. He was hiding it."

Just then there was a knock at the door. The sheriff got up and opened it to see his dispatcher standing there. He told Billy Ray he had to take a phone call and would return as soon as he was finished.

The interruption was to inform the sheriff that the D.A. had arrived and was waiting for him in his office. Now he could have him review the tape and take it from there. Hopefully, they had enough so he would not have to continue questioning Billy Ray. He suddenly felt drained and in need of a shower. He did not want to face the evil in that room again.

The Final Truth

Chapter 53

Danny, himself, was exhausted. He left the sheriff and headed back to the hotel. Once he was in his room, he took the hottest shower his body could stand. He scrubbed his body until his skin hurt. He felt he would never get clean or get Billy Ray out of his mind. As he toweled off, the phone rang. Max and Josie were anxious to meet him and find out what happened. He agreed to meet them in the bar because to be honest, he needed a stiff drink.

Once they were settled in a booth with their drinks, Danny swallowed a shot of whiskey. He had ordered the shot along with a beer. If Max or Josie disapproved, neither one commented on this. They could tell from his face that he was upset.

"Ok Danny, are you going to tell us anything?"

"I cannot get his face out of my mind. More than that, the evil I saw reflected there."

"Ok, we will give you a few minutes. Drink your drink and then we will go to get something to eat."

"Sorry, I just need to be around normal people for a while. What have you two been doing today?" He laughed "I see you are dressed for a change."

Josie reached over the table and punched him in the arm and Max laughed, "What are the chances you will ever let us live this down."

Danny stress now gave way to laughter, "Never, would be my guess."

Once they finished their drinks, Danny was starting to feel better. He suggested that they call TJ and see if she wanted to join them for dinner.

Max said, "TJ has been gone from the office all day. Josie reached her on her cell phone earlier but she rushed her off saying she was busy."

Josie took out her cell phone and tried to reach her again. This time TJ answered but told them she had a pizza delivered to her office earlier and was not hungry. She made plans for them to come over to her office after they finished dinner.

Danny was ravenous. He was surprised at how much appetite he had after the day he experienced being around Billy Ray. He even ordered desert and immediately thought of Lily and how he loved eating with her. She was so different from most women. She enjoyed her food and did not worry about calories. Not that she needed to, but never the less, it was nice to be around someone like that. Then he thought, *Who am I kidding? I love being around her no matter what we do.*

Josie noticed the faraway look in Danny's eyes. She knew he was thinking of Lily because she was too. Lily loved deserts. She told Josie she guessed it was because she had never had any before moving to Relay.

After they had all finished and paid the check, they headed over to see TJ. Josie noticed the air had a chill and wished she had worn a sweater. *Funny she thought, it was warm when I first arrived here. Now the season has changed.*

TJ led them into the conference room. She had a pot of coffee brewing and a folder sitting on the table. She asked Danny if he felt like talking about his day at the police station.

"I take it; you and the sheriff have resolved your differences." She smiled at him and somehow he suspected she knew all about it. He was glad he didn't need to explain that part anyway. Talking about Billy Ray would be enough to handle right now.

He tried to stay calm as he relayed the information. They could all see from his facial expressions, that it was difficult but he continued. They stopped once or twice to refill their coffee or use the bathroom. Danny seemed glad for the interruptions but he wanted to finish. He thought once he had gotten all this out of his system, he may begin to feel more removed from the events of that day. He hated even saying Billy Ray's name out loud and giving him the time it took to tell the story. He wished he never had to see or think about him again. But he knew this wasn't possible. He was still involved with him because of the crimes committed in his town. Soon almost two hours had passed and Danny came to the end of the story. This is when I left..............I couldn't stay any longer around him. I had to get away. I have to tell you all, it got to me in a way I never thought it would. What scares me most is the thought that Lily married his father. I am so afraid that he may have been like his son. How could Lily have survived that?

Josie looked at Danny and her heart broke. "Danny, believe me. From what Lily said about Clyde, he and his son were nothing alike. If he was, Lily would have come to us broken. We would have noticed. Lily is still the sweet person she always has been. That I'm sure of."

Danny looked at Josie. "Thank you for that. I know. But it still makes my heart break for her. It scares me. How some people are so mean yet others can remain so kind and caring."

TJ suggested they take a short break. She said she needed to take a walk and asked them all to join her. She said she thought they all needed to get away from the office and clear their heads. They still had some things to discuss and they needed to do it tonight. They all headed out the door and walked along the deserted streets. Danny suggested they stop and have a drink at the hotel before heading back. Josie and Max looked at him, but he insisted that after the day they all had, a drink was called for. "Don't worry. I am not turning into an alcoholic. Just one beer. No hard stuff."

They stayed in the bar and had beers and munched on popcorn the bartender set out for them. They kept their conversation neutral and did not discuss anything important. Josie relayed some stories of customers she had as a waitress and TJ talked about her life in the big city before moving here. Max and Danny were content to listen. In fact they welcomed it.

Soon they returned to the office. Danny automatically went to the coffee maker and started to make a fresh pot. TJ was the first to speak. "Josie, tell us about your childhood."

"Why? Where did this come from? Why now?"

"Just thought it may be nice to know. If you are uncomfortable, we will understand."

"Well.........Ok, I guess. What do you want to know?"

"Just start as far back as you remember. Your Mom, Dad and any siblings you have."

"I don't really remember my birth father. I was very young when my mother left him."

"So tell us about your mother. What do you remember?"

"We moved a lot. Stayed in hotels. She did tell me my real dad drank a lot. They never had money and then he got mean and started to hit her. She met a man and ran off with him. Guess I'm lucky she took me, huh. Anyway they didn't stay together long. He left her. She said he didn't want kids. But Mom was pretty and also resourceful. She soon found another man. At first things went ok. We moved into a small house when mom got pregnant. She had a boy this time. Did I tell you my name was Joe? My father was furious when I was born a girl. Called me Joe just to spite my mother. She changed it to Josie."

"Did your Mom ever say much about you real dad? Did she ever hear from him?"

"No, not that I remember. I always knew Tom was my step-father but from what my mother told me about my real father, before she died, I was sure he didn't want me back in his life. So I never gave that a thought."

"Do you remember his name?"

"Huey, something. Give me a minute............Yeah, like someone famous. Huey Long.... no, that's not right. Huey Lang. Yes, now I remember. I always thought it was so similar to the famous guy. You know the congressman or senator, Huey Long. But my father's name was Huey Lang. When my mother first told me, I wondered if he misspelled his name and it really should have been Huey Long, you know how kids fantasize, but the time frame was all wrong. "

"TJ looked around the table and took a deep breath. "You all know I have been busy the last two days. Unlike Max and Josie, I kept my clothes on." Josie blushed and Max glared at Danny. Then they all laughed.

"Good, now that we had a laugh, I need to get serious. I found out some interesting information. I have Danny to thank for finding the file and giving it to me to verify before either of us shared the information. Now I feel confident that what was in the file is true......."

Josie interrupted her. "Please do not tell us Lily is guilty. I don't care what you found out. I know she did not kill anyone."

TJ looked at her. "Josie, let me finish. Danny is the only one who is prepared for this because he already knows about it. But I think it may actually be good news."

Josie was getting frantic. "For God's sake spit it out!"

"Ok. I found a file that my Uncle had on Clyde. Apparently he was hired to get Lily a birth certificate. A copy is in the file. Her father's name was Huey Lang."

All eyes were on Josie. Her mouth fell open. This was certainly not what she was expecting to hear. Max reached out and put his arm around her. Danny went over and gave her a hug.

"Well Josie, I find it strange that you cannot think of anything to say. You of all people always have something to say, whether or not someone wants to hear it."

"This is not what ....hell, this never entered my mind. I always felt close to Lily. A special kinship to her, even though we were not a bit alike in either looks or temperament. I never would have suspected. Does she know?"

"None of us has told her yet." She glanced at Danny. He threw up his hands as if in surrender.

"I was tempted but I kept my word. I swear Lily does not know. Besides, I should not be the one who tells her."

TJ looked at Josie. "I suggest we do DNA test to confirm this."

Josie shook her head. "Unless Lily wants to, I am fine with your information. I don't need further proof. I know it in my heart."

"Well then, I'll see if Sheriff Axelrod will give us permission to meet with Lily, all together, tomorrow. Is that ok with you?"

They all agreed. Danny looked around the table. "I feel TJ should be the one to explain this to her. What are your thoughts on this?"

Max and Josie looked at each other. Josie said "That sounds like the best idea. I'll probably be too emotional by that time." They all laughed.

Max, Josie and Danny left to head back to the hotel. They were all exhausted. Max was anxious to share the news with his mother and Bea but promised he would wait until Lily was told. Then he would call them and Josie would call Millie. They were all smiling on their way back to the hotel. Josie told them she swore she was floating and that her feet were not touching the pavement. Max and Danny laughed at her comment but understood because they were feeling much the same. They all knew they would sleep tonight. Things were starting to come together. Tomorrow they would work on getting Lily out of jail.

Chapter 54

Once they left the office, TJ headed back to the hidden file room. When she was talking to Josie, she had a thought, but was afraid to voice it and get their hopes up. Now she started looking for files on Lily Lang, Huey Lang and Josie Lang. Most of the files were in order thanks to Josie's hard work. She spent over an hour looking with no luck. She decided to go home and look again in the morning. As she went to close the door, she looked back in the room and noticed the file drawer ajar. That must be the one Josie fought with. She smiled and started to leave. She was sitting in her car; the key was in the ignition, when she stopped. *Shit, I have to go back and check. It is possible we missed this before.* She turned off the engine and went back inside, all the time telling herself how it was a wild goose chase.

She had to get on her hands and knees in order to get a good grip on the folder. Josie must have missed this. It was wedged beneath the drawer. Only the edge of the folder was visible. As she grabbed it, she heard it rip, so she started to try to wiggle it free. No need to rush and miss most of what was inside the file. She was so close. She forced herself to remain calm. Finally, she worked the edge free. The folder was bent at the corner; it was wedged in the side of the cabinet. Just keep sliding it back and forth; she said to herself, *You can do it.* She kept telling herself to get enough leverage to free the edge. Finally, it worked and the folder came free. That knocked her backwards. She started to laugh and laugh. *This job is getting to me, I'm losing it!* She jumped up, shoved the file in her briefcase without looking at it and headed home exhausted.

The next morning, they were all sitting in the restaurant having breakfast. All looked rested. Josie cheeks were glowing. Max told Danny she had a twinkle in her eyes that he was afraid was not because of him.

They were all laughing and joking. Something they had not done in a long time. Success was within their reach. They all felt Lily would be free soon and they could return to their lives. They all agreed they would appreciate life more by living through this.

TJ called Josie on her cell phone. "I just talked to the sheriff and we can meet with Lily at ten o'clock. Is that convenient for all of you?"

Josie shouted "Yes". Danny, Max and several customers looked at her. She shrugged her shoulders at them. She hung up and told Max and Danny what TJ had said. They were all excited to see Lily. Josie reached out and hugged Max and then Danny. "This is one of the best days of my life!"

At precisely ten o'clock, Lily was led into the conference room. They were all thankful to see she was not in handcuffs. Once the deputy left, after informing them he would be just outside the door, they all hugged Lily. They squeezed her so tight she thought she would not be able to breathe but it felt so good she didn't want them to stop. Once she was released from the group hug, Danny leaned over and kissed her. Now she knew she couldn't breathe. Her heart felt like it had stopped beating and she felt dizzy. She could not remember how long it had been since she felt this way.

TJ was the first to speak. "Ok, ok, we need to talk to you, Lily. The sheriff gave us permission to meet with you, but we need to use this time to get information. Lily, sit down. We have some heavy stuff to talk about. Don't worry; I think you will agree most of it will be good news."

Josie reached out and took Lily's hand in hers. She held on tight, as if trying to communicate with her, and give her strength to hear what TJ was about to say.

Lily listened intently as TJ repeated what she had found out about Lily's father. Her face was frozen and no emotion was readable, yet everyone knew the information she was hearing was so shocking to her, that she would require some time to absorb the full impact. TJ stopped talking after a while to inquire if Lily was ok. If she should stop for a while? Lily quietly told her to please finish. She was anxious to hear everything. Once TJ finished, Lily had tears running down her face. Josie looked at her and said, "Please don't tell me you are sad. It would break my heart."

Lily looked at her. She reached out and hugged her tight. She started to cry even harder. "Of all the things in my life, Josie, you are best thing that came out of my childhood. I never dreamed I would have a family. Now I have a sister and one that I love dearly. These are tears of happiness."

TJ wiped the tears gathering in her eyes and glanced around to see if anyone noticed her weakness. She was surprised to see Danny and even

Max wiping their eyes. This was one of those days that being a lawyer actually made her feel good.

The deputy knocked on the door and told them the sheriff had sent word for Danny to come to his office and that Lily needed to be returned to her cell. They all assured Lily that she would be out soon. They were confident of this and she needed to be too. She smiled and for the first time, she realized it was her wish too.

Max and Josie left, Danny went to meet the sheriff and TJ remained in the room. In all the excitement, she realized she still had the file in her briefcase from last night. Suddenly, she was anxious to take a glance at the contents before heading back to her office. As if driven to look at it now, instead of waiting. She felt a sudden chill run down her spine as she reached for the folder. TJ took a quick glance at the contents. She frowned and decided she had read it wrong. Better to read it again, more slowly and make sure she understood this correctly. The second time she read it, she realized she needed to get to Danny and the Sheriff immediately. She ran out of the interview room and headed to the sheriff's office. She knocked but did not wait for a reply. She rushed into the office and told them she needed their full attention. Now.

The sheriff clearly was not pleased with the interruption but Danny said "Chuck, let's hear her out. So far she has been right on target."

TJ explained how she had found the file, took it home and just remembered to look at it. In fact, how the need to look at it now had overcome her in the interview room after everyone left. That was why she was still here. Then she told them what was inside. Danny and the Sheriff read the file themselves. The sheriff immediately called his deputy. "Get the car ready. We are taking the prisoner Lily out to Clyde Hill's farm."

The sheriff told TJ and Danny to follow them. They would check out the information and see if Lily remembered anything.

Chapter 55

Once they arrived at the farm, they all got out of the car. The banker was already there with the house key. The sheriff had called him before they left and told him to meet them there. He was confused when he saw all the people accompanying the sheriff, but did not ask any questions. He noticed TJ and went over toward her.

"Hello TJ, does this by any chance have anything to do with what we discussed recently?" TJ responded quietly "Don't be surprised if it turns out that way."

Lily was handcuffed because the law required it, but she was treated with more respect than she had been given, since she had been in jail. She was confused with the sudden change in the sheriff's demeanor. She glanced over and saw Danny with her lawyer. *Why were they here? What did they expect?* She had not been told anything before being hustled into the police car. She was eased out of the car. Once out, she stood still. The memories of her life came flooding back. She turned away from the house and glanced at her tree. It surprised her at how much different it was from her memory. Although she was sure it had grown, as trees do, it looked small in comparison to the trees in Relay.

She was startled out of her thoughts when Danny placed his hand on her arm. She immediately glanced at the sheriff to see if he was going to remind Danny that he was not to touch the prisoner. She was surprised when nothing was said and the sheriff still had a friendly look on his face.

"Hi Lily. Please don't be afraid. You are not in trouble or in any danger right now. The sheriff wants your help in finding something. I want you to listen to him and try and help him. I will be here if you need me."

Lily was confused. How could she help now? She had told them everything she knew. She looked at Danny and nodded her head. She couldn't seem to get her mouth to form words. It had been so long since she had breathed fresh air or walked on fresh ground. She immediately had the memory of walking barefooted right where she stood now, and had the urge to kick off her shoes.

The sheriff walked over to her. "Lily, we are going to ask you to come into the house with us." He placed his hand under her elbow and started guiding her toward the door. She immediately froze. The thoughts keep flooding her mind. Images of the man who hurt her, flashed before her. She started to shake. Danny and the Sheriff immediately sensed her distress. Her face paled and she felt lightheaded. The Sheriff told the Deputy to hurry into the house and get a kitchen chair for her to sit on. Danny reached down and scooped her up in his arms and carried her inside. Once Lily was sitting down, Danny and the sheriff each chose a chair at the table and joined her.

"Lily, are you ok? If not, we can go back to the jail right now and come here another time. If you are ok now, we need to ask you some questions. I'm sorry if you are upset. We felt it would be better to bring you here. See if allowing you to move around inside, might cause you to remember the thing we need to find."

Lily looked at the sheriff. She was now very confused. How could she help? What did they need to find? She started to shake. Was she expected to show them the baby's grave and have that dug up? She didn't think she had the strength to endure that too.

Danny's voice brought her back in focus. "Lily, are you ok? Answer us."

"I'm fine."

"Are you up to this?"

"Yes." She was not sure what she was saying yes to, but she knew she needed to finish this. It had hung over her head and weighed heavily on her heart for too long now. Better to see it through.

The sheriff reached out and took off the handcuffs. "Since we are inside, no one will likely report me for this. I think you need to walk through the house on your own. Touch things, feel things and see what you remember. If you want company, I'm sure Danny will walk with you. If you want to do this alone, we are fine with that. Once you are done, come back and sit back down with us. Then I'll tell you what I need."

Now, Lily was uncertain. What was she supposed to do; what was she was expected to find? Part of her wanted to go through the house, and part of her realized it was in the past and she had no desire to be here. She glanced up at Danny. She was struck at how his eyes reflected his feelings for her. They seemed to be telling her that he trusted her to make the right decision. He would be here for her.

"Danny, please stay close, but I think I want to walk in each room and confront the feelings encountered in them, by myself. I'm not sure what I'll feel, but I will let you know if I need you."

He reached over and kissed her forehead and she left the kitchen.

Lily looked around the living room. Her memories of her time in here were pleasant ones. She smiled remembering her first Christmas. *Funny,* she thought, *the room looks the same, yet different. I guess the years have not changed the room from when I left it.*

Her next stop was in the bedroom. She felt herself tense. *The memories were not always pleasant ones. The room appears much smaller than what I remembered.* She felt tears form on her eyelashes. *I never knew love here.*

As she walked out of the room, she saw Danny standing just outside the doorway. She immediately threw her arms around him and the tears found their way down her cheek. He held her for a few minutes and then looked down at her face. "Lily, what is wrong? "

"I just realized how little I had living here. Not material things. I never knew what love was, until I found out with you."

Danny was so surprised to hear the words she spoke, but also felt fear that her life had been much worse that he knew. "Come in and sit down. "

Danny and the sheriff gave her a time to relax before asking her any questions. When the sheriff noticed her face finally relax, he said, "Now you have had some time to look at everything and refresh your memory of this house, I need you to go through each room in your mind. I want you to try and remember if Clyde had a place where he hid money or valuables."

"But I never knew he hid money. That man that came here wanted money and Clyde told him he didn't have any. That's why he beat us up."

"Ok. Just humor me. Close your eyes and think through each room. See if anything comes to mind."

Lily did as he asked, but could not come up with anything. She opened her eyes and shook her head. "Nothing is coming to me. I can't remember anything."

Danny asked the sheriff if they could walk around outside. Maybe something out there, either in the barn or the surrounding area would stand out to her.

"That's fine. I have to handcuff her. Tell you what, how about I handcuff her to you, and I hold the key? Of course, I have a gun too, so you won't have a chance to run off."

Danny looked at the sheriff. "Chuck, I want Lily free the legal way. I guarantee we are not going to run and jeopardize that chance. And thanks, for letting us look together."

They walked around the outside of the house. She showed Danny where she had her vegetable garden. They stopped and looked, and then both remembered this was the spot the body was buried. They went into the barn. Lily walked over to where the animals were kept and explained to Danny the chores she used to do in the barn. They walked over to the hayloft. Lily told him of her time sitting up there and the peace she felt just being by herself.

The Deputy was standing outside watching them but did not intrude. Lily looked at the area inside the barn with disappointment. "I don't think Clyde hid anything in here."

They walked back over to the house to join the sheriff. Fortunately, TJ had brought an ice chest with coke and water. Lily and Danny were glad to have something to drink. They walked into the living room. Danny suggested she sit on the sofa by herself and drink her coke. Maybe then, she would remember just one thing that would help. The sheriff removed Danny's hand from the handcuff and left the one remain on Lily. They would be leaving soon.

Danny was shaking Lily. "Wake up. You were having a bad dream. You must have dozed off and had a nightmare." Lily's eyes flew open and her hands flew out as if to defend herself. Everyone was standing over her and the fear was evident in her face.

Once she realized she was safe, she relaxed. "Yes, I must have fallen asleep. The last thing I remember was closing my eyes. I heard you all talking in the kitchen then the next thing I knew, I was watching Clyde hiding money while I was being beaten by that man wanting to know where the money was. Why do you think Clyde would not give him money? He could have kept us both from being hurt?"

"Well, honey, a lot of people defend what they have, but some make the mistake of placing value on the wrong thing." The sheriff looked at Lily with compassion in his face as he answered her.

"Lily, do you remember where he was hiding the money?"

She looked at Danny. Then she smiled. "Yes, in the bedroom."

"Tell me what you remember about the hiding place."

"One day by accident, I walked into the bedroom and Clyde was on his knees. He had slid out the dresser and it looked like he had the boards pulled up. Somehow, I knew I shouldn't say anything about this. I quietly left before he noticed me."

"Come with us and show us where it was. Sheriff, have the deputy move the chest. I shouldn't touch anything that could be evidence."

"Good thinking Danny."

Chapter 56

Everyone stood around the room watching as the chest was moved. On first inspection, nothing was visible to indicate anything was hidden there.

"Get down on the floor and give it a closer look."

Lily was holding her breath. She looked down at the floor. "I think that is the spot. The sheriff is right; Clyde was on his knees when I saw him."

The deputy got down on his knees. The space was tight and he had difficulty bending over to inspect the floor. "Can you give me a hand to push this chest further out of the way? I can't move down here. It's too tight."

The sheriff and Danny each grabbed an end of the chest and moved it to another wall. The sheriff said, "Clyde was a real small fellow. Thin, not very tall. He fit better than us." He then joined the deputy on the floor. His knees cracked when he bent down but no one commented.

"Run your hands along the planks and see if you feel anything." The deputy did as the sheriff requested. He was unable to find any difference in the wood.

"Well, if memory serves me right, Clyde was very handy with wood. He made a lot of stuff, so he knew his way around building things. Try pressing down on the floor. He may have used a spring latch" suggested the sheriff.

The sheriff got back up on his feet to give the deputy more space. After a few tries, the boards sprung up and hit the deputy in the face. The sheriff was the only one to laugh and he made a quick save by disguising it with a cough. Lily did a quick intake of breath when she saw the hiding place was found. Danny reached out and grabbed her hand. As the deputy reached into the space beneath the raised boards, he felt a box. "Do you want me to bring it out?"

"What is the matter with you? Of course you need to bring it out. Can't see much by leaving it in there." The sheriff muttered, *dumb ass*, under his breath and questioned himself again, how he got stuck with such imbeciles.

The box was lifted up. It was hard to see what kind it was because it was coated in dust. The deputy blew on it and dust flew up. As luck would have it, it went right in the sheriff's face and caused him to sneeze and cough. "Give me that damn thing. We'll look at it in the kitchen."

They all followed as the sheriff carried it as gentle as a mother carried an infant child. Danny felt the tension build and almost laughed at the sight. Once on the table, the sheriff dusted it off with his sleeve so he could see how it was fastened. There was no lock. The box appeared to have a side latch. Once it was unlatched, the lid was able to be removed. Everyone moved closer to have the ability to see what lay inside.

There was not a sound uttered as the sheriff lifted the contents. A tin can. He opened the can and pulled out a bag made out of material. "This is heavy. I'll open it first." The bag was tied with string and the knot was tight.

"Just cut the damn thing", Danny was surprised at his impatience as his words came out.

"Don't reckon, I need this as evidence. Got plenty of witnesses." He did as suggested and took out his knife. It cut easily enough. He dumped the contents on the table. Everyone did an intake of breath. The wad of money was surprisingly thick.

Lily was the first to speak. "Clyde never told me he had money. I never knew he had so much."

The sheriff told TJ and the deputy to count it while they were all there. He wanted it documented and witnessed. Danny looked at him and remembered another sheriff who had not been so honest. Look where it got him, he thought.

He then re-examined the box. "Looks like the rest is only papers." He pulled them out and looked at them. He spent some time reading what looked like a letter. He looked at Lily, and then glanced at Danny before saying "This here appears to be a letter from Clyde. Seems to me it explains a lot. TJ or Danny, I want one of you to read it out loud to the rest of us."

Danny and TJ looked at each other. "Danny, you have been through so much, I think you should do the honor, if Lily agrees." Lily looked at them and nodded her agreement because she could not get the sound to come out of her mouth. She had no idea what the letter contained. She noticed the sheriff had relaxed his face as he read the letter. He appeared to be relieved with the contents.

Danny took the letter and started to read.

MY LILY

If you are reading this, you must know I'm dead and you are searching the house for something.

Lily is innocent of anything you may have found and I want to set the record straight. I was not a good man. I did a lot of wrong in my life. Lily was the only good thing that I had. I have to tell you about Lily.

Her papa sold her to me. I met the bastard in town at a bar one day. He was bragging about his daughter's looks and body. He wanted to get rid of her because he didn't want her anymore. Said she was not too smart but was only thirteen. I got the feeling he couldn't get it up or he would have had her himself. Soon there was a contest in the bar going on to see who bought her. I don't know why, but I found myself bidding on her. It wasn't that I wanted her, more like I just wanted to win. Who knows why men do things like that? Just the desire to win, I guess. I finally won with a fifty-five dollar bid. I got directions to his house and said I'd pick her up the next day when I brought the money. In the meantime, he said he'd get her clothes and stuff packed up.

As I drove home that night, I wondered what in tarnation I had done taking on a girl this young. But as I said, I was not a nice man.

Not being a trusting man, I rode over the next day to check out my purchase. I was shocked at the rubble they lived in. He called his daughter in from outside so I could get a look at her. I was amazed at how beautiful she was. It was hard to believe that old buzzard could have sired someone like her. We talked and I told her father I would be back tomorrow to pick her up.

The next day I went back and I could tell by the look on her face, this was the first she knew that she was leaving with me. He told her to get a sack and take her stuff. She only had a hairbrush, nightgown and some old school books. We drove into the nearest town and got married. You ask why? I don't know why. It may have been because she was only thirteen, although we lied on the marriage certificate. It may have been a pang of guilt to make her into a whore instead of a wife. You decide.

I had two no good sons that had run off soon as they were able. Never gave them much thought, once they left. I settled into a life with Lily. Until one day, one of my sons showed up wanting money. I gave him some, but it was not enough. He beat me unconscious and went after Lily. He raped her and beat her pretty bad too. From then on, I kept my rifle by the bed at night and with me during the day. I knew he would come back. He did. I saw him coming so and I had my rifle in the barn with me. He caught Lily first and tried to rape her again. He didn't see me at first. He threatened us both with a gun. I shot him dead in the barn. Am I sorry about that? No, and I'd do it again. He was a mean son of a bitch and I never regretted it.

I didn't think he was good enough to bury in the family plot so I buried him under Lily's vegetable garden. Lily helped but I don't think she knew there was anything else she could do. Raised like she was, she didn't know much about the law or God for that matter. She just did what she was told.

I told her we would never mention it again. The devil has a way of coming back to torture you. One day about five months later she started to have pains. She and I never gave a thought she could be pregnant. I was pretty sure I was shooting blanks. She didn't know anything about the facts of life and how babies were conceived. She just viewed the act as the sex thing. I can still hear her voice now. Anyways, the baby was born dead. Too little to survive. It was my son's alright. It had the six toes on him just like my son's mother. It isn't something anyone in my family ever had. All hers did.

I made a little coffin and buried him under the tree. Didn't feel right putting him with his daddy and didn't want him buried in the family plot. Lily and I agreed on the spot because she always felt close to that tree for some reason.

I'm telling you this, so you understand how Lily suffered. I left her the farm. Made it legal with the lawyer in town because I got sick and knew I was going to die soon.

I didn't want her staying here by herself because I still had a son out there somewhere. She would never be safe out here alone.

I gave her what money I felt she would need and put her on a bus. I didn't want to give her too much as to get her in trouble. I made my coffin and left money with the Doc in town to see that I was buried in the family plot. This here money is what I got from selling off the animals and what I saved over the years. The lawyer rented the farm for me and Lily should have money in the bank from what rent money was left after taxes and expenses.

I was not a nice man. Remember that. But, I loved my Lily.

The letter was signed with Clyde's name and witnessed by the Doc's son.

Danny could not contain his excitement as he read. This was just the good news they needed to get Lily out of jail. He handed the letter back to the sheriff when he finished reading. Then without saying a word, he went over and took Lily in his arms and kissed her.

TJ reached for the letter. "Well sheriff, it looks good to me. Maybe we can find the Doctor' son and get a statement from him. That way, we can verify that this is his and Clyde's signatures."

"Yeah, I can find him. Looks like we need to head into town and get the D.A. on this so maybe Lily can be released."

The sheriff sent the deputy out to the police car for an evidence bag. The box, money and letter were placed inside and sealed with the sheriff's initials.

The Truth
becomes Reality

Chapter 57

Lily was sitting on the floor with Rosie, playing a board game. Josie was in the kitchen with Madge preparing dinner, when Danny ran through the door allowing it to bang behind him, shouting, "Where is Max? Did Bea and Millie get here yet?"

Madge heard his entrance and came in to see what was going on. "Danny, I find it hard to believe your mother did not teach you better manners. Now, I hope you didn't break the glass in my door." Rosie giggled and enjoyed the exchange between her Uncle Danny and Grandmother.

"You won't be scolding me once I tell you what I just got a call about. In fact, I bet I'll rate a hug and kiss." Just then, Bea and Millie came to the door.

"Come on in and don't slam the door" said Madge. They all looked at her. Something was bothering her right now. Max came down the stairs. "I just got home from work. Now I hear all of this racket. Mom, did something happen to dinner? You sure are in a mood."

"Sorry, I just cannot understand you and Danny. You both have women in your life that I love, but neither one seems ready to make a commitment. I'll be in a wheelchair before I attend a wedding in this family."

Max and Danny exchanged glances at Madge and then each other.

"Well," said Danny, "Lily and I decided to wait until the nasty business with Billy Ray was finished before we made plans. Funny you bring this up, because you all need to sit down and I'll tell you about the phone call I got from the D.A."

Max looked at Rosie. "Honey, looks like we are in for some adult discussion. Come upstairs with me and I'll put a movie on, Princess or Mermaid, you get to decide."

Rosie looked at him. Her child's curiosity got the best of her. "I want to stay. I want to know what is going on."

Lily went over to her. "I'll make you a deal. I'll go upstairs with you to start the movie. Once we are done, we will tell you what the news is, but we might have to leave out the bad parts, ok?"

"You mean the bad words?"

"Exactly."

Everyone laughed and moved into the dining room to sit down. Josie came in carrying coffee. "You can take the girl out of the waitress job but you cannot take the waitress out of the girl", she said.

Max leaned over and kissed her. "I will never look at a waitress without thinking how grateful I am that I found you."

Lily returned and sat beside Josie. They reached out and held hands, gripping tightly to prepare themselves for the news. Danny had sounded like it might be good news. But, the old fears still haunted them.

Danny stood up so he could see all their faces. "I wanted you all here together because I wanted you to hear what I have to say. You have all stood behind Lily and me during the unpleasant business with Billy Ray. You never gave up hope it would all turn out ok. Lily and I will never forget it. Some of what I am going to tell you, you already know. Bear with me if I repeat myself, but I don't want to leave out anything."

He looked around the table and could see the anticipation on their faces. "I have just confirmed the story with Sheriff Chuck or Sheriff Axelrod as you know him. I'll try and start at the beginning. Clyde had two sons and according to him, they were always in trouble. Not just the juvenile mischief. He had files on them back to the age of thirteen. Bullies and thieves. Never enough to send them away, but the entire town hated those boys. The boys always blamed someone else for starting trouble. They also blamed their father for their lot in life. Once they were of age, they left town, much to the relief of everyone. As far as he knew, neither one came back, even for a visit."

"Where did they go? Didn't they get in trouble again?" asked Max

"Well, from what the sheriff has been able to piece together. The oldest one, Buck, went to work for one of the carmakers in Detroit. He got fired for stealing car parts and spent two years in jail. Then he wandered around after that. Finally ended back at the farm, to get money out of his father and that's when he attacked you, Lily, and his father. I'll skip that part. Anyways, his brother Billy Ray got in trouble and the judge gave him the option of the service or jail. He chose the Army. He was sent overseas and actually did pretty good as a soldier, at least at the fighting part. He was a loner and according to his military record, was not liked. Most of his unit considered him unstable and were afraid to trust him. The least little thing would set him off. Most feared he would not hesitate to shoot any one of them. They finally had enough on him; sent him back stateside for a dishonorable discharge. The trail ends for a while and then one day he calls the sheriff looking for his brother. Figured they could go into business together. That's when the sheriff came out to your farm."

"He was already dead by then." Lily explained. "Not too long after that visit, Clyde got sick. Guess that's why he never had time to show up before that. He was either in jail or in the service."

"That's right, Lily. He moved around a lot stealing and committing crimes. Didn't get caught but came close a few times. He'd target a place, rob it, and move quickly out of town. Always chose the small poor towns so he didn't get much. Finally hit it big by accident. One of the towns was building a discount store and the company had transferred funds to the local bank to pay the construction workers and help. Can't say he had the brains to pull it off, just dumb luck he robbed the bank at the right time in the right town. That was the money we found in the car. Bolstered by his good luck, he decided to go after Lily."

"How did he know I was here? Or even what I looked like?"

"Seems he had a friend in town that he kept in contact with and who also kept an eye on Clyde and saw you in town a couple of times with him. He was the deputy at the farm with us. He is now in jail. Chuck said he never fully trusted him. This all came out after Billy Ray sold him out. Even though he had never seen you, he knew your description and name. After the car wreck, and Sheriff Bates stealing from him, he started to blame everything on you. It was easy for him to kill the sheriff because he never valued life. Doubt if he even thought it was wrong. He was just getting even; taking back what he felt was his. Even though, it was still stolen money, and not his."

"What about Karen Brown?" injected Max.

"Well, apparently she had the misfortune of looking similar to Lily. He took his failure to find the right person, out on her. He killed her because she was the wrong girl. No other reason. He hated Lily so much because he felt she had what he should have had, the farm and his father. He followed her to make sure he had the right one the next time. His attack on Lily was not well thought out; so again, he failed. So he left and went back to the town of Greenwood. He found out about the body found on the farm and went to the sheriff to convince him it was Lily who murdered his brother. He broke into the Lawyer's office, which was TJ's uncle. He tried to find the deed to the farm. The lawyer refused to give him any information, so he killed him. "

Danny stopped and took a drink of coffee. "As luck would have it, Lily and Josie arrive in town soon after that. He starts to follow Josie thinking she would lead him to the money or deed that he assumes Lily knows about. Then Max, you and I come into the picture. Once we arrive in town, he is afraid we will get to the money first. That's why he tried to run you and Josie off the road. Wanted to scare you off."

"Guess he didn't find anything because Lily found the hiding place in the bedroom and the money was still there", said Josie.

"It was a good thing he was in jail by then. Things could have gotten ugly if he had followed us. Between him and the deputy, we could have been in danger. But for once, we were lucky. Sheriff Axelrod called the D.A.'s office in Relay. He felt I was too close to the situation because of Lily. He arranged for Billy Ray to be taken to our County Seat for questioning on Sheriff Bates and Karen Brown. Now they were able to get a confession out of him, and he will be tried there. They are looking at the death penalty for the murder of a police officer. That along with the rape and murder of a minor should ensure death or at the least life behind bars. We will not have to be afraid of him ever again."

"Now you and Lily can make a life together", said Madge, "I have been waiting for this day to finally get here."

"But what about the man we killed? Well, Clyde's other son? Don't I still have to get punished for that?" Lily has tears on her eyelashes threatening to spill down her cheeks.

Danny walked over and put his arms around her. He wiped the tears and kissed her eyelashes. "Honey, the sheriff and the D.A. assured me you are clear on that. Taking into consideration Clyde's letter, the rape, and the reason you were Clyde's wife in the first place, plus the fact that Billy Ray was captured, they dismissed all charges."

"Is that true?"

"Definitely. Your case was dismissed and it was filed as the wrong person arrested and the murderer confessed. Clyde's letter was confirmed as his handwriting and signature verified by the Doctor's son, Vernon Higgs. Case closed."

Everyone started to applaud and shout. Max hugged Josie, Danny hugged Lily and Madge hugged Bea and Millie. Just then, Rosie came running down the steps. "What's wrong?"

"Everything is right." They all answered in unison.

"Good because I'm hungry and my movie is over."

Madge called Danny out into the kitchen. "I've been keeping this ring for you since Lily left. Now, don't you think it is time for you to move along and take up where you left off before all this happened? Go in there now, and put it back on her finger. Maybe my son will follow your example."

Danny returned to the dining room, knelt down on one knee and took Lily's hand in his. He bent over and kissed her fingers. "Lily, will you be my wife? I love you and want to spend the rest of my life with you."

Lily held out her ring finger and accepted the ring. "I thought you'd never ask."

The Final Chapter

Chapter 58

Three months later

Rosie was dancing around the Living Room. She loved her new dress and she especially loved the reason she was wearing it. Josie had fixed her hair and weaved ribbons and artificial lilies of the valley in and out of her hair. She couldn't wait to hold her flowers of real roses and lilies with the red and white streamers.

Madge was upstairs helping Lily and Josie get dressed. She called down to Rosie "Don't get into anything and get your dress torn or dirty because we don't have a spare one for you to wear." Rosie knew she was now a big girl and would not do anything to damage the dress. She also knew that grandmas felt it was their job to keep reminding little girls, so she yelled back, "ok". Just then Millie and Bea arrived. She opened the door for them. They both hugged her and told her how beautiful she was. More like a princess every day. Millie handed her a box. "This is for the bravest and most beautiful girl I know. I want you to have something to remember this day."

Rosie ran upstairs to check if it was ok for her to open the present. She knew the packages that kept arriving in the house were not hers and she was not allowed to open them without permission. But that was ok, because she soon realized they were all dumb grownup gifts. Toasters, sheets, towels, stuff that did not interest her like when she got Christmas presents.

Madge told Rosie to run back down and tell Millie and Bea to come up to Lily's room. She could open her gift up there, so all of them could

22222222

watch her. Once they came into the room, they exclaimed over Josie and Lily. Both were breathtakingly beautiful. Rosie grew impatient and asked if she could have permission to open her gift now. They all laughed and turned their attention on the gift. Rosie unwrapped the box and peeked inside. She giggled and reached in to remove the item contained inside. She pulled out one of Millie's fairy collection.

"It is beautiful. I will keep it forever and ever." Rosie immediately came over and gave Millie a hug.

"Rosie, look at the bottom. This fairy has a name. She is **Rosalily.** I commissioned just three of these. Guess who is getting the other two?"

"Lily and hum…………..Josie!"

"Right, each will be painted a little different. You will each have an original one that no one else will ever have. This is your special day and although just like this fairy, everyone can share it, no one can own it but you."

Lily and Josie enveloped Millie in a hug. They were so glad they have gotten through this together and grateful for having each other. Madge and Bea, not to be outdone joined in the group hug.

An hour later, Danny and Max arrived at the church. They had spent the night together in Danny's apartment. Max felt the muscles of his back regretting the time on the sofa already. He smiled at Danny, "I hope there is never a next time but I'll tell you now, I'll get the bed and you'll get the sofa."

They walked to the front of the church and glanced over at the amount of friends that filled the pews. They looked at each other and knew that shortly their life would change forever. Both knew they had no regrets at the prospect.

Soon the music began. Rosie walked down toward the altar. She was grinning so wide, Max was afraid she would either start running or skipping the rest of the way. Millie walked down the aisle with Josie and Madge followed with Lily. Neither one would have it any other way. They were with the women that meant more to them than words could ever explain.

Both Max and Danny reached out to take their bride's hand in theirs. Josie and Lily had told them there was no way they would get married if they could not share the day. They had missed too much as sisters, not to do this together.

Chapter 59

Millie was unpacking a new shipment when Lily can running in. "Danny and I wanted you to know before you found out from Madge or Bea. We are having a baby!"

"Oh honey, I know you have been trying. I'm so glad you took my advice and saw a specialist. I know Josie must be beside herself with joy."

"Yeah, with twin boys she is hoping we have a girl. But Danny and I will be happy with whatever we have."

"If you need to cut back on your hours here, I will understand."

"For now it's business as usual. I won't take any chances and I'll let you know if I get tired."

"Good girl. Let's walk upstairs and see Josie."

Millie had bought the store next door to Max. She had remodeled the top floor into an apartment with a porch and she loved living close to her business and especially living close to all the people she loved. Danny and Lily had moved in next door to Madge, when the house came on the market. Josie and Max lived with Madge so she could help with the children. Josie opened a Beauty Shop over Max's store when Danny's apartment became vacant. She had hired someone to help her out so she could be more flexible when the boys were born.

Josie never got to meet her father and Max was glad that was behind them. When the sheriff tracked the house down, to confront him about selling a child, he discovered him dead inside. From the looks of things, he had been dead for quite some time. According to the autopsy report, the alcohol and lifestyle was to blame.

Millie invested the money that Lily received from the sale of Clyde's farm and the money left in the box. Not much by today's standards but Millie said it would grow over the years and provide for the education of Lily's children. Lily insisted that the money would also be used for Josie's children. After all, they were sisters...................... *And sisters look out for each other............*